Light The Way

Light The Way

Published by Mountain Hill Press
Email contact: steppcom@aol.com

This is a work of fiction. Although numerous elements of historical and geographic accuracy are utilized in this and other novels in the Smoky Mountain and SC coastal novels, many other specific environs, place names, characters, and incidents are the product of the author's imagination or used fictitiously.

Scripture used in this book, whether quoted or paraphrased by the characters, is taken from the King James Version of the Bible.

Cover design: Katherine E. Stepp
Interior design: J. L. Stepp, Mountain Hill Press
Editor: Elizabeth S. James
Cover photo and map design: Lin M. Stepp

Library of Congress Cataloging-in-Publication Data

Stepp, Lin
Light The Way: First novel in the Lighthouse Sisters series / Lin Stepp

ISBN: 979-8-9853681-2-3
First Mountain Hill Press Trade Paperback Printing: April 2022

eISBN: 979-8-9853681-3-0
First Mountain Hill Press Electronic Edition: April 2022

1. Women—Southern States—Fiction 2. South Carolina—Coastal—Fiction
3. Contemporary Romance—Inspirational—Fiction. I. Title

Library of Congress Control Number: 2022900622

Light The Way

1st Novel In The
LIGHTHOUSE SISTERS SERIES

LIN STEPP

DEDICATION

This book is dedicated to all my fans and readers who loved my Edisto Trilogy of books set in the Lowcountry of South Carolina and who asked for more!

ACKNOWLEDGEMENTS

"Always have an attitude of gratitude." – Sterling Brown

Gratitude and thanks to everyone at Edisto Island, South Carolina, who shared their memories and stories, making the island, its people, and its history come alive as I worked on planning my new Lighthouse Sisters novels.

Special thanks to Sharon Welch, business owner, Planning Commissioner, and active Realtor at Seabrook Island, South Carolina, who lives at Seabrook and is a partial owner at Botany Bay Island across the river on Edisto. Sharon added greatly to my knowledge of Seabrook, Johns Island, and Botany Bay Island, the latter now in a conservatorship. Her information and contacts were a great help as I gathered research for my new book series.

Gratitude also to the staff at St. Christopher Camp and Conference Center at Seabrook on Johns Island, who graciously allowed me to tour the camp, answered questions, and shared the history of the camp with me.

Thanks to Karen Carter at the Edisto Island Bookstore for her help with information, island maps, and for introducing me to Charles Spencer's two books on Edisto's history. These and other historical books, found at the bookstore, greatly helped solidify facts about Edisto and fanned my imagination.

Extra thanks, also, to Wey Camp at Trinity Episcopal Church on Edisto for allowing me to tour the church and grounds, sharing information, and sending me the church's newsletter to continue adding ideas for my new Edisto books. He was a blessing and you will find Trinity featured in my books.

Final thanks to the Lowcountry bookstores carrying my South Carolina titles and many of my other books in their stores—Buxton Books on King Street in Charleston, Beaufort Books on Boundary Street in Beaufort, Barnes & Noble Bookstore at Sam Rittenberg Blvd. in Charleston, The Edisto Island Bookstore, and many others.

Acknowledgements to all those who helped with this book:

- Elizabeth S. James, copyeditor and editorial advisor
- J.L. Stepp, production design and proofing
- Katherine Stepp, cover design and graphics
- And ongoing gratitude to the Lord, who helps me in all my books.

A BRIEF EDISTO HISTORY

2000 BC	Archaic cultures inhabited the island
1550s	Edistow Indians lived on the island
1663	SC Colony founded by King of England
	Lord Proprietors granted lands from Charles II
1700-1770s	Plantations grew, importing rice and indigo
1775-1783	Rev War; planters fled; property destroyed
1780s-1860s	Plantations thrived growing cotton
1800s	Edingsville Beach formed for wealthy planters
1861-1865	Civil War years; slaves freed; property destroyed
1870s	Many families returned; cotton still a big crop
1893	Hurricane destroyed Edingsville Beach
1920s	Boll weevil ended cotton production
	Drawbridge to island replaced Dawhoo Ferry
	Intercoastal Waterway dredged, linking rivers
	Truck farming and fishing grew on the island
1925	Resort development on Edisto expanded
	Early cottages built, no electricity or water
1935	Edisto Beach State Park built with CCC help
	Palmetto Boulevard paved for cars
1940	Hurricane destroyed most all homes on Edisto
1941-1945	WWII slowed growth; military patrolled island
	Coast Guard patrolled park; reports of spies
	Edisto S.C. Hwy 174 straightened and paved
1950s	Development on Edisto Beach resumed
1954	Big pier built near park entrance; later burned
1959	Hurricane Gracie did heavy damage
	Groins built to hold sand, stop erosion
1970s	Edisto tourism grew and expanded
1973	Oristo resort and golf course opened
1976	Beach changed fr Charleston to Colleton Co
	Remaining Island stayed in Charleston Co
	Many businesses and beach homes built
1976	Fairfield Resorts bought Oristo Ridge
1993	McKinley Washington replaced drawbridge
2006	Fairfield Resort bought by Wyndham
2008	Botany Bay wildlife preserve opened
	Growth continued with beauty remaining

DEVEAUX BANK

ATLANTIC OCEAN

WATCH ISLAND

MAIN BEACH

CABANA

LIGHTHOUSE

Pavilion

INLAND cottage

GUEST COTTAGES

GIFT SHOP

DEVEAUX INN

STOR

FOG HOUSE

GAZEBO

Lighthouse ROAD

The LODGE

NORTH EDISTO RIVER

MARINA (Ferry Pickup)

MARSH AREA

Estuary

MAP for
WATCH ISLAND
Townsend INLET
EDISTO ISLAND
SOUTH BEACH
MARSH AREA
INLET
TOWNSEND CREEK
ISLAND LOOP ROAD
TWIN LAKES
MARITIME FOREST
BOAL's HOUSE
BOAT HOUSE
MARSH
GEORGE'S HOUSE
RAMP
OCELLA CREEK
BOAT DOCK
SCOTT CREEK
FIG ISLAND

CHAPTER 1

March 2017

Burke paused, cloth in hand, to look out at the line of brown pelicans crossing the sky in neat formation. She leaned on the rail of the gallery near the top of the tall lighthouse to watch them. The pelicans dropped closer to the waterline after a few minutes, dive-bombing when they spotted a fish, then lifting back into formation again.

She watched in awe as the lead bird rose up and down in flight, the other birds following in a perfect rhythmic wave. Burke knew the pelicans in formation behind the lead bird rode the wave of the bird in front of them, conserving energy and cooperatively helping each other. Myron Andric, the ornithologist staying with them at the Lighthouse Inn, had pointed out to her, too, that not the same bird always led in the formation. The lead bird would drop back after a time to rest, letting another bird take the lead in its place.

Burke sighed, moving to sit down on one of the narrow benches against the gallery wall. "I wouldn't mind a little rest and help right now," she said to herself. "It's been hard keeping everything going since Dad died. I never realized how much he did until I had to pick up so much of his work load."

Hearing a noise on the quarter-turn stairs leading to the gallery, Burke stood as Hal Jenkins came through the door. "Good morning, Hal. What brings you to the island so early?"

He waved her back to the metal bench and sat down beside her, heaving to catch his breath. "Your mother said I'd find you here," he offered, drawing in another long gulp of air. "Good grief, it's been a while since I climbed to the top of this thing. I think I walked up a million stairs."

"No, only 120 stairs to the gallery here. There are twenty more to the high catwalk and lantern room, but this is as far as the public is allowed to come." She smiled at him. "The majority don't make it to this point. They stop at the gallery on the fourth level at seventy-two stairs. With the lighthouse situated on a rocky rise at the end of the island like it is, that balcony offers a stunning view across the ocean that satisfies most."

He glanced at the cloth lying beside her and the spray bottle on the floor. "I gather you've been housekeeping?"

"Yes. I cleaned all the glass panels around the lantern room already and am wiping off the benches and rails now." She laughed, nodding at the white splotches on the gallery railing. "The seagulls like to party here. On one of the lighthouse tours this weekend, a tourist asked me what I thought was the most important trait for a lighthouse keeper to possess. I told him you needed to like washing windows, rails, and stairs."

Hal chuckled. "Beach life is alluring but the salt and grit in the sea air builds up and creates more work and maintenance than most folks think about when they buy property here. Still, an old sea dog like me wouldn't live anywhere else. The sea gets in your blood."

"Dad used to say you only need to stand near the ocean to feel the power of the universe and a closeness to the One who created it. I think it's an old quote but I'm not sure who said it."

Hal grew quiet for a moment, looking out across the expanse of ocean, his eyes following a boat on the horizon.

Burke studied him, their familiar friend and neighbor, with his tanned sea-weathered face, strong stocky build, worn jacket, and battered ball cap with Jenkins Tours embroidered across it.

"I miss your dad," Hal said after a moment. "He was one of my best friends, and I know losing him has been hard on your mom, and on you and your sisters. I know it's been especially difficult for you, since you picked up so much of Lloyd's work load."

"You've helped, too," Burke put in. "I hope you realize how grateful Mother and I are for all the ways you've kicked in to help us so many times."

"Well, that's what I came to talk to you about. I spoke to your mother first and she said to come talk with you, too." He hesitated, shifting in his seat.

Burke waited.

"It's March now and we're all heading into the busier season of the year with the winter past. That will mean more work for you at the inn and the lighthouse and more work for us with the ferry, the tours, and the fishing trips."

She leaned toward him. "Look, I know we've imposed on you since Dad died unexpectedly at the end of September. It's pushed more workload than usual on Clifford and Henry, too. Mother and I have been talking about hiring Joe Lewis to work more for us. He's been helping us part time…"

Hal held up a hand to interrupt her. "I think I have a better idea. Waylon is coming home. As a commissioned officer in the Navy, he can retire after ten years and it's been twelve now. He'll get a reduced pension, coming out before twenty years, but it's still good regular money, and he's ready for a change." Hal paused, rubbing a hand over his neck. "You remember Waylon did the Citadel's Naval program on that four year NROTC scholarship. That meant he owed them some time. He's more than paid it now, but he won't be happy to sit around the house for long doing nothing at only thirty-four."

"Wouldn't you want him in the family business?"

Hal frowned. "Waylon might need to ease his way back into that over time. He and my brother Dewey have never gotten on well. There's a lot of story to that. You know some of it. Dewey's already smarted off enough about Waylon coming home for me to see there's likely to be more tension."

A barrage of little memories skittered across Burke's mind.

"I suggested to Etta that Waylon come work here at the lighthouse, live at the lodge down by the dock on South Creek where the boats and ferries come in. Like Etta said, it's rare the lodge rents out. If a group does want it for a weekend, Waylon can stay up at the inn or over at our house with Aileen and me. As you know it's only ten minutes up the North Edisto River to our place at Jenkins Landing."

He hesitated, looking out to sea again. "Aileen and I talked about this a good bit. We're real pleased our boy is coming home—although I imagine he'd prefer the word *man* now. We want Waylon to be happy and stick around, to not get himself upset and take off again. My brother Dewey's a fine seaman, good with the fishing tours—none better, really—but he can be a little outspoken and difficult for some to deal with."

Burke remembered all too well how hard he'd been on Waylon. She'd never understood it.

"As a boy Waylon started coming over here to the lighthouse a lot, bringing our girl Sally Ann to play with you and your sisters, then staying to tag around after your father. He loved Lloyd, and Lloyd loved him. Waylon was always happy working here at any task Lloyd gave him."

"I remember."

"The point is Waylon knows the work here. He's strong, smart, capable, solid, and generally easy-going."

Burke smiled at him. "You don't need to sell me on Waylon's character, Hal."

He grinned back at her. "I guess not, with you two growing up together."

"What does Waylon think about this idea? Is he home yet?"

"He is. I suggested the idea to him, in a way I thought would best appeal to him, before I came over." Hal stopped to rub his neck again. "You know I've got no disrespect for women doing anything they want to do, but I don't like you, your mother, and Lila living here on this island with no man around to help with things."

Burke frowned and crossed her arms.

"Now don't be getting riled up at me. I know what all you can do. You're a strong woman. But you can't do everything, and Lloyd used to handle most all the pickups with the ferry—bringing guests over, taking them back. I know he did a lot of the physical labor here at the lighthouse and around the property, worked with you and your mother with the tours, events, and at the inn. He was a big man, not only in size but in personality and leadership. Anybody trying to fill his shoes would meet a hard time. So don't get testy on me. I love Etta, and I love you like my own daughter, but it worries me there's no man here."

"Henry Boals is our caretaker and Clifford George our groundskeeper. Both live here with their wives on the island, Hal. You know that."

"Yes, and both their places are not near the main marina either. Anyone could pull up there at night or onto the beach with not a soul to see or hear them." He took a deep breath. "You might not know it, but a woman went missing up in Hollywood this week. Lived on her own near the Dollar General. She was last seen walking down the road toward her house. There's not a clue as to where she is or what happened to her, and she lived closer into town. You live out here on an island that a person can only access with a boat."

"You make it sound like we're miles out to sea, isolated from the world. It's only minutes up the river to your place from the marina and a short distance further to the Calhouns we know as well as your family. It's only ten minutes by boat to the Bohicket Marina on Seabrook, too, and as you can see from looking across the river from where we sit, swarms of people live in the huge Seabrook Resort. As you well know, Watch Island is a part of Edisto Island, only separated from it by the Townsend Inlet, creeks, and marshland. We're not isolated from the world here."

Hal rubbed an arm. "Well, all that aside, you need some help and Waylon could use a job and a new direction right now. He could help you and Etta, and you could help him. Etta thought it sounded like a good idea. She's fond of Waylon, glad he's coming home again. She seemed excited about the idea of him being interested in working here. As she commented, it would be hard to find anyone who knew the island, the business, and the lighthouse any better. She said she'd be thrilled to let Waylon take over the ferry runs, deliveries, and other trips out, and she mentioned it would be right nice to have a strong arm and a strong presence around every now and then. She admitted the weekly and day-to-day physical upkeep of the lighthouse wasn't an easy task for her or you either. She also reminded me Clifford doesn't like heights."

Burke grinned at that. "No, he doesn't. I imagine with Waylon working on a ship all these years, he wouldn't have any trouble hanging on a ladder to clean the glass panels at the top of the lighthouse like I did this morning. For most, that job might seem a little intimidating."

"So?" he asked, pulling the discussion to a close.

"So, it's a good idea. Mother and I had already decided we needed to hire someone else with the busier tourist season starting. If Waylon thinks he can put up with us and doesn't mind staying at the lodge, I'm agreeable to the idea. He can take his meals at the inn, like Clifford and Henry do."

She paused, wrinkling her nose. "No one has stayed in the lodge since last summer when a group of fishing buddies rented it. We'll need to get it cleaned up. I'll start on it this afternoon. I don't want to put any additional cleaning responsibilities on Rita Jean. She gets testy if things don't rock along in the normal pattern."

"Waylon won't mind cleaning up the place himself, Burke."

She nodded. "I know, but I'd feel better to get it cleaned a little, at least. When does Waylon want to start? You didn't say. Does he want some time to relax first, spend time with the family and such? It's fine with us if he wants a few weeks of vacation before he comes over to settle in."

"I'll tell him that," Hal said, standing. "I'd better get back to work, and let you get the rest of your cleaning done." He eyed the splotches around the gallery deck and on the rails. "Those gulls can sure leave their calling cards."

"Yes, they can." She gave him a hug before he left.

After hearing the sound of Hal's footsteps disappear on the

stairs, Burke sat down on the bench again for a moment to gaze across the expanse of the sea, closing her eyes and letting the ocean breeze roll over her.

"Well, well," she whispered after a time, smiling. "Waylon's back home. It's been a long time. I wonder how much the same he is." With that thought, she got up to finish her cleaning. Starting from the top of the lighthouse, as she always did, she still had the other gallery deck, the stairs, rails, and windows along the way to do, plus the museum rooms on the lower levels to clean.

She'd talk to her mother at lunch more about Waylon. They'd need to think out the work responsibilities they most wanted him to do and talk about a pay scale. Knowing her mother as she did, Etta would probably have a list made, itemizing it all, by the time she saw her.

About an hour later as Burke moved outside to sweep and clean the covered pavilion on the hill behind the lighthouse, she glanced down the beach to see her sister Lila sitting on a rock with her sketchbook in her lap. Putting away her broom and cleaning supplies, Burke walked down the wooden stairs from the high point of land where the lighthouse stood, through the gate, and along the sandy pathway to the Atlantic Ocean. She then followed the beach to the spot where she'd seen Lila earlier.

Moving closer, Burke stopped in her tracks, stunned to see hundreds of starfish lying on the beach and swirling in the wash of the surf. "What in the world?" she exclaimed.

"Sad, isn't it?" Lila said, looking up to see her coming. "I walked down this morning and found them. I've thrown back all I could find that still had life. It took me hours. Most of the ones you see now are dead."

"I've never seen anything like this before." Burke paused, simply amazed, watching the remaining starfish tumbling over each other in the incoming tide.

"They look like stars fallen from the sky, don't they?"

Burke walked closer, picking her way around the masses of little five-legged creatures scattered across the beach. "I read once that a storm at sea or some disturbance causes this. It doesn't happen often though. I remember starfish washed up on Folly Beach like this once and at Myrtle Beach. I don't recall it ever happening here."

"Me neither, but when we were girls I remember a sweep of jellyfish washing up on our beach." Lila's eyes swept over the starfish. "Gwen got impulsive and tried to pick up some of the dead jellyfish to toss back out to sea and got stung. She forgot that jellyfish can sting even after they are dead."

Burke grinned at the memory. "I'd forgotten about those jellyfish."

"Jellyfish stings really hurt. Gwen had red whip marks for about a week."

Seeing movement in a few more starfish, Burke leaned over to pick them up and toss them far into the surf. "I remember we always called the starfish sea stars when we were girls, and Celeste said we'd all grow up to be stars one day."

"Well, she did." Lila smiled. "Do you remember that British man, the goldsmith, who visited at the inn when we were teenagers? The one who sent us matching gold starfish necklaces he handcrafted in his shop?"

"I do remember him, and we still wear those necklaces." Burke perched on a rock beside Lila's and fished out her necklace from under her shirt to display it. "What was that man's name? I can't seem to remember."

"Gurveen Fitzpatrick." Lila looked out toward the Deveaux Bank in the distance, an island bird sanctuary about a mile off shore. "Do you remember why Gurveen made those necklaces for us? It was because of that old legend Novaleigh told us, that if you see a starfish jump at full moon then your wish will come true. We told him that story out on the beach one evening when he found a starfish in the sand."

Burke shook her head. "It's rare that starfish ever jump high enough to be seen, if they jump at all."

"I know, but Gurveen believed our story and said he saw one jump that night while the moon was full—or he thought he did—and he made his wish." She laid her sketchbook and pencils down as she told her story. "The woman he loved had dumped him and Gurveen wished he could meet someone kind and true. That weekend a sweet little schoolteacher came to stay at the inn. Do you remember her? Marie Jones, a quiet woman, kind, nice, and polite. They struck up a friendship and wrote to each other afterward. Then Marie went to see Gurveen in England and they got married. Gurveen felt we'd been responsible for them finding each other, because we told him the starfish story, so he sent us the little starfish necklaces he'd crafted as a thank you."

Burke smiled at her sister. "Thanks for reminding me of that story. You always remember the sweetest things. I'm so glad you decided to come back home."

Lila's eyes moved over the starfish still on the beach. "I plan to gather up many of these dead starfish to spread across my porch railings to dry out. They'll dry white and we can sell them in the gift shop later. I might even make jewelry from some of the smaller ones." She pointed at her sketches. "I think I'll do some paintings, too. People like beach-related paintings to take home as souvenir remembrances of their vacations."

Burke picked up Lila's sketchbook to look through it. "You do such beautiful, detailed, and intricate drawings. I've always marveled at your gift."

Lila smiled. "I'm getting some good commissions already from some of the galleries around here for my work. It's nice to enjoy the freedom now to simply do art and to help run the lighthouse gift shop."

"You help in other ways, too, but I love how you've repainted and redecorated the gift shop since you got back. It's never looked so good before. The new items you ordered sell well, too." She hesitated. "Are you sure you're not lonely living at that little cottage behind the inn? Inland Cottage is only a small place we offer to unexpected guests. You know you could move back into your old room next to mine in the family wing."

Lila laid a hand on her arm. "Don't feel for a moment my choice not to move back into my old room has anything to do with you. I lived a quiet, contemplative life these last years and wanted my own space and time alone. I still need the quiet, if for different reasons now. It energizes me for my work."

Burke shrugged. "Well, if you're happy, I'm happy."

Lila's eyes moved to the starfish again. "I think the starfish washing in to our beach are a sign that something is coming. Some changes we haven't anticipated."

Burke laughed. "You've always had those little knowings about things, but this time you're right on. I came to tell you Waylon has come back home. His father Hal came to talk with Mother and then with me this morning about Waylon coming to work with us and living at the lodge. Hal thinks Waylon can keep a better watch over the marina, living there, and over our end of the island, plus he can pick up a lot of the work Dad used to do. Mother and I already decided we needed to hire someone with the tourist season starting soon. We've managed through the winter but it's been hard for us all."

"That news is a blessing. I love Waylon and I can't wait to see him again. I know he'll be a fine help. There is so much Dad did you're trying to do now by yourself, Burke, and it's been difficult for you. It will be good to have Waylon helping us."

She wrapped her arms around her knees. "Waylon was five years older than you, with Gwen and Celeste next, making him eleven years older than me. I was only six or seven when he left to go in the Navy, but he was a really sweet, good person. Do you remember how kind he was to Edward? Goodness knows, Edward needed kindness with the father he had. When Waylon brought Sally Ann to play with us, he would pick Edward up over at the plantation, bring him along and keep a watch over him."

Burke shook her head. "Perhaps you've forgotten that Edward's mother Clarice paid Waylon to bring him over to play with us, to watch him, and to bring him back home. She wasn't much of a loving, involved mother. She used every chance when her husband Sam was gone to foist Edward off on somebody so she could go to Charleston and gad around."

"I doubt Clarice was very happy married to Sam Calhoun, even with all the money, help and servants, and their big plantation house. Sam wasn't an easy man."

"No, but he was powerful and generally respected around Edisto. He could get things done, too. Few people seemed able to withstand him when he made up his mind about something."

"Yes, and because of that he hurt a lot of people," Lila said quietly.

Burke frowned. "Dad liked him though, despite his arrogance and bossiness."

"Well, birds of a feather."

"Maybe, but Dad was always kind. Even when he seemed a little overbearing you knew he meant well." Burke paused, thinking. "Do you think that Edward might come home more often now with his father gone? I couldn't believe it when Sam Calhoun died this fall after Thanksgiving, not long after we lost Dad. Mother told me Clarice is considering selling the plantation. She doesn't want to live over there alone."

Lila smiled. "Perhaps the sea will draw Edward back like it did Waylon and me."

"Maybe, but not everyone is suited to live the life we do. It's different living a remote life. Even the plantation where Edward grew up was away from most of the life and activity on Edisto. And the job opportunities are limited here."

Lila ran a hand over her long, wavy dark hair, caught up in a big clip today to keep the sea breeze from blowing it. "It was different, the way we grew up here on the island, even with the tourists coming and going. We were always different at school, too. Everyone called us the Lighthouse Sisters, and it wasn't always said kindly."

Burke shrugged. "Well, children are seldom kind."

"I think we were kind though," Lila argued, gathering up her art supplies to stuff them into a tote bag.

"It's true you were always kind and you always saw life in that sweet good way, but Celeste and Gwen were a different story, both strong-willed and outspoken. Don't pretend you don't remember. They still are."

"Perhaps." Lila stood and brushed the sand off her shorts. "Come help me gather up some starfish to take back with us. I brought a bucket down earlier."

"Okay," Burke answered, glancing at her watch. "We have time before we head to the inn for lunch. As you well know Novaleigh gets testy if we're late."

"Who would want to be late for any of her meals? I missed her artistry in the kitchen while I was away."

CHAPTER 2

Aileen Jenkins stood on the broad front porch of her home the next day watching her son bring out another box. "Waylon, just because Etta and Burke are agreeable to you working for them doesn't mean you need to start moving over there today. Etta said you could take time for a vacation and a break first."

Waylon turned to smile at her. "I've had nearly a week for a break. I'm used to being busy, Mom, and from what Dad says, they need help now."

She leaned against the porch rail, looking out toward West Bank Creek that wound its way behind their home to the North Edisto River. "It has been difficult for them. Etta and Lloyd were close, their love and friendship evident to everyone. Continuing the work at the inn and the lighthouse hasn't given Etta much time to grieve. Your dad and I tried to help in all the ways we could through this fall and winter since Lloyd died, but with the busy tourist season coming, they'll need more help." She paused. "Are you sure moving over there to work with them is what you really want to do? Your dad and Dewey could easily find work for you in the business. They stay swamped through the tourist season with boat tours, fishing tours, and the ferry runs from the landing."

"You know I'll help here as needed." Waylon sat his box on top of the other he'd brought out to the porch earlier. "I told Dad that, but I'm needed more at Etta's right now. She and Burke can't keep carrying all Lloyd's roles, even with Clifford and Henry to help. They need someone to fill Lloyd's place and I'd feel better if it was me. I know the lighthouse, the inn, the island, its work and business. I spent a big part of my youth there tagging around after Lloyd Deveaux and later working with him after school and in the summers. I know he'd want me to step in. The family business here runs itself smoothly with Dad and Dewey doing the tours and you and Sally Ann running the office."

She looked around with a wistful sigh. "This is a big old house for only your dad and me. We've missed you, Waylon. Maybe I need someone here to spoil a little and cook for."

"You can do plenty of spoiling and cooking for Sally Ann's three boys." He pointed at a basket full of toy trucks and cars on the porch. "The boys stay here after school when Sally Ann runs the dock office. Living across the road, they're back and forth here all the time, too." He paused. "I can't believe how much they've grown since I last saw them. From what I've seen, Todd, Bobby and Sam, at nine, seven, and five, keep you busy enough when you're not working at the office. And they eat like crazy."

She smiled. "They are a handful but they bring me a lot of joy and laughs."

"I've enjoyed them, too, and I'll be back and forth often with the ferry runs," he assured her. "You'll see me enough. I won't be far away either, and I know you go over to the inn to visit with Etta."

"It isn't your Uncle Dewey that's causing you not to stay with us here, is it?" She frowned. "I know he can be a little outspoken, and the two of you have never gotten along well."

"That's true, Mom. We don't get along well. I regret that. Dewey changed after his wife died. He drank for a time, had a hard time getting his life back together. He held no patience for little boys. I seemed to provoke him at every turn when he moved back to live here, and I didn't admire him. He knew that and resented it. I was glad he straightened out after a time and I admit I felt glad when he and dad remodeled the dock office and added the apartment above it for him. That helped. Dewey is better now but still critical and thin on patience. Judgmental too. He thinks he's right in every opinion he holds. He still carries a grudge against me, too, for leaving home to go in the Navy. He made a sarcastic remark to me yesterday about being a Captain now, but not much of a Captain loyal to my family and the business."

His mother winced. "That was wrong of him to say. You followed the call of your heart. You got your education, traveled, put in your time with the Navy, won honorable awards. Your father and I are proud of you. I hope you know that."

"I do. Perhaps in time Dewey will see me in a different light, but I doubt any words of mine will change his mind right now. He's stubborn once he gets a viewpoint set in place." Waylon leaned closer to give his mother a kiss on the cheek. "It will be best for me to live and work at the island. I can be of real value there."

She smiled. "You always used to tell me you wished you could grow up to be a Lighthouse Keeper like Lloyd Deveaux. He was a Naval Captain, too, before he came home to keep the Light and to take over the bulk of the work at the lighthouse and the inn from his father. He loved you, too. I think he'd be happy you're stepping into his shoes."

"I'd like to think that." Waylon picked up the two boxes on the porch. "I'm going to take these boxes and all the other items I already packed in my car to my skiff at the dock and run them down to the island. Etta sent me a key to the lodge and told Dad I'd find ample cleaning supplies there. I'm sure the old place will need some work, but unless I discover it in too rough a shape, I'll stay on."

"Well, don't make yourself scarce."

"Don't worry." He grinned. "After being abroad for so many years, I'm glad to be home and near family again. I've missed it here."

Waylon had realized that fact even more as he drove down the family road earlier in the week. Although he'd been away at college and then in the Navy, Edisto Island in South Carolina was still his home, the place he loved and where his heart belonged. He thought when he hit the ten-year mark in the Navy he'd stay on for twenty years and full retirement, but he found himself restless the last year or two, pulled toward home again. He'd always expected Lloyd to still be at the island when he came back. It hurt to realize Lloyd was gone, that he wouldn't share any more good times and talks with the big, warmhearted man with the hearty laugh and broad smile.

Backing the car out of the driveway, Waylon followed the tree-shaded lane back to the main road, turning right to head toward the Jenkins boat dock and family business. A gated entrance off Clark Road led into Jenkins Landing Road and directly to the marina and docks on West Bank Creek. From the landing, the inlet opened into the main channel of the North Edisto River and led to the Atlantic Ocean. Two side-roads wound off Jenkins Landing Road, one to his mother and dad's big, white house, the other to his sister Sally Ann and her husband Don's place. Don was a veterinarian with a practice on the main highway in Edisto, but they'd decided to build their house on family land near the dock and river.

Waylon slowed as he reached the end of the road. The Jenkins boat ramp and long docks lay ahead, with the marsh to the left and the two-storied office to the right with its covered patios. The Jenkins family business, inherited by Waylon's dad and his brother Dewey, occupied the bottom part of the building with a flight of stairs leading up to an apartment above where Dewey lived. It had been a good decision adding the apartment when they rebuilt the office after a bad storm, so someone could keep better watch over the dock, the boats, and the covered parking pavilion where guests, who were enjoying one of their tours or staying at the Lighthouse Inn, kept their cars.

The Jenkins and Deveaux families had worked together for many years. Anyone staying at the Deveaux Inn, who didn't own their own boat, left their cars at the landing and rode a ferry over to the island. Scheduled ferry runs also delivered tourists to the island for tours of the Deveaux Lighthouse. Working for Etta now, Waylon would pick up a lot of that ferrying business. Visitors could only get to the island to tour the lighthouse or stay at the inn by boat, either in their own craft, or on one of the ferry runs.

Waylon parked his car in the family parking area and loaded his boxes into one of his dad's former skiffs—now his—a nice Sea Chaser. Then he settled in at the boat's helm, started the engine, eased his way out from the dock, and headed into the inlet and out into the river. The short route to Watch Island was a familiar one, and he soon pulled up at the main marina, tied his boat to the dock, and walked over to a small covered carport to load his boxes and gear onto the back of one of the golf carts always kept there. On the key ring, along with the lodge keys Etta sent over for him, was a key for the cart. Waylon soon angled the vehicle out of the carport and drove it up the Lighthouse Road to turn onto a small sandy lane leading through the trees to the lodge.

As Waylon drew closer, he barely noticed the long rustic building at first because up on a ladder propped against the house was Burke, cleaning out the gutters. Hearing the golf cart, she turned to smile at him in welcome, and his heart flipped over. She wore an old blue T-shirt and cut off jean-shorts that showed off her long tanned legs. As typical, she'd tied back her dark hair, which always lightened in the sunshine, into a ponytail behind her neck.

Watching her climb down the ladder, Waylon remembered the first time he'd noticed Burke Deveaux with physical attraction like this. She'd been walking up the beach path in a well-worn black bathing suit, laughing, smiling, and lifting a hand to wave at him. Waylon suddenly forgot the words he'd been saying to Lloyd as he stood there rooted to the spot, his heartbeat kicking up. How had he missed seeing she'd started growing from a girl into a young woman?

Lloyd cleared his throat breaking Waylon's focus. "It's a good thing you're heading to the Citadel and the Navy soon," he'd said in a firm tone. "Burke's only twelve years old; you're seventeen. You may be like a son to me, boy, but I'll beat you to a pulp if you touch that girl or act on these feelings hitting you. I'd advise you to keep any of your thoughts locked up well. She's only a child yet and you're barely starting to be a man. Don't do anything foolish, you hear me?"

Embarrassed, Waylon had shuffled his feet, looking down at his shoes, feeling his face flush.

"I want your word you won't let that child know you've suddenly noticed her. You've been raised with Burke, Gwen, Celeste, and Lila like a brother. Don't let your mind be going in some other direction just because your male hormones are starting to kick in. You'll have time enough off at college next year to test out being a male amongst women who interest you. But with Burke you're her brother. Understood? I'll expect you to keep that thought in the forefront of your mind."

"Yes, sir," Waylon had mumbled, humiliated beyond belief. Funny how those words came back to him, even now, checking him, causing him to push his feelings down and rearrange his thoughts.

"I didn't think you'd come so soon," Burke said, interrupting his memories and coming to give him a hug. He steeled himself to pat her fondly on the back as she did, not hugging her back in the way he really wanted to.

She pulled away and studied him. "You look good, Waylon. Tough, handsome, and solid, very much the Naval Captain. I wish Dad was here to see you. He'd be so proud."

"Well, I'm having a hard time believing he's gone. You know how he could fill up a room with his personality, hold people in the palm of his hand with his stories."

"I remember." She looked away.

Waylon tried to think what to say. It seemed disloyal to Lloyd's memory somehow that he still felt his feelings rise at the first sight of Burke, that she still attracted him after so long a time. He thought with time and all the years he would feel differently. But on every occasion when he'd come home for a visit, the old feelings tried to surface at just the sight of Burke. He'd need to work on that, living and working here now.

Waylon glanced toward the lodge, a two-storied building, sitting on a rise of land beside Scott Creek, a wide tributary of water that circled the backside of the island. The lodge, a soft weathered tan, with the same red roof of the inn and other island buildings, sat at an angle so the broad front porch and screened porch to one side looked out over the water and down to the marina and dock. From here, as his dad said, he'd see anyone pulling up, and a bell rigged between the lodge and dock rang a warning whenever a boat touched the dockside. He assumed it still worked. If it didn't he'd fixed it. If there was one thing Waylon had always been good at it was fixing things.

"I hope the lodge will be all right for you." Burke wiped her hands on her shorts. "You know it's a little rustic and mannish since it's rented out primarily to hunting and fishing groups. It was built originally as a lodge for men, although a few groups of women have used it, too."

Waylon lifted his eyebrows and grinned at her. "Since I'm a man, too, I think that will work for me."

"Well, sure." She blushed. "I only meant it isn't fancy like the rooms at the inn."

He enjoyed seeing the flush on her cheeks, having her at a disadvantage. Of all the Deveaux girls, Burke was the more solid one, the least rattled, the reliable older sister who usually took charge of her younger siblings. Gwen and Celeste had always been more impulsive and adventurous, Lila the quieter, shy dreamer of the group. Like a mother hen Burke had usually kept herd over them all and over any visiting children, keeping order, organizing their play, reminding everyone of the time, calming disputes. Except with him, of course. So much older, even than Burke, he'd played the older reliable role, too, especially since he'd often been assigned to watch over his little sister Sally Ann and Edward Calhoun. Someone once suggested he and Burke were like the mother and father of the brood of kids on the island, and Waylon had quickly pushed down a few of the implications of that idea that tried to surface in his mind.

"The lodge will be fine for me, Burke. You know I've always liked it."

"Well, it's a mess right now and I don't really have it cleaned up enough for you to move in." She glanced pointedly at the boxes and duffle stuffed on the back of the golf cart.

"I can clean the lodge, Burke. You have enough to do."

She sighed. "Well, I suppose you can help me." Her eyes shifted over his jeans and gray T-shirt with a Navy emblem on the front. "You'll probably get that nice shirt dirty."

"It'll wash." He glanced toward the golf cart. "Tell me where to put this gear and then I'll get up on the ladder and finish cleaning out the gutters."

"Are you seriously worried about me getting up on a ladder?" she asked with a smirk. "A little height like this will hardly be a problem for me after cleaning the lantern glass at the top of the lighthouse this morning."

"I was simply suggesting a way to help, not implying you couldn't do something, Burke. Don't go all feminist on me. Surely you know I'm aware of all you can do."

"I suppose." Her voice softened.

He waited.

"Get your boxes. I'll carry your duffle," she said then, walking over to the golf cart to reach for it. "I cleaned the downstairs bedroom for you already and put fresh sheets on the bed and towels in the bath. It's the best room in the house." She grabbed the duffle and started toward the lodge.

Waylon followed her carrying the boxes and enjoying letting his eyes travel over her, with her back turned.

"We've modernized the lodge a time or two since you left," Burke continued as she walked up on the porch to push open the front door for both of them. "The kitchen and baths especially needed it and we refinished the floors throughout."

"It still feels and looks about the same though," Waylon said, following her into the big living area, mostly in browns and neutrals, focused around a floor-to-ceiling rock fireplace and opening into a rustic dining area. That space, with a round captain's table, seating twelve when all the chairs were crammed in, looked out into the trees behind the house. The kitchen seemed about the same as he recalled, the little table for two still by the window, but with some new light fixtures, different countertops, and fresh paint.

"I haven't cleaned much yet," she said again as they moved through the main area of the lodge to the big downstairs bedroom in the back. It held a king-sized bed with a new spread but otherwise the same rustic furniture, wall art, old Persian rug, and paddle-fan he remembered.

"Everything looks great," he commented. "I don't see any cleaning I can't manage."

"That's because I've already cleaned part of the downstairs and aired the rooms out," she argued. "Everything was dusty and musty earlier. I'm sure the upstairs bedrooms and baths still need a lot of work."

"Don't worry about it. I doubt I'll be up there much."

She dropped his duffle on the bed while he sat the two boxes he carried on the bedroom floor.

Waylon glanced out the window to the table and chairs on the porch. The back of the lodge looked out into the maritime forest that covered much of the island. The island's beach areas, broadening and narrowing with the tides, circled the ocean and river side of the island, with the southern end of Watch Island a wide marshy estuary, filled with sweeps of sea grasses and narrow inlets. There Townsend Creek, more like a small river, branched its way through the estuary and down to the Atlantic Ocean, separating Watch Island from the rest of the larger expanse of Edisto Island, Botany Bay Wildlife Management Area, the state park, and Edisto Beach.

"I don't mind to finish cleaning," he repeated, turning back to Burke.

"I know, but it will bother me if everything isn't nice and the way I like it, Waylon. There's no use in arguing with me about it."

"There never was," he replied back, making her grin.

"Well, you know I like things neat and orderly."

"I remember."

"You probably remember, too, there are four bedrooms upstairs and two baths. The bedrooms all have twin beds, since guys on a getaway generally don't want to sleep in the same bed together. We made an exception down here for the few times we allowed a couple to stay at the lodge when the inn and cottages filled up. When the coast guard workers come to paint the lighthouse or do work at the Light, they usually stay upstairs, but they only come to inspect a few times a year and seldom stay over."

"I can go back to mom and dad's place anytime the lodge is needed," he assured her, peeking into his new bedroom's adjoining bath, glad to see a good shower there.

Burke opened a side door off the bedroom. "We turned this old storage room into a small office when we renovated." She pointed to a cabinet across the wall with shelves above and a desk with a computer below. "Everyone seems to want a place to work at the computer today."

"I'm glad to see this change," he said, admiring the well-lit space. "I brought a laptop with me, but this will be nice for other work I might need to do."

"Mom and I will try to plan a time tomorrow to talk to you about job responsibilities. She said at lunch she'd already started a list. You know Mom and her lists; I'm sure it will be thorough. I'll take you around and show you changes at the island, too, and remind you of everything else. I hope that will work for you. We have a full house coming to the inn on Friday, most for a two-week stay. Like your dad said, things are starting to get busy again with spring moving in."

He leaned against the doorframe, watching her. "I'm easy to work with, Burke. You should remember that."

"My memories are from a long time ago, Waylon." She lifted her chin. "Except for an occasional trip home and a quick stop to see us once in a while, I haven't spent time with you since we were kids. I'm sure we've both changed a lot in all that time."

He couldn't help adding, "You've certainly changed in one way. You've become a very beautiful woman, Eugenia Burke Deveaux."

She rolled her eyes. "Flattery will hardly get you out of any work needed around here Waylon Arthur Jenkins. In case you've forgotten it takes a lot of work every day to keep the inn and lighthouse running—to keep the visitors happy, to deal with the daily problems that inevitably occur, to do the tours whenever scheduled, to get away to pick up supplies, go to the bank, post office, and grocery store when needed, to police and clean the beach and all the other areas around the island, to check all the inlets, the Twin Lakes area, and the back marina where all the kayaks, canoes, and boats are kept. You may start wishing right away you hadn't taken on such a big job for your retirement."

"Trying to run me off?"

She blushed. "No, just being sure you remember what life is like here."

"I suppose I could give you a rundown of what a naval officer's life is like daily so you might realize I'm hardly accustomed to a soft life."

She looked away. "I didn't mean to be offensive."

"Didn't you? If you'd rather I'd not come to work here all you need to do is say so, Burke. I let Dad come to present the idea to you and your mother, thinking it would be easier for you to tell him no if you didn't think it a good idea."

"I'm sorry. We need help, Waylon. I don't know why I said those things."

He put a hand on her cheek. "I know we haven't been close in the years since I left. But old friends have strong, rich ties that new friends will never know. Deep down, you know me, Burke, and I know you. It won't take long for us to grow comfortable with each other again. We always worked well together when young and we got along easily. Surely you know I'll do all I can to help fill in the void Lloyd left behind, that I'll work hard to help you and Etta keep the inn, lighthouse, the business, and the island going."

She leaned her face into his hand. "I've been scared," she admitted in a soft voice. "And I miss Dad so much."

It was all he could do not to take her in his arms, not to kiss away the tears he saw seeping out of the edge of her eyes. Instead he cupped her face, leaned over and kissed her forehead. "It will be all right, Burke. We'll keep the Light going and the business."

"What if we get used to you and you leave again?" she whispered. "It would be so hard for Mother to face another loss. To lose someone else."

He liked knowing she also meant she wouldn't want to lose him again either. Holding her earlier, being close to her now, made Waylon aware that the feelings he held for Burke ran deep and true, and that it was Burke who had drawn him back as much as the call of the Lowcountry he loved so much.

He stepped back, watching her now. Did she feel something more for him, too? Burke had always held her feelings in close, so he had no way of knowing. And she'd been excited about her upcoming thirteenth birthday when he left to go to the Citadel. Only a girl. Perhaps with time, though, her feelings would grow for him. He'd certainly work to see that happened.

CHAPTER 3

Burke woke the next morning to the familiar smell of coffee filtering into the family wing from the inn's kitchen. The Deveaux Inn had originally been the lighthouse keeper's home. Early lighthouse keepers often birthed large families of eleven or twelve children, so the houses built for them were spacious ones. Over the years the two-storied house on Watch Island had been remodeled and repaired, often following hurricanes and storms, as had the cottages, outbuildings, and other structures around the lighthouse station.

When the Deveaux family took over the inn and light station in the 1930s, after the lighthouse was decommissioned, the family extensively remodeled the house again to make it into a bed and breakfast business that could support the family. Lighthouse properties in that era either reverted back to family owners, were sold to private individuals willing to keep the lighthouse open for tours, or got taken over by state parks or other organizations. The five hundred acre property where the Deveaux Light and Inn stood had been in the Townsend, and later Townsend-Deveaux, family since the 1700s, long before the lighthouse was built and established in 1870. Burke's parents, Lloyd and Etta, were the sixth Deveaux generation to live at the island and keep the Light.

Glancing at the clock on her bedside table, Burke climbed out of bed to dress. A short time later, in navy shorts and a yellow button-up shirt, she headed through the passageway from the family wing into the inn's kitchen.

"Good morning, Novaleigh," she said, walking over to give the tall Black woman with short white hair a kiss on the cheek.

Novaleigh, wearing one of her usual bibbed calico aprons, pushed a dish into Burke's hands. "Take these scrambled eggs into the dining room and put them on the buffet for me. It's nearly eight and our guests will be making their way down for breakfast."

"All right. Is there anything else I need to take out?"

She pointed to another dish by the stove. "Get that plate of sausage patties to take out, too. I've already put out fruit, juice, coffee, and all the rest, and I'm nearly finished with this gravy." She turned to stir it on the stovetop. "Biscuits will be coming out of the oven in a few minutes."

"We're lucky to have you here at the inn," Burke said picking up the plate of sausage.

Novaleigh grinned. "I feel blessed to be here, as well." She turned to catch Burke's eye. "Your mother said a full house is coming in on Friday. Our workload is about to get busier with spring arriving."

Burke had no worries as to whether Novaleigh George could handle any number of guests they needed to serve. She'd worked here as a young girl with her mother and then taken over her mother's job later. When her husband Clifford retired from working at the park service, Lloyd offered him a job as the island's full-time groundskeeper. Novaleigh and Clifford then moved to one of the island's larger cottages on Scott Creek, making it easier for both of them without needing to boat in and out daily.

"Etta told me this morning that Waylon Jenkins is back home and coming to work and live on the island. I always liked that boy—solid, steady, with a good Christian character." She shifted the skillet of gravy off the stove eye. "You and your mama were needing more help around here, too."

"Where is Mother?"

"Sitting out on the screened porch talking to Waylon. You might want to go tell them they can come fix a plate of breakfast now."

"I'll do that." Burke turned to take the sausage and eggs into the dining room to put them on the buffet.

The Deveaux Inn, typical of most bed and breakfasts, operated on a well-oiled schedule. Breakfast was always served from eight to nine, lunch from one to two, and dinner from six to seven. Because the Deveaux Inn was larger than many smaller inns, with guests sometimes staying in the cottages as well, they'd long ago decided to serve meals using a heated buffet line. It kept the foods hot or cold as needed and made them available to guests in the portion sizes they preferred.

The dining room was a big, open room with a long row of windows to let in the light and a big fireplace at one end to offer cheerful warmth on cold evenings. Six round tables sat tucked around the room with four chairs to a table, giving ample seating space even when all six guest rooms in the inn and the four rental cabins were full. The long buffet table, now ready for breakfast, spanned the wall near the kitchen. The family and staff alternated sharing meals with their guests or eating in the family wing's dining room or on its screened porch, when the weather was fair.

Burke glanced around the dining room before going to find her mother. Etta had already set the tables, as she usually did every morning. Burke ambled around, out of habit, straightening silver and plates, checking to see if each table had salt, pepper, and other breakfast condiments. Yesterday, Burke arranged a few early daffodils in small vases on each table, and she smiled to see they still looked fresh and nice.

Novaleigh came into the dining room with a bowl of sausage gravy and steaming homemade biscuits to put out. "Go tell your mother and Waylon this breakfast is hot and ready. Tell Clifford too. He's working in the side yard trimming some ivy that dared to creep into one of his flower beds."

"I'll do that." Burke headed out of the dining room, through the inn's screened porch and out to find Clifford. Then she came back through the kitchen and cut across the side passageway to find her mother and Waylon on the family end of the porch. As she expected they sat looking over one of her mother's lists of chores together.

"Breakfast is ready," she called. "Novaleigh said to tell you both to come fix a plate." Burke could see Etta had put a pitcher of juice and a carafe of coffee on the side table beside them, along with mugs and juice glasses.

"Good morning, Burke." Waylon grinned at her as he got up. "You don't need to persuade me to head to the dining room. Novaleigh promised me earlier she was making homemade Southern gravy and biscuits. I'm sure looking forward to that. It's been a long time since I ate Novaleigh's good food."

"Well, go fix a plate," Etta said. "We'll eat breakfast out here instead of in the dining room today so we can talk a little more. I'll follow as soon as I move these papers off the table."

As Waylon headed to the buffet, Burke helped her mother gather up all the paperwork. "It looks like you've been talking with Waylon about the work around here."

"I have." She smiled and came to give Burke a hug. "I'm so pleased Waylon is joining us. He immediately picked up on everything I needed to discuss with him, knowing the lighthouse, inn, the island and its business so well. I can't believe our good fortune that he wanted to come work with us. No disrespect intended, but in comparison to Joe Lewis, Waylon is a godsend."

Burke grinned, recalling all the times Joe, a personable but not exceedingly bright man, mixed up directions Etta gave him or simply forgot to take care of tasks he should have remembered to do.

Etta paused, biting her lip in the way she did sometimes to stem tears. "I know Lloyd would be so pleased to know Waylon is here. He loved him like a son."

"I'm sure Dad's looking down with pleasure to see Waylon back."

Her mother gave her a small smile. "I'm sure you're right. I need to keep that comforting thought in my mind that Lloyd's always with us. Grief still hits me at odd and unexpected moments though."

"I know the feeling."

Burke glanced at her mother as she stuffed notes, brochures, and lists neatly into folders. Etta was tall and slim like her daughters, her dark hair silvery white and cut short now, but her brown eyes were still lively, her health strong. Her mother's life at the inn had never been an easy or idle one, but Burke knew she loved it as her father had, too. The two found a joy few could understand in faithfully carrying on the work of the lighthouse, in the Deveaux family for so many years. Burke felt the same pride and joy.

"Let's go get some breakfast," Etta said then, starting toward the door.

Burke, Waylon, and Etta soon settled down at the table on the screened porch again to eat their breakfast and to talk more about how they'd break up the responsibilities of running the inn, the lighthouse, and the island's business. Etta and Waylon argued about pay for a time, with Waylon insisting he needed less with Navy pay coming in, but the two finally compromised in the end.

After finishing breakfast Etta took Waylon on a tour through the inn while Burke took care of emails and other business at the computer. She'd gone to Trident, one of the community colleges in Charleston after graduating from high school, to get her two-year degree in Information Technology and to gain new skills the inn needed. She'd become fluent in several new computer programs, learned graphics skills, and had built a new website and kept it up since graduating.

After Waylon finished his tour indoors, Burke walked with him out into the sunshine. "I think Mom's gone over most everything you really need to know by now, but I thought I'd take you around the property, like we talked about yesterday, to remind you of anything else you might have forgotten."

"I'd forgotten much of what the inn looked like inside. It's been so long. Mostly as kids we played outside, rode bikes, ate picnics on the beach or out on the screened porch, played games in the pavilion, and raced into one of the empty cabins when it rained." He hesitated. "I followed your dad around then and helped in any way he asked, too."

"Mom said earlier she knew Dad would be pleased you're back

and working here."

"I like to think that."

Boonie, the family's black-and-white border collie, came dashing around the corner of the house then with a happy bark.

Burke watched the collie run up to Waylon with no hesitation. "He remembers you."

Waylon squatted to pet the dog. "I remember when your dad brought him home after visiting with Sam Calhoun at his plantation one day. He was only a little pup. I'd come home for a visit then. I think it was about four years ago. Right?"

She nodded. "Milo, the cat, showed up that same year."

"That brown striped cat I saw sleeping on the chair on the front porch?"

"The same. And don't underestimate that cat. He rules the roost around here. He rules Boonie too." She laughed. "Someone must have dropped him off on the island. Dad found him crying at the back door one night." She paused. "Mom threw a fit at first about keeping both Boonie and Milo. She holds fast to the 'no pets' rule for anyone staying at the inn or visiting at the lighthouse. When our old lab died, she didn't want more pets."

"Your dad loved that old black lab—Reuben I think his name was."

"We all loved Reuben. Mourned him when he died." She reached down to scratch Boonie's ears. "But we've grown crazy fond of Boonie now, too. I hope you don't mind if he walks along with us."

"Do we need a leash?"

"Not on the island except when it's real busy. Dad worked hard to train Boonie so he wouldn't be any problem. It's a mistake not to, especially with the inn, the lighthouse, and all the people coming and going. Boonie needed to be well-trained, and it was the deal Dad made with Mom to keep him."

Waylon stopped to glance back at the inn. "The Deveaux Inn is a beautiful place, clean, white, and welcoming, with its deep red roofs, family wing and garages jutting out at appealing angles. I love that gracious, shady porch spreading across the front with the rockers, paddle fans, and plants everywhere. On the upper porch you can see the ocean over the trees."

"We remodeled a lot indoors, too, over the years."

"I saw some of those changes, but much was the same. That wonderful old living room, peaceful with all those sea greens, the old ship paintings, bottles, shells, and rock fireplace, and that library with books from floor to ceiling and cozy arm chairs. Made me want to curl up and read."

"I need to remember some of your nice words for the inn brochures I create and for the website."

"Your dad was proud of all the computer and business skills you gained."

Burke changed the subject. "Did Mom take you upstairs?"

"She did. I saw some of the empty bedrooms and a few of the changes your mother felt proud of, like the renovations to the upstairs sitting room." He grinned at her. "The guest rooms still carry the names I always liked so much—The Seaside Room, The Marsh Room, The Sand Dollar Room, The Blue Sky Room, and The Sunrise Room."

"Plus The Bird Watch Room, don't forget that one. We usually simply call it the Bird Room though. Our ornithologist is staying there now. Appropriate, huh? He'll be with us until summer, working on a major project about seabirds for the university. The College of Charleston is letting him take a partial sabbatical to do the work, going back and forth to teach a class or two and to supervise his grad assistant who is handling the rest. The articles and book he's working on are especially focused on the brown pelican."

"There are a lot of them on the Deveaux Bank."

"Yes. They come and go there daily and build their nests there."

"I'd like to go out to the Bank one day. Will you go with me?"

"Sure," she answered. "Right now I thought we'd walk to the cabana and the beach, then follow the loop road around by the cabins, past the lodge, the Georges' place, and on to the boat dock and the Boals' house. We can cut over to Twin Lakes after that point when the road curls and then walk down to South Beach and the Inlet before we head back."

"Sounds good. I look forward to seeing everything again up close."

"Well, ask me anything you want while we walk. It will be mostly the two of us keeping a watch around this island, along with Henry and Clifford. I know you remember we put fencing in several places to deter trespassing and posted signs to remind beach visitors the island is private property. People often ignore the signs though. They climb over the fence and up to the lighthouse and inn. They use our banks for fishing or playing in the ocean and pull their boats up to our docks."

While they talked Burke and Waylon followed the winding pathway from the front of the inn toward the beach. A neatly landscaped side road wove from the main road to the front of the Deveaux Inn, where passengers unloaded from the trams that brought them from the marina.

"Clifford keeps all the landscaping and gardens around the inn looking beautiful," Waylon commented.

"He knows what everything is, too. Ask him if you want to know the name of anything. He'd love talking to you about it."

"I'll enjoy spending time with Clifford again. He's another favorite of mine. I trailed after him, too, when younger, helping him with one task or the other—mostly to hear his stories."

She laughed. "He and Novaleigh know enough stories about the island and its history, the land and its creatures, to write several books."

"Perhaps you should write one."

"No, that's not my gift." She shook her head. "Lila might write one, though, with her beautiful illustrations mixed in."

They stopped at the large covered cabana, a pavilion with picnic tables and benches. On one side was a storage room filled with beach chairs, umbrellas, and other beach paraphernalia and on the other side two restrooms.

Burke spoke to the dog to sit and then jumped up to settle on a picnic table where she could look down the sandy pathway leading through the dunes to the beach. "Be sure to check the locks here when you make your rounds. We always keep the restrooms and storage room locked. All the beaches in South Carolina belong to the state, and thus to the people. Tourists and locals with boats, kayaks, or canoes can find their way to our beaches and have a right to enjoy them."

"They don't have the right to come further into the island, though. It's all private property." Waylon sat on the picnic table beside her, enjoying the view out over the ocean.

"Yes, but seeing the cabana, people slip up here anyway. They go through the gates and climb over the fences to walk up the hill to the lighthouse and pavilion, too. Sometimes they don't know they shouldn't venture into the island; other times they know and don't care. Part of your job daily, unfortunately, is playing police officer. We try to tell people in a nice way about the law when we find them far into our private property, but occasionally the people we speak to aren't always nice."

"I remember times when Lloyd had to deal with trespassers," Waylon added. "Most were nice—like you said—simply not paying attention to the signs, but some got ugly."

"I've always hated making people leave. I know they're curious and attracted to the lighthouse, but there are legal risks if people are harmed while roaming around on the island and many leave trash behind and do damage."

"You have a right to protect your property. We deal with those issues over at the landing, too."

Burke shifted to her feet from the table where she sat. "Unless you want to walk to the beach from here, we'll move on." She glanced down the path winding through the dunes to the ocean. "I don't know if Etta mentioned it to you but hundreds of starfish washed onto the beach here yesterday. I've never seen anything like it before. Lila found them first, early in the morning, and spent hours throwing live starfish back into the sea. Henry came later to clean the beach further, carrying the rest of the poor creatures away that died in the wash-up. Myron, our ornithologist, properly reminded several of our guests at dinner, when one asked if starfish were really fish, that they're technically called echinoderms in the Asteroidean class and not fish at all, despite their name."

Waylon laughed. "I guess having the professor around isn't always an asset."

"Oh, he's gracious about it." She shook her head. "Anyway, if there are still dead starfish washing in, I'd rather not see them. Henry said they only washed up on the main beach here below the cabana and not further down at the inlet at South Beach. We'll walk to the beach there later, if you want."

"You're the tour leader," he replied, pushing off of the table and landing close to her as he did. Burke noted he was only a little taller than her now, where once at five years her senior, he'd been so much taller. She watched him pause for a moment looking at her, and she felt her heartbeat kick up in an odd way. Did that look of his mean anything? Did he see her differently now? Burke had often imagined how he'd view her and how she'd feel spending time with him again. Before he'd left, and in the times when he came back for visits, she'd sometimes seen him watching her and wondered.

CHAPTER 4

Waylon enjoyed seeing Burke's awareness of him as he stood close to her, studying her, enjoying the rich brown of her eyes, the flush on her checks. He caught a whiff of some light tangy scent, too, with a hint of ginger, spices, and vanilla. The scent could be her cologne, but knowing Burke it was probably from a soap or lotion she used instead. She'd never cared much for wearing perfumes or more than light makeup, but with her natural fresh complexion and looks, she'd never really needed anything to enhance her beauty.

She rubbed at her cheeks, frowning. "Do I have something on my face?"

"Only natural beauty," he said in a soft voice.

Her eyes widened before she turned away. "Funny, I don't remember you being the complimentary type before."

"People change over time, Burke. Maybe I held those compliments in before, thought better of saying them."

She shrugged, starting to walk up the path toward the road. "I can't imagine a reason anyone wouldn't enjoy hearing a few compliments."

"Sometimes between a man and a woman, words and compliments can lead to more. And it isn't always the time between two people for that."

"Hmmmph," she said, not turning back to him, but Waylon could see the flush rising up her neck.

He smiled to himself, following her.

Deciding to help her past her discomfort, Waylon asked, "What brought Lila back home? Mother said she came home for your dad's funeral, left again, but then suddenly decided to return before Christmas for good." He paused. "Wasn't she a nun or something?"

Burke turned to frown at him. "We're Episcopal, Waylon. Being at Sewanee in the Community of St. Mary was different from being a Catholic nun. It's more a chosen vocation, a place to work and serve God."

Waylon hardly saw the difference but decided not to say so. "I didn't see her at breakfast this morning."

"She eats by herself some mornings. Lila asked to live at Inland Cottage when she came back." Burke stopped and pointed down the road to the small cottage they could see through the trees behind the inn. "Lila said she got used to a quiet life and wanted to live separately, to keep some of the ways she'd come to know. She still spends a lot of time in prayer, in contemplation and stuff. Growing up, Lila always lived close to God. She still does, but maybe more so now."

"Why did she leave that community?"

"Mother and I aren't really sure. We know she began to spend a lot of her time as a volunteer at the Community of St. Mary while in college. She went to Sewanee to study art. The two properties are close. After Lila graduated, she decided to stay on in an internship of some type at the Community and then decided to make it her vocation."

Burke rubbed an arm, still looking toward the cottage. "We visited her there a time or two. I honestly couldn't be happy in a life with so much structure, but Lila seemed content. The Community of St. Mary puts a lot of emphasis on caring well for body, soul, and the earth. They do organic gardening and emphasize care for creation. They believe in leading healthy, valuable lives and in improving the world through their actions. Lila especially found her place working in the gift shop they run and in creating art to share and sell to benefit St. Mary's Community. She seemed to find her niche in that ministry work and in helping people spiritually, like students or people coming to visit the area or retreat center, hoping to find peace. The setting in the mountains is incredibly scenic."

"Is Lila doing all right since she came back?"

"I think so. She's been very private about her decision to return home from Tennessee, but she's pursued her art with a passion since coming back. She's practically taken over running the gift shop at the lighthouse, too. Wait until you see all she's done to improve it since getting back."

"I hope no one hurt her at the Community in some way."

Burke sighed. "Mother asked her about that. She said no, that she simply came to realize the life there wasn't her genuine calling, that another life called to her more."

Waylon kept pace as they walked on. "This life here on the island, this place, can call strongly to the heart. Perhaps it simply called her back home."

She smiled at him. "That's a kind way to put it. I'm happy to have Lila back. You know she's the youngest of us."

"You took care of her a lot when she was little, too."

"I did. We shared a room, and Celeste and Gwen shared a room. Lila and I always seemed to suit each other in personality."

He laughed. "And Celeste and Gwen were usually the ones to get in trouble. They always filled up a room with their presence and talk, a lot like your father."

"Yes," she agreed. "Lila and I are more like Mother."

"Maybe in some ways. In others you and Lila are totally unique. I saw that in Gwen and Celeste, too, in all four of you Lighthouse Sisters."

She punched his arm. "We got called that enough in school, and as Lila said the other day it wasn't always spoken kindly." Her face softened then. "I remember many times you stood up for us at school though, got into a few fights protecting us."

"I'm glad if you think I was a hero." They paused as the other cabins, all in a row along the street, came into view. "Do you still rent these four cabins closest to the inn? I think I remember Etta telling me that."

"Yes. Like the rooms in the inn, they each have their own names, too. The Seaside Cottage here is closest to the beach path, the Redfish Cottage beside it. Lakeview Cottage follows, set back a little from the road with a view of Twin Lakes from its back deck, and Sunnyside Cottage is the final one. We let the Georges have the Scott Creek Cottage, the largest cabin on the island. It's further away from the inn complex on the creek. And as I mentioned, Lila is staying at Inland Cottage. We always kept Inland only as a backup for unexpected guests anyway and seldom rented it out. It's rather small and plain. Lila seems to like that about it. She turned the upstairs attic room into a studio, said the big skylight there provided good light for her painting."

"Where the inn is white with a red roof, most of the cottages are red with white roofs and trimmings. I always thought that made them special."

"Dad always said all the light station buildings were designed in red and white to match the stripes of the lighthouse. That coloration is the Deveaux Lighthouse's Daymark, its daytime identifier. A ship or boat seeing the red and white stripes of the lighthouse from a distance, or even the red and white colors of the buildings, knows they are near land, near Watch Island and the North Edisto River. The light flashes of the lighthouse at night, called a Light Signature, are distinctive, too."

Waylon smiled. "I watched and timed the flashes last night—five seconds on, five seconds off, five seconds on, and then twenty seconds off, before it began to repeat."

Burke slowed her pace to glance at him. "I've always found the repetition and continuity of the light comforting, the regular rhythm of it peaceful. I like order. It's comforting to me. I like the easy pattern and rhythm of life here, of the sea, the weather."

"Life doesn't always flow along in an easy rhythm though, Burke. Even here. There are hurricanes and storms, sorrows and disappointments, that come to us all."

"Perhaps, but after time, the rhythm returns, the comfortable patterns of the weather, the tides, the rising and setting of the sun, the migration of the birds, the coming and going of the seasons. People always seem to be seeking something, yearning for something beyond what they know and have, but I've always been content right here."

"Your dad told me he found new strength and purpose leaving the island, going into the Navy, traveling and seeing the world. He said doing so satisfied a deep sense of adventure in him and made him content later to return, enriched from his journeys. So perhaps we each have our own course to chart. Some boats stay close to shore; some travel afar and then perhaps return."

Burke stopped to prop her foot on a bench by the road to tie her shoe. "You've developed a poetic streak I don't remember."

He grinned at her. "You see? Sometimes breaking from the comfortable patterns of life can bring change for the good. I needed the changes I've walked through. They've made me a better and stronger person, I believe."

"Lila said that finding oneself fully and realizing one's purpose is an aspect of spirituality, a part of life's journey. She said some people find their way and purpose early; others find their way and purpose after experiences and change. She believes many people need those changes. Like you, she said some boats are meant to sail further off to sea to teach people courage and confidence. For many their lives and hearts were not in the pattern they were pressed to conform to when young. Lila insists each person has to find his or her own destined way and path."

"Lila is a wise woman now. It looks like leaving home as she did took away much of her earlier timidity. She sounds stronger and surer about herself."

She nodded. "Actually she is. She wrote a quote in pretty calligraphy and framed it on the wall at her cottage. It says: Life isn't about finding yourself, it is about discovering who God created you to be." Burke glanced at her watch. "We're pausing and talking so much that we're not making good time. Novaleigh will not be happy if we're late for lunch."

"Let's go down to the lodge and get the golf cart that I left in the garage. We can make better time riding around the rest of the island and stopping wherever we need to."

"Good idea. Let me take Boonie back to the inn though. I see Clifford in the yard working. Boonie can hang out with him." She waved at Clifford, taking Boonie over to him and then they walked on down the road and through a side path to the lodge.

As they drove up the road in the golf cart a short time later, Burke asked, "Did you settle in and sleep okay at the lodge last night? I forgot to ask earlier."

"I slept great. The lodge is close to the mouth of the river and not far from the ocean. I could hear the sea rolling in the quiet."

"That's a good sound." Burke pointed to their left as they drove along. "I'm sure you remember there are several trails cutting through the island like this one going to Twin Lakes and ending up on the other end of the loop road near the estuary. Henry and Clifford try to keep the trails cut back and safe but much of the island is still maritime forest with marshy areas. We try to encourage visitors at the inn and lighthouse to stay on the maintained trails if they go exploring."

"People forget that except for the lighthouse station and buildings that the bulk of this island is undeveloped and basically wilderness."

"I guess that's right."

"I'm going to meet with Henry and Clifford to talk about what I can do to help them to keep the grounds up and keep everything safe."

"That's good." She gestured to a house in the trees to their right. "That's the Georges' house. Their son Gavin lives in their old house now on Point of Pines Road near Novaleigh's parents. Gavin married Maizie Jessup, one of the Jessup daughters from Edward's family plantation. You know the Jessups manage and take care of all that plantation for the Calhouns—they have since forever. Gavin and Maizie have a little girl named NellaJune now. She's a cutie. You'll see them over here some time I'm sure."

Walyon drove the cart on, pleased that Burke hadn't argued with him over who would drive. She used to vie with him about it.

"There's the Boals' House on the right." She waved a hand in that direction. "Let's turn down that side road by their house to stop at the Boat Dock."

A few minutes later, Waylon parked the golf cart by the paved boat ramp and near the two long wooden walkways that wound through the marshland to the docks. At the far end of the longest dock sat a long covered pavilion with U.S. and South Carolina flags flying above it on a tall flagpole. He spotted a few small jonboats pulled up to the side of the pavilion on one side and behind the pavilion noticed several colorful kayaks and canoes in piles, waiting for use.

"It looks much like I remember," he commented.

As he followed Burke out across the boardwalk to the larger dock and pavilion, he noted that the other long walkway, across from them, led to two covered sheds where several larger skiffs and boats were kept.

"Our problem here is always safety, seeing that our guests, not used to being around the water, get into a boat properly without taking a dunk in the water," Burke said as she walked into the pavilion. "All these locked storage bins contain life jackets, paddles, and other equipment. Our other problem here besides safety is theft, as you might imagine. You'll notice the chains attached to the canoes and kayaks we rent to our guests."

Waylon glanced out over the water to where South Creek ended, splitting into Ocella Creek heading north and Townsend Creek winding south. "I remember these back creeks as great places for canoeing and kayaking."

"Yes, the creeks are scenic but not without their dangers. Henry Bouls, a former shrimper and at home on the water, usually goes with most of our inexperienced guests to paddle down any of the creeks. Dad used to love to do that, too."

"I can help with that," Waylon put in.

"Good." She sent him a smile. "Henry still likes to shrimp when he can with his son Calvin on their boat the Della Belle. They're out today, which means we'll get fresh shrimp for dinner tonight or tomorrow at the inn."

"I remember Calvin. Didn't the Boals used to live over at Rockville?"

"They did. Kind of like the Georges, Henry and Rita Jean used to commute to work. It wasn't far, but when Calvin graduated from high school, they moved here to the Boat House."

Waylon glanced back at it, sitting further inland from the docks but with a good view down to the water. "Their place looks like a good sized house."

She nodded. "It's newer than many of the buildings around the island, built later when the increase in tourism demanded someone live at the backside of the island. Ralph Cavett lived here for many years before the Boals. He was a wily old codger. When he passed away, Henry suggested he and Rita Jean move here. Calvin and his wife Maggie live at their old place now. It's a nice property in Rockville with acreage on the water. Henry wanted to keep it in the family. Calvin comes over to help Henry with big tasks; so do Calvin's boys Eddie and Joe. They're fifteen and thirteen. Calvin's wife Maggie fills in with housekeeping and cooking at the inn, too, so Rita Jean and Novaleigh can take days off when needed. Mother and I help, also."

"It sounds like everything runs like a well-oiled machine."

He saw her smirk.

"Well, not always," she said. "Rita Jean, although a meticulous housekeeper, can be testy to work with. She and her daughter-in-law Maggie don't get along very well sometimes. You'll see that soon enough. Maggie is the happy, warm-hearted type—sings in the kitchen, hums while she works, is gracious and friendly to everyone. Rita Jean is all business and somewhat stern in nature. Maggie's sunny disposition seems to annoy her."

Waylon laughed. "Funny how those serious, grumpy types, often get annoyed at the people who look on life with a happy, positive attitude instead."

"Well, mostly we all work harmoniously, getting around the little problems that are inevitable with different personality types."

Burke glanced toward one of the covered storage sheds off the other walkway. "You can keep your skiff down here under cover if you want. I've been thinking we should build a covered area for unloading at the main marina where the ferry comes in and where our tram picks up our guests staying at the inn. They get a little testy loading and unloading when it rains. The tram is covered, of course, and we have a big van for cold or rainier days …"

He interrupted. "But people still have to get out of the ferry and walk to the cabana or van. I noticed in past that can be a problem in bad weather. I helped your dad a number of times to move baggage in the pouring rain. A wet and nasty job. Your dad talked to mine a couple of times about collecting some estimates to build that addition to the marina dock."

She turned to start back down the walkway. "Could you work on getting estimates to build that? I'm sure your dad knows some good contractors who could do the work."

"Yeah. I'll see what I can do," he said, following her.

As they walked past the Boals' neat white house with its red roof, Waylon noticed several other storage sheds around the area for equipment and a small house a short distance from the Boals' home where Townsend Creek cut along the south end of the island.

Burke noticed his glance. "That's the old original boathouse. Ralph lived in it for a time before this better house was built. The old boathouse is rough but sturdy. Eddie and Joe love to stay in it when they come for a weekend or in the summer."

Climbing into the cart, they set out again. The Island Loop Road wound into denser maritime forest on this back end of the island, the trees shading the smooth, sandy road. Remembering Burke's plan, Waylon pulled over at the start of the Twin Lakes path when he spotted the old trail sign. They walked along the narrow woods trail, shaded and quiet, soon spotting the first side trail to the lake.

Waylon slowed.

"Let's walk on to the second trail that leads to the large section of the lake," Burke said. "The fishing dock is there. I try to keep a watch on it to be sure it stays in good shape."

"I remember that dock. I used to fish there a lot. Your dad said both the lakes were probably fed underground from the nearby estuary."

After turning down the second trail, they followed along the narrow path through the woods until the trail opened to a clearing beside the lake. Twin Lakes, more like two large connected lagoons, sprawled across a marshy area. The water was a fresh and salt water mix, its consistency depending on the rains and tides. Only fish and sea animals that had the ability to thrive in both fresh and saltwater lived in the lake.

Spartina or cordgrass lined the sides of the banks and Waylon caught the familiar scent of pluff mud on the air. He walked out onto the fishing deck to get a closer look. "If I remember right you can find clams and crabs here and catch a few fish, if you're lucky—mullet, small red drums, perch, sea trout or croakers."

"Raccoons like it here, too, as well as snakes and a few turtles. You'll also spot some water birds, like that egret." She pointed at one standing a distance away in the water's edge. "Myron has seen marsh wrens and Saltmarsh sparrows back here, too, along with herons and other birds."

Burke walked closer to the deck rail as she talked, but Waylon reached out to grab her arm and pull her back as she started to lean her arms on the rail.

"Whoa. Keep a distance, Burke. We have another visitor here today—a very big alligator." He pointed to the reptile, partially submerged in the dark murky waters below the pier.

"Well, great," Burke said with annoyance. "I wish he hadn't made his way over here. It causes trouble with the tourists."

She shifted then, realizing Waylon still had his arms wrapped around her—and rather snuggly, too.

"You can let me go now, Waylon. I'm not planning to leap into the lagoon with that alligator."

Waylon let her go with reluctance, letting his hands drift down her arms as he did.

She turned to look at him. "If I didn't know better, I'd think you're trying to flirt with me, Waylon Jenkins."

He grinned at her words. Burke had always been perceptive—and candid.

Deciding to be honest, he said, "Actually, I've been trying really hard not to do that, Burke, but it's difficult."

He watched her eyes widen with surprise, as she backed away from him.

"I know." Waylon shrugged. "We work together and it's inappropriate."

She walked carefully off the pier, keeping an eye on the gator and on him at the same time. "We probably need to head back to the cart," she said in a matter-of-fact tone, changing the subject. "I still want to stop by South Beach before we head back for lunch."

Waylon followed after her, annoyed at her total evasion of the issue. "So you're going to avoid making any other comment back?"

Burke slowed to turn and look at him again. "I don't know what to say back, Waylon. You're confusing me. We've known each other forever and now …" She looked away.

"Listen. I know I'm older than you, Burke, but have you never felt anything for me but just comfortable friendship?"

"I really don't want to talk about this," she snapped abruptly, walking on.

Oh, well. Waylon let it go. Obviously he'd moved in too fast on Burke. But he thought he'd picked up on some feelings earlier that pushed him to hunger for more.

They drove on in an awkward silence around the winding road, with marshland now on their right, the maritime forest soon disappearing as they drew nearer the southern end of the island. Waylon parked the cart at a trail sign and pullover, and they followed a winding pathway through scrub grass and the dunes to the far end of the island where the Townsend Creek separated Watch Island from the rest of Edisto Island beyond it.

"I remember your dad telling me the island used to connect to the mainland of Edisto before Hurricane Gracie roared across the Lowcountry in 1959," Waylon said, trying to break the silence. "This channel of the Townsend Creek broke through during that storm. With all the rain, wind, and flooding that occurred then, this whole new wide tributary formed, totally separating Watch Island from the rest of Edisto Island and the end of Botany Bay Beach we can see across the water. There was only a narrow creek between the two before. Your dad said you could walk across easily, especially when the tide was out."

Instead of responding, Burke stalked across the beach, passing one of the No Trespassing signs on her way. "I'm glad we came down here today." She snapped out the words. "Look at all this trash someone left behind. It makes me so mad."

She pulled a folded piece of plastic out of her pocket, shaking it out to reveal a small garbage bag. "I always carry a folded up garbage bag in my pocket. I never know when I'm going to run into a mess like this." She leaned over to start picking up cola cans and other paper litter left behind.

Waylon moved in to help her. When they finished and Burke stood up, he saw tears in her eyes.

"This isn't worth crying about," he said, surprised at the tears.

"I'm not crying about this." She glared at him, crossing her arms defensively. "I'm crying about you flirting with me. Just because I'm older now doesn't mean I don't have feelings, Waylon Jenkins. I don't like you playing male-female games with me. It hurts."

He started toward her but then stopped as she pulled back.

She shook a finger toward him. "I'm saying this once and once only. I had a crush on you forever when I was a girl and of course you never noticed me or anything." Her voice rose. "Why should you have? I was five years younger than you, only a scrawny kid when you started becoming a man. I know it was stupid, but I couldn't help it. I mourned when you left, too. Then whenever you visited home, even when at college nearby in Charleston, you only came to the island for short visits anymore and mostly to spend time with Dad."

Waylon couldn't help smiling as he listened to her words.

"Don't you smile and laugh at me." She dropped the garbage bag and moved closer to push him in the chest. "I won't have it, do you hear? And I don't want you playing games with me now that you're home again. It makes me remember how much that time hurt. I don't care how silly and stupid to you this sounds, it's how I feel."

He grabbed her arms, looking down at her. "You need to know your dad warned me off, Burke. He saw I was starting to notice you and have feelings for you and he warned me off."

Waylon watched her eyes widen with shock.

"Dad warned you off?" she repeated, her voice breaking.

"Yes, he reminded me you were twelve years old, just a little girl, when I was seventeen. He said it was a good thing I'd be leaving for the Citadel and the Navy soon. He made it clear to me I was to think of you only like a sister and not make any moves to take my feelings beyond that."

Her mouth dropped open. "You had feelings for me?" she asked in a shocked voice.

Waylon put a hand to her face. "I had big feelings for you that never went away, Burke. Every time I came home I had to push them down. I tried to stay away from spending time with you for that reason." He stroked her cheek. "I think you drew me back home as much as anything else, Burke Deveaux. I told myself that maybe with time I could begin to change our relationship, let you know how I felt, see if I could move it to something more than only an old friendship."

She began crying now, putting a hand to her mouth.

"I'm sorry I upset you. Have I waited too late, Burke?" He hated to see her crying. "I can pack and leave again if this seems wrong to you. Maybe I should."

Burke stood there quietly for a few moments, then her eyes met his. "Do you know what my mind is saying over and over again right now? It's saying: Waylon Arthur Jenkins likes you; Waylon Arthur Jenkins likes you." She gave him a small smile. "Like one of those silly childish notes the kids used to pass in school."

He grinned. "Be assured that Waylon Arthur Jenkins more than likes you, Burke. I think I'll show you how much more." He leaned in to kiss her then. How could he resist, learning she, too, had cared about him all this time?

It was a sweet moment and better than he'd ever even imagined, feeling her lips under his, holding her close against him, feeling her heart beating and her breath catching. He shouldn't have waited so long to come home.

Burke grabbed the front of his shirt as he pulled away. "Don't you ever leave me again, Waylon, do you hear? And don't you ever let anyone tell you not to care about me again."

"Your dad meant well," he whispered, pulling her close again and kissing her forehead. "You were only a child. He should have warned me off."

"No, he should have known you were a good person and would never have done anything to hurt me."

"Fathers don't think like that about their little girls. They want to protect them, keep them safe. Don't fault him for caring. I probably shouldn't have let his warning stay with me so long, kept me from seeing if there could be anything between us but friendship."

She gave him a small smile. "Well, I guess you've got your answer to that."

"Yes, and it's a good answer, too." He kissed her again and then pulled her down to sit beside him in the sand. "Let's sit here for a minute and just revel in this, okay. I still can't get over the shock of finding out you've cared for me all this time, too." He hesitated. "Or at least cared for me part of the time. You spent time being mad at me, too. Did you fall for a lot of other boys and men in between? I'm lucky I didn't come home to find you married."

"I had some offers," she said, leaning against him when he tucked his arm around her. "But something always seemed to be missing, even when I liked some of them a lot. Most didn't want to consider living here on the island either, and I didn't want to leave."

He leaned his head against hers. "I can't say I'm sorry to hear that."

She punched at him. "So what about you? I kept thinking one

day your mother Aileen would come over to tell Mother and me you'd gotten married. I so dreaded that day."

"No one I met compared with my memory of you, Burke. It must have been destiny we both waited." He paused. "You'll be thirty this September."

She frowned at him. "Thanks for that cheerful reminder. May I remind you that you'll be thirty-five in May."

He winked at her. "Well, think of us as simply well-seasoned."

She laughed and he wrapped her in his arms to kiss her again. It was a heady, stirring thing being close to Burke like this after dreaming of her for so long. He pulled away after a time, breathing deeply and drawing in his control, but pleased to see Burke struggling with her emotions, too.

They sat quietly for a few minutes before Burke turned to him.

"Could we just enjoy getting to know each other like this for a while without letting everyone else know, too?" she asked in a soft voice. "I'd like some time for us to explore our developing friendship without everyone offering their thoughts about it."

"I like those words developing friendship." He leaned in to kiss her again. "Let's develop it some more."

They kissed until a group of boys in a passing boat hooted at them, reminding them they sat in a somewhat open spot here on the beach.

Burke glanced at her watch. "We'd better get back."

"Come walk on the beach with me tonight. I know you walk Boonie most every night. Your mother mentioned it. I'll meet you at the cabana and walk with you."

She smiled, getting up to brush the sand off her shorts. "I like that idea. I'll see you then." She picked up the garbage bag and started up the path.

"Burke, I'm going to get Novaleigh to make me a boxed lunch and supper to take to the lodge. I'll tell her I have work to do there." He grinned at her as he caught up with her on the path. "If I sit in the same room with you right now, or later this evening, in front of your mother and sister, they'll know from the big smile on my face—and from the fact that I won't be able to keep looking at you every minute—that something has happened with us."

She stopped by the golf cart to look at him again, putting a hand on his face. "I love those words, too, that something has happened with us. Aren't those the most wonderful words?"

"They are." Waylon kissed her again before they climbed in the golf cart. "We're a good better-late-than-never story, too."

"Who first said those words better-late-than-never?" Burke asked.

"I don't know." Waylon shrugged as he started the cart. "I think it's been attributed to a lot of people, but right now I'm just glad it's happened to us."

CHAPTER 5

Burke floated through the entire morning the next day. She and Waylon had walked on the beach at length last night, talking and falling in love. Even if they hadn't said the words yet, the emotions were there. Burke simply reveled in the wonder of it.

At dinner last night and at breakfast this morning, she had eaten in the dining room with two couples who were leaving on Friday, spending time letting them share memories of the week, answering their questions, enjoying their company. As giddy as she felt in her heart, Burke was surprised everyone didn't notice and comment about it. She imagined her mother, Lila, or Novaleigh might notice the change in her right away but everyone seemed oblivious to this new secret buried in her heart.

Her mother came to join her as breakfast ended. "Aren't those two couples the nicest people?" she asked, looking after them as they left the dining room. "They've known each other since they used to double-date in high school. It was nice of you to eat with them."

"I like them, too," Burke said, occupying herself with finishing one of Novaleigh's apple muffins.

Etta passed Burke a list. "These are our guests coming in tomorrow. The three Ellis sisters and their husbands, all from different states up north, will be taking three rooms." Etta pointed at the couples' names on the list. "They are the Orrs, Shaddens, and Wells. They're all retired and decided to plan a little two-week holiday here together. I imagine they'll travel around the area, as well. They're real excited about seeing Charleston."

Burke smiled to see, as usual, Etta's little personal notes about their guests scribbled in below their names.

"I've scheduled the other two inn rooms, besides the one Myron is in, to two other couples coming in from Wisconsin, the Jacobsens and the Hartsells." She laughed. "Rebecca Hartsell, who called to make the reservation, said they were all sick of ice, snow, and freezing cold weather and wanted to get away to some place warmer. All these couples plan to stay two weeks with us—good money for the inn."

"Yes. That's happy news."

Her mother smiled. "We always forget that March here in the Lowcountry, even if chilly some days and evenings, seems like paradise to visitors from the north."

"The weather reporter on television last night gave updates about some blizzard or other roaring through the northern states. Seems like Wisconsin had temperatures below freezing and about eight inches of snow."

Etta nodded as she made a note on her list. "They love the mild weather here right now."

"Who's coming to the Lakeview Cottage?" Burke asked, spotting one of the cottages on her mother's guest list.

"A young couple, Neila and Perry Ormont, bringing their kayaks. They have all sorts of expeditions planned. I doubt we'll see much of them except at meals."

"Looks like we'll be busy."

Rita Jean walked into the dining room with a frown on her face. She plopped a paper bag onto their table. "I found this tucked in Evelyn Berle's trash while cleaning her room this morning when she was at breakfast. It's booze bottles. You know we don't allow liquor at the inn or food or drinks in the rooms. Obviously she's been tittling all week while she's been here. I kept thinking there was an odd smell in the room."

Rita Jean, their housekeeper—a fine, fastidious one—was a small stocky woman with short curly hair, helped along with a little reddish-brown coloring. One of those individuals with a natural bent toward cleanliness and order, she had been an asset to the family ever since she first came to work at the Deveaux Inn.

She lifted her chin now. "I didn't say a thing to the woman about this. It's your job to handle it."

"I didn't pick up on the fact that Evelyn had a drinking problem. She conceals it well." Etta sighed, fingering the bottles in the sack. "I remember she confided when she made her reservation that her husband passed away recently. Perhaps she's taking it hard and not handling her grief well."

"Well, I haven't seen you taking to the bottle over Lloyd's loss," Rita Jean said.

Burke watched her mother wince at the reminder. "Evelyn will be checking out in the morning. Perhaps we can simply overlook it this time and not confront her."

"I think that might be best, too," Etta agreed. "I'll make a note by her name in our records, though, in case she decides to return again."

"Handle it as you will, but it isn't always a help to someone with a problem to overlook it and not call it to their attention," Rita Jean stated.

"I know," Etta agreed. "But we can't resolve everyone's difficulties here at the inn. This time I think we'll let it pass. She hasn't caused any difficulties for us."

"Speak for yourself." Rita Jean put a hand on one hip. "I'll need to spend extra time cleaning her room and airing out any liquor smells left there. And I have enough to do today and tomorrow getting ready for all the new guests coming in to the inn without more work to deal with. Plus I have one of the cottages on my cleaning list to get ready."

"I'll take care of cleaning and getting the Lakeview Cottage ready," Burke offered.

Etta smiled. "Thank you, Burke. I'm going to work in the kitchen with Novaleigh, as well, to help her get extra salads and desserts ready to make her food preparation load lighter."

Satisfied in part, Rita Jean glanced at her watch. "Well, I'd best head upstairs to start getting the empty rooms ready for new guests tomorrow." She picked up the sack. "I'll take this to the dumpster outside. No sense in it stinking up our garbage indoors anywhere."

As she left, Etta drummed her fingers on the table. "I guess we can be glad Evelyn didn't cause problems this week with her drinking."

"Some people conceal alcoholism well," Burke added.

"Are we wrong not to confront her?" Etta asked.

"No. I feel sorry for her, but I think you're right to let this one go. She is leaving tomorrow morning."

"I'll keep a watch on her until then," Etta added.

Burke could recall many times in past when her father or mother enforced their rules at the inn and asked people to leave over inappropriate behavior. "Rules are made so things run well," her father used to say. "But they're of no use if not enforced."

Glancing at her list, Etta brought up a new subject. "Waylon said at breakfast he is meeting with Clifford and Henry today at the lodge. They're sharing lunch at the lodge while they talk and Novaleigh is sending food down for them. Waylon told me he's going to start getting estimates for the work to add a covered pavilion to the marina. He mentioned you talked with him about it yesterday. I hope he can get someone to work on it soon before we get even busier here." Etta smiled. "It will be nice not to hear whining and complaining from guests arriving in the rain. Your father and I talked for years about adding a pavilion but never got around to it."

"I'm sure Waylon's dad Hal knows people to recommend for the job."

"Waylon said he can help with a lot of the work, too. I imagine Calvin might also help. He's young and strong, good with tools."

Burke felt pleased to know Waylon had already started getting information about the project.

Her mother idly rearranged silver on the table. "Waylon assured me he'd pick up all the guests at the landing on time tomorrow and get them back here by 4:00 to check in. He also said he'd help the young couple get their kayaks and gear up to the cabin. Isn't it wonderful to have some of that load off our shoulders?"

"It is," Burke said, not adding more.

"I mentioned to Waylon that you'd be heading over to the Bohicket Marina to go to the post office and pick up some needed groceries today and he offered to go with you. Waylon said he was good at hauling bags." She grinned. "I told him I felt sure you'd be glad of his help. He asked me to tell you to walk down to the lodge after lunch, that he'd run you over to the marina. That was nice of him wasn't it?"

Burke kept her voice noncommittal. "Yes, it is, but remember Waylon is working for us now, Mom. It's the sort of thing we hoped he'd help with."

She nodded. "Well, that's true. Be sure to show him where we keep our old van at the marina so if he needs to run errands for us he'll know where it is."

"I'll do that." Burke piled up her dishes to take to the kitchen. "I'd better get over to the cabin to start cleaning it up."

Grateful to slip away from more conversation with her mother, she headed to the cottage. The temperature had dropped and Burke wore jeans today and a blue and tan striped shirt. As she headed out the door she slipped on a favorite tan denim jacket, too. The ocean breeze blew cool in the morning and the cabin would probably be chilly until she turned on the heat to warm it up.

Burke followed the path from the inn across to the cabins, and let herself into the Lakeview Cottage with her key. The old cabin had a covered porch on the front, leading into a living, dining, and kitchen area with a bath and bedroom downstairs and a broad deck on the back with a view of Twin Lakes through the trees.

Humming a happy little tune to herself, which had been floating through her mind all morning, Burke stood inside the cabin for a moment, lost in sweet memories.

"Need some help?" A voice called from behind her.

Burke turned to see Lila at the door, dressed in neat, black slacks and a grey sweater.

"Mother said you offered to clean the cabin to help Rita Jean get ready for all the guests coming in."

Burke hesitated. There was no polite way to refuse time with Lila.

"Well, sure, you can help if you want to," she said after a moment. "I can do it easily myself though if you need to work in the gift shop. I'll be doing tours at the lighthouse tomorrow on Friday and on Saturday, as usual, and we'll probably have more visitors with fair weather expected and all our new guests coming in."

"I already cleaned the gift shop well yesterday. I can help you here now." Lila stepped inside giving Burke one of those soft sweet smiles of hers. "You sounded happy when I walked up, humming away. I heard you humming earlier this morning, too."

"There's nothing wrong with humming." Burke walked over to turn up the heat in the cabin to warm it.

"No, humming is a very self-soothing activity and often an unconscious way of expressing inner happiness. You hum when you feel good, and you feel good when you hum."

Burke tried to decide if Lila meant anything in particular with those words as she went to the closet to get out the vacuum. "I'll dust and vacuum if you want to clean the kitchen. Then we can make the beds in the bedroom and put out fresh towels."

"That sounds fine." Lila headed to the kitchen and both busied themselves working. It didn't take long to get the little cottage spic and span and ready for guests. As they finished spreading sheets on the two twin beds, Lila said, "Let's go sit down to rest for a minute. I found some cold bottles of water in the refrigerator. I want to ask you about Gwen and Celeste. They usually come home for Easter, which isn't that far away now, but I haven't heard if they will come now since both were home this fall for Daddy's funeral."

Deciding the focus of this discussion safe, Burke agreed and soon relaxed in one of the living room's comfortable chairs, propping her feet on the coffee table.

Lila grinned. "Don't let Mother see you with your feet on the table."

"I think we're safe here." Burke leaned back to relax.

"Do you think Gwen, Alex, and the children will drive home for Easter?"

"I don't know. It's a long trip from Little Rock, Arkansas, well over twelve hours. They usually fly when they come and I don't blame them for that. A lot of times Alex can't get away from the restaurant and Gwen comes with the kids by herself."

"Are they doing all right?"

"They're fine as far as I know. Gwen isn't big on writing letters. She finally finished her teaching degree and has been subbing while she looks for a job."

"I remember Gwen used to write letters before the children came. With her life so busy she likes to text more now, like Celeste. Mother showed me a picture of Gwen and Alex's house yesterday. It looks really nice. She showed me some photos of the kids, too. Mother said Alex's restaurant stays busy all the time and that the downtown area near the river where they opened The Riverside Grille is booming."

Burke crossed her ankles. "Yes, everything seems to be going well for them. Chase is eight and the twins, Leah and Rose, six."

"They're beautiful children." Lila paused. "Do you ever wish for children, Burke?"

"Well, it's best to be married for that, and neither of us is, so it seems to be a moot point," Burke replied.

Lila sighed. "I guess I've simply been thinking about it more, looking at pictures of Gwen's children."

Surprised at this turn of Lila's thoughts, Burke decided not to answer. After all, her sister had only recently come out of a religious life. She hadn't even dated for years, so Burke wasn't sure how to reply.

"Mother said she hasn't heard from Celeste in a long time, and that even when she's called or texted her, Celeste hasn't replied," Lila said, changing the subject.

Burke shrugged. "She's a nationally known country singer, Lila. Her life is really busy. She travels on the road, works hard, performs, records. I think she and her husband Dillon were working on another album together, too. She's never been one to keep close touch with us either."

"When did you last talk to her?"

Burke thought back. "I don't remember. At Christmas, then back in the winter sometime."

"I'm worried about her." Lila frowned. "About Gwen, too."

"Why?"

"Just a feeling when I pray."

Burke could hardly dispute that without sounding unbelieving.

"Well, write and tell them your heart is concerned," she said instead.

"I will." She smiled then. "I'm not worried about you at all though."

"Well, that's good. Especially since you told me worry is a sin and that we should be anxious for nothing. Seems like you read me the scripture."

Lila had the grace to giggle. "That's true. I did. I'm glad you remember those words. I need to re-read that scripture myself. We're told not to worry about our lives, but to trust God in all things."

"Yes, and to look at the birds to see how well the Lord cares for them," Burke finished for her. "You told me many times we're supposed to take all our cares to God in prayer and not dwell on them afterward. I've tried to take that advice you offered me and not grow overly anxious about the inn, the business, and all the work to learn and do since we lost Daddy. He carried so much responsibility I didn't appreciate before. I've tried to pray for Mother, as well, to have peace and comfort and not grieve too much." She smiled at Lila. "Your strong faith has had a good effect on me."

"I can see that." Lila sat her water bottle down. "God is bringing sweet, happy changes for you, Burke. Please don't feel you can't share with me because I've been living in a religious community."

Burke looked away, not sure how to answer.

"I saw you and Waylon walking on the beach last night. I'd come out to sit at the pavilion to pray. The moon was full, beautiful on the water, lighting up much of the shore." She smiled. "It's sweet that God brought you two back together. I'm happy for you."

Annoyed at this change of conversation, Burke leaned forward. "Listen. Don't say anything to Mother or anyone else yet, Lila." Burke frowned. "I know it looks like all this happened fast, but Waylon and I found we'd both carried strong feelings about each other for years. So in some ways it doesn't feel fast." She closed her eyes for a moment. "Actually, it feels simply wonderful."

"I can hear your joy even in the air. Don't wait too long to share it, Burke. Everyone loves you and loves Waylon and will be happy for you."

Burke sighed. "It may sound silly but I wanted to revel in it privately for a little while first. Our lives here on the island are such public ones in many ways. I wanted this joy to be mine alone for a short while at least."

"Your wish is safe with me, but do realize joy is not easy to contain or conceal."

Burke groaned. "I hear you. I practically hid out from you and Mother, knowing you would see it. You know Novaleigh will notice it, too."

"Falling in love is hardly like getting scurvy, Burke. Revel in it for a little while alone if you wish but then share. There's no reason to keep your life so secret."

"You can hardly preach to me about being secret about things." Burke crossed her arms. "Mother and I still don't exactly know why you left the Community."

"I told you," she said.

"A very concise and un-detailed answer."

Lila looked down at her hands in her lap. "I began to feel restless at St. Mary's, oddly discontent living with a community of women, even after choosing that life and feeling right about it before. Several of the older women I'd grown close to helped me to examine my feelings, to realize I wasn't truly called for the vocation as I'd once thought. There's more to the story I'm working out, of course. You might say I'm in a transition phase, praying and waiting for clarity. Sensing something is coming that may bring even more change for me, for all of us in some way. I felt that again when the starfish washed up on the beach, that a sweep of changes is coming. I don't see the rest clearly in any way, but I keep feeling unrest. Before the starfish washed in I was actually beginning to feel calmer and more settled."

She reached out to put her hand on Burke's. "When I understand more, I'll share more. I'm not concealing anything from you that happened at St. Mary's. It was a little bit embarrassing to think you belonged so perfectly somewhere and then to realize—and to be lovingly told so, too—that you didn't."

"Did they ask you to leave?"

"No, they simply helped me to see that I should, but it was still a little embarrassing. They could see and sense that I was restless, even when I tried to conceal it."

"A week ago I was feeling restless," Burke confided. "I never imagined in a million years Waylon would suddenly come back home though. I thought he'd stay in the Navy twenty years until full retirement. I never imagined for a minute either that he held any feelings for me. He never showed them on any of his visits home."

"Why did he never speak to you before?"

"He said Daddy warned him off, that he saw Waylon starting to notice me when I was only twelve. Waylon said every time he came home he felt the same, but that he had no idea I'd ever felt anything for him except friendship."

"Hmmm. Daddy always was protective, maybe a little too protective in some ways." Lila looked at Burke. "I think I was too young to notice any of this and you always hid your emotions well. To me this is a happy surprise."

Burke leaned forward. "I didn't even know how to pray for what my heart really yearned for. I thought those feelings still locked inside me were silly and childish. But look how good God is." She smiled at Lila. "And if He's been this kind to me, not praying right or anything, He'll be kind to you and show you the right way, too. How can you doubt it? You've always been the strong one of faith among us."

Lila gave Burke another little smile. "It's easier to discern things, to discern truth for others than for yourself. But thank you. You've been helpful to me today, and I believe I will see my way clearly soon." Lila stood up, shifting the conversation and mood. "Come over to my place now and let me show you some of my new paintings and the sketches of the jewelry pieces I plan to make with the starfish when they totally dry out. Henry brought more to me and we spread them over boards behind the house."

Burke glanced at her watch.

"We have time before lunch and I want to show you some of the preliminary sketches I've started doing for Myron Andric, the ornithologist staying with us. He asked me to start doing a series of bird sketches and paintings for the book he's working on. I might even design the book cover. Isn't that exciting?"

"It is," Burke said, glad to see Lila back in a happier mood. "Let's go look at them before lunch."

CHAPTER 6

Waylon enjoyed time with Henry Boals and Clifford George over their lunch at the lodge. He hadn't heard any of Clifford's old island stories or Henry's booming laugh and sea tales for a long time.

His eyes moved over the two older men as they talked now about the ongoing problem on the island of visitors trashing the beach and what to potentially do about it.

"It's a continuing aggravation," Henry said. "I wish we could find a way to resolve it."

Now white-haired with a matching white mustache, Henry had the swarthy skin of an old shrimper. He was handy with tools, too, good at fixing things and enjoyed work out of doors. Clifford, employed with the park service at Edisto Beach State Park most of his earlier life, had developed a specialty in landscaping he'd brought with him to the island. A Black man with a warm smile and a full, stocky figure—probably from his wife Novaleigh's good cooking—Clifford worked hard with Henry to see that all of the island stayed well-kept.

"Well, here's the thing to remember," Clifford added. "It's always people, more than any other thing, that create the most problems around the island. All we can do is the best we can do."

"That's true," Henry agreed and then changed the subject. "I like the idea Waylon brought up about adding a pavilion at the marina. I think we should place it close to the road, too, if we can. On bad days the ferry can pull in close to load and unload, keeping people more out of the weather."

"A pavilion is a good idea," Clifford agreed. "There's no way to ensure though, that even with a nice pavilion, folks won't get wet sometime. Rain and sleet often have a mind of their own."

Henry laughed. "Yeah, that's for sure. A gale storm can blow wind and rain sideways. I've seen it enough out in the boat, even when under cover."

Waylon made a few more notes on the pad of paper in front of him. "My dad already suggested two area contractors he thought would be good to consider. I think I'll ask both of them to come and give us an estimate and talk about what they can build that would work. We can all sit in on that meeting, if you like."

Henry finished off the last bite of chocolate cake in front of him. "You know, I liked the three of us meeting today. Maybe we can get together like this on a regular basis every week, go over work, problems, and such."

"I like that idea," Clifford put in. "This is a good place for it, too, here at the lodge away from all the activity." He turned to Waylon. "Do you mind hosting us if we do this again?"

"No problem." Waylon smiled, pleased at the easy welcome from these men he'd long admired.

As they started getting ready to leave, Henry added, "I wanted to mention that a news report this morning said they still haven't found the missing woman in Hollywood. A witness came forward, though, who saw her heading down river our way in a boat with a man. The witness knew the woman well and he recognized her. The police said they planned to start a broader search of the waterways closer to the ocean based on this new information. We may see them cruising around the island and creeks near us."

Clifford frowned. "What caused that woman to set off in a boat with someone unexpectedly? Makes you wonder if it was someone she knew."

Henry shook his head. "I guess we won't know until they find her. But it's troubling. Sounds like the police are wondering if there might be a link between this woman from Hollywood missing and another one missing a month ago."

"Did that woman live in Hollywood, too?" Waylon asked.

"No, she lived on Yonges Island closer to the Wadmalaw River. There's no real evidence the two women have any link, only the coincidence that both went missing recently and haven't been found." Henry carried some dishes into the kitchen and came back. "I think we need to keep a special watch over the women and guests around our island, knowing this."

"There's wisdom in being careful," Clifford agreed. "I'll talk to Etta about the updates I heard. There's no sense in anyone being out and about by themselves too much, until this gets settled. It's sensible to use caution."

"I agree. I'm taking Burke to Bohicket to the post office and store at Freshfields in a little while," Waylon added. "I'll talk to her, too, about this."

"Good," Henry said as he and Clifford got up to leave.

"Is there anything else we need to discuss?" Waylon asked.

"No, I think we've covered everything for now." Henry offered a little salute. "Welcome on board, Captain," he said to Waylon with a grin. "We're glad to have you back around here. I'm going to head out now and get my mowing started. I've got a lot to get done today."

Clifford helped Waylon clean up the rest of the dishes from lunch, then picked up his battered straw hat to leave. As they stepped out on the porch, they could see Burke walking down the road from the inn.

Clifford smiled in her direction, and then turned to Waylon. "Does Burke know you've always fancied her?" he asked.

Waylon knew his mouth dropped open in surprise.

The old man laughed. "Lordy, you should see your face, boy. It's not as though an observant person couldn't see there's something there—the same as it's been for a long time." He chuckled again. "I'd say it's about time to act on it, too, don't you? I know Lloyd warned you off back when Burke was only a child, but those days are long past. You should keep in mind others have tried to win

Burke and that more will come. Don't dilly-dally around too long now you're back. Burke's strong and independent, but it would be a fine thing to win the love of a woman like her."

Stunned, Waylon couldn't think of a thing to say.

"Well, you have a good day, boy," Clifford said, ambling off.

"Are you ready to go?" Burke called as she started up the drive.

He found his voice after a moment. "Yeah. Let me run in the house and get my keys." A little space would give him time to collect himself, too.

A short time later they headed out from the dock in Waylon's skiff, turning up the North Edisto River toward Bohicket Creek that led to the marina.

"I like it that you named your boat Home Again," Burke said from her seat beside his at the helm.

He laughed. "Actually, Dad named it. He'd gotten a larger boat a few months ago and decided, when he knew I planned to come home, to give me this one as a welcome gift versus selling it."

"Well, it's a good name, and I'm glad you are home again."

"Me, too," he said, letting his eyes roam over her, from her hair gleaming in the sun, down her trim figure to her long tanned legs. She wore Bermuda shorts today with the weather warming back up, although she'd put on a lightweight jacket for the ride to the marina.

"Nice shirt," Waylon commented, glancing at her white T-shirt with a colorful red-and-white striped lighthouse and the words Deveaux Lighthouse on the front.

"We sell the shirts at the gift shop—might as well advertise when I go out. The T-shirt often leads people to ask questions and I can tell them about the lighthouse tour and the inn if they query more."

She pulled a visor cap on over her hair as the wind picked up and began to toss it. He wore a visor himself, too, along with good sunglasses. As always, Waylon enjoyed the pleasure of being out on the water, of skimming along over the waves, with the sound of the boat's powerful motor like a song.

Burke looked across to smile at him, mirroring the contentment he felt. They'd always shared so many of the same pleasures of living here close to the sea, appreciating the beauty and the timeless rhythm of this special place.

"How often do you give tours at the Light?" he asked.

"The regularly scheduled tours are always offered on Fridays and Saturdays at 2:00 pm, year round, like we advertise in our brochures and on the Internet. A footnote in our literature and media explains, too, that inclement weather might cause cancellations and advises checking the website before setting out."

"Do you do all the tours yourself now?"

"Most of them. Lila doesn't like to do them at all. Mother occasionally fills in if I can't do one of the tours for some reason." She hesitated, looking out over the water. "Dad used to do a lot of the tours. He taught me little by little to take them over by letting me follow him around when he conducted them. Gradually he started asking me questions in front of the tour groups, letting me add pieces of information and repeat the details I'd heard so many times. Eventually, I learned to handle the tours simply by helping him so many times."

"Maybe you can start teaching me," he suggested. "If I trail around after you, I can start memorizing the spiel. Then maybe I can help you out with tours when needed."

"I love that idea." She smiled at him. "I keep pinching myself to realize you're home again for good, and that it seems likely you'll stay around this time."

Holding a firm hand on the wheel, Waylon leaned over to catch her chin and kiss her. "Wild horses couldn't drag me away after realizing you love me." He slowed the boat. "You do love me, don't you, Burke? I love you with all my heart and breath. I know it might be too soon to say the words, but in other ways it seems far too late to say them."

She dropped her gaze to her lap and then reached a hand across to lay it over his on the steering wheel. "I do love you, Waylon. My heart was yearning for you to say the words. I've dreamed of hearing them so many times."

"Then I'll be sure to say them often." He winked at her.

They skimmed from the river into Bohicket Creek and soon drew near the marina.

"Our boat slip is on the second dock." She pointed ahead. "You don't need to go to the Charter Dock today where you pick up passengers for our lighthouse tours or your family's different tour offerings. The nice thing about having a slip here at the marina is that we can leave the boat as long as we like, even to go to Charleston for the day if needed."

Waylon slowed to ease his boat into the slip. "I'd forgotten your family owned a place here at Bohicket with a slip."

"Dad got an opportunity, when Seabrook was young and Bohicket Marina just developing, to buy one of the townhouses here. A friend of Dad's persuaded him it would be a good investment, that he could rent it out to pay for it—which he did long ago. The chaplain at St. Christopher's Camp, Dean Anderson, rents it now. He's been here about six or seven years. Our family has always held a close association with the camp. We sponsor special tours for the camp children every summer and ferry visitors from the retreat center, too. I'm sure you recall the camp is only a little way down the road from the marina here."

"I remember."

She smiled at Waylon. "If you haven't met Dean Anderson he comes over to the island often to eat with us at the inn. He and Dad were great friends. Dad, Dean, and Wiley Barnwell, who also works at St. Christopher's, fished together and hung out. You'll meet both Dean and Wiley sooner or later. Wiley grew up around the area like Dad and he knows all the best creeks and streams for fishing."

As they secured the boat and climbed out, Burke pointed down the long dock toward the row of townhouses set behind a walkway by the marina. "That townhouse on the end is ours. It has a two-car carport. Dean uses one side; we use the other. It turned out to be an excellent decision buying the townhouse when we did. It allows us a much faster way of getting to the stores and shops on Johns Island and into Charleston when needed. We all got really excited, too, when Freshfields Village opened right up the road. It's a little trendy and yuppie in flavor and prices, but the shopping complex has a post office, grocery store, gas station, and banks."

He grinned, walking along the dock beside her. "My mother loves Freshfields, too. She and your mom come here often to shop, eat lunch, or to pick up the van to head into Charleston and its outlying malls. Do you still own that old VW Routan van?"

"Yes. It has some age on it now, but dad always kept it in good shape."

"I can pick up keeping the van in good shape; I'm good with cars and fixing things."

"Just another good reason to keep you around," she teased.

"I come with a lot of fringe benefits," he quipped back, loving this new ease with Burke, glad to be enjoying happy times with her again, old tensions gone.

Freshfields Village, built and opening around 2004, had brought a wide variety of shops, restaurants, and services to the residents of Seabrook, Kiawah, and Johns Island. Tourists loved it, of course, for its shops and restaurants, but so did locals. It brought not only new shopping close to them but, as Burke mentioned, banks and other services including attorney and real estate offices, a computer center, doctors' offices, a dentist and an optician, a cleaners, barber shop, hair salon, and spa.

Waylon, not a man ordinarily fond of shopping, enjoyed walking around with Burke today nevertheless. Unlike his sister Sally Ann, she didn't drag him into every little store while she tried on countless pairs of shoes or sorted through dresses and clothes. Burke made her way quickly instead to the spots she needed to hit—the post office, the bank, and into the Harris Teeter market to pick up a few needed groceries from a list in her purse.

"Let me know if you want to stop somewhere," she said, as they came out of the grocery. "I do little of our real shopping here other than picking up a few groceries occasionally, probably because I'm so prudent and practical." She laughed. "That's what Gwen and Celeste always say to me. They love coming here."

"I'm delighted you're prudent and practical," he said. "What else is on your To Do list?"

"We need to run up the road to the Rosebank Farms Market on the Parkway. They have a farm stand there and Mother asked me to pick up several items they keep on hand, even before their garden produce starts to come in."

Waylon glanced ahead to spot Vincent's Drug Store and Soda Fountain on their left. "Let's stop at Vincent's and get a Coke float."

Burke laughed. "They call the Coke float with vanilla ice cream the Brown Cow. I'd forgotten how much you like those. They even have one with root beer in it, but I don't think they offer a cherry cola one."

"It's been hard to find a good Coke float in some places where I traveled." He opened the door ahead of them into the drugstore, with its vintage interior and checkered floor. "You want one, too?"

"Sure," she said agreeably. "A break would be nice about now."

Waylon told her about some of the places he'd traveled while they enjoyed their floats, each served in chilled old time soda glasses.

"Did the Naval ships you worked on have names, like our boats around here do?" she asked at one point.

"They did. Most of the Naval Aircraft Carriers I served on were named after U.S. Presidents. The Navy has about 480 ships in active service and in the reserve fleet. I served much of my time on ships in the Indo-Pacific. I'd usually be at sea for about six months or more at a time." He smiled at her. "Spending so much time in the company of mostly men, this time with a beautiful woman is especially nice."

Her brow furrowed. "Did you serve in any battle situations?"

"The U.S. hasn't been at war while I served, but we faced a few testy situations with Iran occasionally."

"I want you to tell me more about that some time. My news mostly came from your family while you were away."

"I'll do that, but let's go finish your errands now, so we can head back to the island."

Waylon and Burke gathered up their purchases, drove to the market up the parkway, and then back to Waylon's skiff at the marina.

Neither of them were especially talkative individuals and they rode down the Bohicket Creek and back to the marina mostly in quiet, enjoying the beauty of the afternoon. At one point Burke pointed to several dolphins following them as they drew closer to the ocean, their dark fins breaking the water. Gulls flew overhead and other craft passed them along the way, including a few shrimp boats heading up the river to Rockville, their day about finished.

Waylon's heart soared, spending time like this with Burke. This was what life would be like with her, peaceful and calm. Happy and comforting. They fit like two matching gloves in so many ways and always had.

The marina and dock were quiet as they pulled up.

"We're home again," she said, grinning as he turned off the motor. "Just like the name of your boat."

Waylon stopped Burke from getting out of her seat. "I am home again in my heart and in my mind since coming back to you, Burke. This is where I belong, where I always want to be, here with you, spending my life with you, taking care of the island, the lighthouse and inn." He reached across to take her hands. "Could you see yourself spending your life with me, too, Burke? Even with some of the misunderstandings that happened between us?"

She bit her lip and looked down at their hands, showing some of the shyness he remembered when she was a girl. "It's still early to talk about the future. You haven't been home but a little over a week."

"It might seem like a short time together for some people, but not with us because we've known each other since childhood, grown up together, played and worked together, laughed together, gotten in trouble together."

He saw her smile at that.

"Let me show you something," he said. He pulled his billfold out of the back of his pocket, opened it and took a ring out from among the bills tucked in the back. "This was my Grandmother Jenkins' engagement ring. When she was ill near the end of her life she gave it to me. She said she wanted me to give it to the woman I found to love and share my life with some day. What do you think of it?"

He held the gold ring out to Burke. It was a pretty ring, with a carat diamond tucked in its center and tiny diamonds decorating the filigreed band in an old fashioned, intricate design.

She looked up at him with wide eyes, biting her lips a little anxiously.

"I want us to get engaged, if you're willing, Burke. I don't need a long time to know you're the one I want to spend my life with. There's no magic number as to when a couple should get engaged. I believe when you know you know, and that's it's never too soon to begin planning your future together when you do. Some people know on the first date, right after they meet, so why shouldn't we know when we've known each other so long?"

He reached to take her left hand and kiss it. "Do you think I could try it on you to see if it fits? You remember my grandmother. You were a similar size and height."

Not hearing her argue yet, Waylon slipped the ring on her left hand. "It's only a tiny bit too large. Not much. We can get it sized to be perfect."

Burke pulled her hand away from his to look at it. "Oh, Waylon, it's so beautiful. I remember as a girl seeing it on your grandmother's hand, especially noticing it when she crocheted. I remember all the pretty things she used to make."

"Does that mean you'll say yes, Burke?" He leaned toward her, taking her face in his hands, leaning to kiss her, pulling her closer across the seat when he heard her sigh. "I'll spend my life trying to make you happy."

She pulled away, reaching a hand to stroke it down his face. "I want to say yes with all my heart, Waylon, but it's so soon. What will Mother think and your parents? We don't want to disrespect them, acting in too much haste."

He smiled at her. "How do you know they won't be happy for us and pleased? Even this morning Clifford said he could tell there were feelings between us." He laughed softly at the memory. "He told me not to wait too long to pursue you."

Her mouth dropped open. "Clifford said that?" she asked with surprise.

"Yeah. I'd brought the ring back from the house yesterday with me. I'd kept it all these years in a safe deposit box with other valuables." He paused. "This moment was on my mind and I wanted to be ready. But I admit Clifford gave me a good push this morning."

Burke studied the ring on her hand.

"We could talk to your mother tonight, Burke. Tell her where our hearts are, see what she thinks about us getting engaged. Then we can take our time getting to know each other well again, deciding when we're ready to think about a wedding. Doesn't it feel right to you to be committed? I like the idea of saying to everyone that we belong together, that we're in love and planning our future together."

"I'm simply swamped with feelings all new to me, Waylon, but all lovely ones. I do know deep in my heart, too, that we belong together. I knew from the other day, with our words and that first kiss." She blushed at the memory.

"Yes, I've enjoyed our developing friendship, too," he teased, reminding her of those words they said to each other. "And you can't deny something has happened between us."

She gave him one of those rare smiles that lit her face. "Oh, why not, Waylon," she said. "Lila already knows. She saw us walking on the beach the other night. She told me today I shouldn't try to hide what we feel for each other. That because we've known each other for so long that everyone would be happy we found each other in a new way."

"We could tell your mother that we want to talk with her about some things at dinner tonight, suggest we eat together out on the family part of the screened porch. The weather has warmed up enough to eat outside again, and I know your mother loves to eat on the porch when the weather is nice." He took Burke's hand in his again. "We could tell her what we've decided and ask her blessing."

He turned the ring on her finger. "I went to the cemetery at the Trinity church this morning to ask your dad's blessing," he said. "I got a sense he thought it was all right, that he felt glad I was going to take care of his little girl."

Burke started to cry.

"Oh, Burke, don't cry." He gathered her close against him to hug her.

"Dad won't be able to give me away later when we get married. It's always hurt my heart to think about that."

"I'm sure my dad would be honored to do it," Waylon said with his mouth against her hair.

She pulled back to smile at him. "Yes, I think he would." She sighed deeply then. "I do want this, Waylon, no matter what anyone thinks."

"So do I. I'm so confident it's the right thing for us to do. The real key is that we both know we love each other and that we're both ready to be committed."

She held out her hand, studying her ring. "Then we'll pray and believe that Mother, my family, and your family will understand and be happy for us."

He leaned over to kiss her again and their kissing went on for some time then.

Waylon smiled at her when they finally pulled away, realizing they'd been out in the boat for rather a long time. "We may be a little late getting started, Burke, but you'll see—the best is yet to be."

CHAPTER 7

Burke admittedly dawdled in her room before dinner that evening. Waylon talked to her mom earlier and said they wanted to discuss a few things with her. Etta knew they'd gone to Bohicket and Freshfields together so she assumed it was about business.

She finally slipped across the passageway from the family room to fix herself a plate. As she walked through the kitchen afterward, Novaleigh stopped her. "Hold on and let me send a few of these fresh rolls from out of the oven with you. I know Waylon loves them."

As Burke walked closer to get the rolls, Novaleigh's keen eye caught the glisten of the ring on her finger. "Well, the good Lord be praised." She put a hand to her heart as she leaned closer to look at the ring. "I was wondering how long it would take you two to realize you're a match made in heaven and overdue to connect."

Burke sat her plate on the counter. "Shhh, Novaleigh. We haven't told mother or Lila yet." She looked toward the door out of the kitchen in concern.

"I can see from your face that's worrying you."

"Yes." Burke sighed and closed her eyes. "Waylon just got back last week and has only been here a few days. It's not like me to be impulsive. Mother may be upset with me."

"Your mother isn't blind anymore than the rest of us. Don't you be worrying about that if you and Waylon are sure."

"We really are. It seems like a dream come true."

Novaleigh leaned over to kiss her cheek. "It's time for some dreams to come true for you. You're a strong, conscientious, good woman but you deserve joy, too. And love."

Burke picked up her plate again, adding the extra rolls on top of it, and then hesitated.

"Run on and deal with this." Novaleigh swatted her gently from behind. "Dread and worry never did solve anything."

Smiling at her words, Burke headed on through the kitchen to cut over to the screened porch behind the family wing. She tucked her left hand in her lap as she sat down, deciding to let Waylon take the lead. He suggested he would.

Etta and Lila continued talking about the bird sketches Lila was making for Myron Andric while Burke began to eat, picking at her food a little, her nerves still on edge.

After a time, Waylon said, "I went over to the cemetery at Trinity Episcopal Church this morning to visit Lloyd."

Burke watched her mother blink back tears and wondered if this was the best approach for Waylon to take.

"You know how much I loved and honored Lloyd and I needed to talk with him about some things." He hesitated. "I needed to tell him I'd fallen in love with his daughter and to ask his blessing to get engaged to her."

Etta and Lila's eyes widened, and Burke heard her mother gasp.

"To be truthful, Etta, I fell in love with Burke before I left to go to college and every time I came home I knew it more. I held back though in saying anything to Burke. Lloyd had sensed my feelings and warned me off, with Burke so young. Later, I knew my life held years of travel with the Navy, long months at sea aboard ship, possibilities of war. Not much of a life to offer Burke. In the last year or two I felt restless, though, could feel the Lowcountry calling me home. As soon as I saw Burke I knew she was what really called me back, Etta."

Lila sniffed. "This is so lovely."

Etta sent her an annoyed glare.

Waylon continued. "Finding Burke still blessedly single, I decided to work a little to see if I could get her to notice me beyond friendship. I started flirting some, testing the waters." He grinned. "Burke got as mad as a hornet with me, warned me off from what she called flirting and playing male-female games with her. She teared up and said she'd carried a crush for me since before I left home and she didn't want me to hurt her further by playing around with her." He laughed then. "I thought my heart would soar out of my chest, learning she'd cared for me, too, all these years. I'll admit I acted on it. A man doesn't get a second chance like that often in life."

Burke's mother sent a glance her way and Burke felt a blush steal up her cheeks.

"Do you have a point in all this, Waylon?" Etta asked then.

"My point is that I love your daughter. I've been blessed to learn she loves me, too, and I asked her if she'd be willing to get engaged to be married. My heart couldn't be surer this is the right thing, Etta. I'll love and cherish Burke all my life, help you and her to keep the lighthouse, inn, and business strong and firm. Hopefully, we'll pass it on to another generation in future."

Burke felt another blush deepen on her neck.

Etta's eyes turned to Burke. "And what did you say to this proposal?"

In answer, Burke held out her hand to show her ring.

Lila clapped her hands. "God be praised. Let me see that ring, Burke." She got up to scamper around the table to get a closer look.

"This is very sudden," Etta said. "Perhaps too sudden." Her eyes turned to Waylon with a frown. "You just moved over here on Tuesday. It's only Thursday now."

Waylon leaned forward to answer before Burke could. "Well, here's the thing, Etta. This is a somewhat public place, despite it being an island, with people coming and going all the time. Whoever and whatever anyone is or does is easily seen around here. With Burke and I falling in love, it's likely to show and be seen. Lila saw us on the beach together the other night already. Even Clifford commented that he'd seen the feelings kicking up between us. I thought it would be easier, and seem more appropriate and proper, if everyone simply knew up front that Burke and I are engaged. If anyone catches us in a moment, there won't be speculating about it." He took a sip of his coffee. "We can take our time getting to know each other more. But we can do that while engaged. I wanted to ask your blessing, as I did Lloyd's."

"It would have been more appropriate if you'd asked my blessing before you proposed getting engaged," Etta put in. "That's customary."

Waylon grinned. "I got a little eager."

Lila giggled. "He's asking now, Mother. Most people don't even ask their parents at all anymore about getting engaged or married."

"I'm aware of that." She glared at Lila. "I'm simply shocked, that's all. I hardly know what to say."

"What are your concerns, Etta?" Waylon asked.

"Getting married, and even engaged, is a serious thing. Before couples take that step there are many matters to consider. Couples need to talk about how they'll handle finances, where they want to live, what values and interests they share, if they carry similar faiths. They need to talk about what they want from life, what balance they think is best between work and family, if they enjoy each other's friends."

Lila chimed in again. "Honestly, Mother, even I know the answers to those questions about Waylon and Burke. And they can continue to talk about all these issues while engaged. It's not as through they ran off and got married without talking to us. You're not making Waylon feel very welcomed into our family."

"And you're not helping this situation," Etta snapped. "I have a right to some reservations. This is an impulsive decision." She looked at Burke. "Of all my daughters I least expected you to do anything impulsive without thought and careful consideration. Celeste and Gwen were always adventurous and frequently too impulsive. Lila was basically more cautious in most ways but that artistic side of hers was unpredictable. And who would have thought she'd …." Her voice dropped off.

Lila put a hand to her mouth, looking away, trying not to giggle.

"I see your point, Mother," Burke put in, "but I also remember the story you and Dad told me of how the two of you met. If I recall correctly, you rather impulsively fell in love, began seeing Dad in secret, and then stood up against the wishes of both your families to get married."

Her mother pursed her lips. "I was a Baynard. Lloyd and I met at a debutante ball in Charleston. He'd filled in for a friend as an escort, hardly the usual young man expected at that sort of soiree, despite his good bloodline heritage. Lloyd didn't live the life my parents wanted for me. The idea of me moving to a remote island to help run a lighthouse and inn was hardly what they envisioned for me. So, yes, they pushed against it." Her eyes softened. "I never wanted what they wanted for my life, though. I hated all that pompousness, those society parties, the gossip, the overemphasis on clothes, material possessions, or who you knew. I escaped to the outdoors whenever possible, was a tomboy my parents despaired of for years. It's hardly the same story."

"Grandaddy Deveaux said they worried you wouldn't fit in with life at the lighthouse, being used to society, coming from what he called so much glitter." Burke smiled at the memory.

"Well, I proved them wrong in time and they admitted it."

Burke waited, not commenting back, giving her mother time to think.

Novaleigh stuck her head in the door. "You ready for me to bring in a refill for your coffee?" she asked, holding up a fresh carafe.

"How much of this have you heard?" Etta asked her.

She chuckled. "Enough to set my mind remembering a strong, self-willed, opinionated young woman who came to this island when I was a girl about the same age. I also remember how much in love she and Lloyd Deveaux were. The two of you had a glow about you not much different from what I see with Burke and Waylon."

Etta scowled in displeasure.

"If I rightly recall," Novaleigh continued, coming into the room to swap out the coffee carafes on the side table, "you told me your own self, Ettarae Catherine, that you knew Burke had a crush on Waylon before he ever left to go to school and the Navy. You also told me Lloyd talked to him and told him not to act on those feelings he'd seen whipping up. Where's your memory? Why are you surprised at these events happening here today? Didn't you ever figure out why Burke kept pushing away every one of those boys coming after her ever since, many of them smart, handsome and well-to-do, and proposing marriage? She still carried feelings for Waylon in her heart. There's no point in you acting all uppity, carrying on like this is such a big surprise to you. I think, if you're honest, you've been expecting this deep down."

"Novaleigh, you're stepping out of line in this," Etta said.

"Some things need to be said." She put a hand on her hip. "A wise mother would praise the Good Lord her daughter had chosen such a fine young man to care for. She'd praise God, also, to be gaining a son-in-law who loved her daughter, this island and business, and who wouldn't be carrying her off to other parts and places. You got one daughter way over across the Mississippi River you hardly ever see, another in Nashville, running all over the country singing, in God knows what sort of places, and married for the second time now."

Etta closed her eyes and sighed. "You certainly inherited your outspoken nature from your own mother."

"I don't see knowing and speaking the God's truth as a negative trait."

"No, and you do tend to nail things and tell them like it is sometimes." She turned to look first at Waylon and then at Burke. "I'd almost forgotten how a boy and a girl see life differently when they're young and in love. And deep down, my heart is happy for you both. Novaleigh is right I need to express that as well as my surprise and reservations."

Burke bit her lip. "Perhaps I should have come to talk to you first before saying yes to Waylon."

Novaleigh snorted.

Etta had the grace to laugh, too. "When a young man pours out his love and heart to you, your first thought usually isn't, 'Gee, I need to go talk to my Mother about this.'"

They all laughed then.

"This is so wonderful," Lila said, sighing.

"How about we get a little party together to announce this?" Novaleigh asked.

"Whoa. Not until we go talk to my parents," Waylon put in. "Perhaps we can include them in any party plans we make. I think they'd like that."

"Sally Ann and her husband will want to come, too," Lila added.

Etta held up a hand. "Well, let's get all these guests settled in at the inn this weekend and then talk about things more next week when everything quiets down a little. That will give time for Waylon to talk with his family. We don't need to be in a hurry. Celeste, and Gwen and her family, often come to the island for Easter. If they plan to come perhaps we can have a special dinner then."

Novaleigh smiled and nodded. "I need to get myself back into the kitchen to check and see if anyone else in the dining room needs anything before I start cleaning up."

Burke wanted to say thank you to Novaleigh but thought better of it. She'd find a time later to thank her for her help and support.

Her mother smiled at her as Novaleigh left. "Well, Burke, come over here and let me look at that ring closer." She turned to Waylon. "Your mother Aileen told me once that her mother gave you her old engagement ring to save. Is this it?"

"Yes, ma'am, I wanted to honor her memory and give it to Burke if she liked it," Waylon answered.

"Well, it's a lovely thing," Etta said, studying it now that Burke had walked over to her chair.

She put a hand to her mouth suddenly, tears coming to her eyes. "It's just hit me suddenly that you're getting married." She squeezed Burke's hand and then got up to hug her, moving next to hug Waylon. "I am happy for you both."

Burke felt like crying then, the rest of their dinner and time over dessert happy and full of warm discussions.

Later in the day, Burke and Waylon met to walk down the beach as the sky darkened and as night begin to slide its fingers over the island. The light of the lighthouse, always coming on at sunset, flashed its long beams out across the ocean in its familiar pattern.

They walked along, holding hands, Boonie dashing out in front of them, the collie simply enjoying being a dog. Although the days at the inn and the lighthouse were often busy, these evening hours on the beach were usually quiet. Further down the beach, where the tourists stayed at Edisto, and across the river at Seabrook and Kiawah, there would be more couples and families out walking, but here on their island things always stayed more peaceful.

Waylon stopped to pick up a piece of driftwood to throw for Boonie to retrieve.

"You may regret starting that game," Burke said, watching the black and white dog race down the beach after it.

"I've missed having a dog all these years." Waylon tossed the stick several more times for Boonie as they walked along, the dog running back to drop it at his feet each time, eager for more.

"I think things went well with our parents overall today, don't you?" he asked.

She wrinkled her nose. "I guess so, but things started out stressful with your parents at first just like with Mother."

He laughed. "My parents came around more quickly though when it dawned on them that by marrying you I'd undoubtedly stay in South Carolina and not leave to go traipsing off somewhere else again."

"You'd better not go traipsing off. Be assured that deciding on me is deciding on a life here. The Light and me are a package deal." Burke turned to look at the sweep of light reaching out into the night sky. "Being a lighthouse keeper gets in your blood like the sea does, Waylon. You'll see and feel that after a time. We may not work as hard and tirelessly as the old keepers of the past, but we hold a responsibility yet—to keep the Light and to let others see it and learn about it. It's a special role."

"I learned that fact working with Lloyd and I've seen that love and dedication to the Light and the Light Station in you, as well as your love for the inn. I'm looking forward to this life here getting into my blood. I'm ready to settle down." He turned to her. "I'm ready to let you get into my blood, too."

Waylon kissed her again then, teaching her more about kissing and its joys. It could certainly stir the blood. The feel of his body, warm against her own, began to stir her blood, too. Despite being nearly thirty, Burke had worked so much over the years, carried so many responsibilities, that she hadn't found much time for experiencing passion. Her knees felt suddenly weak now though and she almost stumbled in place.

Stepping back, Waylon gave her a little smile. "Our developing friendship is coming along rather well, isn't it?"

She knew she flushed a little and could feel the heat rise in her neck.

"We have a lot of intimacy to explore, Burke, but I won't step past the boundaries I promised myself and vowed to your father and mine, until we're married. If it starts to get too difficult for us, being close and wanting more, we'll set a date to marry and move things forward."

She studied his brown eyes and sturdy, familiar face. "I've read a lot of romance books. Is it as exciting as they make it sound?"

He laughed. "It's better, Burke, if only because it's real. And especially when two people really love each other and are committed. Surprisingly, your father, even more than mine, gave me a lot of talks like that."

"Do you think my Dad was always worried about you hanging around his girls so much?"

"A man with four beautiful, smart daughters should worry. Or at least be very watchful over them. This world has thrown so many of its old values away today and cheapened many of the sweetest things life has to offer."

She leaned over to pick up a shell. "A visitor to the lighthouse got mad at Mother recently and used some hateful words to her, because she wouldn't let him register to stay at the inn with his girlfriend in the same room. I listened to Mother inform him, in that direct, no nonsense way of hers, that the Deveaux Inn belonged to her—not the government or the state. She reminded him that she could make any rules here she desired and could expect them of the people who came to the inn. She added to him, 'This inn is also my home and I can run it any way I wish.'"

"She's tough, your Mom."

"You have to be tough running an inn, doing all she does. She and Dad created firm rules for the Deveaux Inn and it is rare if she breaks them."

"I know she doesn't allow children or pets to stay at the inn or the cottages."

"Yes, and it isn't that she doesn't love them. It's that they are a liability." She slowed to study the moon hanging over the ocean, a big ball of yellow tonight in the darkening sky. "You saw that alligator in the lake this week. If a dog yipped and barked at it, climbing down the bank too near it, or if a small child got too close, poking a stick at it, that gator would attack. You know that. We've heard too many stories all our lives about it. Here at the island we just can't take that risk."

"Yet you have Boonie." He pointed to the dog, prancing along ahead of them, enjoying the evening.

"Boonie gets times of freedom like this with supervision, and Boonie has been well-trained. He follows commands like one of your Naval cadets or ensigns. Even in an unexpected situation, he minds." She turned to smile at him. "We ran into a big snake, acting aggressive on the trail the other day, but both Boonie and I turned around slowly and walked the other way. After the first bark to warn me, Boonie didn't bark again."

"What kind of snake?"

"A black racer, but as you know they will bite and they will dart at you sometime to protect their territory. The best thing to do is to leave a snake or any wild creature alone." She smiled at him. "Snakes, gators, and a lot of other creatures are something we constantly deal with here, Waylon. It's a five hundred acre island bordered by a vast protected wilderness area. Wildlife are more in the majority than we are. I try to respect that."

She could see Waylon thinking about her words.

"There's an old hunter's instinct in me that wants to take out some of the dangerous members of the animal kingdom when I see them, even though I know they're legally protected," he said.

"I hear you. I always think that one of our city guests may be the next one to run into one of our wildlife friends and not have a clue what to do."

"I could do some talks about that, as Lloyd used to do, when they arrive."

"That might be a good idea, Waylon. We want to keep everyone safe."

"Speaking of staying safe," he said as they came to the inlet and turned around to start back. "I forgot to talk to you earlier today about that missing woman at Hollywood."

She listened to him fill her in on the ongoing story. "I suppose we need to find a way to mention this to our guests, to suggest caution, but there's no point in kicking up unnecessary fear."

"I agree but do be watchful, Burke," he said. "We don't want to think the worst, but two women are missing with no trace found of them."

"I'll keep that in mind," she said.

Changing the subject she added, "Mother reminded me before I came to walk with you that I need to call Gwen and Celeste to share our news. With them both living in the Central time zone, I can call them when I get back. It won't be too late yet."

"Sounds like a good idea." He chuckled. "I can't wait to hear what they have to say about this. As your dad said, I grew up like a brother to them. I'm sure it will be difficult for either of them to think of me another way."

She leaned over to kiss his cheek. "After we get married, Waylon, you'll actually be their brother by marriage."

He laughed out loud this time. "Well, heaven help me then."

CHAPTER 8

April 2017

March slipped away into April, as time does. Waylon found his new life at Watch Island a full and busy one. He'd settled into an easy relationship with Clifford, Henry, and with Henry's son Calvin and his boys Eddie and Joe. Calvin, especially, had been a tremendous help with the new covered pavilion at the dock now fully built and only needing a little final sealant. Once they'd talked to and decided on a contractor, it amazed Waylon how quickly a pavilion structure could be constructed. The design they decided on included a long covered walkway on the last piece of the main dock, which abutted right into the new pavilion beside the roadway. Without plumbing aspects in the plan and only needing to hook the structure into some outdoor lighting already in place, the contractors were able to construct both the walkway on the dock and the pavilion in less than two weeks' time.

"This pavilion sure looks fine," Henry said as they worked this afternoon adding sealant over both structures. "That construction crew worked fast getting this up. I didn't realize how many pavilions today came in prepackaged sections. They just hauled everything down river on a little barge and set to work."

"The Greenlee Construction group puts up pavilions and buildings like this all around the South Carolina coastal area. They had great references, the time available to work with us, and we all liked them."

"Yeah, top notch people." Henry stood back to check the line of sealant he'd painted on a long beam supporting the roof rafters of the big pavilion. "It will be real nice for guests at the inn and visitors to the lighthouse to just get out of the ferry, walk down the now-covered dock and right into this pavilion. If they need to wait a minute or two for the tram to get here or if it's a bit rainy, they'll be under cover and can sit on one of those benches I found in the storage barn. Etta suggested getting a couple of picnic tables, too, to put under the pavilion, and that's a good idea, I think."

"I agree." Waylon looked around picturing it. "There's plenty of room."

Henry paused to gaze out across the long dock. "I like that stain we used for the walkways and pavilion with an old weathered look. Staining and resealing the rest of the dock kind of made it all blend together nice. I wouldn't mind doing some staining and sealing at the other docks before winter sets in. They could use freshening."

"We'll talk to Etta and Burke about it. The cost for this proved less than expected, and we could all kick in and do the work of staining and sealing this fall when things aren't so busy."

"Yeah, there's always work to do around here."

Myron Andric pulled his boat up to the dock while they worked and walked with a quick angry stride down the walkway toward them, a scowl on his face.

"What's wrong?" Waylon asked him.

"There's a bunch of folks over at the Deveaux Bank on an area of the beach that's off limits. They're playing loud music and partying. Worse, they've got a dog with them, a big dog. You know dogs aren't allowed over there at all. He's been running loose, chasing off the birds. I tried to talk to them but they basically told me to bug off and mind my own business." He shook his head. "I was hoping you would know who we might call. That's a designated Seabird Sanctuary. No dogs are allowed. People aren't allowed to enter any of the designated nesting areas for the birds either. You know that whole area is closed year-round above the high water line, too, except for a few areas for recreational use. And that's not where these folks decided to set up their beach camp for the day."

He looked back in the direction he'd come from, pacing and

obviously upset. "They're in the zones around the back of the island, in areas off limits between March 15 and October 15. The tide is out and I know the beach looks pretty and pristine, but the breeding and nesting season is beginning for several bird species. If they abandon their nests, as people walk by or make too much noise with music, boat motors, and such, it leaves the eggs, and any chicks that might have hatched, unprotected. Eggs can quickly overheat in the sun, predatory gulls can swoop in, and the feet of dogs or people can crush the eggs underfoot. Most of the birds build their rough nests directly on the ground. There's pelican, tern, red knot, and skimmer nests over there and the whimbrels are here on their migratory route. They're an endangered species. It's a shame I tell you. We've been working hard to protect the birds at Deveaux and to keep their populations from diminishing more."

Henry nodded. "I have some contacts with the Coastal Conservation League and with the South Carolina Department of Natural Resources. I'll make some calls."

Myron shook his head. "The League offices are in Beaufort and Charleston, a long way from here. Even if we contact someone who can head out now, it will take a while for them to get to the Deveaux Bank. We need to do something."

"What are you all talking about?" Burke said walking up. "What do we need to do?"

Listening to Myron ranting away, Waylon hadn't even seen Burke coming down the winding road from the inn.

Myron filled her in on the problem.

Burke turned to Henry. "I came to help you and Waylon finish the sealing, but we need to stop and deal with this situation first. Henry, go call any of the agency contacts we have for infractions of the trespassing laws at the Deveaux Bank. Call the state park, too, and the Edisto police department. They often send someone to clear off the no trespassing areas." She glanced at Waylon. "We'll go over in your boat and remind them of the laws about the Bank, let them know agencies with the legal right to prosecute are on their way. A lot of times people don't know the severity of the trespassing violations on the Deveaux Bank. They can get fines of up to $465 or more with the potential of thirty or more days in jail. Many times if they know the law has been called, they'll disperse to avoid prosecution."

Waylon glanced at his watch. "I have the ferry run to do soon for the 4:00 pm pickup at the landing. Several of the guests went touring over in Charleston today."

"Don't worry about that," Henry offered. "I'll do the ferry run for you today after I make my calls."

"Thanks, Henry," Burke said, turning back to Myron. "Did you see any signs of firearms at the Deveaux Bank? Some people like to shoot at the birds for kicks. Occasionally they even try to trap them. I'd like to know if we're dealing with those types."

"No, they were only a bunch of kids, probably high school and college age, out for a lark, wanting a place to party," Myron answered. "I saw beer cans, but I don't know if they had drugs or not. It's Spring Break for a lot of schools right now."

"You be careful anyway," Henry said.

He'd cleaned his and Waylon's paintbrushes and put the tops back on their cans of sealant while they all talked.

He turned to Myron then. "Head up to the inn and tell Etta where Burke and Waylon are going. Trespassing happens around here more often than you know. A pristine, private beach like the pretty stretch at the Deveaux Bank attracts folks, and they don't like being told there are laws telling them they can't play and party there."

"Tell her Henry is doing the ferry pickup, too," Burke added.

"Sure thing." Myron turned to head up the road to the inn. "I have calls I want to make, too."

As Myron left, Henry turned to Waylon. "Before you leave, go in the lodge and look in that back closet. You'll find a couple of Turtle Patrol caps. You and Burke can wear them. It might give you a little muscle. If anyone pins you down about the hats, we do volunteer work with the Seabrook Turtle Group across the river. You can add, in addition, that you're keepers at the Deveaux

Lighthouse, maintained by the Coast Guard. The Guard does all the big maintenance of the Light here, so we do have an affiliation."

Waylon grinned. "Good idea. I'll get those hats while I run in to get my keys and change my shirt."

A short time later, he and Burke rode out from the marina into the North Edisto River heading toward the Deveaux Bank. He and Burke both wore Turtle Patrol hats now and Waylon had pulled on a clean T-shirt with a Naval emblem on it.

Burke grinned at his shirt, reading the words out loud. "U.S. Naval Captain—Pride Runs Deep. I haven't seen that one."

He winked at her. "I thought it might lend a little more authority." Looking ahead he asked, "Where can we safely pull the boat in close to shore?"

"Myron said the kids settled on the ocean side. We can pull into the authorized area facing Seabrook, near the restricted zone. I know a good spot. We can anchor the boat and walk around the beach to look for them. Legally, people can be on the island below the high water mark, but I'm sure they've probably carelessly set up some of their chairs, coolers, and such above the designated marks. And there is the dog issue. Dogs are totally illegal at the Deveaux Bank."

"Does Myron have special privileges to be in the restricted areas?"

"Yes. He carries paperwork from the South Carolina Department of Natural Resources showing he's part of a research project with the college and authorized to be in restricted areas on the Bank. He parks his boat, as we will, on the non-restricted side of the island and walks around to different parts of the Deveaux Bank, observing nesting sites, counting numbers of birds' nests, identifying types of birds regularly on the island as well as noting numbers and types of migratory birds coming in. He takes pictures, and sometimes works with groups that come over to do bird banding."

She chuckled. "He probably got indignant and bossy with the group he found, carrying on about the danger to the birds and the environment. Myron gets a little upset about that sort of thing. He probably ticked them off."

"Even if they found Myron annoying doesn't make it all right for them to be there on the Deveaux Bank breaking the law."

"I know." She lifted her eyebrows and grinned at him. "That's why we're on our way to see if we can get these folks to move on to another spot."

A short time later, they anchored the boat on the horseshoe-shaped island, waded to shore, and began to walk along the beach toward the ocean side of the Deveaux Bank.

"I'd forgotten how beautiful it is here," Waylon said, looking around. "Look at all the birds. The place is teaming with them—gulls, pelicans, terns, skimmers. Obviously they love this place."

"It's home to them. We're the intruders. With so many beach areas to enjoy around the South Carolina coastal region there's no reason not to respect the laws in place to protect this bird sanctuary. Myron can fill you in on how many species of sea and shore birds call the Deveaux Bank home. Many fly here every night to roost or to forage, breed, and nest, and others stop here on their migratory routes."

She pointed to an area with yellow tape near a dune. "Sea turtles nest here sometimes, too. The patrol from Seabrook usually keeps a watch for nests here at the Bank and on the beach at our island. They can get to both sites more quickly than the Edisto Turtle Patrol can by simply kayaking across the river. You'll see members of the Seabrook Turtle Patrol walking along our beaches sometimes, especially in the evening. We work and cooperate with them."

She paused, pointing ahead. "There are our trespassers."

Waylon saw a good-sized group of young people, most college-aged, with two boats pulled up and anchored off the beach.

As they drew closer, one of the young men walked toward them. Spotting Waylon's shirt and hat, he said, "If you've come to tell us to head out, some old guy already came by and read us the riot act. We're packing up. I thought legally it was okay for us to be on the beach, that South Carolina's beaches belong to everyone. That man pointed out the problems with our stuff being above the high-water line and having the dog with us."

Burke smiled. "Myron Andric, the ornithologist you met, is staying at our inn. He's doing research about the birds here and is passionate about keeping the island safe for them."

"No kidding," the young man said. "Well, like I said we're packing up."

"That's good," Burke smiled again. "A lot of people don't realize there are fines to almost five-hundred dollars for trespassing in undesignated areas here or in bringing a dog to the Deveaux Bank. Dogs are totally illegal here. The South Carolina Department of Resources of Law Enforcement can add up to thirty days in prison. I thought you might want to be warned they've been called."

"Thanks, and like I said we're heading out."

Another boy came running out of the thick bushes behind the beach then. "I found the dog at last," he hollered, dragging the big dog along by his collar. "Dang dog went way back in the brush and scrub, but he led me to something we don't want anything to do with. Believe me. We need to get out of here."

He paused, eyes widening as he realized Waylon and Burke weren't a part of their group. "Who are they?"

Waylon answered. "I'm Waylon Jenkins and this is Burke Deveaux. We keep the Light over on Watch Island." He gestured in that direction to where the top of the big striped lighthouse was clearly visible. "What kind of problem did you run into?"

As the boy shifted his eyes to the older man, trying to decide whether to answer, one of the girls came up to snap a leash on the dog, taking it away.

"You'd better tell them," the man said.

The boy's eyes widened. "There's a body back there, or what's left of one. It isn't nice to see. Creeped me out when I spotted it. Looks like it's been there a while."

Their friends, now loading into their boats, waved at them. "Come on," one called out. "We're ready to go."

"I'll leave this new problem for one of you to report," the older man said, turning to walk away. "We're heading out. You can tell them we started packing as soon as we learned we shouldn't be here and that we didn't know the dog was a problem."

Waylon sent the younger man a stern look. "Tell me where you saw this body before you cut out. It might be a good idea, too, for you to leave me your name and a way to get in touch with you."

The boy pointed toward a break in the scrub and myrtle behind the beach. "Cut through there and follow back on the only path you'll see."

The other man grabbed the boy's arm, pulling him toward the boats. "I don't think we'll leave any names with you. We didn't have anything to do with what's happened here, and we don't want to get involved."

Waylon, annoyed, started to follow them, but Burke put a hand out to stop him. "Let them go. We'll stick around until a couple of the agency people show up and report to them what the boy said. We'll let them check it out. Not us. If there is a body we don't need to get involved with that either."

She pulled out her phone and snapped a couple of shots of the boats, zooming in to catch one of the boat's validation numbers on the hull before the two pulled away. "These photos will help if any of this group need to be questioned later."

Waylon looked behind him toward the break in the thick scrub the boy indicated. "Do you think we should check to see if the claim about a body is even valid?"

Burke shook her head. "No. We might add more unneeded footprints and contaminate the scene. I know you'd like to check it out, but I think waiting until someone comes would be best. I'm sure Henry made calls to all our usual sources. Someone will get here as soon as they can. We've been asked by these agencies to contact them if we see trespassing at the Bank." She paused. "Usually one of the police officers from Edisto boats over here, too. We are a part of Edisto Island, and they don't like flagrant breaches of the law. "

Waylon spotted a large driftwood log and gestured to it. "If we need to wait around, let's sit down for a few minutes. No sense in walking around and upsetting the birds anymore than this group probably already did."

They settled on the log stretching their legs out.

"We didn't even get any names," Waylon grumbled.

"We're lucky we still found them here at all," she replied. "As you saw, they were packing up to leave. Even if they mouthed off at Myron, they knew he'd go call someone. I hope the dog didn't run around and cause too much damage. Maybe Myron can come over later, walk around and check. I wouldn't know what to look for."

"If there's a body, the police may make the area off limits while they investigate."

Burke frowned. "The boy said it looked like the body had been there a long time. Do you think it might be that missing woman?"

"I have no idea. I hate to think so. But it seems likely there's been some sort of foul play. Who would come here alone to the Deveaux Bank and wander around? And what else could happen to them except something criminal?"

She shrugged. "There are snakes and gators here, too. Sometimes people come to isolated places to commit suicide."

"Those are gruesome considerations."

"You grew up here. You know bad things happen, even here."

He rubbed his neck. "Yes, I do. I've never liked seeing the dark side of people though. No matter your occupation, it's always a reminder of the more depraved nature of humanity."

After watching for watercraft for a few minutes in quiet, Waylon asked, "You never did tell me what your sisters thought about our engagement."

Burke pulled her Turtle Patrol cap off, to tighten the band on her ponytail, and then put it back on before answering. "Gwen was shocked at first but then laughed and said she'd always thought a little more than friendship surfaced in the air between us." She shifted to get more comfortable on the log. "Gwen sent her congrats and said she wanted to come for the wedding later when we planned it but she didn't think she could get away sooner for

Easter this month with work at the school going on. I know Mother was disappointed to hear that. She loves Gwen and loves seeing Gwen and Alex's children, too. They're Mom's first grandkids and it's a shame they don't live closer."

"What about Celeste?"

She frowned. "Celeste didn't answer the call I made or any calls Mom made after. It's troubling that we haven't heard anything from her. Lila likes writing letters and wrote one to her, too, put little drawings in it. She didn't hear back either."

"I know Celeste travels a lot but such a long absence without keeping in touch with her family isn't the norm for her from what you tell me."

"No, and Gwen said she hadn't heard from Celeste either."

"Is there anyone you can call to try to check on her?" Waylon asked.

"Not really. We don't know any of her friends personally. She and Dillon moved into a house back in the fall and she put her old condo up for sale. I think it's still for sale. We have the new address for her house, but we don't know any of her neighbors there." Burke sighed. "We don't really know what else to do. But it isn't like Celeste to go for so long without contacting us. As Gwen suggested, she could be touring or traveling abroad, but she usually tells us when she travels."

Waylon pointed out to sea. "There's our police boat coming. Looks like the Edisto Island Police decided to respond."

"Good," Burke said, standing to wave at the incoming boat. "With a possible body here, they'll be the appropriate ones to investigate."

Two officers in navy Edisto Police uniforms walked over to talk to them after pulling their custom-built sea craft into shore and anchoring it with a spike in the sand.

"Hey, Burke," one of the officers said. "Henry told me, when he called in the problem, that you and Waylon Jenkins were coming over here." He stuck out a hand to Waylon. "I'm Lonnie Culler, grew up around here like you. I know your father well and remember you as a boy."

"I think I remember your dad, too," Waylon replied. "Didn't he run the gas station up near Adams Run?"

"Still does." Lonnie turned to the officer with him. "This is Ben Sutherland. Did our trespassers take off before you got here?"

"No, but they were packing up when we walked over from the non-restricted side of the Bank and encountered them."

"Did they give you any trouble?"

"No, but they might have found some trouble," Waylon replied. "One of the boys went back into the scrub to find the dog they'd brought. He came back, white-faced and upset, dragging the dog, to say he ran into a body. He said it looked like it had been there a while. It's the main reason Burke and I waited for you to come, so we could report this to you."

"Did you go check it out?" Lonnie asked.

"No. We didn't think that would be wise," Burke answered. "The boy pointed to that break in the scrub, myrtle, and cord grass there." She gestured toward a break in the dense shrubbery a short distance past the high water mark. "The boy said if you followed what looked like a trail, you'd find it."

Lonnie scowled. "Did you get any of their names?"

Waylon shook his head. "No, they weren't eager to provide any, but Burke snapped a few photos of their boats as they left. She also zoomed in to get a photo of one of the boat's ID numbers on the hull."

"Good thinking." Lonnie added.

"Should we call for backup, Lonnie?" Ben asked.

"Let's walk back there and see what we've got first. Sounds like the situation isn't a current or dangerous one. But we'll need to call in a forensic team if there really is a body." Lonnie turned to Waylon and Burke. "I don't see any reason for you two to hang around and lose more of your work day here. You can head on back. Email me those photos if you would before you leave."

Lonnie pulled out his phone, giving Burke his email address so she could send them on to him. He nodded as they came through in a few minutes.

He turned to Ben then. "We'd better get back in there and see what we've got."

"Will you call and let us know what you learn?" Burke asked.

"I'll do that or send you a short email. We appreciate your involvement in this case. If you hadn't come over to the Bank, that group of kids would have taken off, probably never called in what they saw."

"Do you think the body might be that missing woman?" Burke couldn't resist asking.

"We'll know after a time. It would clear up a lot of concern and speculation if it was, but it might grieve folks who knew the woman well." He rubbed his neck. "She has family in Alabama who've been pushing on all the police departments in this area. We'd like to get some resolution."

Waylon and Burke walked back to their own boat, waded out to climb in, dried off, pulled anchor, and set off back to the island. "I'm glad we wore shorts today since we had to wade in and out."

"Yeah." Waylon steered out into the ocean heading toward the mouth of the North Edisto River and the island, neither far from the Deveaux Bank.

"It's nice the police and Coast Guard have those boats, made to skim right up to the shore," she commented.

"The military has those, too."

"You know, we'd better call Mother," Burke said, pulling out her phone.

"I'm sure she'd appreciate it."

"Hi, Mom," Burke said when her mother answered. "Just calling to say we're fine. Waylon and I are on our way back. We'll fill you in on the details later."

Waylon could hear Burke's mother's reply. "I'm glad you called. Gwen just phoned me. She and the children are at the Jenkins Landing. I was stunned to get her call. Could you and Waylon run up the river and pick them up while you're out? The children are tired and hungry, Gwen said. I was getting ready to call Henry to see if he'd go get them but I hated to ask. He did the ferry run for Waylon not long ago and then came back and finished the sealing work on the pavilion."

Burke lifted her eyebrows in surprise. "Did you know Gwen and the children were coming? Is Alex with them?"

"No to both questions, and Gwen sounded evasive and upset."

Burke frowned.

"Tell your mother we'll head up to the landing right now," Waylon put in. "We should be there in about fifteen minutes. She can call Gwen and tell her to watch for us at the dock. Gwen will know where to park the car."

Burke gave him a worried look as she hung up. "I wonder what's wrong? It's not like Gwen to drive all this way from Arkansas alone with the children without phoning us first. That's a long trip."

Waylon leaned over to give her a kiss as he maneuvered the boat toward the mouth of the North Edisto River. "We'll know soon enough. Try not to worry."

CHAPTER 9

Burke knew she grew quiet on the way to the landing to pick up Gwen. She had so many questions roaring through her mind. Why had Gwen suddenly come home without calling? Why did she drive alone, with three small children, all the way from Arkansas instead of flying? Granted, Gwen could be impulsive, but not this impulsive. Something was wrong. Burke could simply feel it.

As they pulled up to the long dock closest to the boat ramp at the landing, Gwen's children jumped up from the bench where they'd been sitting to wave and shout greetings.

"Looks like someone is glad to see you," Waylon said, smiling as he pulled back on the throttle and eased the boat up to the pier.

Burke saw Gwen stand, too, lifting a hand in greeting, putting on a smile.

"Welcome to Edisto," Waylon called out.

Burke jumped out to tie up the boat. Then she ran straight into her sister's arms, hugging her fiercely, before squatting to hug the children, exclaiming over them.

"Is that all your gear?" Waylon asked Gwen, gesturing to four duffle bags and a box sitting on the dock.

Gwen stepped closer to the boat, handing Waylon two of the bags. "It's enough for now," she spoke in a low voice but Burke heard the words. "The rest is in my car. Maybe we can come get it tomorrow."

"Sure thing." He winked at her. "And you sure have turned out to be a beautiful woman."

"Thank you," she said, and Burke saw tears in her eyes.

Climbing back into the boat, Burke passed Waylon the other two duffle bags.

"I'll get the box," he said, stopping her before she started to climb back to the dock again. "It looks heavy. Get some life jackets out and settle the kids into the seats in the bow of the boat. Belt them in well. We might hit some swells on the river as we head nearer the ocean."

He climbed out, helped the children and Gwen into the boat, and then went to retrieve the box.

Burke couldn't resist stroking her hand down the children's hair as she helped them into life jackets and buckled them snuggly into seat belts in the bow of the skiff. Chase, at eight years old now, was growing taller, looking less like a little boy, his hair a sandy brown streaked with blond like his father's, his eyes a warm brown. Leah had the same honey blond hair and brown eyes as Chase, but Rose, nearly identical in looks, had Gwen's blue-grey eyes—the easy way to tell the twins apart.

Gwen pulled elastic hair bands out of her purse. "Girls, let me pull your hair back into a ponytail or the wind will whip it in your face." She made quick work of slipping the bands on their hair and then pulled her own dark chestnut hair back to secure it, too.

Waylon's Sea Chaser wasn't a large craft, so Waylon had to tuck the duffle bags around the children's feet and put the larger box in the back near the motor.

Burke climbed into her seat by Waylon again, while Gwen settled into one of the seats behind them. The skiff had seats for four in the interior of the boat with the only additional seating in the bow.

"We'll be a bit tight, but we'll be fine to just run down the river to the island," Waylon said, starting the boat.

As the Sea Chaser pulled into the river, Gwen leaned between them. "I forgot to say welcome to the family, Waylon, and congratulations to you and Burke."

She shook her head as Burke started to ask her a question. "Let's don't talk about anything right now." Gwen nodded toward the children. "They've had a long trip and they're tired and hungry."

"Surely you didn't drive straight through?" Burke asked before she could help herself.

"No, we stopped at a motel outside Atlanta last night. Nearly eight hours on the road was enough for all of us. We drove the rest of the way in today."

The children drew their attention then, excited at spotting dolphins in the water, keeping pace with the boat, and then they laughed and exclaimed over a group of noisy gulls following a shrimp boat.

Etta was at the dock when they arrived a short time later, battling back tears as she welcomed Gwen and the children. These last months since Lloyd's death had lifted her emotions closer to the surface, and Burke noticed her mother cried more easily. Deep within, Burke knew Etta was still in mourning. She was, too, to a certain degree, but of course it wasn't quite the same.

"Gwen, this is a lovely surprise." Etta pulled back to study her daughter as Waylon recruited the children to help him unload their bags and carry them down the dock to the new pavilion.

Tall, like all the Deveaux girls, Gwen had more of a pixie, heart-shaped face, her dark brunette hair inherited from Etta, her blue-grey eyes from her father. Gwen also had a curvier figure and a touch more beauty, or at least Burke had always thought so. She also possessed a more vivacious, energetic, and outgoing personality, which seemed subdued now.

"I'm sorry I didn't call and that I missed the usual ferry," Gwen said. "Road work on the interstate slowed us down arriving."

"It's no problem." Etta stroked a hand down Gwen's cheek. "I'm simply glad you're here," she said softly. "For now, let Waylon and Burke take your bags up to the Seaside Cottage. It's empty and I know you like that little cottage closest to the cabana and the path to the beach."

"Thank you. Is it going to be a problem putting us there?"

"No. The inn is full right now, but only one cabin is rented." She smiled at Gwen. "You stay as long as you can. Always remember this is your home."

Burke saw tears again at the corner of Gwen's eyes.

Waylon had walked back to the boat to retrieve the box, stowing it and the duffle bags in the tram Etta had driven down from the inn. "Where are you putting our welcome visitors, Etta?"

She smiled at him. "In the Seaside Cottage. Drop me at the inn on your way. While Burke helps Gwen and the children settle in, I'll help Novaleigh get dinner finished and help to set up at the evening buffet tables. I'll also put extra chairs around the big table on the screened porch for the family. We'll eat there rather than in the dining room tonight."

Burke giggled. "That woman who wanted to bring her little granddaughters may get testy when she sees Chase, Leah, and Rose go through the buffet."

Etta lifted her chin. "A vital fact that will always be true is that this inn is my home as well as a bed and breakfast for guests. I raised my children at the inn, and any of my grandchildren will always be welcome here."

"Mom, you know I'll keep a watch on them," Gwen said.

"Of course you will," Etta added.

With eagerness the children climbed into the tram now, seeing the long vehicle as a fun novelty, like children always did.

Etta glanced at her watch as she climbed into the tram herself. "It's almost six now. Give the guests a little time to go through the buffet and settle in to their dinner, if you would. Then come on over to the inn. A short walk to the beach will keep the children's minds off their tummies until then."

"We'll do that. Thank you, Mother," Gwen said, climbing into the tram, as Waylon started it to head up the road toward the inn and cottages.

The Seaside Cottage stood closest to the ocean, red with white trim like all the Deveaux rentals, with a small covered porch in front and a comfortable screened porch off the back that caught the sea breeze.

Lila met Gwen and the children at the door with enthusiastic hugs. "I'm so excited to see you. What a wonderful surprise." She held the door wide for them to bring in their bags. "Mother sent me ahead to open the cottage and get it ready. I didn't have a lot of time, but I did tidy up and turn on the fans to air the cottage out. Burke and I cleaned all the cottages last week though so everything still looks nice."

"You are sweet," Gwen said, kissing her cheek. "I love the little letters you write to me and the children, and all your wonderful drawings. Thank you."

Lila drew back and put her hands on Gwen's cheeks. "Healing and direction will come for you, sister. Everything will be all right. You are loved and God will help you through any problems if you reach out to Him."

"Thanks," she whispered back, sniffling and wiping away a few tears. "You've always been such a comfort."

Waylon cleared his throat. "You know, I think I'll take the tram back and freshen up before supper," he said. "I'll see all of you later on."

Burke walked out with him.

"It seems obvious something has gone wrong in Gwen's life in some way," Waylon said. "She used to get mad and refuse to cry even when a bee stung her."

Burke couldn't help laughing. "Well, whatever it is we'll help her through it." She leaned in to give him a quick kiss. "Thanks for all your help today."

He winked at her. "I aim to please."

She looked down at the ring on her hand. "I find myself amazed and pleased with my life every day now, even in the midst of all the unexpected events we've faced today."

Waylon turned her hand over and kissed her wrist. "Only sweet things are coming our way, Burke."

"I hope so." She glanced back toward the cabin.

He paused before leaving. "I hope we'll hear something from Lonnie about the woman later on. I may take dinner to the lodge and let you, your mother, and Lila enjoy family time with Gwen and the children tonight. I'll come walk on the beach at our usual time, though, once dark falls. If you can get away, come join me."

"I will," she said, letting him leave and walking back into the cabin.

"The children want to walk to the beach before supper," Lila said. "We won't go far, but it will be good for them to run and play for a little while after sitting in the car all day."

The three sisters and the children soon started down the sandy path past the cabana.

"The tide's out," Gwen commented, stopping to look across the broad sweep of beach to the waves washing in, the ocean beyond it azure blue under a clear blue sky.

Lila paused as they neared the end of the path. "Gwen, why don't you and Burke stop here on this bench and simply enjoy the view and the sound of the ocean. I'll walk with the children along the beach and keep an eye on them."

Gwen's eyes followed Chase, Leah, and Rose, already scampering along the sand.

"Don't let them get in the water," Gwen cautioned.

"No need to worry about that." Lila sent her a sweet smile. "It's April. The sea hasn't warmed up yet; it's too cold even to wade in the surf right now."

Gwen sighed. "I'd forgotten."

Burke waved Lila on with gratitude. She knew Gwen needed a few minutes of quiet, a time to let loose all that steely reserve she'd been holding in.

They sat quietly, watching Lila play with the children on the beach, enjoying the soothing sounds of the waves washing in, listening to the gulls calling and squabbling, and feeling the soft ocean breeze sweep over them. Burke could see Lila picking up shells to show the children as they walked, pointing out things they might miss otherwise, teaching in that gracious way of hers.

"Look how she already has the children in the palm of her hand," Gwen said after a moment. "She's always had such a gift with children. I never could understand why she chose a religious life." She turned to Burke. "Has she said why she left?"

"Only that what once seemed like the right path no longer felt the same anymore."

"Bless her heart, I know that feeling." Gwen put a hand to her mouth, trying not to sob. "My life's a mess right now, Burke. I don't know what I'm going to do."

Burke put a hand on her knee. "Has Alex cheated on you, been unfaithful?" She couldn't imagine any other reason Gwen would leave him. The two had always been so passionately and obviously in love.

Gwen sighed. "He's been unfaithful in a worse way, I think. For the last year or two he's lied to me, told me the restaurant was doing great when it wasn't."

She closed her eyes. "You know we finally moved from our little two bedroom condo to a house three years ago. Chase got his own room, the kids a yard to play in. I actually stopped working in the restaurant after we moved, too. Chase and his partner Josh Vine hired a receptionist to replace me. I went back to school to finish my coursework in Elementary Education and did my internship in the schools last year. I took my Praxis exams and finally got the teaching degree I started all those years ago before Alex and I ran off and got married. This year I've been subbing and applying for teaching jobs."

"So the restaurant really isn't doing well?" Burke asked, remembering Gwen's earlier words. "Wouldn't you want to stay and help Alex until things are better?"

Gwen frowned at her. "If I'd known about the trouble all along, that's exactly what I'd have done. But Alex concealed everything from me. He lied to me, never let me know there was a problem. He took out heavy loans, one against our house. Alex's partner in the restaurant, Josh Vines, lied to me, too, and he's been like a brother to me all these years. This week it all caught up with them. Alex had to come tell me we were going to lose the business and the house."

Burke wrapped an arm around her. "I'm so sorry, Gwen."

"I was so shocked, Burke. I trusted Alex. It hurt so much to know he'd lied to me like he did. I couldn't bear to even be in the same room with him. I made him pack some bags and go to stay at Josh's place. I needed time to think, to cry, to try to figure out what to do." She hung her head, with tears dribbling down her cheeks.

Burke waited, shocked and hurt, too. How could Alex have done such a thing? Not shared with her?

"Josh called me when I wouldn't answer any of Alex's calls. He apologized, too, and he tried to get me to understand Alex didn't want to worry me, that they thought they could turn things around. Josh said they were putting the restaurant up for sale; he assured me he and Alex would find other jobs."

She hesitated. "When I still wouldn't let him put Alex on the phone, he advised the best thing to do about the house was to put it on the market quickly before it went into foreclosure. Josh said we could move into his condo, next to our old one, and that he would move home with his folks for a while. I couldn't believe he kept talking away, like Alex had earlier, as though I should simply understand everything and go along. Like it was no big deal they lied to me, deceived me, that the children and I were losing our home."

Burke couldn't think what to say.

"The children were at school, thank goodness," she continued. "I wept and cried the whole morning and then made a decision. I wrote a note to Alex, put it in the mail to him at Josh's address, and when the children came home, I had the car partly packed to head to the island here."

Burke's eyes followed the three children turning to walk back up the beach with Lila. "How have Chase, Leah, and Rose dealt with this?"

"We often come to the island for Easter and their Spring Break. You know that. They were disappointed when I told them earlier we probably couldn't come this year. So I just cheerily said I'd changed my mind. We finished packing that evening and headed out the next morning. You know the rest."

"I see. They think you're simply on vacation."

"Yes." She turned to Burke. "I'll need to figure out how to get my teaching license here in South Carolina. I'm sure it will involve some paperwork and stuff, but I should be able to get a job to teach elementary school somewhere in the area. I'm licensed for kindergarten to sixth grade in Arkansas. I feel confident the schools I subbed in will give me good references."

"You've always been good with kids."

Gwen smiled at Lila galloping up the beach with the children. "Maybe not as good with them as Lila but I am a good teacher. I already know that." She closed her eyes. "Alex told me there would be money when they sell the restaurant. Hopefully, there will be more if he can sell the house before they foreclose. Even separated I should get part of it. That will help me and the children get resettled to wherever I can find a teaching position. I plan to apply in Charleston, Summerville, Walterboro, and Beaufort. I don't want to live so far away from all of you anymore."

"That fact sounds like a happy idea to me," Burke said, trying to stay positive, even while she felt overwhelmed with all this news.

As Lila and the children drew closer, Gwen turned anxious eyes to Burke. "Do you think Mother will let me and the children stay here for a time? I can help with the inn and maybe get a part-time job nearby. Everyone will need extra help with the tourist season coming in. I know restaurant work really well. I helped Alex and Josh all the first years with the Riverside Grille. I think I did every job in the restaurant at one time or another."

Burke turned her eyes to Gwen. "How can you imagine for a minute Mother wouldn't let you stay with us? You're our family. Mother will be heartsick over all this sorrow you've had to deal with. I am, too." She leaned over to hug Gwen close. "We'll see you through this. Let that be one thing you can be totally sure of."

Hearing the children's chatter grow closer, she added, "You'll need to share all this news with Mother after dinner. Lila and I will bring the children back to the cottage so the two of you can talk alone." She looked at the children's happy faces as they held up shells they'd collected. "You'll need to find a way to talk with the children, too. And soon. Remember how you felt being lied to, how we all hate to be lied to, even children."

"I'll find a way," Gwen said, standing up. "One thing at a time, Burke."

They went back to the cottage to clean up and soon started across the pathway to the Deveaux Inn for dinner.

Burke glanced at her watch as they neared the inn. It was nearly seven. Most of the guests would be finished with their dinner or settled comfortably in the dining room eating. Their timing was good to be less intrusive.

Burke hoped she'd get a chance to walk with Waylon later, too. Already he seemed such a part of her life.

CHAPTER 10

Waylon was pleased to see Burke coming down the path to meet him later that night, with Boonie dashing ahead to greet him with happy barks. He and Burke had established a routine over the weeks, meeting at the bench behind the old Signal or Fog House, which held the island's foghorn and bell. It was a beautiful night with a pink and golden sunset settling over the ocean.

He scratched the dog's ears in greeting and then grinned at Burke. "I still remember as a boy when Lloyd let me ring the bell or sound the foghorn here to warn boats of a dense fog moving in. Do you still do that?"

"Yes. Sometimes. When fog moves in, it can really reduce visibility for boat pilots. It's especially dangerous for casual boaters. They're not used to navigating safely from the sea into the river. Ringing the bell or sounding the fog horn can provide an alert to them so they don't run into rocks or land as they try to make the turn."

"I've seen accidents like that."

"Sometimes the Coast Guard or one of the other agencies will send us a message asking us to provide a warning," she added. "A boat rammed into the Deveaux Bank not long ago, marooned for several days after. The night was dark, with heavy fog, no visible moon, and the pilot not a seasoned one."

"It's sad when that happens." He reached for her hand as they started down the pathway to the beach.

She smiled at him. "We still serve an important purpose here at the mouth of the river, with the low sandy spits of the Deveaux

Bank not always spotted by inexperienced pilots. There are some dangerous shoals off Seabrook Island, too, and more at Stono Inlet a little further north by Kiawah. Heavy fog, rain, snow, ice, or storms often create unexpected problems."

His eyes moved to the lighthouse on the hill, its sweep of light arching out across the ocean in regular rhythms.

"How many miles out does the light reach?"

"In good weather twenty-six miles, less in inclement weather. But if you're a small craft, without a knowledgeable pilot or a good navigational system, seeing the light alone can be a lifesaver. We still have our stories, too, of rescuing boats that founder in the sea during a storm."

Surprised, Waylon asked, "Do you head out in bad weather alone?"

"I used to go with Dad sometimes when we spotted a small boat in trouble not far out to sea." She stopped to pick up a shell. "Once last month I went out to pick up a jet skier whose craft hit a corner of the Deveaux Bank in the dark. The hit damaged his craft and left him stranded there. He was smart enough to take off his shirt and wave it, trying to get attention. I was walking Boonie on the beach and saw him. It's only a mile to the Bank, not a problem for me even in the dark."

Waylon felt himself flinch. "What if the man hadn't been an honorable person? People sometimes set up situations like that to take advantage of others."

She stopped and turned to him, obviously provoked at his comment. "Part of my job is discerning situations that occur, contacting the Coast Guard when there's trouble and sometimes helping people when I can. Don't start going macho and overprotective with me, Waylon. I'm a businesswoman. I do my job in the way I've been trained to do it."

He smiled at her, trying to restore peace. "You did mention you usually went out with your dad for rescues. Two is better than one in most situations. Perhaps you might call on me as a help with future problems."

He watched her consider his words.

"I could do that." She walked on. "The man I rescued that night was bruised and cut up with his leg bleeding. A little help to get him into my skiff would have been nice."

Waylon decided not to say more.

"How's Gwen?" he asked instead, changing the subject.

"Tired, upset, and angry. She impulsively loaded up the children and left Alex yesterday, not even talking to him before she took off."

"Had he cheated on her?" Waylon asked.

"That's the first thing I asked. As crazy as they've always been about each other, it's the only reason I could imagine for Gwen to leave Alex impulsively."

She paused to call to Boonie, investigating a sea creature washed up on shore. The dog ran back on her command before she continued. "Gwen says Alex's business was in trouble but that he kept it from her. He took loans to try to stay afloat and then it all imploded. He had to come tell her then he'd lost the business and their home."

"Ouch." Waylon whistled. "That's tough."

"Gwen says they have time before foreclosure on the house. Hopefully, they can sell it before that happens. I imagine Alex is in a similar situation with the business. I know he and his partner Josh have it for sale, too." She sighed. "Gwen felt totally betrayed and blindsided. She couldn't believe Alex didn't share with her about any of this and lied to her for well over a year, letting things grow worse and worse."

She turned to him. "Don't ever do that, Waylon. Whatever it is—a business problem, a health concern—you share with me. Lying and deception can destroy a relationship."

He took both her hands. "I will share with you, Burke, good and bad." He knew this situation with Alex and Gwen had left her reeling, envisioning the hurt that could come with marriage as well as the joys. He gathered her close to kiss her until he felt the tension begin to slip away.

She sniffed and brushed tears away from her eyes. "My heart hurts so much for her, Waylon, and for the children. They love their daddy. You should hear them talk about him. It's so obvious how foolish they are about him."

"Hasn't she told them anything yet?"

She shook her head. "No. They think they've come for Easter break at their grandmother's. But she plans to talk to them soon. She doesn't plan to return to Arkansas."

Waylon tossed a stick for Boonie to chase. "Will she stay here?"

"For a time. She says she's going to do the paperwork to get her South Carolina teaching license and look for a job nearby. Gwen was always eager to leave the island but she says she wants to settle closer to the family now after she finds work."

Waylon thought about this as they walked on. "What does Alex want?"

Burke shook her head. "I have no idea. From Gwen's story, he planned to look for another job. His friend Josh told Gwen that he could move home to his parents' place in Little Rock and let her, Alex, and the kids use his condo for a time."

"But she left without talking to Alex, without telling him goodbye or letting him see the children?"

"Yes. It sounds harsh, but she was hurt."

They walked along, quiet for a time. "I can't help but feel a little sorry for both of them and for the kids," Waylon said.

"Me, too."

"Do you think there's any chance they might reconcile?"

"Not from listening to Gwen. She seems to have made up her mind, and if you remember, she's always been headstrong and stubborn when she does."

Waylon couldn't help laughing at old memories popping into his mind. "Gwen was always a little spitfire, that's for sure. I imagine she gave Alex what-for."

"I'd love to have been a fly on the wall when she talked to Mother after dinner." Burke grinned. "Lila and I took the children back to the cottage, played a game with them, got them ready for bed.

With the three of them still awake when Gwen got back, Lila and I didn't learn more. I'm sure we will later."

"I hope your mother wisely counseled Gwen there could be legal ramification for taking the children without talking about it with Alex. They aren't divorced or even legally separated. Alex has the right to know where his children are and to see them. His actions would probably not be the kind, either, to deny him parental rights or partial custody."

"Well, acting impulsively has always been one of Gwen's problems if you remember. She tends to act without thinking things through, although you can't blame her for being emotionally upset in this situation."

They turned around as the broad Townsend Inlet came into view, the beach ending. Waylon whistled to Boonie to start back with them.

"Should I go talk to Gwen?" he asked.

"Not tonight," she answered. "I know she's exhausted, and I imagine Mother's had strong words with her. Not that Mother wouldn't be loving and sympathetic, after hearing everything, but she will have considered many of the things you mentioned. I'm sure she will insist Alex be contacted."

"I don't envy them this hurtful time to go through."

"Me neither." She squeezed his hand as they walked along. "Thanks for letting me share with you."

"We'll be sharing everything for the rest of our lives, Burke."

"That's a nice thought," she said softly, reaching out to touch his face. "I do love you, Waylon."

"And I you, Eugenia Burke." He pulled her into his arms to show her how much, loving the soft sighs he heard as he kissed her, and reveling in the wonder of holding her in his arms.

A little later, their walk finished, they climbed the pathway up to the Signal House again.

"With that old bell tower on top, I've always thought the Signal House looks like a little chapel, painted white as it is," Burke commented as they drew closer to it.

"Is the building locked?"

"Always." She laughed. "If we left it open visitors and pranksters might try to sound the fog horn—which, believe me, is really loud—or they might ring the bell for sport or fun."

He felt glad to hear her laugh again. "Try not to worry too much about Gwen. Things will work out. She has a loving family to help her through whatever she might need to face."

"That's a comfort, but it still doesn't make this time an easy one. I'm so sorry this has happened. I know you've never met Alex, but he's smart, kind, and charming, and there's always been so much love and passion between him and Gwen. You could almost feel the sizzle between them in the room sometimes. It seems such a shame their relationship has to end."

"It's going to be awkward, too, that Gwen's taken the children so far from him. I'm sure if a separation proceeds the kids will soon have a back-and-forth life between South Carolina and Arkansas."

"I never thought of that. I wonder if Gwen did?"

"I'll bet your mother did. My guess is she'll haul Gwen down to her attorney right away, unless Alex is agreeable to allow them space to think this through before starting any legal action. Even then they may need an attorney's counsel to make a verbal agreement stand."

"Wow. How do you know all this?"

He shrugged. "You deal with a lot of personnel problems in tight quarters on a ship. I often got involved in legal issues."

She shook her head. "I guess I was so overwhelmed I didn't think about any legal aspects relating to this."

"My guess is Gwen probably didn't either."

Waylon's cell phone rang. Seeing the caller, he answered. "Hello Etta. Is everything all right?"

"Hardly. Could you come up to the house with Burke? I'd like to talk with both of you."

"We'll be right there," he said.

"I'll be in the family wing where we'll have some privacy."

CHAPTER 11

"I wonder what's happened?" Burke asked as they found the path toward the inn.

"I'm sure your Mother will tell us soon."

A few minutes later they cut through the back porch to the family wing. As the demand for more guest rooms had grown at the Deveaux Inn, Burke's grandparents added a wing off the main inn with a private family wing on the ground level and more guest suites and accompanying baths above. The family room, like a spacious apartment, had a living area, opening to a small kitchen and dining room, with two bedrooms and two baths. It was a comfortable, relaxing space, decorated informally in blues, creamy white, cozy chintz fabrics, sea paintings, nautical decorations, and a hodge-podge of furniture.

"I'd forgotten what a nice place this is," Waylon said as he and Burke came into the main room.

Etta sat in an old wing-backed chair, her feet on a stool.

Burke studied her. "Are you all right, Mom?"

"I'm fine," she answered, gesturing to the sofa nearby. "I just needed to talk to you both for a few minutes."

Burke and Waylon settled on the sofa.

"First off, Lonnie Culler from the Edisto Police called. The woman they found was named Cloris Epson—not the missing woman from Hollywood, but the other woman who went missing before."

"The one from Yonges Island?" Waylon asked.

"Yes. She's been positively identified and she was raped and murdered. Lonnie confided this might mean a killer is living or staying around the area who targets women, assuming there's a link between the woman found at the Deveaux Bank and the other woman."

Waylon frowned. "I'm sorry to hear that."

"Aren't we all?" Etta agreed. "As much as I hate to do it, I think I may need to caution our guests arriving tomorrow." She turned to Waylon. "You, Clifford, and Henry may need to do more security checks around the island regularly, as well. I'd hate to think one of our guests comes across a criminal or a dead body, since the woman from Hollywood is still missing."

Burke's eyes widened. "Is there reason to think the woman from Hollywood might have come here?"

"Only that someone saw her and a man in a boat on the river near our marina."

Waylon frowned. "They could have been heading out to the ocean. From what Dad told me, no one actually saw the boat on any of the creeks or inlets around our island."

"I'm aware of that, but we still need to take this issue seriously until it is resolved," Etta replied. "Lonnie said the news of the murder would probably hit the newspapers and other media in the morning." She looked across at both of them. "He said to tell you he purposely left your names completely out of the report."

"That's good news," Waylon said.

"Yes, it is. We have enough problems already." Etta sighed. "I also need to talk to you both about our new family issue."

Burke turned to lift her eyebrows at Waylon while her mother reached for the glass of iced tea on the table beside her. He winked at Burke before she turned her attention back to her mother.

Etta heaved a sigh. "Waylon, I'm sure Burke has told you by now that Gwen has left her husband, angry because he left her out of the picture about their financial affairs. It's my opinion he handled that situation poorly. It's also my opinion Gwen handled learning about the situation poorly, packing up and taking off with their children without discussing it with Alex at all."

"She sent a letter," Burke offered.

Etta frowned at her. "Would it satisfy you if Waylon took off without talking with you and merely sent you a letter in the mail to receive afterward?"

Burke winced. "No," she had to admit.

"It's probably not my place, either, but I called Alex," Etta continued. "I know Lloyd would have done the same. I wanted to hear what Alex had to say about things."

Burke leaned forward. "What did he say?"

"He candidly admitted he had not handled things well in his business affairs or in his personal life. He said he and Josh Vines had hoped to turn things around without upsetting Gwen over their problems but he realizes now that decision was a mistake."

"Mother, he lied to her repeatedly, told her everything was fine."

"Gwen told me that; so did Alex. He's deeply remorseful, not that his remorse changes anything. It's still a mess."

Waylon cleared his throat. "Although the wrong is all on Alex's side in this, Gwen taking off with the children wasn't the wisest move on her part. Legally, of course."

Etta rolled her eyes. "Tell me about it. I've called our attorney, and he's writing up an informal separation agreement to give both Gwen and Alex time to cool down, think and consider what they want to do before either begin any legal actions. We mainly need this for Gwen's sake and her legal protection. I'm taking her down to talk to Ralph Maybank at the Maybank-Calhoun Law Firm on the highway on Edisto tomorrow. Sam Calhoun, a family friend, was a partner there before he died. The firm has always handled all of our legal affairs. At this point they can take care of this, and if Gwen decides to later proceed to a divorce, they can refer her."

She looked across at them. "We have a full house coming in tomorrow at the inn and a busy weekend coming up. Burke, you will need to do your usual Friday tour at the lighthouse and you and Waylon will need to help in any way you can while I take Gwen over for her appointment tomorrow afternoon. Lila is keeping the children so she won't be able to help much in any way. Burke, you'll need to handle ringing up any sales in the gift shop since Lila can't help and since I'll be gone."

"I can do that," Burke assured her.

"I can help, too," Waylon added. "And I'm glad Gwen is getting some legal advice on how best to handle this situation."

Etta sighed. "I hate this has happened. It will be difficult for Gwen, and for Alex and the children. Starting over after hardship is tough for any family, but starting over alone, and bitter, is harder. As you can imagine, Gwen is not open at this time to any other alternatives."

"What will Alex do?" Burke asked.

"Right now, he'll stay with Josh and work to sell the business and the house as expediently as possible. He said that a potential buyer had approached them in past about the restaurant. I imagine they'll reach out in that direction first. They've been wisely counseled that selling out is better than trying to declare bankruptcy in their situation. They're both young. They can start again. I gather Josh Vines' father has a business in the area they both might go to work for. It's all I know at this time, but when things settle down a little, Alex will want to see the children. My guess is he would fight if necessary for joint custody."

"Do you think Gwen thought any of this through?" Burke asked.

"No." Etta shook her head. "Even when she was a little girl, Gwen would act first and think later. I'd hoped she would mature and outgrow that tendency, but evidently she has not at this point."

"She's really hurt, Mom," Burke said.

"I'm aware of that and I hurt for her, but someone has to stay level-headed and handle things. With Lloyd gone, that's me now."

"What can I do?" Waylon asked.

Etta smiled at him. "At this time, only what I've asked already. I guess you're getting a quick dose of what it means to marry into the Deveaux family."

"It's no more challenge than the problems I faced regularly in the Navy, Etta."

She gave him a considering look. "I imagine not. And I admit your solid comfort is a help right now."

Waylon stood after glancing at his watch. "It's late. I need to head down to the lodge and check the marina, especially with this new knowledge."

"I'll see you out," Burke said, starting to get up.

"No need." He waved her back in place. "Visit with your mother a little longer and then both of you settle into bed with a good book. We all have a big day tomorrow." He paused, looking back at Etta. "You did well jumping on this situation with Gwen so quickly, calling your attorney, and even calling Alex."

"Thank you. I doubt Gwen will be especially grateful when she learns of it in the morning, but it had to be done."

He left, winking at Burke on his way out.

"I do like that man," Etta said after a few moments. "Smart, steady, calm. He always tended toward that direction as a boy—easy-going and reliable. But he's grown into a fine man now."

"Yes, he has." Burke agreed, smiling.

"You look like the cat that swallowed the cream, even in the midst of all these problems," her mother said.

"I feel like I'm simply floating above the clouds sometimes, Mother."

"Well, young love is a sweet time. Savor it well." She got up, taking her glass to the kitchen to wash it out. "I'm going to head to bed. I'll see you in the morning." She came over to kiss Burke on the cheek before she left.

Burke went into the kitchen after her mother left to fix herself a cup of hot tea, coming back to sit in the quiet for a few moments. It had been a stressful day, and yet she felt such a wash of joy within at the lovely turn her life had taken, in bringing her and Waylon back together. Everything seemed so much easier to face with him in her life now.

She remembered her mother's words about needing to handle the problem with Gwen on her own, with Lloyd gone. It was one of the first times Burke fully understood her mother's pain in losing her father, being alone, not being able to lean on him or share with him. Of course she was here for her mother, as were the Georges, the Boals, and other good friends, along with Lila now. But it wasn't the same.

How quickly two people became one. Burke had always seen the unity, love, and warmth between her mother and father, even when they squabbled a little and disagreed. She knew how often she pictured her father even now when she was giving tours. She could easily remember him laughing and telling his sea stories to their guests. Often it hurt and brought back a rush of fond memories, seeing her father's favorite chair now empty or running across an old sweater of his with a touch of his bay rum scent still lingering on it. How much harder this time had to be for her mother, missing her father's love, their shared intimacies.

Burke took her cup to the kitchen, washed it out, and headed to her room for bed. Originally Burke's grandparents lived here in the family wing with Lloyd before he went away to school and the Navy. When Lloyd returned and married, his parents—Burke's grandparents—had moved into the big master suite on the main floor of the inn and gave the family wing to her father and mother. When she and her sisters came along, they'd occupied various spots in cradles and cribs around the apartment, and later beds in the spare bedroom.

When her grandparents passed away, with Burke and her sisters only small, her parents moved to their big master suite in the inn so the girls could have the two bedrooms in the family wing. She'd been nearly nine then, Gwen seven, Celeste five, Lila only two. Before that, she and her sisters shared one bedroom, but when her parents moved, Burke moved into their room, taking Lila with her. She'd been caring for her youngest sister a lot already and a bond already existed. Living with Lila was quieter and more restful than rooming with Gwen and Celeste, both so talkative and dramatic. Burke smiled now remembering that, as she dressed for bed and settled under the covers, like Waylon had mentioned, with a book she'd been reading. He knew her well already.

Burke's bedroom had been altered some through the years, but it still looked much the same—a spacious, comfortable room with two four poster twin beds, several pieces of matching dark cherry furniture, and a soft wallpaper on the walls. Sea prints established the color scheme for the room, and shelves of books and personal belongings adding warmth and individuality, as did two old trunks at the end of each bed.

Burke wondered for the first time where she and Waylon would live when they married. Would he want to stay at the lodge or move here with her into the family wing? They simply hadn't talked about it yet. She suddenly realized, too, that he would want to bring many aspects of himself with him. She looked around imagining it. And then she grinned, knowing two twin beds so far apart would hardly do for a married couple. Like her mother had said, there were still a lot of things she and Waylon needed to talk about.

CHAPTER 12

As Etta predicted, Friday proved to be a busy and hectic day. On Friday guests moved in and out of the Deveaux Inn. Guests checked out at ten in the morning and checked in at four in the afternoon.

Waylon had learned from Etta that guests arriving on Friday, for the weekend, left on Sunday, where guests arriving for a week's stay left the following Friday. This morning he'd drive the Deveaux Inn's ferry up the river to Jenkins Landing to drop off the inn's guests checking out. This afternoon he'd drive the ferry back to the Landing to pick up the new guests coming in. Along with helping to load and unload baggage, Waylon quickly realized the importance of his role as an ambassador for the inn. For those leaving, he was their last impression, sending them off with friendliness and the hope they'd return. To new guests arriving he was the first representative they met, when excited and bubbling with questions.

Waylon had ridden the ferry back and forth with Lloyd Deveaux many times as a boy, and he found he fell naturally into his old mentor's role as ferry Captain, even telling some of Lloyd's stories for entertainment on the morning trip. Now in the afternoon, he was returning to the Landing to pick up the large group of new guests arriving, most for a two-week stay.

When he arrived, he found his dad chatting congenially with many of the guests waiting for pickup while others talked with his mother working in the office. Dewey had already left, taking a fishing charter out on the ocean.

The incoming guests waited for the ferry under a broad covered patio by the Jenkins Landing Office. Picnic tables and chairs were scattered around the waiting area with bathrooms, a water fountain, and vending machines nearby.

"Friday's always a busy day at the Deveaux Inn," his dad commented as he helped him load baggage into the Jenkins tram to drive down to the ferry. "It's a fine sunshiny day, too, and it's a boon the marina's new walkway and pavilion got completed so quickly. I remember miserable days loading and unloading people and baggage in the midst of a nasty storm."

"So do I. The Greenlee Construction crew did a great job."

His dad hopped on the tram with him to take the baggage down to the ferry. "Etta told Aileen about the woman found over at the Deveaux Bank," his dad added. "Sorrowful thing to hear. Aileen knows some of the woman's family. They're torn up, of course, and I'm not too pleased to think we might have a killer hanging around our area. We've started taking extra precautions; I know you have at the island, too."

"Yes. Henry, Clifford, and I are doing extra security checks, staying alert and watchful. There may not be any link between the two women though."

"Well, simply knowing the killer of the woman they found hasn't been arrested is worry enough."

At the dock, his dad hopped off the tram to help transfer the baggage to the back of the ferry. "I heard they found a dead dog at the Deveaux Bank, too," he added. "Killed like the woman."

Waylon glanced up. "I hadn't heard that."

"Family said it was her pet, that she was foolish about it. No one can figure why she took it over to the Bank with her. Locals know dogs are illegal there."

Waylon frowned. "That is odd."

"Yeah, well this whole thing is odd and irregular. I hope it soon gets settled. Makes everyone nervous and skitsy."

Heading back to pick up the guests to transport to the ferry, his dad asked, "How is all that business with Gwen coming along?

Yesterday Dewey let Gwen in at the gate when she called from her cell phone. Aileen and I'd gone into town for groceries or we'd have welcomed her more." He rolled his eyes. "Dewey was into some football game, so he just released the gate for her and went back to it."

Waylon laughed. "Sounds like Dewey. Always the cordial, welcoming type."

"Well, he didn't know Gwen like we did either." Hal excused him. "Aileen says Gwen's left her husband. We're sorry to hear that, for her sake and for Etta's." He paused. "Etta's got enough on her plate right now simply getting past Lloyd's death."

"How did Lloyd die exactly?"

"Dropped dead with a heart attack. Real sudden." Hal frowned. "Just one of those things. You know Lloyd was about ten years older than Etta but he was still too young to check out at his age. It's a shame."

Back at the office, Waylon drove the tram around to pick up the incoming guests, waving goodbye to his dad as he pulled away again.

Six couples had arrived to catch the ferry, with five headed to the inn and the younger couple, Neila and Perry Ormont, checking in at the Lakeview Cottage. Neila and Perry brought kayaks with them, along with other outdoor gear, that Waylon stowed in the back of the ferry. He answered a barrage of questions on the way back, then delivered all the guests, with their baggage, to the appropriate destinations.

Waylon had hoped to follow Burke around on her lighthouse tour earlier in the day so he could help her in the future more with the tours, but an issue came up with a man and lady stopping at the marina, arguing with him about taking their dog to the lighthouse.

"Our Bitsy is only a little Pomeranian," the woman argued. "She won't be any trouble."

Waylon had spotted her and her husband starting up the road to the lighthouse from the marina where they'd docked their skiff, and he soon caught up to them.

"I'm sorry," Waylon told her. "Dogs are not allowed on the island or on the lighthouse tour."

The man scowled. "Well, since we already boated over from Seabrook, the least you could do is make an exception this time."

"I can't do that," Waylon replied. "The 'no dogs ruling' is a legality here. It's printed on all the Deveaux Inn and Lighthouse brochures, on the official website, and on the sign right by the marina." He pointed back toward it.

"I saw that sign," the man admitted. "But I assumed there would be an exception for small dogs like our Bitsy that can be carried."

"No, there aren't any exceptions. I'm sorry." Waylon shook his head.

"Do you own this place?" the man snapped back. "Who else can I talk to about this?"

"If I let you walk on to the lighthouse, Burke or Etta Deveaux would tell you the same thing and you'd simply have to walk back again." He paused. "If you're staying at Seabrook or Kiawah, you can come back tomorrow at two without your pet. The family does tours on both Friday and Saturday."

The woman cuddled the dog. "Where we go our Bitsy goes. If she can't come with us then we're leaving."

Waylon thought about offering to keep the dog while they toured the lighthouse but he knew it a risk he shouldn't take. And against the island's regulations.

"Why don't you allow dogs?" the man asked. "Especially little ones like Bitsy. What would it hurt?"

"Small or large dogs can be injured or killed easily if they get free from their owners. There are alligators in the lake and lagoons, snakes, and other dangers. Much of Watch Island is basically wilderness. It's easy for an animal to run off and get lost." He paused. "The lighthouse poses its own set of problems, too, with steep stairs, high balconies, historic relics to protect, and the additional problem of multiple people on every tour, some allergic to or not comfortable with dogs."

"Well, I can see you're not going to be reasonable about this and make an exception," the man said, frowning. He turned to his wife. "Let's go, Ethel. You wanted to go to see the Angel Tree on Johns Island, too. We can drive to see that before we meet the Franklins for dinner."

They huffed off, still grumbling.

Then as Waylon headed toward the lighthouse again, Henry called him on his cell phone to help with yet another problem.

"While I was weed-eating near the dock, I spotted a couple of kayaks pulled up on the bank with nobody around. From the tracks they left, I think they decided to explore the island's trails, ignoring the No Trespassing signs." He sighed. "Could you go hunt them down? I really need to finish the job I'm working on."

"Sure," Waylon said. "I'll go get my golf cart and head over right now." About forty-five minutes later he finally found the two young men, sitting on the dock by the lake, their legs dangling over the side, laughing and smoking cigarettes. After Waylon pointed out the tip of the alligator's nose not far away in the weeds, they agreed to head back to their kayaks more readily.

"We were only exploring. Taking a break," the older of the two men said. "We didn't think it would be a big deal to look around. It didn't seem like we'd be bothering anyone."

Waylon was beginning to see that most people decided No Trespassing rules weren't really enforced. He wished he knew an answer for it.

Burke's day had proved equally busy and even after dinner, she got tied up, helping to settle their guests in at the inn and couldn't get away for their usual walk together. Waylon missed his walk down the beach with her, but he used the time to check the island again carefully for any problems. It was unsettling to know a murder had occurred so near them, with the other woman still missing as well. The whole business gave him an uneasy feeling.

As Waylon was checking the cabana, in a final drive around the island on his golf cart, he saw a small figure dashing down the path to the beach. In a few moments, he heard a woman's voice, "Chase, come back here. You can't take off down to the beach in the dark."

Gwen came into view, spotting Waylon at the cabana as she drew closer. "Did you see my son head down the path here?"

Waylon nodded. "Yeah. Is everything all right?"

"No. Things are a mess in my life right now. You know I went to talk to an attorney with my mom today, and tonight after dinner I finally talked to the children. It was probably an overdue conversation, and they didn't take it well, especially Chase." She sighed. "He ran out of the house crying."

"It hurts kids when their parents split up."

"Well, it's hardly my fault, Waylon Jenkins." Gwen crossed her arms and glared at him. "With you planning to get married, let me advise you that open communication, sharing, and trust are critical factors to a healthy marriage. Lying and shady dealings don't have any place in a good relationship. Don't be so quick to judge how you might feel in the same situation."

"I don't think I mentioned how I'd feel or how you should feel, Gwen, only that when parents have problems of any kind, kids are impacted by it." He looked down the pathway to where he could see Chase walking up the beach. "Let me go get the boy and bring him back. You shouldn't leave the girls alone, and a little walk will help cool Chase off if he's upset."

She sighed. "Chase loves his dad, is foolish about him, and he's angry with me."

"More reason to let him take a walk right now. I'll watch after him and bring him back after a little while."

"Thanks, Waylon." She turned to start back to the cottage.

Waylon watched the boy walking down the beach for a few more minutes, and then started down the path to follow him.

He eventually caught up to him, with his strides longer than the boy's. "It's only me," he said as he drew closer, catching the boy's attention.

He saw Chase turn to glance at him, before walking on. "Did Mom send you to look for me?"

"I was checking the cabana, told her I'd come walk with you. She mentioned you were upset."

He turned eyes awash in tears to Waylon. "She's left my dad. She told us we were coming to the island for Easter, but now she says we're not going back home, that she and my dad are splitting up. We didn't even get to say goodbye." He sniffed. "She always tells me when I have a fight with my sisters, a friend, or with her or dad, that I need to forgive, work it out, be loving. Somebody needs to tell her that. It's wrong to get mad at dad and run off and leave him."

Waylon wisely just walked along with the boy.

"She said Dad and Josh's business had failed, that Dad took a lot of loans trying to save it, including one against our house. She said he didn't tell her or us anything about what was going on, that he lied about it all, saying everything was all right when it wasn't. Then he came in the day before we left, while I was in school, and told Mom he was losing everything, the business and our house."

Chase rubbed his fist across his eyes. "They're having to sell our home real fast, if they can, before it gets taken or goes into some big word I can't remember."

"Foreclosure."

"That's it. What does that mean, Waylon?"

"It's a legal process when a lender tries to recover monies he's loaned by taking ownership of any property put up to take the loan. If your dad pledged the house to get loans and then couldn't repay the loans, the lender has a right to take the house."

"That sounds mean."

"It's only business and they might have given your dad a lot of space before taking this action at all."

"Is that what happened with dad and Josh's business, too?"

"Probably. I don't know any of the details exactly. Only that your dad is facing a really hard time."

Chase kicked at a shell on the beach. "Yeah, and Mom just made us walk out on him, not even sticking by him in trouble."

"If you found I'd lied to you for a really long time, caused you to lose your house you loved and maybe other things, would you want to stick by me in trouble?"

Chase winced. "I don't know. I guess I'd be mad and hurt."

Waylon put an arm around Chase's shoulder. "That's it. Your mom's mad and hurt."

"Do you think they'll try to work it out?"

"I don't know. It's a rough one. Your mom's got good cause to be upset, to feel betrayed and mad. You need to keep in mind she's hurting, too. Relationships are built in part on trust, as well as love. This is a hard time for her."

"It's a hard time for me, Leah, and Rose, too. We're losing our home and our friends and we've got to move to a new place and a new school whether we want to or not."

"I can see why you'd be upset and mad, but here's one thing for you to know for sure. Your mom loves you and she's going to work hard to take care of you. Your dad loves you, too, and when he gets on his feet again, I'm sure he'll help to take care of you and see you whenever he can. In addition, you've got good family here that love you and will stand by you. Not everyone has that much love and caring in their lives when things go wrong."

He sniffed. "I just want everything to be like it was."

"Sometimes that can't happen, Chase." They'd come to the end of the beach and to the Townsend Inlet. "See that big inlet in front of us as wide as a river? It didn't used to be there. This island used to connect right over to the land across from it."

"No kidding?" Chase looked across the broad expanse of water.

"A big hurricane swept through here in 1959 and tore up jack along the coastline. The water that swept in and flooded much of the land caused a new inlet to form from the Townsend Creek, cutting off Watch Island from the mainland of Edisto Island."

"I didn't know that."

"You can still get across the inlet in a boat or kayak. I'll take you one day, but it will never go back to the way it was."

"You're trying to tell me my mom and dad probably won't get back because of the problems that happened with them."

"Whether they do or don't, your life will go on, full of good times. Hating your mom or your dad won't help anything get better though." He hesitated. "You being sort of the man of the family now, your mom could use your support. You might want to think about that and step up. She's always had your dad before and now she's on her own."

"I don't feel like I want to step up and help her right now." Chase frowned, turning to start back down the beach with Waylon. "Right now I'm just mad."

"Yeah, I would be, too."

They walked along in silence for a while.

"Waylon, if I need to talk sometime, can I come talk to you? My dad's gone and my grandpa is gone, too."

"You come talk with me whenever you want."

Chase nodded.

"You about ready for me to walk you back to your place?"

"Yeah, okay." He turned to Waylon. "Do you think Mom would get mad if I asked to call and talk to my dad?"

"No. I'm sure she'd understand and let you do that. I'm sure, too, as soon as your dad gets some things worked out in his life that he'll want you, Leah, and Rose to come visit him. He'll always be your dad, Chase, and he'll always love you. Just like your mom will."

"Life sucks sometimes, doesn't it?"

Waylon couldn't help laughing a little. "Yeah it does. And we all have our hard times. But the bad times never last forever. Life has a way of balancing out eventually. You'll see."

They climbed up the path from the beach and started down the road toward the Seaside Cottage where Chase was staying.

"Will you really take me in a kayak or a boat across that big inlet, Waylon?"

"Sure," he said, glad the boy was already looking ahead to something and not so upset anymore.

After dropping Chase off, Waylon backtracked, picked up his golf cart and drove back to the lodge. He fixed a cola and took it out on the screened porch to sit and look out over the ocean. A wisp of moon hung in the sky like a cradle, and Waylon wondered, looking at it, what it would be like to have a son like Chase to raise. He and Burke hadn't really talked about family yet, but the few times the subject came up, she hadn't made any comments to suggest she wouldn't like to have a child or two. Waylon wanted children.

He thought of Alex Trescott as he sat and looked out at the dark. He couldn't imagine the man wasn't missing his boy and his two beautiful little girls. He hoped Alex could make some good decisions and get his life back together. He had to be missing Gwen, too. Those Deveaux girls got into a man's blood.

CHAPTER 13

Burke felt a little sorry for herself Friday night as she settled into bed late. She'd missed having any special time with Waylon, with both their afternoons full of work problems. She sighed. Having Gwen home had brought a whole new set of difficulties, and she could tell her mother worried over it. Tired, Burke finally drifted off to sleep.

The next day after lunch, she felt pleased to see Waylon walk into the gift shop by the lighthouse.

"I hope I can follow along with your tour today," he said.

"I'm glad to have you." Burke smiled at him.

Glancing around the gift shop, Waylon winked at Lila. "You've sure made this shop a little showcase since I last visited. New paint, new shelves and arrangements, new sales items, and some of your beautiful paintings on the wall." He walked over for a closer look. "The talent you showed as a young girl has blossomed into a fine gift, Lila."

"Thank you," she replied. "I learned and grew a lot at Sewanee studying art. But mostly I believe practice improves any art skill. After I left home I developed my art more than at any time in my life, and I began to see it then as a career, as the gift God wants me to use and develop."

"I'd say you're on the right track," he replied.

"Isn't the detail in this painting incredible?" Burke asked, walking over to stand with him in front of the lush painting of flowers trailing along a winding path to the ocean. She started to say more but the door opened to let in the tour group.

Burke counted fourteen as they came in with her mother, a mix of guests staying at the inn plus the tourists Waylon had picked up earlier at the Jenkins Landing and Bohicket Marina. When she could, Etta enjoyed taking the group on a short tour around the inn and its grounds before the lighthouse tour, telling them about the Light Station's early history.

She'd done that today and as the group filed in she added, "This little gift shop was once the Lighthouse Station House. The keeper or his assistant stayed here in quarters directly by the lighthouse at night or in inclement weather." She smiled at the group. "After the tour you can come back to the gift shop to look around, but for now, let me turn you over to my daughter Burke for the tour."

After a little further chitchat and introductions, Burke led the group through the covered passageway that connected the small gift shop to the lighthouse and its wide first floor museum. "Please note, if you haven't picked up on the pronunciations yet, that Deveaux is pronounced in two syllables, *de-voh*, with a long o and the accent on the second syllable, like you'd pronounce the word Bordeaux in Bordeaux wine. The word Edisto is pronounced with three syllables, *ed-i-stow*, with the accent on the first syllable, pronounced like the man's name Ed."

"Oh, thank you," one of the women said. "I'd been trying to figure out how to say both correctly."

"Deveaux is French in origin, and the word Edisto comes from the Edistow Indians who once lived in this area long before white settlers."

"When was this lighthouse built?" one of the men asked.

"The Deveaux Lighthouse was established in 1870," she answered. "There were thoughts of building a lighthouse here earlier, at the mouth of the North Edisto River, but other lighthouses along the coast took priority and then the Civil War disrupted all plans of building more lighthouses for a time."

"How many lighthouses are in South Carolina?" the man asked.

"Eleven plus this one. However, only two others still function as lighthouses and are taken care of by the Coast Guard."

The man laughed. "The Folly Beach lighthouse is sitting out in the ocean now."

"Yes, and many other lighthouses are now surrounded by the sea after years and years of erosion. Coastlines are always changing over time. They're not stable. This island used to have a broader beach and it used to be connected to Edisto Island where the Townsend Inlet separates it now."

"I read they had to move the Hunting Island Lighthouse."

"Yes, they did," Burke replied. "Visiting that lighthouse and the Hunting Island State Park is a nice day trip you could make while staying in South Carolina. You could also explore historic Beaufort at the same time. We have brochures about both in the gift shop you can pick up before you leave."

Burke gestured around the museum room they'd gathered in. "Lighthouses come in all sizes and shapes. The Deveaux Lighthouse is wider at the base than most and rises 125 feet to the top of the light tower. Instead of having a single spiral staircase winding to its top, the Deveaux Light has levels with staircases leading to each. The levels, like the room here, once served various purposes over time but today the three lower levels in the lighthouse have been made into museum rooms."

She walked across the room to a large glass-covered display on a tabletop. "This is a replica of what the entire Deveaux Light Station looked like back in the early 1900s. The lighthouse was built on the higher rocky end of the island, set back from the ocean, to withstand storms better and to be more visible from sea. The Deveaux Lighthouse's distinctive color, its deep red and white stripes, called a Day Mark, help identify it in daylight, and by night the distinctive flashes, called a Light Signature, help sailors and pilots recognize the location at night. The Deveaux signature is five seconds on, five off, five on, followed by a twenty second rest before it repeats."

Burke had always been proud of the glassed display, artfully created with exact building replicas, landscaping, and roads—a treat to look at. She pointed out the different buildings in the display now as she talked.

"My mother Etta took you through the inn and talked to you about its history, so I know you're aware it was once the Lighthouse Keeper's home. Of course, it's much larger now than when originally built and has been added to and updated multiple times, but many of the old buildings around the Lighthouse Station remain."

One lady on the tour laughed. "I liked hearing about the Necessary House when Etta took us outside around the grounds. I'd never heard that name before for an outhouse."

"Well, as you saw, we use it for a little garden shed now," Burke replied. She pointed out other buildings around the grounds in the display—the Signal House, various storage buildings used in past for fuel or supplies, the old cistern, the boathouse and marinas, the cottages, and when and why they were built, and she told the history of the lodge, originally built as a hunting lodge.

"The Townsend family, land rich in the 1800s when the lighthouse was built, not only owned the land the lighthouse station now occupies, almost 500 acres, but the family owned several plantations—most now in the Botany Bay Heritage Preserve, covering 4,600 acres. An early planter, John Ferrars Townsend and later his son Daniel Townsend, also owned all of Seabrook that you can see across the river. The family mostly used that land as a hunting grounds."

She saw Waylon watching her as she fielded questions from the guests. Growing up at Edisto, he could probably answer many of these questions, too.

Burke walked her tour group over to a wall filled with photos and informational plaques next. "We are blessed to actually have photos of all the lighthouse keepers of the Deveaux Light. The first keeper was Wellford Jacob Deveaux who married Miranda Margaret Townsend. Wellford had been an acclaimed Naval military leader in the Civil War."

She pointed to the old sepia photo of him and his family lined up beside the lighthouse. "Marrying one of the Townsend daughters made Wellford an appropriate choice as the first keeper. He knew the sea, the area, and he was family. This land was leased to allow a lighthouse to be built here with the written understanding that the family govern the lighthouse and live here, if willing, capable, and available, and that if the lighthouse was ever removed or decommissioned, the land would revert back to the family. Which is exactly what happened in the 1930s. That's when the Deveaux-Townsend descendants gradually began to turn the old keepers' house into an inn."

"Doesn't the Coast Guard help care for the lighthouse?"

"Yes, it does. We do the daily care of keeping the Light, the inn and the island, and the Coast Guard does the larger maintenance needed for the actual lighthouse, major repairs, painting, equipment checks, and replacements. They come by several times a year, or when needed after a severe storm or problem affecting the lighthouse." She smiled. "There are actually many decommissioned lighthouses for sale right now that you could buy, but they usually come with an obligation to offer public tours, as most, like the Deveaux Light, are on the National Register of Historic Places now."

She turned back to the other photos of the keepers and their families again. "My family is the sixth generation of Deveaux-Townsends to keep the Light. The early keepers had a far more difficult life than we do, without electricity, water, and communication aids so common now. They endured adverse hurricanes and weather, national wars, the Depression, and more. The island here was only readily accessible by water, as well, which made a keeper's life limited in many ways." She paused. "Early keepers lived on the edge of the land and on the edge of the life other people knew."

"I've read some stories about their harsh lives," one woman commented.

"Their stories are memorable." Burke turned back to the photos. "These are the six keepers of the lighthouse starting with the first, Wellford Deveaux, I mentioned before, with his wife Miranda and their ten children. This next photo is of his son Aston Lee Deveaux, the second lighthouse keeper, with his wife Nelia and their eight children, followed by Hiram Elijah Deveaux, the third keeper in the early 1900s, with his wife Francis and their seven."

Burke waited a moment while the visitors studied the stern sepia and black and white photos of the old keepers and their big families, before moving on to the clearer, more congenial photos to come.

"Hiram's son Captain John Daniel Deveaux, along with his wife Sarah Rachel, and their four children, became keepers in the transitional years of the lighthouse when the Light was decommissioned in the 1930s," she continued.

"Tourism grew greatly in this era, and they began altering the keeper's house into an inn. Their son Morgan Burke Deveaux, and his wife Eugenia Talia continued their work."

Burke reached out to touch that photo with fondness. "They were my grandparents, and their son was my father Lloyd Andrew Deveaux. He and my mother Etta became the next keepers. This last photo is of my parents with their four daughters, including me, when we were much younger." She smiled at the last shot of her father in his Naval uniform, with Etta and her sisters clustered around him, the lighthouse in the background.

One of the ladies on the tour, Rachel Hartsell, looked toward a mannequin dressed in an old lighthouse keeper's uniform nearby. "Did the keepers always wear these uniforms?"

"No, keepers' uniforms were created in 1884." She smiled. "On an interesting note many keepers' wives and daughters became official Lighthouse Keepers after their husbands or fathers died. They'd always worked and helped to keep the Light and they knew the job. It was one of the first government jobs women in the United States ever held."

"Did they wear a uniform?" Rachel asked.

Burke laughed. "No, and they had to wear the multiple layers of clothing and long skirts of women of their day. It made it difficult for them—doing their job and making rescues at sea. One of our upper museum levels has photos of some of the more famous women lighthouse keepers, telling about the difficult lives they lived and the often heroic rescues they made. There's a great photo of Ida Lewis there, who kept the Lime Rock Lighthouse in Newport, Rhode Island. She saved more than eighteen lives and was awarded the Congressional Medal for bravery and heroism."

She walked them toward the original Fresnel Light that had once been at the top of the Deveaux Lighthouse. "Early keepers climbed the steps with a lamp in one hand and a pail of whale oil in the other. Their job in keeping the light lit was arduous. Later with the invention of the Fresnel light, the work of keeping the light burning at night grew somewhat easier. This is the Fresnel light that once beamed its rays over the waters from our lighthouse. Now our lighthouse, like others, is automated. We have two electric lights with high-powered, 1000-watt light bulbs that rotate and send out the light. They come on automatically at dusk and turn off at dawn."

They walked around the room then looking at old rescue boats and life jackets, wooden paddles and painted buoys, and nautical flags. There were also early photos taken around the island with plaques explaining bits of interesting history.

"We'll head upstairs now," Burke said, checking the time on her watch to keep on schedule. "As I mentioned, many lighthouses are tall and narrow, with a spiral staircase to the top. The Deveaux Lighthouse is wider with sets of stairs alternating to landings, or rooms, like this one, but naturally each level grows smaller as the lighthouse rises and narrows."

Burke herded the group toward the stairway. "We'll follow twelve steps to a small landing, cross it and then follow twelve more steps to the second museum level. It holds photos of early lighthouses and keepers and it contains artifacts of a more personal nature, like old books, keepers' logs, fog trumpets, checkerboards, and dice that keepers used to pass the time."

She started toward the stairs to lead the way upward. Waylon followed at the rear. At the next level, his attention was drawn almost immediately to the ham radio operator's station in one corner that the lighthouse once used for communications.

One of the men staying at the inn, Isaac Jacobsen, stopped at a glass-enclosed display of boats in a bottle. "The plaque here says many early lighthouse keepers used to make these. How in the world did they get the boats into the bottles?"

Burke laughed. "Early keepers and sailors had a lot of time on their hands. Many filled it by creating detailed ship replicas and they put them bit by bit into bottles, pulling them into place with wire and string. A few artisans still create boats in a bottle, but these are early originals." She pointed to a group of bottles with messages tucked inside them in a second glass display case nearby. "Many keepers' lives were very lonely and to pass the time, and to try to reach out to others, they put messages into bottles, tossing them out to sea."

She pointed to a photo. "This is Robbie Goldsmith. He was stationed for much of his career at a remote lighthouse on an island a mile from land in the English Channel. He often spent months alone, not seeing a single soul. He wrote and put many messages into bottles, tossing them out to sea afterward, and believe it or not he got answers from as far away as France and America."

"That's some story." Isaac laughed.

"What's this photo of a dog?" his wife Margie asked.

"That's a Springer Spaniel named Spot, who belonged to the keeper at the Owl's Head Lighthouse in Maine. He's famous for several rescues he was involved in, leading rescuers to save lives that might have otherwise been lost. Spot would bark when he heard ships at sea in storms or fog and he'd ring the fog bell by pulling on the rope with his teeth."

She told more of the humorous stories then that she knew the tour group always loved. In her mind she could almost hear her father telling the same stories, his booming, contagious laugh bellowing out afterward. His laugh alone made her smile to hear it. In many ways Burke felt she kept her father's memory alive, telling his stories, continuing his work.

The third lighthouse level, that Burke next led the tour group to, was a narrower room, filled predominately with art, the walls covered with old paintings of ships, schooners, and famous lighthouses. In one display were photos of all the South Carolina lighthouses, and in another display photos of early lighthouses built in the U.S., including the first, the Boston Light, established in 1716 and destroyed by the British in the Revolutionary War. Under glass in various cases around the room were collections of shells, fossils, and sea items, with a marvelous framed collection of shark's teeth on the wall.

Nodding at Waylon, she let him talk about the shark's teeth, knowing it a subject he loved.

"More than a dozen kinds of shark and ray species can be found along the coast of South Carolina," he told the group, "including white sharks, bull and tiger sharks, hammerheads and more. Occasionally sharks are sighted near shore but most are found miles out to sea. They can live twenty to thirty years in the wild and they lose thousands of teeth in a lifetime. Some sharks lose teeth every single time they eat, with new teeth moving into place right after. Those shark's teeth, that fall into the sea and fossilize, often wash up on the beach where you might find them, like people did these."

One lady shuddered. "I always worry about sharks when I get in the ocean."

"You shouldn't worry about that. Sharks have a bad reputation from movies and they generally want to avoid you as much as you want to avoid them. The odds of even seeing a shark are slim and the odds of being bitten by a shark about one in four million." Waylon paused. "It's smart though if you ever see a shark or hear a report of sharks being spotted to get out of the water. A few other smart tips to remember are to stay in groups when in the ocean, to avoid swimming around areas where people are fishing with bait, to never enter the water if you have a wound of any kind, and to get out immediately if you get cut on a shell or anything and start to bleed."

"I read sharks have a great sense of smell," said Perry Ormant.

"You're right about that. Up to two thirds of a shark's brain is dedicated to smell. They can smell blood, or prey, from about a quarter mile away." He laughed. "But most sharks don't really like human meat; they'd much rather have fish, mollusks, or sea birds on their menu."

Burke let the visitors look around a little longer and then led them up yet more stairs to the last, and fourth, level of the museum. As usual, she noticed most of the tour group huffing and puffing at this point and slowing down on the stairs.

She smiled as they gathered in the narrow, rounded room. "We've climbed seventy-two stairs to this fourth level and about sixty feet. You'll notice rest benches scattered around the room here and a door leading to what we call the Seaview Gallery, a walkway several feet wide with a railed balcony around it. You can walk out on the gallery to see some fine views across the ocean. If a few of you are game, I can walk on up with you two more levels to the High Gallery at about one hundred feet. I do warn you the stairs grow much steeper as the lighthouse narrows toward its top. Many people find this spot the perfect turning around point."

Only the young kayaking couple and two of the men wanted to venture higher.

"I'll walk up with them," Waylon offered to Burke. "You can stay here with the larger group and tell them some more stories."

She smiled at him. "I'll take you up on that offer and I'll tell them about the Deveaux Bank, that they can see clearly from here, and more about Seabrook, Kiawah, Johns Island, and the St. Christopher Camp they can see as they walk around the gallery."

About twenty minutes later, Waylon led his group back down to join them again and they all started the walk back to the floor level of the lighthouse. Burke concluded the tour with a few final words and then led them back to the gift shop, so they could look around, pick up brochures, buy postcards, gift items, hats, T-shirts, or souvenirs before they left.

Waylon walked over to stand by Burke in the doorway as she

kept an eye on the group. "I'm going to ferry the tourists back to Jenkins Landing and the Bohicket Marina in a few minutes," he said. "Etta gave me a list of some items to get for her at Freshfields at the market. She wants stamps from the post office, too, and asked me to drop off a deposit at the bank before it closes. I'm going to run up the highway afterward to meet two old school friends for a catch up visit and a pizza. John heard I was home and he and Richard want me to drive to Richard's place on the river for a little while. I won't be at dinner tonight, but if you can get away to walk Boonie I'll join you later."

She smiled at him. "You're talking about John Castle and Richard Myers aren't you, that you went to high school with?"

"Yeah, I haven't seen either for a long time."

"Well, enjoy yourself. And I should be able to get away to walk with you and Boonie tonight. Boonie pouted a little last night when we didn't take our walk."

"Pouted?"

"Oh, you know, gave me that disappointed look dogs give you when you break a routine they like and enjoy."

"Well, the weather's nice and clear tonight. It will be good to get out and take a walk." He leaned closer to her. "And to have some time alone with you."

Later that evening as dark fell Burke texted Waylon to meet her at their usual spot. After she and Boonie followed the path to the bench behind the Signal House, Waylon didn't waste any time moving in to gather her close and kiss her. Burke wrapped her arms around him as he did, glad to be close to him again, too.

Boonie, eager to move on after a few moments, pushed against them a little as they lingered.

"I guess we'd better walk," she whispered, her breathing heavy like his.

"Boonie can wait another minute," Waylon said against her neck, nuzzling her skin, kissing his way back up to her mouth, and pulling her tighter against him.

A little later they walked down the beach, smirking a little over their moments behind the Signal House.

"I feel like a teenager sneaking off to make out sometimes," Burke said. "But it's fun, isn't it?"

"Yeah," Waylon agreed. "My heart loves it, but I admit I sometimes imagine your dad might come around the corner, clear his throat and glare at us."

"Do you think he'd be happy we've gotten together?"

"I do. Clifford helped me see your dad's early warning wasn't meant to last a lifetime. For a while I actually felt like he always wanted me to keep a distance, stay like a brother to you."

"I regret that misunderstanding. It caused us both some unnecessary heartache and hurt."

"Maybe, but perhaps this is a better time for us to get together and marry. I'm finished with the Navy now and wouldn't need to ask you to leave your home and travel to places far away with me."

"Perhaps that would have been exciting. My grandmother traveled with my grandfather for a number of years while he was in the military, before they came back home to the lighthouse. I loved the stories she told of the places she'd lived, in Sicily, Guam in the South Pacific, and in Toulon, France."

"Well, I've seen those places and some more."

"You see? That must be exciting."

He leaned over to kiss her cheek. "Not as exciting as being here with you. Much of the time I was on ship when I traveled and I couldn't have been with you at all."

"Well, I suppose you can tell me stories anyway."

He picked up a piece of driftwood to throw for Boonie. "I enjoyed your stories today. Many of them I remember hearing your dad tell."

She smiled. "I always think of him as I tell them. It still hurts that he died so young. I know Mother especially misses him. They were a close couple, working together as they did, living remotely on an island versus in a busy city or suburban neighborhood."

"Would you prefer that? Living in a city or suburban area?"

"Me?" Her eyes widened. "Never. But Gwen would prefer that

life. She's already restless and antsy here, as are the children. They're used to a different kind of lifestyle now."

He told her about talking with Chase.

"That was kind of you. Despite his mistakes, Alex is a good person. I really liked him, and he and Gwen were such a comfortable match. All of this is such a sorrow. I hate to see their little family broken up, Gwen so angry, hurt, and bitter, the kids grieving, not really understanding their parents' problems. It's just sad."

Waylon changed the subject. "Easter is coming up next weekend. I thought it might be fun to have a cookout next Saturday evening at the lodge with an egg hunt for the kids. If it's okay, I'd like to invite my sister Sally Ann, her husband Don and their three boys. Sally Ann and Gwen were practically best friends all through school while growing up. I think it would do Gwen good to spend time with my sister, and Chase will love time with Sally Ann's boys. He's only had his sisters to play with since he came. At eight, you know he wants guys to spend time with, too."

"That's a great idea. I know Lila would love helping me with an egg-dying party for the kids. They need some fun and normalcy." She slowed to walk around a jellyfish on the beach. "Mother and Lila will love helping Gwen make some baskets for Easter morning, too." She sighed. "I wish Celeste could come."

"Have you still not heard from her?"

"No. Mother is getting troubled about it, too."

He looked out to sea thinking about this problem. "I could drive to Nashville to look for her."

"Actually, Gwen suggested that if we don't hear from her this week, that the two of us drive to Nashville on Monday after Easter to look for her."

"Perhaps that's a better idea. Celeste doesn't know me like she knows both of you. If she's having personal problems, it's family she'll want."

Shifting the subject again, they talked about ongoing issues around the island, updates on the woman who was killed and the other still missing. Waylon told her about the dog they'd found.

"That's really queer," Burke said. "Why would she take a dog to the Deveaux Bank? She was a local and would know it's illegal. That doesn't make sense."

"None of this makes sense, "Waylon added. "Crime often doesn't, and neither do the motives of the people who commit them."

"Well, I hope they find who killed that woman and find the woman that's missing. Everyone will feel better when that situation is resolved."

"Did you talk to the guests about this?" Waylon asked.

"Mother and I did, encouraging care and watchfulness."

They walked along quietly for a time. "If you go to church tomorrow, I'd like to go with you," he said. "I talked to the rector, Wey Camp, at Trinity when I went to the cemetery that day. I really liked him, and I'd like to go to church where you do." Waylon slowed to look at her. "It's important that we have faith in the center of our lives and marriage. Lila actually reminded me of the importance of that the other day when I ran into her sketching down at the beach."

I agree," she said, touched by his words. "We always try to make Sunday breakfast and lunch easy meals at the inn so we can go to church on Sunday morning. Henry and Rita Jean Bouls are Catholic. They go to mass with Maggie, Calvin, their boys, and others in their family on Saturday evening at the big Catholic church on John's Island. So they cover for us, and for Novaleigh and Clifford, on Sundays at the inn. Novaleigh and Clifford go to church and dinner with their family on Edisto and they take Sundays off. Then the Georges cover for the Bouls another day so they can take a day away from the island."

"That sounds sensible."

She put an arm around his waist. "I'd love for you to go with us to church and I'd like us to be married at Trinity, if you don't mind. Not something large but maybe only a small service, possibly outside using the pretty gazebo in the garden."

He grinned at her. "We'd need to do that in nice weather, long before winter comes."

Burke felt herself flush as she said, "I was thinking in terms of September when the tourist traffic begins to diminish."

He winked at her. "I like that idea."

"We still have a lot of things to talk about."

"And a lot of time to do it," he added grinning. "Remember we have a developing friendship going here."

She laughed. "You'll never let me forget that one."

"No, and our relationship will always be growing, developing, and getting richer and stronger over time. You can count on it."

They parted a little later at the path to the Signal House, kissing goodnight, Waylon whispering sweet nothings into Burke's ear, making her giggle.

Walking back to the inn, Burke couldn't help smiling the whole way, thinking how good her life had become in so many ways. "Thanks, God," she decided to say out loud, remembering their earlier conversation. "I'm so grateful to You for so much and I hope You'll help Waylon and me grow more in our faith. Lila's right that we need You at the center of our lives, and we want to start out right in that way."

Glancing up at the sky, she saw a small cloud pass over the moon and then watched the moon pop out bright and clear again. Like my life, she thought, despite an occasional storm or cloud, it just gets brighter and brighter every day.

CHAPTER 14

Waylon looked around with pleasure to see Chase, Rose, and Leah, along with his nephews, Todd, Bobby, and Sam, running around the yard with plastic baskets looking for Easter eggs, with Boonie racing along behind them. As he'd expected, Chase was thrilled to share time with boys near his own age and all the children were enjoying playing and exploring around the lodge and grounds.

Although the Deveaux Lodge had an old outdoor fireplace, Henry had helped Waylon earlier to find two Weber kettle grills to cook the hamburgers and hotdogs on he'd decided to serve. While Waylon manned one grill turning thick burgers and putting them on a side platter when done, Don Nagel, Sally Ann's husband, handled the other grill, covered with sizzling hotdogs. The Deveaux women and Sally Ann had divvied up bringing the other menu options for their cookout—potato salad, baked beans, chips, colas, and assorted cupcakes and cookies for dessert.

"This was a great idea," Don said, smiling at him. "I've been wanting to see where you're living and working now and Sally Ann is over the moon to spend time with Gwen again. She says they've been best friends since childhood."

"Yeah. They hit it off right from the first." Waylon remembered. "Living somewhat isolated from most of Edisto at the landing, Sally Ann didn't have close girlfriends to play with, so she loved getting together with the Deveaux girls. I brought her down here often to play with them, and she and Gwen especially bonded, being the same age. At school, growing up, they were usually in the same class together, too."

Don pulled some hot dogs off the grill. "Sally Ann wanted our boys to go to the old Country Day School in Meggett where you, Sally Ann, Edward Calhoun, and the Deveaux girls went to school, but it closed."

"We were all sorry when that happened. Sally Ann says she likes the private school your boys go to on Johns Island, not far from the Bohicket Marina, though."

"Yeah, my mom is an administrator at the school and my parents live just north of the marina. Their home is a nice old place, right on Bohicket Creek. It's been in my family a long time."

"Isn't your dad a doctor?"

"My dad's a pediatrician with a practice nearby."

"Sally Ann told me you usually take the kids over to their place on school mornings to ride into school with your mom. Or she takes them."

"It's only about seven minutes by water from Jenkins Landing. It isn't far. If mom has scheduling problems I run the boys to school from there in an extra car we keep at my folks' house." He turned the hot dogs on the grill as he talked. "It's worked out well."

Waylon studied Don while he talked, a tall, lanky brown-haired man, smart, kind, and good to Sally Ann and the boys. The veterinarian clinic he'd opened on Edisto had been greatly needed and everyone took their pets there now. Dr. Nagel was beloved around the area, with a true, good heart for animals.

Don glanced toward Gwen's children. "Is Gwen going to put her children in school soon since she's not going back to Arkansas?"

"Burke told me, since Gwen's an elementary teacher, that she's home schooling the kids until she gets a job and resettles. She doesn't want to stay at the island though. She wants to live closer to a town."

"I'll ask my mom if they have any openings coming at her school or if she knows of anything. She might be able to help Gwen get her license updated and to network around the Lowcountry area.

She knows a lot of people in the school systems."

"That would be a help to Gwen. Be sure to tell Gwen that and give her your mom's contact information."

"I will." Don pulled the last hot dog off the grill. "It looks like we're ready to add these hot dogs and burgers to the buffet set up and to enjoy a good dinner."

Everyone soon loaded a plate with food and settled around the yard at the various tables set up. Waylon noted the kids all took their plates to an old picnic table under a big shade tree, glad to avoid adults for a time.

He settled into a chair by Burke at one of the tables on the patio. "Everything looks good," he said, eyeing his loaded plate.

"It does. Thanks for hosting." She smiled at him. "You were right that Chase, Leah, and Rose would really love an evening like this. I've enjoyed watching them run, play, and laugh."

Waylon slathered mayonnaise on his hamburger bun. "It looked like you and Lila were having a lot of fun hiding Easter eggs for the kids, too."

"We did have fun," Lila agreed, sitting down with them and putting her plate and drink on the table. "I've been doing entirely too much adulting these last years, acting so mature and responsible." She grinned. "It was starting to make me feel old."

Waylon wrinkled his nose at her. "I can't imagine you ever being old, Lila. You're one of those people I think will always be young at heart."

"From your lips to God's ears." She giggled. "I hope that stays true."

He glanced across to where Etta sat at another table. "Who's that man with your mother?"

"Oh, I should have introduced you," Burke said. "That's dad's friend Dean Anderson. He showed up at the inn this afternoon, planning to join mom for dinner to catch up. So she invited him down to our gathering."

"He's a lovely man," Lila said. "As an Episcopal minister, he's been a help to me in this transition time I'm walking through."

Waylon searched his memory. "Isn't he the man who lives at your family's condo at the Bohicket Marina, the one who works at the camp?"

"Yes. He's the Chaplain there," Lila answered. "He was formerly rector at a church near Summerville. When his wife died about ten years ago, he wanted a change and moved here. Dad met him when he rented our villa and they hit it off right away."

Burke glanced across to where Dean and Etta visited with Gwen, Sally Ann, and Don. "You remember I told you Dean, Dad, and Wiley Barnwell fished together all the time and that Dean often came over to the Inn to eat dinner with Dad and Mom. It's been good of him to continue his friendship with Mom, now that Dad is gone."

Seeing Dean's attentiveness to Etta, Waylon wondered if there was more to it, but he wisely said nothing. Dean may have been widowed for ten years but Etta had only lost Lloyd this fall.

"It's been great for Gwen to get together with Sally Ann again," Burke said after eating part of her hamburger. "I've already heard them planning weekend trips where they can take the kids and have some fun."

Waylon told Burke then about Don's offer to ask his mother to possibly help Gwen in her job hunting.

"Oh, that's a wonderful idea," Burke said. "I'd forgotten Don's mother was a school administrator. I imagine she knows a lot of people who might be a help to Gwen."

"I'd love to go over to Don's parents' place to paint," Lila added. "They have this gracious two-storied plantation home on the river, with a long green lawn sweeping down to Bohicket Creek, mature trees everywhere with moss draping off the oaks, and lovely flower gardens."

"When did you go to Don's parents' home?" Burke asked.

"I went with Gwen and Sally Ann one day years ago, back when she and Don first started dating." Lila paused. "Sally Ann married into a nice family. Don has a sister, too, but she lives out west somewhere. I forget where. I think her name is Angela. His mom and dad are Robert and Elizabeth Nagel. Robert is a pediatrician. The family has money and I'm sure that helped Don to attend veterinary school and open a solo practice on Edisto."

Burke's mouth dropped open. "For someone who's been living off in a religious community you sure do remember a lot."

Lila smiled. "I notice things. Artists do."

"Have you noticed if Gwen is feeling less angry yet?"

Lila sighed. "She's holding tight to her anger and bitterness toward Alex. He's tried several times to communicate with her but she'll barely talk to him, if at all. Since they are still married, there are a lot of decisions to be made about the house, its furnishings if it sells, joint accounts and assets. Gwen usually snaps at Alex, telling him that since he handled everything behind her back before that he can figure out how to handle everything now."

"Ouch." Waylon frowned. "That sounds petty. Surely Gwen realizes that Alex is trying to work with her and make peace, knowing the mistakes he made before."

"Well, Gwen isn't giving him even an inch to work with," Burke added. "I've heard her say similar things."

"Is she letting Alex talk to the kids?"

"She is doing that, at least," Burke answered. "She lets Chase and the girls talk to Alex every Sunday evening. They're doing Skype together on my laptop in my office at the inn. I help them get set up to do it." She sighed. "Gwen says she doesn't even want to look at Alex, so she won't even come to the inn with them when they Skype. I usually hang around nearby though. Alex is being really sweet with them. He told them how sorry he is that he made mistakes and caused problems in their family. He listens to all their stories, answers their questions, laughs with them. And he never says a negative or bitter word about Gwen."

"Unforgiveness is an ugly spirit," Lila put in. "I've tried to talk to Gwen about that but she gets mad at me for even bringing it up."

"Hurts go deep and take time to heal," Burke said softly, looking toward where Gwen sat. "Can you imagine how we'd feel if someone came and told us their actions caused us to lose the inn and lighthouse?"

Lila smiled at her. "It's a place, Burke. Although we love it dearly and hold deep roots here, it's only a place. We would still have each other and the love of the Lord."

Waylon saw Burke roll her eyes and tried not to grin. "I think I'll go get seconds," he said, getting up to take his plate to the buffet table.

Later he hid eggs again for the kids and walked around with Leah and Rose, giving them hints to help them in their search. From a distance he could hardly tell the girls apart, but up close their eyes gave them away—Leah's a warm brown like Chase's and Rose's blue-gray like her mother's. They were pretty little girls, warm and affectionate, hugging easily, sweet and eager to please. In temperament, he didn't see much of Gwen's impulsiveness or outspoken nature in the girls. But he saw some of her quick temper and stubbornness in Chase. He could see, too, that Chase still felt angry with his mother for leaving his father.

As darkness began to fall, the children played hide-n-seek and night tag around the lodge, while the adults sat on the lodge's screened porch talking companionably, away from the inevitable mosquitoes that came out in the evening. Dean had walked Etta to the inn and then planned to head back across the river to his own place.

Don gave Gwen the information about his mother as they talked, and Sally Ann promised to take Gwen to the school to meet her on one of her days off.

"We can go shopping at Freshfields while we're at Johns Island and maybe have lunch," Sally Ann suggested.

Gwen frowned. "Well, even though your boys are in school, I'm homeschooling my children right now. I don't want to take too much advantage of Mom, Burke, or Lila's time to look after them."

Lila smiled. "I'd be happy to stay with them, Gwen, and if you'll show me what lessons they're working on I'll help them with their studies." She hesitated. "Mother and Burke carry so many more responsibilities than I do. Please ask me anytime if I can help you.

I know it's important that you find a job for the coming year so you can begin to feel settled about your life."

"Thanks, Lila." Gwen reached a hand across to squeeze her sister's hand. "That is kind of you."

After Sally Ann and Don gathered up their children and dishes to head home, Waylon, Burke, Gwen, and Lila lingered on the porch talking, while Gwen's children went inside to watch a favorite television show in the lodge's living room.

Burke glanced up the road toward the inn. "You know the real reason Mother went back early was to finish making the Easter baskets for the children. She's planning to put them on our table on the porch in the morning at breakfast so she gets to watch the kids find them. She even hinted to them that the Easter Bunny always puts his baskets on the porch."

"That's sweet," Lila said. "Mom's been so excited about making Easter baskets again. Sillier even than me. I went with her into Charleston one day this week to shop and we had so much fun buying little candies, toys, cute stuffed Easter bunnies for the girls, and a kite for Chase to fly on the beach."

Gwen closed her eyes, leaning her head back. "All of you are being so nice to me, and I know I've been a shrew."

"You're going through a difficult time," Waylon said. "We all know that."

"It's worrisome and stressful to have your life turned upside down." Gwen reached to get her glass of cola. "I'm still worried about Celeste, too. I tried to call her again today. I even tried contacting her agent, Gary Feinstein. He wasn't in his office, but I left him a message with my number and told him we were really concerned about Celeste, that we hadn't heard from her in a long time. I hated to go behind Celeste's back like that, but we need to find out if she's okay."

"Do you still want to go to Nashville on Monday to look for her if we haven't heard anything back?" Burke asked. "I talked to Mother about it and she seemed relieved we might go."

Waylon leaned forward. "I'll help Etta watch after things here while you're gone and I'm sure Lila will stay with the children."

"I'd be happy to," Lila put in. "I feel something is seriously wrong in Celeste's life or that something bad has happened. I hope you'll find her."

"Well, we can try," Burke added. "We have the address for her new home, her old condo, and her agent's office downtown. Surely someone will know where she is."

Gwen pulled out her phone to tap in some information. "It's a nine hour trip to Nashville, Burke. We'll need to leave early to get there before dark. I'll drive my SUV but I don't fancy trying to find my way in rush hour traffic in Nashville. It we could get there before four that would be great."

"Just tell me what time you want to head out and I'll be ready," Burke said.

"I can spend the night at your place, Gwen, so the children won't be alone when they wake up," Lila added.

"Thanks." Gwen glanced down at her phone. "I already know how to get to Celeste's old condo. I drove there from Arkansas to visit Celeste and Nolan once. And she took me downtown to her agent's office. I can find it again, if I need to. I've never been to Dillon's new house where she moved after they got married last year though."

"Did you like Dillon?" Burke asked.

"I only met him when we all went to the wedding," Gwen replied. "But we all knew and loved Nolan." She turned to Waylon. "Nolan Zeller was Celeste's first husband. They married when Celeste was barely eighteen and Nolan thirty-five. He was not only Celeste's first husband but her manager. He made her career, believed in her talent from the minute he heard her singing in a club in Charleston. It broke her heart when Nolan died two years ago."

"Perhaps she married Dillon Barlow too soon afterward," Burke added. "They were both entertainers and had performed and sung together, but Celeste didn't really know much about Dillon's life outside the industry, didn't know his family like she'd known Nolan's."

"Maybe that's where the problem is," Lila said. "Celeste always loved to share her happy times and successes but she was always secretive when something went wrong."

"That's true. I remember that, too." Gwen agreed. "But it's wrong for her to shut her family out, no matter what."

"Perhaps she'll call before Monday, realizing it's Easter and knowing she usually comes home to see everyone," Waylon said.

"We can only hope so," Burke added.

CHAPTER 15

Easter Sunday proved a blessed and busy day, but Celeste still hadn't phoned by the evening, nor had Gwen received a call from Celeste's agent. So as the day waned, Burke and Gwen packed clothes and other items for a trip to Nashville. They'd pinpointed a couple of Nashville motels where they could spend a night, or even two, if needed. Both were purposed to locate their sister. It had simply been too long since any of them had heard from her.

At Gwen's request, Burke set her alarm to get up before dawn so they could leave at five and get to Nashville by the afternoon. Waylon insisted on getting up early, too, to take Burke and Gwen to Jenkins Landing to see them off and to help load Gwen's car.

"It was sweet of you to get up and see us off," Burke said as they made their way up the river in the dark to the boat dock.

"No problem," he said, winking at her.

After easing his skiff into a spot by the dock, Waylon tied off the boat and helped to carry their bags to Gwen's car, parked in the Jenkins lot. He paused before leaving to reach out a hand to touch Burke's face gently and then he leaned in to kiss her goodbye, kissing Gwen on the cheek, too.

"You girls drive safe and call or text to let us know when you get to Nashville." He paused. "You know your mother will worry if you don't."

"So will you," Burke said, kissing him again, ignoring Gwen's giggles as she did so.

Heading the car out of the parking pavilion, they were soon on their way, both too tired to talk much as they drove through the darkness from the island toward the interstate that would take them to Nashville.

As the sky began to lighten, driving into Columbia, Gwen said, "I could use a potty stop and another cup of coffee. Look and see if there's a Starbucks up ahead."

Burke got out her phone to search. "There's one off Piney Grove Road as we move out of Columbia. Will that work? We'll be out of the worst of Columbia's traffic by then. There's a gas station down the street, too."

"Great. Watch for that exit for us."

Burke put her phone away. "We could just grab a cup of coffee at the Waffle House next door or at the gas station."

Gwen gave her a pointed look. "No, we couldn't. I haven't had a Starbucks Coffee since I left downtown Little Rock, and I could use a treat about now. We still have a long trip ahead."

They found the Starbucks off the freeway, Burke trailing Gwen into the store.

Gwen smiled at the clerk. "I'll have a Cinnamon Dolce Latte with an Almond Croissant." She turned to Burke.

Burke studied the board of options, wondering what to order.

Gwen giggled. "I'll bet you hardly ever go to Starbucks."

"It's not exactly an option near where I live," Burke replied.

"You like plain coffee with a little milk. Order a Caffe Misto. It's coffee with a little steamed milk. You'll like it." Gwen glanced back at the menu board. "And get a Vanilla Bean Scone. You'll love it, and if you don't, I'll eat it later on the road."

Burke nodded to the clerk to accept Gwen's suggestion.

They sat at a table a few minutes later to drink their coffee and eat their breakfast snack before moving on.

In Knoxville, about four hours later, they stopped briefly at a Chick-fil-A off I-40 and took another quick break before heading on to middle Tennessee.

Two hours later they began to see Nashville signs.

"I'm going to cut around the 840 Bypass and take Interstate 65 to Brentwood, and the address I have for Dillon's house, to see if Gwen is there first. I Googled it last night and think I can find it, but I'm going to put the address in my GPS, too. We don't need to lose any time getting lost in a city we don't know."

She turned on the GPS and entered the address. "If Celeste's not at her house and if we can't find anyone who knows where she is, we'll head north into Nashville to her agent's office I guess."

Burke, living such a quiet life at the island, marveled at all the traffic and businesses along the road as they headed into Brentwood later. Gwen, following the GPS directions, soon drove down an assortment of side streets off the main highway to eventually wind her way into a broad road lined with homes that looked like estates to Burke, with long green lawns and huge sprawling houses.

Slowing, Gwen turned up a driveway leading to, in Burke's mind, a castle-like chateau on a shaded hillside. It looked like it belonged in France somewhere.

"Good grief. Who would need so much room?" Burke gaped. "This place is humongous."

Gwen brought the car to a stop near the front door. "You forget that Dillon Barlow and our sister are award-winning, famous country music singers. They both make millions, Burke."

She shrugged. "Well even so, there are only two of them. No two people alone need a house this size. Celeste and Nolan just lived in that big condo downtown in Belle Meade."

"In a gated development. It was posh, too."

"Well, it was nothing like this."

They climbed out of the car and walked to the door to ring the doorbell. After a time, a small Hispanic woman in a gray uniform answered it.

"May I help you?" she asked.

"We are looking for Celeste…" Gwen began.

"She is not here," the woman interrupted abruptly, starting to push the door shut.

Gwen aggressively stuck her foot in the door and held it open. "Listen. We are Celeste's sisters and we've driven a long way from

South Carolina today. We haven't heard from our sister for some time and we're worried about her. I know it's your job to be discreet about your employers' whereabouts but please help us if you can."

The small woman studied them and then sighed. "She has moved out, and wisely, I might say. Mr. Barlow is not a nice man sometimes."

"Do you know where she moved?" Burke asked.

"No. The last time I saw her was when the ambulance came to take her."

"What happened to her?" Burke gasped.

Now the woman put her hand to the door again. "This is enough for me to say. I need this job; I have four children. All I can tell you is that you will not find her here and I do not think her husband is someone you want to reach out to for help." She paused. "Now please go. I do not need trouble."

Gwen let her shut the door then before turning to Burke with wide eyes. "Mercy. Let's go downtown right now. We have to find Celeste's agent or someone at his office to help us, and we need to find Celeste, wherever she is."

Getting back in the car, Gwen dug out her phone and called Celeste's agent again. "Listen, Gary Feinstein, this is Gwen again, Celeste's sister. I don't know where you are, but you need to call me back right now. I am in Nashville with Burke. We've come looking for Celeste, and the housekeeper at Dillon's home in Brentwood just told us Celeste doesn't live there anymore. She also let it slip Celeste had been taken to the hospital. If you don't want a scene in your downtown office in Nashville you'd better call me soon, because we're on our way there right now."

On the way into Nashville, Gwen's phone rang.

"Put it on speaker," Gwen said, handing it to Burke.

Gary Feinstein's voice soon came on. "Is this Gwen?"

"Yes and Burke, too. I'm on the road and I put the phone on speaker. Where is Celeste?"

They heard a deep sigh. "She's at her old condo. I called her when I heard from you the other day and she told me she'd get back with you."

"Well, she didn't."

"Listen. Celeste has been through a hard time. Dillon roughed her up when drunk about a week ago. It wasn't the first time but it was the worst time. I finally got her to leave him and to get a restraining order against him. I'll need to call the gate at her condo community to give them your names to let you in. I posted a paid guard there. Dillon's angry and I didn't want to take any chances he could get to her again."

"Oh, my heavens," Gwen said. "Why hasn't she called us?"

Gary sighed again. "I don't know. Women in her kind of situation get ashamed and embarrassed. Celeste is not in a good way emotionally right now as well as physically. Be kind."

Burke leaned toward the phone. "You should have called us. Celeste is our family and we love her. She shouldn't have needed to go through this alone."

"It's what she wanted. I'm her agent, not her keeper. And she trusts me. I try to help her live her life as she wants."

Burke watched Gwen wrinkle her nose distastefully. "Well, this time I think you made a mistake." She snipped out the words. "But thank you for making the calls so we can get into Celeste's condo development. Will we have a problem getting into her door?"

He hesitated. "She might not want to open the door. She's stayed in close since I brought her to the condo from the hospital. She didn't want to come home with me, although I offered. The condo was still furnished, except for some things she took to Dillon's when she moved there last spring."

"Has anyone gotten those things?"

"I did, with a court order."

"Do you need to come to let us in her place? I hate to make a scene but I will if necessary."

He sighed again. "I'll have Mike, the guard we hired, take you up. He has a key in case of emergencies. Where are you now?"

"Heading up 65 and getting ready to turn off the interstate to head over to Belle Meade."

"Then I'd better get off and make my calls."

Before hanging up, Gwen added, "Thanks, and if I ever call about my sister again, you call me back, you hear?"

He replied in the affirmative and hung up.

Burke and Gwen both sat stunned with the news about Celeste for a few minutes as they drove up the freeway.

"I'd like to wring her neck for not calling us," Gwen said, watching the exit signs to move into the upcoming turn lane. "When you have problems, you reach out to your family. Especially if you have close loving family."

Burke shook her head. "I don't understand why she didn't want us to know."

"Pride, I guess, and maybe shame like Gary said."

"Well, don't fuss at her," Burke said as they worked their way toward Woodmont Boulevard to the condo where Celeste lived.

Gwen raised an eyebrow. "I won't promise that. We'll see how things go."

Burke's eyes widened again as they pulled up to the black gate at Celeste's big condo development a short time later. Behind the tall iron fencing and lush landscaping, two tall condominium buildings rose to either side of a tasteful entrance, each with balconies and a sense of elegance oozing from the entire complex.

"I always feel impressed driving up to this place," Burke commented. "And yet the street leading to the development is lovely and gracious, not as ostentatious as this posh place."

"This is simply how most monied people live," Gwen commented as she showed her ID to get clearance to enter.

They drove around a circular drive before stopping again at another gate that would lead them behind the building's north side to Celeste's condo. Gwen guest-parked as she'd been directed, and they were soon met at the side door by Mike, the uniformed guard.

"I'll take you up to Celeste's apartment," he said, starting toward the elevator. "Gary said he'd call her to open her door for you, but if she doesn't answer, I have a key."

He turned to glance at them as they started down the second

floor hallway to Celeste's condo. "I'm glad you've come. She's been in a bad way."

At Celeste's door, Mike knocked.

"It's open," a voice called.

Mike nodded, and turned to walk away as Gwen and Burke let themselves inside.

"Where are you?" Gwen called.

"Back in the den behind the kitchen," Celeste's voice came again. "Turn left at the rotunda and walk straight back."

Burke glanced around wide-eyed, forgetting as usual the elegance of Celeste's place, so different than the homey, comfortable rooms in the Deveaux Inn. Everything here looked like a photo shoot from a decorator magazine.

They paused as they passed through the kitchen, looking across the spacious den-like room to where Celeste sat in the corner on a long sectional sofa, wrapped in a blanket.

"You look like the very devil," Gwen said with candor, starting across the room.

"I've met the devil and gotten more acquainted than I'd like," Celeste replied, trying to smile.

Gwen went to hug her as did Burke right after. Then they sat down on the sofa beside her.

"God bless your heart. You've been through some sorrows," Burke said, studying her sister, one arm casted and bruises turning yellow and brown around her eyes and on her chin. Her face, free of the usual, artful makeup she wore, looked sallow, with bags under her eyes. Her glorious blond hair wasn't beautifully styled today or her outfit a fashion statement.

"Do I look that bad?" Celeste said, watching Burke's examination.

"Yes, you look awful." Burke leaned over to hug her again. "I'm so sorry, Celeste. Why didn't you call us? Why didn't you reach out to us?"

Gwen laughed. "Burke told me not to say that before we got here."

Celeste looked away from them. "I started to call so many times but then I couldn't think what I'd say. I'd sit in Dillon's house, afraid, often curled up on the floor, hurt or bleeding after he vented out his anger jerking me around, hollering hateful things to me, or hitting on me. It was always so shocking. And he seemed like such a nice, personable, normal person other times. Talented and charismatic. Loved by his fans. Who would even believe me about how he could act?"

Celeste closed her eyes and leaned her head back against the sofa. "After Dillon roared out of the house mad and drunk in the bad times, blaming me for one thing or the other, usually saying it was my fault he'd even gotten mad, I'd sit there and try to think what to do. It's stupid that I didn't pack up and leave even after the first time he backhanded me. No one had ever hit me like that. I was so surprised and cried so long after. Of course, he came home later, actually the next morning, bringing flowers, so repentant, saying he was sorry. That became his pattern. I soon felt like I lived in some ongoing nightmare I didn't know how to get out of."

Burke felt like crying just listening and she noticed Gwen had moved closer to Celeste, putting her hand over hers.

"You know all those childhood stories we read about how clever and subtle the devil can be?" Celeste asked. "I never knew how true they were until I married Dillon. He was like two people, one a talented, likable man I worked with, performed with, who chauffeured me around to parties and shows or to recordings, always popular and sociable, the life of the party. But at home I began to see the other side of him."

She sighed again. "I lived every day on edge, scared, and that annoyed Dillon. He'd insist I hadn't forgiven him or I wouldn't act as I did. He often got testy with me about that, and he claimed I still loved Nolan and not him. I began to freeze up when he got close to me or wanted to make love to me. Sometimes that triggered one of his anger fits, that I wasn't responsive anymore."

"Why didn't you talk to anyone?" Gwen asked. "It's not like you to let anyone keep hurting you like that."

"Somehow, Dillon had gradually pulled me away from most of

my friends and even my family. He became possessive, controlling. I'd always been spoiled with Nolan taking care of all aspects of my life, but Dillon took over my life in a different way." She shook her head. "I know I married him for the wrong reasons and too soon after Nolan died. But I felt so alone. Nolan had always taken care of me, taken care of everything, since I was only a girl. I felt so lost, and I'd been recording and working on a lot of songs with Dillon for an album we were doing when Nolan died. I sort of drifted into a relationship with him to ease the loneliness."

She hugged a pillow to herself. "Now I've got to find my way out of all this, legally, physically, and emotionally. Dillon really messed with my head. I seemed to lose my sense of self along the way, began to go through the motions in my work and performances. I started dreading going home when not traveling, fearing time alone with Dillon. He seemed to sense that and to enjoy it, and that was sick, too."

"Didn't anyone notice after he worked you over?" Gwen asked. "My heavens, look at you—bruises all over your face, your arm broken and casted."

"He was careful most of the time to hit on me and hurt me where it didn't show. Like even now I have a broken rib, too. You can't see it but it hurts." She sighed. "Dillon also seemed to pick times to go after me when he knew I had a big space between performances. He also often attacked me when he knew I'd made plans to visit with friends or family."

She sent Gwen a sad smile. "I told Dillon last week I wanted to fly home to the island for Easter, knowing you and the kids would be there, that Lila was home, that Burke and Mother would be there, all the people I love most. It set Dillon off, that I wanted to leave him, not spend Easter with him. He stormed out of the house when I made a quiet little stand that I planned to go, needed time with my family."

She hesitated. "I guess it shouldn't have surprised me he came home doped and liquored up later and went after me. Except this time it was worse than usual. The little housekeeper we use was still there, a Hispanic woman named Martina. When Dillon stormed out after, she came in and found me in the floor, passed out. She called an ambulance and she called my agent, Gary. I learned he'd given her his number and said if anything bad happened again to call him."

Burke shifted in her seat. "Gwen and I met Martina at the house where we first went looking for you. She was afraid to tell us much but she did say you'd been in the hospital and that the last time she saw you was when the ambulance took you away."

"Maybe later I can help Martina but I'd need to be careful in doing so. I wouldn't want Dillon to target her." Celeste blew out a long breath. "He's really angry right now, carrying ugly tales around town, trying to diminish any damage to his reputation, but not concerned about damaging mine. Some pictures got out, too. I guess someone in the hospital got bribed. I don't know. Close facial shots, bloody and bruised ones. Gary says the media started to dig into Dillon's past then and found previous times when he was named in domestic violence reports. He was never prosecuted but the old reports were there, and some of the women have begun talking again now."

"That can only help you legally that he has that past."

"Yes, but it makes him angrier, that because of me it got stirred up, brought out. He sees that as my fault, not his."

"Then he is definitely sick," Burke said.

"I actually worried about any of you coming here, afraid he might hurt one of you." She smiled at Gwen. "I knew you'd go after him with your claws out if you heard even a little of what he'd been doing to me. He's dangerous, Gwen, so don't."

"I can well see that," she said. "But you're not staying around here for him to come looking for you again. Burke and I are taking you home with us to the island. He won't come there. You need time to heal and you can't perform beaten up like you are with your arm in a cast, all bruised up, and with a broken rib." Gwen paused. "How else did he hurt you?"

Celeste put a hand near her heart. "I have a lot of bruises in a lot of places. I had a little concussion, too, but that's okay now. I also banged up one of my knees bad when he knocked me down. It's made me limp around but it will be all right."

Gwen sat up straighter. "Burke, why don't you take my keys and go down to the car to get our bags. We'll stay here tonight but then we need to head back to the island in the morning. Celeste, you can tell us tonight what to pack for you, and don't even think about arguing. You need your family right now and you need a place away from here and all the hurtful memories. You need to get back to you, to get strong again, to be yourself again."

Burke saw tears trickle down Celeste's face.

"Mother has enough to deal with right now," Celeste said, "still getting over Daddy's death. I hate to add more trouble to her plate."

"As a mother myself I can tell you that logic doesn't compute," Gwen replied. "Mother has been worried not hearing from you, and when she knows what you've been through, what her heart will want most is for you to come home so she can love you, take care of you, and support you."

Celeste began to cry in earnest now.

"I really want to go home," she whispered. "I wanted to go home last week. I've been so afraid for such a long time."

"Well, that's not like you at all," Gwen said, standing up. "But you'll get better. Mother and Novaleigh will fuss over you, even Rita Jean in her brusque way. You know Lila will pray for you, give you her sweet love and wisdom. I've had my share already."

Celeste glanced up at her. "What for?"

"That's a story for another day. Right now I want to know if you have food here so I can cook something for us for dinner."

"Gary has kept people sending things in. I'm sure you'll find stuff in the refrigerator, freezer, and cabinets. Check around to see if anything looks good. If not, I can order something. There are restaurants everywhere in this part of Nashville. A lot of them deliver. Others have take-out."

Gwen grinned at her words. "The idea of gourmet, city food sounds lovely. I love our little island and Novaleigh's good cooking but the city life has gotten into my blood, too."

Celeste actually smiled a little then. "I remember we used to save our allowance money for weeks as girls so we could go to eat at one of the gourmet restaurants in Charleston or Beaufort."

"We'll go again soon," Gwen assured her, grinning back. "But this time I'll let my rich sister treat."

"I do admit money is nice. I always wanted a lot of it," Celeste acknowledged. "But it isn't worth anything if you're not safe and happy and loved."

Gwen headed toward the kitchen. "Well expect to be safe, happy, loved, and unduly pampered for some time to come. All the Lighthouse Sisters will be home together again for a while. Sally Ann lives nearby, too, and Waylon is back." She paused. "You do know he and Burke are engaged, don't you?"

Her eyes flew open. "Is that true?"

"Haven't you been opening and reading your mail?" Burke asked.

"I was traveling and had a bunch of shows up north and then I came home before Easter week and got into it with Dillon. I don't think I've even been to my post office box to get my mail." She paused. "I started having everyone send mail to my P.O. box so Dillon wouldn't get into it."

As Gwen got her car keys out to pass them to Burke, she said, "One good thing you have going for you, Celeste, is that you didn't legally change your name when you married Dillon."

"No. Long ago Nolan carefully took care of me in that way and taught me the importance of keeping my stage name intact even when I married him and of protecting my finances. I have so much to thank Nolan for. He left me well taken care of when he died, between my assets and his that I inherited. Dillon can't touch any of my money. I am blessed in that."

Celeste looked around. "I really think God was looking out for me, too, with our old condo not selling. It gave me somewhere to go. Actually I refused several offers this fall, with the idea in the back of my mind already that maybe I could find a way to get away from Dillon and come here. Dillon owned a house, totally furnished, when we married, so I left most everything of mine here. The realtor advertised the condo as furnished. A lot of people like to buy a second home already furnished in Nashville near the city and the entertainment industry."

Burke went down to Gwen's car then to get their bags, putting them on a little cart afterward to trundle them into the elevator. The cart would come in handy tomorrow, too, when they got ready to pack and leave. She'd remember to come get it.

In the hallway, she pulled out her phone to call Waylon. She filled him in briefly on the situation and that they'd be heading back tomorrow with Celeste. "We might arrive late," she said.

"Just call me when you get to the landing and I'll come get you," he replied. "Tonight you and Gwen get some rest. You'll have another long travel day tomorrow."

When Burke got back, she saw that Celeste had curled up on the couch for a nap while Gwen worked making them dinner.

"I found lasagna from one of the local restaurants nearby in the freezer. I thawed it a little in the microwave and now it's heating in the oven for us. It looks good."

"What can I do?" Burke asked.

"Find some dishes and silverware while I finish making this salad." She paused. "Did you call Waylon?"

"I did. He said he'd fill Mother and Lila in on the situation and come to get us at the landing when we arrive tomorrow."

Gwen smiled at her. "You picked a nice one, Burke."

Burke bit back her reply that Alex was a good man, too. She doubted Gwen wanted to hear that right now.

Instead she said, "When we get back to the island, Celeste can have her old bedroom by mine in the family wing that you used to share with her. With my room right across the hall, I can keep an eye on her, too."

"That sounds like a good plan." Gwen looked toward the sofa where Celeste slept. "She's really been through an awful time, hasn't she? Do you think she'll be all right to make the trip?"

"She can sleep in the car," Burke said. "We'll put some pillows and blankets in the back seat for her. I think simply getting away from Nashville and the fear that Dillon might hurt her again will help her. What a horrible man he turned out to be."

Gwen looked thoughtful. "I think we should call Gary and let him in on our plans to take Celeste home for a time. He might need to come over to talk to her before she leaves. I'm sure any performances he's scheduled for her, for several months ahead, will need to be postponed. He's probably already taken care of that. If he's been helping Celeste with legal matters, too, we need to get contact names from him and learn any other facts Celeste will need to know."

"Why don't you go back in the bedroom and call him now?" Burke suggested. "I'll finish the salad and check on the lasagna."

"Good idea. I'll call Lila, too, and check on the kids."

In the kitchen, Burke kept glancing toward Celeste, huddled on the couch under the covers, so unlike the strong, decisive, confident sister she'd always known. Bruised and broken not only in body, but in heart and spirit right now. Life could surely send some blows and sorrows.

CHAPTER 16

Nearly a month later on a warm Saturday afternoon in May, Waylon walked down the path by the cabana to the Atlantic Ocean, sparkling in the sunshine under a deep blue sky. He unlocked the storage room to get a chair and a towel to take to the beach with him and then stood for a moment looking toward the scene spread out before him.

Colorful umbrellas dotted the beach, with chairs tucked beneath them or beside them. Coolers sat around nearby, along with beach bags stuffed with towels, sun lotion, sunglasses, and snacks. Children's toys lay scattered around on the sand or tumbled across old quilts, and Waylon could see the twins, Rose and Leah, working to build a large sand castle. The boys, Chase, Todd, Bobby, and Sam, were racing in and out of the waves, with the ocean now warm enough to play in. As Waylon walked closer he could hear the happy chatter and laughter of the women he loved—Burke, Gwen, Celeste, Lila, and Sally Ann—a good sound that made him smile.

"It feels like old times coming down here to find you girls all together again," he said, settling his chair beside Burke's. The other girls sat clustered around nearby.

"You look good," Celeste said, as he pulled off his T-shirt. "A lot more filled out and handsome that when we were young girls."

"Already getting a good tan, too," Gwen added.

"He's already taken, so don't get any ideas," Burke teased.

"It still seems so sweet to me that you and Waylon got together,"

Lila put in. "The two of you were always the older responsible ones who took care of us, kept us out of trouble, and settled our squabbles."

"We didn't always keep you out of trouble." Waylon laughed.

"If we'd kept your good sense and wisdom more in mind it might have saved us some heartache," Celeste said in a soft voice.

"You're looking more like your beautiful self again," Waylon said to her. "Your color is better, your bruises fading away, and I see you got your cast off last week."

"I'm a little less scary to look at now." She offered him a smile. "I know some of the guests at the inn raised eyebrows over my looks this last month."

"We told them she'd been in an accident," Gwen said. "It wasn't a lie and we didn't add details."

"People were basically kind though," Celeste said.

Waylon stretched his legs out, enjoying the warmth of the sun and glad to relax after a busy workday. "So catch me up on all the news," he said.

"Mine is easy," Sally Ann offered. "Simply the same old life as usual working at the office and keeping up with the boys. I think life is much more interesting here with people coming and going at the inn all the time."

"There was a big turnover at the inn yesterday." Gwen dug into the cooler beside her for a cola. "Who are the new people who came, Burke? Several had British accents and two of the women sounded very New Jersey."

Burke laughed. "The British guests are Royce and Adelind Dearborn from Worcestershire in the UK. Royce owned some sort of automotive company in England but, according to his wife, sold it recently, so now they have time to travel. Their two grown daughters Natalie and Verona are traveling with them. The four of them are spending an entire month in the U.S. They stayed two weeks in the Captain Nichols Inn by the sea in Searsport, Maine, and now they'll be with us for two weeks. They're really lovely people."

"What about the New Jersey women who look alike?" Gwen asked.

"They are Betty Camden and Joan Erwin, two sisters from Trenton, near Philadelphia—both widows who take a spring trip together every year."

"Well, they're a fun pair," put in Celeste. "Certainly more fun than the whiney widow, Connie something. I got stuck at her table one evening and she complained and felt sorry for herself the entire meal."

"Mother picked up on that, too," Burke said. "She worked to pair her with the minister's wife, Karen, along with Betty and Joan, to take day trips around the area. That will give Karen's husband a chance to do some fishing with the men staying in the Lakeview Cottage, too."

"I'd forgotten how mixed up we all get in other people's lives here," said Celeste.

"It's inevitable whenever you work in any type of people industry, I think," Waylon said. "Didn't you get involved with people all the time as an entertainer?"

"No, not in the same way," Celeste answered. "It was more surface in some ways, your life always more a part of the show. People saw what you presented and they interacted with you in relation to that. I'd forgotten how much fun it is to sit around the dinner table, on the porch, or in the living area simply talking, visiting, and getting to know people in a real way."

"It was nice of you to play the piano and sing for the guests a couple of evenings," Lila said.

Celeste shrugged. "Well, they knew who I was. It would have been rude to say no."

"I remember you used to play and sing at the inn when we were girls, too," Sally Ann added.

Gwen laughed. "Honey, Celeste would sing for anyone who would ask back then—at the inn, in shows at school, at the church, or anywhere she got invited."

"I remember when Celeste first started to sing at some restaurants in Charleston that Daddy would go with her," Burke said.

Celeste laughed. "Yes, he watched over me like a Papa Bear, growling if any man dared to flirt with me. He was very protective of me, actually of all of us."

"I don't think that's a bad thing, do you?" Lila said and Waylon wondered at a small pained look that crossed her face as she said it. Lila had always been one to keep herself to herself.

Gwen dug some sun lotion out of her bag to rub over her legs. "I remember Daddy was really upset with me when I ran off to marry Alex. He let me stay in housing on campus at USC in Beaufort with reluctance but I loved it and I fell in love with Beaufort." She paused. "Then in my sophomore year I also fell in love with Alex Trescott. When he was ready to graduate, and told me he was moving to Little Rock with Josh to open a restaurant, it didn't take much persuading for me to marry him and go along. We ran off because we knew Daddy would try to stop us." She sighed. "Maybe it would have been better if he had."

Lila put a hand on her arm and said softly, "Look at those three beautiful children playing on the beach and see if you can say those words again."

Gwen rolled her eyes. "I hear you."

"How are things going with Alex?" Waylon asked.

Gwen sighed. "Through some correspondence he's let me know he's sold the house and that he and Josh are fielding an offer on the business. There will be loss and big debts to pay from any profits, but he and Josh can begin again when it's all settled."

"What did you decide about the furniture in the house?" Burke asked. "I know Alex wrote to see what you wanted to do about it."

"I sent him a list of the things I wanted him to ship here, like clothes, toys, and personal items, but I told him to sell the furniture. I talked to Mother about it. It's expensive to ship furniture and I'd have to pay to store it. Right now, I have no idea where I'll be moving until I get a teaching position. I imagine I'll need to get an apartment or something and the space will be smaller. A lot of the furniture might not fit."

She hesitated. "Also I'm not personally crazy about having any of the furniture with all the memories attached to it." She looked away. "Alex and I shopped for it and picked it out together."

"I know that feeling," Celeste added. "I never want to see one item of furniture at Dillon's place again or to even drive by his house in Brentwood."

Gwen nodded. "Mother has a lot of furniture in our storage buildings here on the island, used in the inn or in cabins before remodeling. Most are stored in the big attic over the garage where the mowing equipment, tools, and such are kept. She and I went up there one day to look around. There are bed frames, chests, dressers, tables, chairs, even sofas that only need recovering. I won't need to buy much to get set up and I like the idea of starting fresh."

Waylon winced, sad to see Gwen hadn't softened in her bitterness toward Alex in any way.

"My things at the condo where I lived with Nolan remind me of him but all in a good way," Celeste put in.

"Will you go back to your condo soon?" Sally Ann asked.

Celeste closed her eyes. "I don't know. Gary's already pushing me to begin scheduling events, but I keep putting him off. I need more time. I told him I wanted the whole summer off. I don't think a few months will hurt and it will let all the negative publicity die down." She offered them a smile, if a somewhat forced one. "Fortunately, Dillon's attorney helped him to see that contesting the divorce would be stupid, as it would mean all his dirty deeds would air publicly. I agreed to a mutual-consent, no-fault divorce, not wanting more publicity either after all I went through, so in June sometime I should be legally free."

Waylon felt glad to hear this and to see Celeste's good looks returning. It was nice to see more smiles and laughter in her days, too. She seemed more stable now after surviving so much emotional trauma.

"I'm sorry you had all that trouble," Sally Ann said.

Burke turned to Lila, probably hoping to redirect the conversation.

"I stopped by that little gallery in Edisto that's carrying some of your paintings when I went shopping last week. Your work looks beautiful there."

"Thank you." Lila smiled. "As I get more paintings done I hope other Lowcountry galleries will handle some of my work, too."

"Don said to tell you he'd like to get a couple of your paintings for the veterinary office," Sally Ann said as she stood to wave at the boys, who'd drifted too far away from their beach camp while playing in the ocean. They waved back to her and began to work their way closer again.

"Well, I've really been wowed at how your talent has grown, Lila," Celeste added. "I want to buy a few of your paintings, too, to put in my place when I go back home."

Waylon saw her frown at the word home. To him it showed she wasn't ready to go back to Nashville and her busy work life yet.

"Your turn, Waylon and Burke," Gwen said with a smirk, sitting back down in her chair. "Have you set a date for the wedding?"

Waylon put a hand over Burke's. "We talked to the rector at Trinity Episcopal Church about a tentative time in September."

"Well, do it early in September before I get too tied up traveling again," Celeste put in. "How about sooner, like this summer, while I'm still here?"

"We'll talk about it," Burke said evasively. "Whenever we hold the wedding, it will be small and simple. But of course we hope everyone in our family can come."

"It will be a wonderful, happy day for sure," Sally Ann said, sending Waylon one of her grins.

Leah and Rose came running up the beach then, their bathing suits covered in sand from playing with the sand castle.

"Come swim with us in the ocean, Waylon," Rose called. "I like to ride on your back so the big waves don't knock me over."

"I do, too," Leah said, jumping up and down. "We can take our noodles with us, too. They're fun."

Both girls, and the boys, swam well, so water wings, foam noodles, rafts, or floats were only for extra fun in the ocean—not meant as safety devices. Additionally, in the boat at any time, Waylon insisted on lifejackets for any children and for the adults riding with him. South Carolina required kids under twelve to wear lifejackets and also required life jackets or PFDs, personal flotation devices, on board for every adult.

Gwen made a face at the girls. "Look at you two, covered in sand. While you're out in the water wash all that ickey sand off. When you come back you both need more lotion and maybe a T-shirt, too. I don't want either of you getting burned."

"Go with me, Burke." Waylon winked at her. "You know the boys will descend on me as soon as I get in the water. I need back up."

She grinned and stood to follow him and the girls to the beach.

While the girls scampered ahead of them, Waylon asked, "Are you enjoying having all your sisters at home again?"

"It's been fun, even with Gwen and Celeste's problems," Burke answered. "But neither of them really pitch in and help with the work at the inn. Celeste has mostly rested or gone to the city to shop. Gwen has been working with the children, homeschooling, and interviewing with schools."

"Was Don's mother, Elizabeth Nagel, a help?"

"Yes. She doesn't have an elementary opening at her school for the fall, but she gave Gwen helpful contact names for schools in Walterboro, Beaufort, Charleston, and Summerville. Gwen got her South Carolina credentials confirmed, too, and that's a big help."

"I imagine Alex will want time with the kids this summer after he gets his other matters taken care of. Has he been hunting for another job in Little Rock?"

Burke shrugged. "I don't know. He moved into Josh's condo with him, and Gwen said Josh's father owns a restaurant supply business of some kind in Little Rock. Josh is going to work for his dad, and Gwen thinks Alex probably will, too."

"Well, at least things are working out to some degree," he replied, but he'd had enough talks with Chase and the girls to know they weren't really happy.

At the water's edge now, he and Burke began wading out into the waves to play with Leah and Rose, the boys soon coming to join them, all talking and laughing, just being kids and having a good time.

Waylon loved spending time with all of them. It reminded him of the good times he'd known here as a boy. Their original group was all back at the island right now, except for Edward Calhoun. Waylon had kept up with Edward to some degree over the years but they'd only seen each other a few times since they left the island.

Putting his thoughts aside, Waylon helped Sally Ann's youngest, Sam, to learn to surf better on his body board. And then Rose was soon climbing on his shoulders to get away from the big waves. Glancing at Burke, her black suit hugging her figure, Waylon decided life couldn't get much better.

CHAPTER 17

The next week moved along rapidly for Burke with the inn full again and tourist season picking up at Edisto, Seabrook, Kiawah, and in the surrounding Lowcountry. Tours of the Deveaux Lighthouse were a popular attraction for visitors to the area, and Burke's Friday and Saturday tours filled up quickly. She kept the tour group numbers limited to about fifteen to eighteen, enough to keep up with at any one time.

This week, they'd also hosted a special tour and brunch for a local historical group on Wednesday—creating a hectic day, replenishing and adding to the early breakfast buffet items to create a nice brunch selection for the visiting group at eleven, then taking it down to set up for the inn's regular lunch again at one. Burke had let Waylon handle most of the lighthouse tour that day. He'd gotten comfortable doing it little by little, following along with her, just like she'd learned with her dad.

Growing up around tourism at Jenkins Landing as Waylon did, with the assorted tours his dad and uncle conducted, Burke knew Waylon had grown comfortable in leadership roles at an early age. His years with the Navy had only strengthened his confidence, ease, and maturity.

Burke readily admitted, too, that her life, and her mother's life, had grown easier with Waylon here. Every day, she also fell more deeply in love with him. Frankly, Celeste's idea of moving the wedding date up to August sounded more appealing every time she thought about it. With Celeste staying in the family wing, Burke and Waylon had decided they would start their married life living at the lodge. Perhaps in the years to come they might move to the inn, especially if Etta needed them there. But for now the idea of time alone at the lodge sounded nice.

Burke was sitting at her computer in the inn's office this Thursday morning, updating the website, when her mother stuck her head in the door. "We've got trouble."

"What?" Burke said, turning toward her in alarm.

"Rita Jean's had a fall. She had driven to the boathouse, after finishing her cleaning this morning, and somehow she fell while cutting across the yard. She twisted her ankle and couldn't get up." Etta leaned against the doorway. "Henry was working nearby at the dock so when Rita Jean hollered he came running."

"Is she all right?"

"No. Because she couldn't stand up, Henry got her to the dock and to his boat and took her to the marina at Seabrook. Then he drove her to Roper St. Francis Hospital in our van. He said Rita Jean fussed about going but with her pain so bad and not being able to walk on the foot, they needed to get it checked out."

Etta came to sit down in the chair across from Burke. "Fortunately, Rita Jean didn't break any bones but she has a sprained ankle—between a Grade 1 and a Grade 2 Henry said. That means she stretched and partially tore some ankle ligaments. She'll need to rest and stay off the foot for a week, maybe two, and then go to the physical therapy center on Bohicket Road so they can help her strengthen and heal the ankle more."

"Ouch." Burke shook her head. "I'm sorry to hear that."

Her mother sighed. "Yes, and we have the weekend coming. So you and I will need to kick in and do Rita Jean's housekeeping work along with our other jobs."

"Maybe Gwen and Celeste can help."

Her mother laughed. "I guess you've noticed Celeste can't even pick up after herself in her own room or in the family wing where she's staying. I know you've been doing all the major cleaning there so Rita Jean won't rant and rave about the clothes strewn everywhere, the makeup all over the bathroom, wet towels left in the floor, and the kitchen never cleaned up."

Burke wrinkled her nose. "With all Celeste has gone through, I hated to say anything to her about cleaning up more."

"Well, my point is, I think Celeste has lost the art of housekeeping, if she ever had it. I'm not sure she could be much help without supervision. She is good with many things, but Celeste is a sloppy housekeeper, and these years since she left home she's been waited on hand and foot, hardly turning a hand to cook, clean, or do a domestic chore."

Her mother rubbed her neck. "Frankly, Gwen isn't much better, but I'll talk to her about helping a little. It would probably be more efficient to get Lila to help us and to simply let Gwen keep up with the children. She's homeschooling them until the end of the month and she's started doing school interviews. I'm sure you've noticed neither she or Celeste have done much to help either of us since they've been here."

Burke tried not to grin. "I hated to say anything, with both of them dealing with so many personal problems."

Etta crossed her arms. "Personal problems, big or small, have never kept the two of us from doing our work. I guess it's just perspective. To you and me, this is our business, but to Gwen and Celeste, they're simply visiting."

Burke pulled out a folder to open it. "Most of the guests who came Friday are staying two weeks with us. That will be some help."

"Yes, but we'll still have beds to make, bathrooms to clean, dusting and vacuuming to do, windows to keep sparkling, and more. You know how much Rita Jean does."

"Do you think Maggie could come help out?" Burke asked. "She and Calvin already work Sundays every week and they know the inn. I know they fill in other times for us, too. It would be worth paying extra if Maggie could do Rita Jean's job for a week or two until she can come back."

"Well, I'll call her." Etta grabbed a piece of paper and began to make a list. "I'll need to talk with Clifford and Waylon about picking up some of Henry's work, too. He'll need to help Rita Jean a lot at first. I'm sure Novaleigh will be happy to provide carry-out meals for them that Henry can pick up." She paused and frowned. "You know, I just realized Maggie may need to do housework for Rita Jean and Henry. She might not be able to help us at all."

Burke smiled. "It's always something, isn't it?"

"Yes, and we'll certainly be busier than normal for a week or two until Rita can come back to work." She wrinkled her nose. "Climbing stairs could be a problem for her even then."

"That makes me wish we'd given more thought to putting in the elevator you, Dad, and I talked about a few years ago."

"We might think about it again this fall when things quiet down." She stood and put a hand to Burke's cheek. "In case I don't say it often enough, I love and appreciate you, daughter. I'm so glad your heart drew you to stay here, that you wanted to continue the work and business at the inn and to keep the Light."

Burke smiled. "There's an old quote that says: Where else would I be when the sea calls to me. That's true for my heart."

Etta laughed. "Well, the sea draws a lot of people here to the Lowcountry but not necessarily to work. As you've seen with our inn, most come expecting to be waited on hand and foot and catered to."

"We'll be all right, Mother. We've been through worse with storms, droughts, building issues, leaky roofs, rutted out roads, trespassers doing damage, problems with snakes, alligators, gnats, flies, and mosquitoes."

"And now this woman murdered so near our island and another missing." Etta frowned. "Is there no further news about that?"

"Nothing that I'm aware of." Burke glanced at her watch. "Let me finish the updates on our website and then I'll do a housekeeping check all around the inn. I'll make sure Rita Jean didn't leave anything undone she meant to come back and finish later."

"While you do that, I'll go call Maggie, speak to Waylon, and then talk to Novaleigh and Clifford." She paused. "I think I'll get Clifford to pick some flowers in the garden, too, so I can make an arrangement to take to Rita Jean's. She won't be happy about this situation. You know she doesn't like her schedule to be interrupted in any way and she won't like the idea of other people doing her job."

"Yes, I imagine we'll hear some grumbling and complaining about it—especially when she gets back—if everything isn't exactly the way she likes it."

Etta laughed. "Believe me, I'll be so glad to see her back I won't say a thing in return, no matter her complaints. That woman is a meticulous, spotless, and thorough housekeeper. Maggie says it's her German blood."

Her mother left then, and Burke closed her eyes and sighed. Tomorrow was Friday, with new guests coming in and others moving out—always the biggest cleaning day of the week. She had the usual lighthouse tours to do at two tomorrow and on Saturday. It would be hard to cram all the new cleaning responsibilities around the work schedule already on her plate. Oh, well. She'd manage.

Burke fought back a big twinge of resentment toward her sisters as she thought about all the extra work ahead. They neither one seemed to realize the additional work both had created for the inn with five new mouths to feed, plus laundry and cleaning. Many days Gwen and Celeste also took off to shop and eat lunch in Charleston, leaving the children with Lila, her, or her mother. Of course, they all loved Chase, Leah, and Rose, but young children had to be watched after carefully and entertained. It wouldn't have hurt either of them to offer to help out more.

It didn't improve Burke's mood, when a few minutes later, she ran into Connie Brachard, the widow from Atlanta staying with them, who'd done nothing but complain and feel sorry for herself since arriving. You'd think she was the only person in the world who'd ever known a disappointment and it especially annoyed Burke when she whined to her mother, also a widow.

"I'm glad I ran into you," Connie said in a testy voice. "I really think you should make more of an effort to keep that dog and cat away from your guests. After all, your inn doesn't allow people to bring their pets so, quite frankly, it hardly seems right that we have to deal with yours. I had to pay to leave my dog, Dickie, at the kennel in Atlanta. And here I am constantly reminded of how lonely he must be every time I go out and your dog comes up to me. That cat of yours hissed at me on the porch today, too."

"Milo?" Burke was surprised to hear that.

"Yes, I tried to shoo him off a chair so I could sit down and he acted quite nasty."

"Was it a red chair?"

"I think so. What difference does that make?"

Burke made an effort not to grin. "We keep two rows of rockers on either side of the front porch, with nice cushions and pillows, for our guests, but we also keep an old red wooden chair down at the end of the porch in the corner for Milo. It's a somewhat ratty chair with an old cushion on it but he loves it and he thinks of it as his own."

She stuck her chin up. "Well, how was I to know that?"

"Actually, next time you're out on the porch you might notice we painted a little sign on the wood slat at the top of the chair that says: Milo's Chair."

"Well, again, the cat should hardly have hissed at me because I didn't notice that. My point still is that if guests can't bring pets, you really shouldn't keep pets here, either."

Burke struggled to remain patient. "All our brochures and website information state that we have a dog and cat at the inn. Most people like that, but for others who are allergic or dislike pets it offers a warning." She paused. "Keep in mind, Mrs. Brachard, that this inn is also our home. We bring guests into our home but it is still our home. Just as you enjoy the pleasure of having pets, so do we."

Connie heaved a deep sigh. "Well, it would have been a comfort to me to have brought my Dickie with me. You know I lost my husband Earl a year ago. Dickie is all I have now."

"We're sorry about your loss, Mrs. Brachard, but if you'll excuse me I need to make some checks in the rooms upstairs here." Burke moved on, not giving the woman time to think of something else to complain about. She found herself glad to remember Connie Brachard would be checking out in the morning.

The entire day afterward seemed to be filled with annoyances. Gwen's girls picked some flowers in Clifford's garden, upsetting him, and they tromped on other plants without realizing it. Mrs. Humbolt, the pastor's wife, ran one of the golf carts into a tree after seeing a snake in the road. She damaged the cart, but fortunately wasn't hurt. Then the air conditioner went on the fritz in the Lakeview Cottage, causing Burke to need to move the two men staying there into the cabin next door.

After supper later, Burke went over to the lighthouse to check everything out, knowing she had a tour scheduled the next day, and then she walked up to the top level of the lighthouse, simply to be by herself for a while, curling up on the old sofa bench to read a book.

About an hour later, as dark began to fall, she heard steps coming up the stairs, and in a few minutes, Waylon climbed into the top room to find her.

"Hey," he said, stopping in the doorway. "Your mom said she thought you'd come this way after dinner."

"Is anything else wrong?" Burke asked, knowing her voice sounded petty.

"No. Not that I know of." He smiled and walked across the room to sit down beside her. "But I hear you've had a hard day. Lila told me you often come up here for a little peace and quiet when life goes sour. If you're wanting to be alone, I can leave."

She leaned her head against his shoulder. "No, I'm glad you're here. I meant to come walk with you later."

"We may have to skip that walk. A storm is moving in. I saw lightning as I came over." He looked around the room. "This is a nice little spot up here."

"The top gallery, spanning around the outside of the lighthouse, is outside the door—as I'm sure you remember. The old bench here along the wall once proved a welcome spot where early keepers could catch a little rest between refueling the light or keeping a lookout during storms. Dad said I "girlied" it up putting cushions and pillows around, but it created a nice place where I could get away when I wanted to think, be quiet, and catch my breath after a busy day."

Waylon looked around the small round room. "I remember that desk across the room used to be the keeper's desk where he kept the daily log. I've showed a few of the old log books to guests on the tour who wanted to walk this far." He crossed his leg getting more comfortable. "Do you still keep a log?"

"There's a journal we make entries to as needed, but we don't write down every daily task or change in the weather, like the keepers used to do. I know they did it in part to keep track of the endless work responsibilities they needed to accomplish, but the log was required then, too."

"Some changes are good."

"I heard you took dinner to Henry and Rita Jean," Burke said, changing the subject. "How's she doing?"

"Hurting, mad, cross as a bear to be laid up. Angry at herself, too, for not watching her feet better. She stepped in a hole in the yard, taking a shortcut instead of going around to the walkway. All the ground around the boat dock and buildings, even at Henry and Rita Jean's house, is uneven. Being near the water keeps it eroded in spots."

They talked about Rita Jean for a few minutes and then about the various problems they'd faced through the day.

"Sounds like your day hasn't been a picnic either," Burke said, looking out to see the beams of the lighthouse sweeping over the water now that dark had fallen.

A streak of lightning flashed across the sky, too, with a deep rumble of thunder following it.

Burke jerked with the noise of it and Waylon wrapped his arm around her, which soon led to some kissing and sweet words. The tension of the day began to ease away, to be replaced with a new kind of tension.

Breathing hard, Burke put a hand to Waylon's face. "I was thinking today about Celeste's idea of moving the wedding to August while she's still here."

He ran his hands down her arms and pulled her a little tighter against him. "Sooner sounds good to me," he said in a teasing tone, leaning over to kiss her neck.

Burke drew in a breath. "We don't have to change the date but we could if you think it might be all right,"

"It's getting harder to wait," he murmured against her ear.

"Yeah, I know," she said, finding it difficult to think with him this close.

He stood to look out the window then, putting some distance between them. "The rain is starting."

"There are raincoats and slickers in the closet on the lighthouse's first level. Some were my dad's. You can snag one before you start back to the lodge."

"I'll do that." He turned to look at her. "I need to tell you more bad news though before I go."

She sighed. "Well, come sit down and tell me."

CHAPTER 18

Waylon walked over to sit down on the cushioned bench a little distance from Burke this time. He hesitated, trying to think what to say.

"Just tell me what it is," Burke said, sending him a smile. "I've had a tough day but I'm a tough girl, too. I won't fall apart and break into a big weeping spree on you."

He ran a hand through his hair. "I hate bringing you more bad news after you've already had a rotten day. I considered waiting to tell you until tomorrow, but your mother already knows, and others will soon."

Burke put a hand to her heart. "Gracious, Waylon, you're almost scaring me now. Has something happened to Mother? Or to one of your parents or one of my sisters?"

"No, it's not family." He realized he was making it worse by hesitating. "The police found another body today, another woman."

"The woman missing from Hollywood?"

"No. The police thought so at first but it's not her. It's another woman, reported missing months ago in November. They didn't think to connect the report of her disappearance to these new problems."

Burke shook her head. "This isn't good news. Tell me all you know."

"They found the woman's remains even closer this time, on Fig Island across South Creek from us."

"What?" she exclaimed. "That's an uninhabited marshland strictly off limits to the public because of the old shell rings there. Those mounds date back three to four thousand years and are being studied to learn more about early Archaic people who might have lived or hunted in this area. It's totally illegal to even venture into any part of Fig Island and No Trespassing and Do Not Disturb signs are posted everywhere." She paused. "Who even found the woman there?"

"A group of archaeologists with the South Carolina Department of Natural Resources along with students from the Institute for Archeology and Anthropology at the College of Charleston," Waylon answered. "They went over for a day of research, ran into the woman's remains, and then contacted the police."

She shook her head. "Access isn't easy to Fig Island, and most people don't even know how to find their way into the little tributaries winding to land. You need to be conscious of the tides when there, too. That means whoever is murdering these women is a local who knows the land and waterways well."

Burke jumped as another streak of lightning flashed outside the window, followed by a boom of thunder.

"The storm's kicking up," she added. "What else did you learn?"

"Lonnie says since both murdered women were found at remote places, they believe the victims were either willingly or unwillingly lured to those locations." He got up to look out the window at the pouring rain. "The media will hit this hard, with a second murder uncovered now. Etta says she'll talk to all the guests staying at the inn in the morning and to new guests coming in tomorrow afternoon. Police will be searching the area, and around the shell rings on Fig Island, for any clues, so we'll inevitably see their boats coming in and out from the river or creek. Lonnie says they may check around on our island, too, since the access is so close. They may also have questions for us."

Her eyes widened. "Surely they don't think we had anything to do with these women."

"I imagine they don't, but with Watch Island squarely between the Deveaux Bank and Fig Island, it would be remiss of them not to ask questions and look around. I'd say they'll be doing the same across the river at Seabrook, at the camp, around Rockville, up Bohicket Creek, and in other nearby places."

"How awful." Burke shook her head. "Do they know this new victim's name? Is it anyone we know?"

"Lonnie said her name is Helena DePratter. They found some identification on her; he didn't say what. She lived near Rockville off the Maybank Highway and worked at the Cherry Point Landing seafood market. She'd been staying in a basement apartment at a friend's, who reported her missing, surprised she didn't take any of her stuff. Questions were asked, of course, a search made, family out of state contacted, but no one had heard anything from her." Waylon shifted to get more comfortable on the bench after sitting down again. "Another Charleston police department investigated the situation, not Lonnie's people."

"It was good of Lonnie to call you." After another bolt of lightning, Burke went to look out the window again. "We're getting a really heavy rain with a lot of wind now, too. That means in addition to everything else, there will be debris and limbs to pick up around the island tomorrow."

"Does it ever make you nervous, being up high like this in the lighthouse, during a storm?"

Burke turned to grin at him. "This is only a thunderstorm, and actually this old lighthouse is often a safer place in a big storm than other buildings around the island. It was built to be strong and to last, and it's withstood a lot worse than this, including major hurricanes."

His eyes moved over her in the glimmer of the light from the window. The intimacy of the darkened room in the storm, with both of them alone high in the lighthouse, made Waylon's mind wander to thoughts he didn't need to focus on. Restless, he got up to walk across the room to stand by her at the window, looking out at the storm. He could see the lighthouse's beam crossing in its regular pattern over the waves.

"When this storm winds down a little, I'll head back to the inn,"

Burke said. "You can go back to the lodge sooner if you don't mind getting a good soaking. Did you drive one of the golf carts to the inn?"

"I did and then I drove it here. The cart has a roof cover. I can give you a lift to the inn and save you getting wet."

She sighed. "I probably should go back. I've hidden out here long enough, and I need to talk to Mother."

A streak of lightning lit the sky and Waylon saw what looked like a boat out in the water near the Deveaux Bank. He leaned closer to the window to look again. "I think I see a boat out there in all this mess."

"Do you really?" she asked, coming to join him. "Is it moving?"

"It's jostling in the waves but it looks like it's grounded on the bank." He leaned in closer. "I can't see much through all this rain."

She frowned as the light from the lighthouse swept over the Deveaux Bank. "I see it, too, and that boat isn't moving," she affirmed. "Where there's a boat there's a pilot, too, and maybe passengers. It's close by and we can get there much quicker than the Coast Guard. We need to go check to see if anyone needs help."

"You're going out in this?" Waylon asked, shocked.

She gave him a studied look. "We're Lighthouse Keepers, Waylon. That's what we do. Even in the rain, we can be there in ten or fifteen minutes. Someone might need help or transport, and if we find a serious situation, we can contact the Coast Guard for more help." She started toward the stairs. "Are you coming with me or not? Dad and I have gone to the Bank or the shoals around the Breakers in a lot of storms to pick up people who foolishly didn't head in soon enough before a storm. The sea will be rough but we can manage. The Deveaux Bank is less than a mile from us."

Burke reached into a nearby closet to grab a bag. "I have medical and emergency supplies in this bag, At least the boat hasn't capsized or is already sinking. I know you have radio equipment in your Sea Chaser. If your boat is down at the marina, we can get to your craft quicker than my skiff parked at the back dock."

"The Sea Chaser is docked at the marina," he said taking the bag from her to carry, realizing it useless to argue with Burke about a rescue check. "We can be at the marina in a few minutes with the golf cart. Can you grab us a couple of slickers from the closet when we get to the main level? Maybe a few extras, in case we need them?"

"I can do that," she said, starting down the stairs.

A short time later, they pulled up to the pavilion by the marina in the golf cart, the storm still pouring rain over the entire area.

As Waylon parked the cart, she said, "I'm calling Henry to let him know we're doing a rescue check. Dad and I never call Mother if we don't have to but we always let Henry know when we go out."

Waylon smiled. In this emergency situation, Burke talked as though her Dad was still with her.

He felt glad of the new pavilion and walkway, giving them cover and protection as they made their way to his skiff. Burke made her call as they climbed into his boat and set out.

It was difficult navigating the boat out into the river and then into the ocean, with the wind fierce and the storm kicking up the waves around them. As they grew closer to the side of the Deveaux Bank, where they'd spotted the craft from the lighthouse, the lights of Waylon's Sea Chaser highlighted the troubled boat, grounded in the sand on the bank.

His mouth dropped open as they drew closer. "I know that boat. It's one of my Uncle Dewey's fishing boats. What the heck is he doing out here in weather like this?"

Waylon moved in a little closer to access the situation. He tried radioing Dewey's boat, knowing all the Jenkins' boats had Marine VHF radios, but he got no answer.

"I don't see anyone on board," Burke said, trying to see through the darkness and rain.

"I'm going to pull in toward the bank over here." He gestured. "I can't afford to get too close to Dewey's boat with the waves and wind slapping us around so hard." He turned to her. "Can you hold the skiff steady while I wade in to shore and make my way over to Dewey's boat to check the situation out? I'll drop an anchor to help, too."

"I can do that," she said, moving to the helm.

Waylon pulled some hip boots out of a storage bin, taking a minute to pull them on, and then worked his way down the ladder to find footing, with the water only a few feet deep. He waded in to shore and then sprinted across the beach to wade in again to reach Dewey's boat. He could see the anchor line, a good sign. Someone had been thinking when the boat hit ground to try to secure it in place to not get overly tossed and beaten by the incoming waves.

Once on Dewey's boat, Waylon began to make a check around the craft and found Dewey crumpled in the cockpit near the console. His head and arm were bloody, but as Waylon knelt, lifting his uncle's head and calling his name, Dewey opened his eyes in a groggy way. "Waylon?" he asked in a raspy voice.

"Yes, I'm here," he answered.

"I tried to get out a signal but a wave hit and threw me around. I didn't think I got through." He looked around confused. "I guess I got knocked out."

"Burke and I saw the boat from the lighthouse. A streak of lightning lit the area around it or I might not have spotted it. She's holding my skiff steady while I came to check on you." He waved at Burke. "Do you think if I help you, we can get you out of here and over to my craft? I can carry most of your weight if you think you're strong enough to hold on to me."

Dewey winced, trying to pull up. "My right side and arm is still good but I banged the left one up real bad at sea with a fall, trying to get equipment in and secure everything when this storm came out of nowhere."

"Do you think your arm's broken?" Waylon asked.

"No, but it's dang near useless. Kept me from handling the boat well while working my way back from sea in this weather. I probably didn't keep my speed level down like I should have, either, so when a wave and gust of wind hit me hard, I got thrown off course and into the bank here." He said a few choice words.

"We can call for Coast Guard rescue if you think you need it."

Dewey shook his head. "I think I can make it over to your boat if you'll help me."

"Well, let's see what we can do." With the wind and rain still thrashing at them, Waylon managed to get Dewey to his feet and down the ladder—not an easy job. Then with his uncle's good arm wrapped securely over his shoulder they waded into shore, back across the sand toward the Sea Chaser and out into the water again to the craft. There, with Burke's help, he managed to get Dewey into the skiff and strapped into a seat for the journey back.

Burke sat down beside Dewey to check him out while Waylon pulled anchor and began to back the boat out into deeper water for the trip back. They were all soaked but at least Dewey was safe.

"Should we head directly to the Bohicket Marina to drive your uncle to the hospital?" Burke asked.

"No!" Dewey hollered. "Just get me back to my place. I'm only banged up and bruised. I've been through worse. I'll be fine."

Waylon saw Burke frown at him.

She mopped some blood off Dewey's arm and then said, "I'll agree to take you to the lodge where Waylon and I can check you out and evaluate your condition, even if that might not be the wisest course."

Dewey glared at her. "You'll take me dang well wherever I tell you girl. You ain't my keeper."

"Actually, in this instance I am," she answered in a testy voice, leaning closer to him. "I'm the Lighthouse Keeper at the Deveaux Light and I have protocol to follow with any of my rescues. In addition, you need to keep in mind that this craft is Waylon's boat, not yours, and that he's also assuming the responsibility of Lighthouse Keeper, engaged to me."

Waylon winced to hear Dewey say a string of swear words he shouldn't utter in front of a woman, or in fact anyone.

"Swearing will hardly help gain you any favor in this or any situation, Dewey Jenkins," Burke said. "And personally, I've never, for one, understood what has made you so cantankerous and difficult when your family are all such nice people. It always made me mad how mean you were to Waylon when he was only a boy."

Dewey pushed at her. "You ain't got no right to talk to me like that."

Burke crossed her arms, ignoring the rain still blowing into the boat. "Why not? Someone needs to. You'd still be lying out there at the Deveaux Bank if it weren't for Waylon. He was the one who saw your boat, drove us out to rescue you, hauled you into his boat when he could have called the Coast Guard and left you there. He may have saved your life and I haven't heard even one thank you from you. Excuse me, but that doesn't make me admire you very much."

Dewy snapped a reply back. "After a little more time, I'd have come to and radioed for help."

"Maybe and maybe not."

"I got a right to ask you to take me back to my own place or to call Hal to come get me," Dewey grumbled, unrepentant.

Waylon eased the boat now from the river into South Creek toward the marina and lodge, glad to get out of the heavy waves of the ocean and river.

He glanced toward his uncle. "I'll need to contact Dad to come with the towing boat so we can go get your Sea Scout at the Bank and bring it in. You know if we leave it there all night the waves will pound it mercilessly and possibly damage the craft. It's an expensive boat and that would be stupid."

Dewey offered a few more unneeded expletives.

Waylon hesitated and then added, "I'm not of a mood to listen to your usual surly behavior tonight, Dewey, and I don't appreciate your rudeness and lack of gratitude to Burke. She insisted we come do a rescue check when I saw your boat. How many women do you know who would risk getting out in weather like this, care enough that someone might be hurt?"

Dewey snarled an answer but then grew quiet.

As they pulled into the dock, they saw Henry watching for them. Despite Dewey's protests, Waylon and Henry got Dewey out of the boat, down to the old Jeep Henry sometimes used around the island and into the lodge. In Waylon's room, the only bedroom downstairs, he and Henry stripped Dewey out of his wet clothes, cleaned him up and got him into a pair of sweat pants and an old T-shirt of Waylon's, then into the bed under a quilt.

While Waylon dried off and changed, too, Burke found an old shirt of his for herself and tossed her wet clothes in the dryer. Then she went to the kitchen to make coffee and heat up a can of soup.

A little later she came to find him, sitting in the big living room after Dewey seemed to quiet and close his eyes. She brought him a cup of coffee.

"Did you get him settled down?"

"Yes, with Henry's help and Dewey complaining the whole time." He sipped the hot coffee with gratitude. "I also sent Henry home to Rita Jean and I called my dad to come down river with our towing boat. Dad says the storm is abating a little now so we can get out to the Deveaux Bank to get the boat, but he agrees we shouldn't leave it overnight. The National Weather Service Marine Forecast said another storm is on the tail of this one. Waves could damage the boat where it is, and if the anchor comes free, it could be worse."

"Dewey seems determined to go back up river with your dad."

Waylon grinned. "Yeah, I guess he doesn't like the idea of staying here and being more obligated to me. With him getting knocked out, someone will have to get up with him through the night to check on him for problems, make sure he can carry on a conversation, isn't dizzy or has slurred speech. I don't think he's had a concussion, but he shouldn't be alone tonight. If he goes back with Dad, he or Mom will need to watch over him. With Dewey so determined in that, Dad will probably take him back with him."

"I hope I wasn't out of line, going after him like I did," Burke said, sitting down beside Waylon with her own cup of coffee. "But he just made me so mad."

"It's okay. Dewey was rude and crude to you. I'm sorry. I don't know why he's like that with me."

"Have you ever really talked to him about it? Asked him about it, told him you wished things could be different? I know you tried when you were a boy but he brushed you off. I know it hurt you, too. You admired and loved him but he was so unkind to you."

"You two about through talking about me?" Dewey said from the doorway.

Waylon almost spilled his coffee. "What are you doing up?"

"Going to the bathroom, a necessary thing." He ambled into the room and sat in the big armchair near them. "Hal on his way?"

"It will take him a while to get the towing boat and equipment out, but then he'll head this way. The weather's still bad so it might be a while." He studied his uncle, partially bald now but still fit in appearance, stocky and strong of build like his dad and himself, but looking a little wane, pale, and bruised right now.

"Think I might have a cup of that coffee?" he asked Burke.

"How about a cup of hot soup instead," she answered.

"Maybe both," he said, grinning at her.

She went to the kitchen, returning with two mugs a few minutes later, putting them on the table beside him.

"Nice shirt." He teased her.

"It's one of Waylon's. There weren't any girl clothes here. Mine are in the dryer."

He drank soup for a few minutes and then sipped at his coffee, while the rain pounded down outside.

"I got a few things to say while we wait for Hal," Dewey said after a moment. "First I owe you both thanks for coming out in this miserable weather to haul my sorry ass in from the boat. I was so mad over getting caught out in the weather, an old sailor like me who usually senses a storm coming in his bones, that I acted irritable and ungrateful."

Waylon knew his eyes widened with surprise.

"I can be nice when there's a need, Waylon," Dewey said, making Burke giggle.

"Then there's the other matter," he said, pausing. "You know my wife Charlotte died years back. I loved her better than life and it was a sorrow and shock to lose her. She had some kind of stroke, died quick and fast. What you probably don't remember, Waylon, is that she was keeping you that day. She was crazy about you. So was I. We both kept saying we wanted a little guy just like you, but it hadn't happened yet. When I came in and found her dead, you were there crying, not understanding anything."

He closed his eyes and leaned his head back. "I didn't handle that time well. Got angry at life, angry at everyone, angry at God." He opened his eyes to look at Waylon. "Angry at you, too. I got some sort of demented idea it was your fault she died and of course every time I saw you, it brought back the memory of coming home to find her with you. It tore me up. I took to drinking for a time, wasn't any sort of good man. I got into bitter, hard ways. It took me some years to crawl out of that hole."

Waylon couldn't think what to say. He'd only been two years old then. He knew Charlotte had died but not that he'd been there.

"I moved back to the family house with Hal and Aileen and let the place go that Charlotte and I rented. You'd been foolish about me before Charlotte died, but you didn't like the new bad-tempered, angry, and often drunken man I became. It deepened the breach, and over the years I couldn't seem to get back into a right place with you. You took up with Lloyd Deveaux later, spent time with him whenever you could, idolized him. Then went in the Navy like he did, got a lot of education, left the island. In my mind it seemed wrong but I see now you had a right to live your life as you saw fit." He paused. "And you've become a fine man. I need to admit that."

Burke shook her head. "It's good of you to tell Waylon all this, although to my way of thinking it's a bit late to be doing it. Why didn't you make more of an effort to right things with him long before this? He was only a child and you were a grown man."

Dewey shrugged. "What's in the past can't be changed. But with you two talking tonight, and with Waylon back at Edisto now, I thought it might be good to clear the air."

Waylon still couldn't think of anything to say.

"Well, I hope this means the two of you will be more civil and agreeable to each other in the future," Burke put in. "I was even tempted not to invite you to our wedding, but I think I might change my mind now."

Dewey grinned. "You got yourself a strong-willed woman in this one, Waylon. Cherish that. My Charlotte was spunky like that, too. Never let me get away with any of my crabby, independent ways without taking me to task. Made a better man of me while we were together."

Waylon finally found his voice. "Thanks for talking with me about all this tonight, Dewey."

Chuckling a little Dewey added, "I do plan to go back to Hal and Aileen's place tonight. They probably won't let me stay at my own apartment even though you can see I'm all right, but at least I can go home in the morning and hopefully get back to work after a rest. I have a fishing tour scheduled on Saturday and another Sunday afternoon. Weekends are busy around here once the tourists start coming in."

"I'll let you battle that out with Dad," Waylon said, as the alert buzzer let them know a boat had pulled up to the marina. In a storm like this, it was unlikely to be anyone but Hal with their towing boat.

Waylon glanced at Burke. "Will you be all right here with this old buzzard while Hal and I go tow his boat over from the Bank?"

"Yeah, we'll be all right. And I think if he takes a rest while you're gone I'll let him go back to Jenkins Landing with Hal."

"I can work with that plan," Dewey said, walking to the front door to let Hal in.

Burke smiled at Waylon when Dewey was out of earshot. "Daddy always said bad times had a way of bringing good after," she said in a quiet voice. "I'm inclined to agree with him tonight."

"Yeah, it seems so," Waylon said, his mind still trying to sort through the story Dewey shared with him.

CHAPTER 19

Burke had little time to think about the night before as Friday moved in, unusually busy with guests coming and going and with Rita Jean's work to do as well as her own.

After breakfast, as the guests checked out, Burke headed upstairs to start cleaning their rooms. She was stripping a queen size bed in the Marsh View Room when a voice interrupted her.

"Looks like you could use some help."

Burke turned around to see Maggie Boals standing in the doorway, her short red hair its usual disarray of wispy curls, her eyes merry, and a big, happy smile on her face.

"I hope you mean that," Burke said, grinning at her.

"I do—no problem at all. You know I work a little part-time with my mom and dad's cleaning business on John's Island but it was easy for them to make some quick adjustments so I could come to fill in for you and Etta."

"That's great news, but what about Rita Jean? Aren't you needed more there?"

Maggie laughed. "Henry brought Rita Jean's best friend Wanda Manning over from Johns Island to stay with her for a day or two and help out. Wanda's a retired nurse, likes a chance to tend someone now and again. Frankly, I get on Rita Jean's nerves. We've always had problems. I'm sure Henry knew he'd see very little peace with Rita Jean and me cooped up together for too long. It was a wise decision on his part, and I love to work over here whenever I can."

"Well, I'm grateful to you," Burke said, already knowing Maggie's ease and skill.

Maggie walked over to help Burke strip the bed. "This is the prettiest room with its soft moss green colors throughout and botanical prints on the walls. I like that each room has its own personality at the inn. Around my house it's mostly a lot of old attic pieces of furniture scattered with pizza boxes and snacks from the boys, along with shoes, clothes, and sports equipment."

Burke laughed. "How are Calvin, Eddie, and Joe?"

"Calvin's out shrimping already," she answered. "Eddie and Joe are still in school right now, but they'll be finished at the end of May. Both are looking forward to spending time here at the island. Henry promised them work cleaning, re-staining and sealing the decks and boathouses near his house. At fifteen and thirteen, Eddie and Joe are old enough to do a good job with some instruction and incentives. Henry promised them money and that they could stay some nights in the old boathouse. The idea of being on their own over there really rang their bell."

Maggie had already started to remake the bed, with Burke's help, while she talked.

"It's hard to believe my boys are both teenagers now, Eddie already champing at the bit to learn to drive." She laughed, a warm sound that always made Burke smile to hear it. "Calvin said he might help Eddie learn here at the island with the old jeep. With no cars or traffic here and only quiet dirt roads, Calvin says at least Eddie can't crash into other vehicles."

Burke grinned as she shook pillows into new pillowcases. "Dad taught us here on the island for the same reason."

"The boys want to kayak, fish, and go out with their dad to work on the shrimping crew some days over the summer, too. With boys fifteen and thirteen you want to keep them too busy and tired to get into trouble."

"They're good boys, Maggie."

"Yeah, and I hope they stay sensible and good. It's such a crazy world today with so many dangers."

The Marsh View Room was a large room with a sitting nook in one corner with two comfortable chairs.

"Come sit down for a minute and talk to me about the cleaning to do today," Maggie said as they finished the bed. "I can take care of everything up here and then downstairs later, too, if you'll just remind me of what I need to do." She sat down in one of the chairs and pulled a list out of her pocket. "Your mother gave me this before I came up to find you. It probably has most everything I need to do written on it, but what I need to know is what you've done already."

Burke smiled to see one of her mother's lists. "I started with Myron Andric's room," she said.

"That's the Bird Watch Room, right? Where the professor who's working on a research project is staying? I met him a few times on the Sundays I work."

A help was that Maggie already cleaned and cooked on Sundays to give the staff a break. Cheerful and friendly in personality and efficient, she could really maximize time and get a lot done.

"After doing Myron's room and bath," Burke continued, "I came here to work. Pastor Humbolt and his wife Karen just checked out to head back to Alabama, but a new couple comes at four. Connie Brachard in the Blue Sky Room checked out, too, this morning. I planned to go there next. Two women are also coming to stay in that room later today. We like to do a big cleaning after anyone leaves. The other rooms only need a light cleaning, the beds changed, bathrooms cleaned, a little dusting and vacuuming done."

"I've cleaned on Sundays for a long time here," Maggie put in, "but to me one of the most important things to remember is that it's expensive to stay at the Deveaux Inn. Because of that the guests expect a little cosseting in their accommodations, meals, and in the gracious treatment your family always gives to everyone."

Burke smiled. "Not everyone is easy to be gracious to. You can be glad Connie Brachard checked out."

"The world is full of difficult folks as well as those who make your life a joy and pleasure." Maggie looked down at her list. "I think I know everything to do upstairs, as well as downstairs in the main rooms, and on the porches and annex areas. I see on Etta's list, also, that there's a cottage to clean, maybe two. I think she mentioned she had to move the two men staying in one? That the AC broke down?"

"Yes. If you have time to get to both cottages that would be great."

"What about the cottage where your sister Gwen and her kids are staying and the family wing where you and Celeste stay? Do you want me to clean there, too?"

"No." Burke shook her head. "You shouldn't need to clean for me or my sisters."

Maggie grinned. "Sounds like there's a note of irritation behind those words. You having some problems with your sisters being home?"

Offering a smile, Burke said. "I love my sisters but they've both been going through a difficult time in their lives right now. It's hard sometimes dealing with that."

"They're also very different women from you. I've seen that easily enough on my times here. I admit, last Sunday I popped in where both are staying to clean a little. Neither would win the housekeeping award for the year." She grinned.

"Mother told them they needed to take care of their own cleaning while here. You don't have to clean Gwen's cottage or do any work in the family wing where Celeste is staying."

"Well, if I have time it might be a help to you. I know you'll do it yourself if I don't. Both of us like to see things neat and nice."

Burke found herself unloading a little to Maggie about her sisters. "I know they have real problems going on in their lives right now and I don't mean to be unsympathetic, but we've got a business to keep running here, too. We could use their help sometimes, but they never offer it." She paused. "Oh, sometimes they do a few things. Carry a few dishes to the kitchen after a meal or visit with the guests. Gwen picked up some brochures for us while in Charleston. Celeste has been kind enough to entertain the guests a couple of evenings. They loved that." She paused, considering her words. "I just don't understand why they don't help more."

"We're all different and that's a fact," Maggie agreed. "Me, I'm the tomboy of the two girls in my family, loved playing with my two brothers and his friends more than with any of the girls who lived near me. But my sister Freya loved girly clothes and fashion since she could barely walk. She works for this fashion magazine over in Charleston now, always looks like a million dollars, has a slick husband who works at a big bank, and two pretty little girls she dresses like fashion Barbies. We couldn't be more different. Freya looks down her nose at me, although I know she wouldn't say so." She laughed. "You know my mother and dad own a cleaning business. A successful one too. They both work hard, have done well but they live simple. I help part time in their business when needed. Freya finds all that a bit of an embarrassment, her family being in the cleaning business, my husband a shrimper. So you see, all families have these things."

"I guess. Thanks for sharing that. It makes me feel less guilty."

Maggie stood up. "You go do what you need to do and let me get to my work now. I can come all this week, next, and part-time afterward for a time, if needed, until Rita Jean is well. Despite our differences, I love that woman, Henry, too. I don't want to see Rita Jean push herself to come back to work too soon, injuring herself worse. I also know Wanda will be better at policing my mother-in-law than I ever could. Plus they're friends. They'll enjoy time together."

With Maggie finishing the cleaning, Burke had time to head into her office to check emails, and answer correspondence. Her mother had left her a few notes about upcoming reservations and she'd left the morning paper Maggie brought, open on her desk for Burke to see. The news about the woman found on Fig Island was right on the front page. Great. It couldn't help bringing concerns to their guests and tourists coming for lighthouse tours. If nothing else, it would bring a lot of unwanted questions.

Remembering that new guests would be coming in later in

the day, Burke headed out to one of the inn's side gardens with clippers and a small bucket to pick flowers for the tables. Clifford's hydrangea were blooming profusely now, and he'd given Burke an okay to pick some blooms to put in the bud vases on the dining room tables. Just one bloom was enough for each vase and Burke knew the big colorful blossoms would look nice for several days.

As she went out the front door, she found Celeste and Gwen sitting on the porch visiting while the kids rode bikes around the roads and paths by the inn.

"Hi, Burke," Gwen said. "Going to pick some flowers?"

"Yes. They look nice on the dining room tables when Clifford will let me pick some."

Gwen made a face. "I'm really sorry about the kids getting into his flower beds the other day."

They talked for a minute about the new murder, the storm last night and Dewey's rescue. Then Celeste asked, "Do you think you, Mother, or Lila could keep an eye on the kids today while Gwen and I go into Charleston? Gwen could use something nicer to interview in and we thought it would be fun to eat lunch at Magnolia's downtown. They have the best tomato bisque soup and a fabulous Caesar salad."

Burke looked at them, casual and comfortable on the porch with big glasses of cold iced tea beside them.

"It's Friday," she said after a moment, trying to keep the annoyance she felt out of her voice. "Mother has new guests coming in this afternoon and she's helping Novaleigh in the kitchen. I have the tour at the lighthouse at two and Mother always takes any visitors around the inn, sharing history with them before the tour. Lila runs the gift shop now and she needs to be there before and after the tour, plus this morning she went to take some paintings to the gallery at Edisto. I don't think that will work out today."

She saw her sisters raise their eyebrows at each other, obviously picking up on her tone of voice.

Burke sighed. "I know you two keep forgetting it, but we run a business here and Mother and I work hard to keep it going. Lila helps in the gift shop and works in the garden and around the grounds with Clifford. It wouldn't hurt either of you to offer to help, too, when you can. You know Rita Jean just fell and got hurt yesterday. You might have offered to help clean this morning."

Gwen lifted her chin. "Quit playing the martyr, Burke. We asked Mother if we could help after you went upstairs to start cleaning this morning, and she told us she'd just gotten a call that Maggie was coming to do Rita Jean's job. She said we wouldn't be needed."

"I know that you work hard here," Celeste added. "As kids we did, too. We all had our jobs and had to do them every day. Working here now is your career, but keep in mind Gwen and I left and made other lives. It's not the same when we come back. We're more like guests. Everything has a well-oiled work pattern and it's hard to see where we might fit in to be of some help."

Gwen nodded. "It is different, Burke. Celeste and I have a lot of emotional mess going on right now, too, problems and decisions to make. Getting away to the city makes things a little better sometimes. Cheers us up." She frowned at Burke. "It wouldn't hurt you to get away a little, too, to go with us to Charleston for lunch and to shop."

Burke tried to think what to say that wouldn't make things worse.

Celeste smiled at Gwen then. "We'll take the children with us today, Gwen. It will be fun. I'll treat for lunch and maybe we'll all go to the aquarium."

"The kids would love that," Gwen said smiling.

"They really would love that," Burke added, already wishing she hadn't acted so cross. "I'm sorry if I seem stressed. All these new worries and the storm last night…" Her voice drifted off.

Celeste studied her. "You really need to make time for fun when you can, Burke. Besides, Gwen and I don't get home very often. Before you know it we'll be gone again and your life will fall right back into its old familiar pattern."

"It's not like we don't know how to work hard, too," Gwen put in. "If you'd followed us around these years since we've been away, you'd have seen that. Maybe that's one reason we're enjoying this time, even with all our problems. Both of us will soon be back to work full-time. Times for sharing lunch or walking around to the shops and stores will be limited."

Burke tried not to glance at her watch. In the meantime, despite their words, she was still working, which they both seemed to always forget.

"Maybe I can take a day off next week so we can all go somewhere together," she offered.

"I'm still homeschooling the kids, but maybe we can make a day into a learning field trip. Like going to Charlestown Landing or one of the historic plantations." Gwen stood to wave at the kids. "Celeste, I need to get the kids cleaned up and changed into something nicer to go into the city."

Celeste glanced down at her shorts. "I think I'll go put on a sundress or something. I'll walk to your cottage when I get ready and we'll go down to the marina from there." She glanced at Burke. "We'll take one of the small skiffs to Bohicket Marina and drive the van into Charleston. I'll tell Mother we won't be here for lunch but that we'll be back for dinner."

As Celeste started into the house, Gwen headed toward the Seaside Cottage, calling to the kids again. Burke stood there as they left, feeling suddenly mean-spirited.

Later in the day after she finished the lighthouse tour and said goodbye to all the guests, Burke walked to the big pavilion behind the lighthouse and sat down on one of the tables for a minute to think.

A short time later Lila came to join her.

"You look troubled," Lila said, sitting beside her on top of the picnic table where she'd settled, looking out at the ocean.

"I think I just had a fight with Gwen and Celeste earlier, but I'm not sure."

Lila giggled. "You're not sure?"

Burke sighed. "They wanted to take off today to Charleston to shop and have lunch again and they wanted one of us to look after the kids. It's Friday, Lila, one of our biggest days of the week around here. We've had extra problems putting strain and extra workload on everyone—Rita Jean getting hurt, the storm last night leaving debris all over the island to clean up, police running up and down the waterways with this other murder occurring. Honestly, couldn't they stop to realize it isn't the best time to ask for favors? Or that it might have been nice if they'd offered to help out in some way versus taking off for a pleasure trip today?"

"Are you jealous?" Lila asked.

Burke's eyes widened. "I don't think so, but I was provoked they even asked and I guess they picked up on that."

"So maybe you said some things you shouldn't have?"

"Probably, but it's phony to always act nice like anything people do doesn't matter when it does." She looked across at her sister, who always appeared so serene and calm. "How do you manage to never have cross words with anyone? And I have to ask how you got along with all those women in the Community of St. Mary's all the time? Surely some of them got on your nerves now and then. Ticked you off or made you mad. Were any of them naturally lazy in nature, shirkers, letting others carry most of the workload? Did any take advantage of other people's time and good nature? Were any sloppy and not neat, causing others to have to clean up for them?"

Lila reached over to pick up a pile of shells one of their guests had left on the picnic table. "Look at these shells," she said to Burke. "They're all different. Some are big, some small. Many are beautiful while others are not pretty at all. Some are more colorful, like this one with the rose pink coloring inside, some simply drab and gray. But God made them all. Every single one of them. They're all beautiful and precious to Him, and they all have value and purpose in His world."

Lila smiled at Burke. "I think of that, too, when I work in the garden with the flowers and when I used to work in the gardens at St. Mary. Sometimes I'd go out after a storm and find all the gladiolas falling over, that I'd worked so hard to plant. I'd wonder why they were made so weak. Or I'd find myself getting provoked when the roses would get that blight they sometimes get, while all the other flowers stayed fine and healthy."

"I think I'm getting a lecture that I need to be kinder and to appreciate the differences in others more," Burke put in, picking up a few of the shells still on the table to study them.

"The Bible talks about how we're all a part of the same body but that each part has different purposes. We're not meant to think or look or act the same, although it often seems like other people should act more like us." Lila's mouth quirked in a smile. "I imagine others think we should act and be more like them, too. There is a natural tendency for us to think the way we live, think, and do things is the right way and the best way, and that others should live and be more like us. But that isn't God's way. He loves and delights in diversity, and we see it all around us."

"I see what you're saying, but that applies most when comparing good to good, don't you think?"

Her sister smiled. "God made Venus flytraps, too, and mosquitoes. I do mean to ask him about mosquitoes one day."

Burke laughed out loud. "If we didn't spray around the island, they'd carry everyone away, I think."

Lila grew quiet for a minute. "At the Community, I lived with the Lilas, the Gwens, the Celestes and the Burkes. With the Sally Anns, the Novaleighs, the Rita Jeans, and the Maggies. I felt more in harmony with some than others. But I learned to love all and to criticize less. To see the differences as individuality more than as flaws. God said we were his peculiar people. I imagine from his perspective, He has his moments with us, like you had today with Gwen and Celeste, but I'd say He handles it differently."

"Yet we're told not to grieve the Spirit," Burke put in.

"You have been reading your Bible, I see." She paused. "But I believe it's a mistake to expect others to be like us and to think like us. Just as God made the great diversity of flowers, trees, and other things in our world … He made us each wonderfully and peculiarly unique. Our obligation is to try to see the unique beauty and potential in others, different from us … but still okay. We can share our thoughts and ask some questions to try to understand others better … but not when we're angry or annoyed. And not to control them or to try to make them over to be like us."

Lila turned the shells over in her hand for a moment. "Loving one another isn't always easy … but we need to keep in mind God made each one according to His design and purpose. And we need to pray for each person in our lives to find God in a deep way and to find His perfect plan for their lives. One thing I've learned is that the more of God there is in a person, the easier it is for us to be comfortable with them, and them with us, because we're like-minded in our faith. Those who don't know God well are always more worldly, seeing things through a different lens."

"I've seen that here at the inn, too. People who don't walk in faith do see life through a different lens." Burke wrinkled her nose. "I have to add that some people are simply more difficult, too, Lila."

"I agree. Some have deep-seated problems, have become hard-hearted and cold, live selfishly only thinking of themselves, not minding the hurt they bring to others. I'm not saying there isn't evil in the world or that sometimes the evil one lives strong in some. Yet we've all read the stories of how God has turned lives around, totally changed people as He came to live in them more fully, or as they found Him for the first time and let Him in."

"So what's the answer?"

"Learning patience. Praying for others more. And not expecting them to be like us simply because it would be easier. Like the shells, we have to trust that God has a plan and purpose for every life and that those plans and purposes are often very dissimilar." She turned a small white shell over in her hand. "A part of learning to find our place in the world and in getting along better with others is to recognize our own uniqueness, to embrace and love ourselves, to see we can't be who other people want us to be if it's not our God given design. Young, shy, and often timid as I was when younger, usually off in dreams, yearning to create, made me different. But God helped me accept who I am and why he made me the way he did. Being true to yourself is a way you live in your own purpose and integrity, without feeling you need to apologize all the time or worry if you're not pleasing other people."

She laid the white shell down by the others. "Actually once you accept yourself it becomes easier to accept who others are. To see their purposes, and to see—with love—when they aren't happy or close to God and haven't really found their way. That's a good time to begin praying for them every day, too."

"So you're saying, in a nice way, that you didn't always like the ways of all the women in your community but that you learned to love and appreciate them." She grinned at Lila. "I imagine that was easier with a group of women all supposedly sold out to God."

Lila had the grace to laugh. "Yes, I suppose it was in some ways. I've been reminded of that difference, too, back on the island with so many different kinds of people coming and going every day—many very worldly. But, honestly, coming to love and accept myself has been a big help in it all."

Burke sat quietly for a time thinking over Lila's words. "Surely you know I love Gwen and Celeste."

"But of course."

"And I see the gifts they each carry, both so talented in their own ways. They've accomplished so much, despite the problems they're both facing right now."

"Keep in mind, too, that they simply both enjoy and like doing different things from you and me. Celeste loves to shop, loves the retail world, always has. It's a delight for her poking around in stores." She laughed. "I can see from that face you're making that it isn't a delight you share."

"True."

"And Gwen has that boundless energy and sense of adventure. She always wants to be doing and seeing. And she likes the challenge of helping people to grow and branch out. She can't get that sense of satisfaction here waiting on people, helping them to have a good time, keeping the inn running smoothly. You find satisfaction in that but she doesn't. She doesn't thrive on routine as you do."

Lila smiled at her, adding, "That's why when a bunch of troubling things come up you get testy, Burke. They interrupt the smooth rhythm of life that you love. The balance, the flow."

Burke considered her sister's words. "That is true about me."

"The point to keep in mind is that Celeste and Gwen, and even me or Waylon, aren't meant to be like you to be okay." She climbed off the table. "Try to pray more for Celeste and Gwen. They're at a turning in the road, a time for decisions. Pray they find the right road and pray they reach out to God to help them find it."

Burke leaned over to kiss her sister's cheek. "You're such a good person. We've been so lucky and blessed to get you back."

She turned to smile at Burke as she left. "Go tell your other sisters sweet words like that, too, later on. We all need to hear and know we're loved."

CHAPTER 20

Several days later after the busy weekend, Waylon and Burke sat on the screened porch of the lodge, while a casserole heated in the oven. The good smell drifted out, tickling Waylon's nose.

"What are you cooking?" he asked her.

They sat in two old wicker chairs where they could look out toward the water, their feet propped on a trunk with a quilt over the top of it. Burke's dog, Boonie, sat on the floor beside them napping.

"It's called South of the Border Casserole; it's a recipe my friend Kiley gave me," she answered.

Waylon lifted his eyebrows, the name unfamiliar to him.

"I forget you haven't met Kiley Wells. She and her husband Robert live in one of the villas at Seabrook. You can see their place from the lighthouse, right across the river. I boat over to visit and sometimes we meet for lunch at Freshfields or at the Bohicket Marina. We met years ago when getting our degrees at the community college in Charleston. When we realized we lived close we started carpooling and hanging out. Kiley does graphics from her home and has a little girl, Lexie, who is seven and looks exactly like her." Burke smiled. "We haven't had much time together with everything so busy lately, but we did meet for lunch earlier this week when I went to Freshfields for errands."

She gave Waylon a shy look. "I told her all about you and she said she and Robert would love to have us over for dinner sometime. He works in an administrative position at Seabrook. Kily and Robert like water sports and are great people. I think you'd like them."

"I'm sure if you like them I will, too."

Burke crossed one ankle over the other. "Kiley was kidding me that I needed to show you I actually know how to cook, since Novaleigh cooks daily for the inn. She dug through her recipes and gave me this one, a favorite of her family's, to try."

"It smells rich and spicy. What's in it?"

"Chuck, onion, chili beans, corn, tomato sauce, taco seasoning, cheese, and crushed up tortilla chips." She ticked off the items. "I'll add fresh tomatoes and green onions on top when it's done. It's like a meal in itself, but I made a fruit salad with fresh pineapple, strawberries, and blueberries, too. I think that, plus the ice cream pie in the freezer, will be enough for us."

He winked at her. "No chance you're getting away from me now since I know you can cook, too."

"We all learned to cook with Mother and Novaleigh, but it was fun to plan a dinner for just the two of us tonight." She gave him a punch on the arm. "I know you can cook, as well. Your mother told me. I'll expect you to fix something special for me one night."

They chatted about small matters while they waited for the casserole to finish baking and then carried their plates out to the screened porch to eat. Burke had brought some food down for Boonie, and she fixed the dog a dish of kibble, adding a little casserole in with it.

"We really had a stressful weekend," Burke said, after a while. "I know, when we walked on the beach last night, that you said Dewey seemed fine now. Have you talked any more with him?"

"Not much, although he's acting more civil with me." Waylon hesitated. "I did talk to my parents, though. No one ever told me I was actually with Charlotte when she died."

"I assumed it was true."

"Yes. Mother said I was napping in one of the bedrooms in a crib that Charlotte and Dewey kept at their apartment. I didn't see Charlotte collapse or fall, but of course when I woke later I cried because she didn't come to check on me. Mother said she'd spoken to Charlotte right before she put me down for a nap and that Dewey came home about an hour later, so I wasn't alone long. They thought I didn't need to know what happened. Mom sort of whisked me out a back door and took me home while Dad stayed to help Dewey."

"And they never told you later?"

"No. Mom said they never knew Dewey associated me with Charlotte's death negatively. They saw Dewey took her death hard, grew angry, negative toward life, drank, and became a more difficult person. They loved him through it all, as Mom said. But it was hard on everyone, especially when Dewey lived with us for a number of years. She said Dewey's angry outbursts and actions scared me so much that I began shying away from him."

Waylon drank some of his iced tea. "We never got it straightened out and I never understood why he acted as he did. In some ways I still don't. Dewey didn't have to take it out on me or the world that his wife died."

"Well, maybe things will be better now."

"I hope so. It's been hard for my parents, too, putting up with Dewey's temperamental ways."

"Families cause problems, don't they?"

"Yes." He smiled. "You've had some of your own lately, too."

"I have," she admitted. "At the inn, when difficult people vex you or get on your nerves, they check out after a week or two, but difficult family we keep through good and bad—or as Lila says, learn to love and deal with."

"She been talking to you again?"

"Yes, and it's always a help when she does. I don't always like her advice and counsel at the time, when I want to stay annoyed, but she's usually right. She's grown wise through the years and her faith is a comfort."

"Having to deal with a lot of different people and their problems helps you. I know my time at school, in the Navy, and traveling so much, working with diverse kinds of men and women in other cultures, helped me."

She smiled at him. "Mother says we're getting a nice crash course in all the problems married life brings."

"Perhaps." He reached across the table to put a hand over hers. "But I'm falling more in love with you every day, and I'm really glad we moved the wedding date to early August."

"Me, too." She glanced away from him, a blush stealing up her cheeks.

The buzzer sounded before they could say more, letting Waylon know someone was pulling up to the marina. He stood to look out the door toward the dock, Boonie jumping up to head to the door with him.

"Who is it?" Burke asked.

"A police boat," he answered. After watching for a minute or two, he recognized Lonnie getting out of the boat to walk down the dock. "It's Lonnie Culler. I'll walk outside and wave to him to come up to the lodge. He was probably heading here anyway."

Waylon spoke to Boonie, letting the dog know the visitor was a friend, and then held the door open for Lonnie as he started up the porch steps. "Hey, stranger. Good to see you again."

"Hi, Lonnie," Burke added. "Have you had dinner? If not, I can dish you out a plate of the casserole I made. It's still hot."

Lonnie sniffed the air with appreciation. "You know, I'd like that. I didn't even get a chance for lunch today."

"Well, sit down and I'll go fix you a plate." Burke headed toward the kitchen, while Lonnie stooped down to pet Boonie and talk to the dog a minute.

Waylon gestured toward one of the extra chairs at the table. He studied his friend as he settled into it comfortably. "You look tired. I guess you've put in some long hours since this second woman was found."

"That's for sure." He sighed as Burke came back carrying a plate of food and a glass of tea to put on the table.

"Thanks," he said. "It has been a rough week."

He forked into the casserole with relish while Burke chatted about mundane things.

After finishing off most of his dinner, Lonnie shifted a little in his seat. "I appreciate your kindness here, but I came to tell you we found another body earlier today over on Pockoy Island on the back side of the Botany Bay Plantation Heritage Preserve. I just got word the victim is the missing woman from Hollywood."

Waylon saw Burke's mouth drop open at the news.

Lonnie rubbed his neck. "We'd asked the SCDNR, the South Carolina Department of Natural Resources, folks to help us do checks around the area after some of their people found the woman on Fig Island. You know Fig Island is a part of the Botany Bay preserve, so it revved up the Department's interest with a body discovered at Fig and earlier at the Deveaux Bank they manage, too. It's bad press and raises concern about employees and such."

"Where did they find the body on Pockoy?" Waylon asked.

"Off Ocella Creek near the Greenway pond in an obscure spot," he answered. "Whoever is taking or luring these women to these places knows Edisto Island and the areas around it well."

Lonnie forked up the last of his casserole before adding more. "The body wasn't found near places where the tourists go while taking the motor tour around the preserve. I'm glad of that and glad it wasn't a random visitor who discovered the woman's remains. So is the Department."

"I read archeologists are working at both Fig Island and Pockoy's shell rings," Burke put in.

"Yes, but the digs on Pockoy are much closer to the beach than where the woman was found. Still, you can be sure anybody who has worked in any of the remote locations at the Deveaux Bank, on Fig or Pockoy, are being questioned." He heaved a sigh. "We've gotta get to the bottom of this. Edisto Island, Seabrook and Johns Island, and all this area are a major coastal resort for tourists. The idea of a killer wandering around isn't appealing press."

"I imagine it really puts pressure on your department," Waylon added.

"Big pressure."

Burke got up to go into the kitchen to cut each of them a piece of ice cream pie, bringing the dessert back on a tray.

"Why in the world do people do awful things like this?" she asked sitting back down. "This makes three woman murdered and raped." She paused. "Lonnie, I assume you learned the woman from Hollywood was murdered and raped liked the other two, didn't you?"

"Unfortunately, yes. We have a very sick killer on the loose." He cut into his pie and took a bite. "Ummm. This sure is good, Burke. Tastes like its got candy in it."

"It does, bits of chopped up peanut butter chocolate cups," she answered.

After eating a few bites of pie, Waylon returned to their subject. "Maybe these three murders will be all that the killer will do now, knowing the police are looking for him everywhere."

"I'd like to hope that would be true, but we know, with three deaths now, that this is likely a serial killer. Nothing's more difficult and heartrending to understand than serial killing," Lonnie replied. "But there's a tendency for them to keep at it until caught. The odd thing is they often seem like normal members of their communities, are usually employed, sometimes have families, although most are loners. The psychology of it's hard to understand and the motivation. Usually its linked back to their upbringing in some way but research has found a mix of life, health, or other psychological issues can be at the base or root of it."

"How could they not see it as wrong?" Burke wondered. Sensing she was upset, Boonie had come over to sit beside her.

"Some psychopaths are so screwed up they don't see killing or other crimes as wrong," Lonnie answered. "I've been in law enforcement for a long time now and you find all kinds of factors behind why people step outside of the law."

He glanced at his watch. "I really appreciate the dinner, the great dessert, and the hospitality, but I need to head home. I'd promised to keep you in touch, Waylon, so I wanted to stop by to let you know what was going on. I'm sure this is going to cause concerns for you folks here until this is resolved." Lonnie paused. "I need to encourage you to be watchful, too. This location near the coast seems to be the killer's focus area. So far we haven't seen a link between the victims except that all were woman, either divorced or unmarried, and lived mostly on their own."

"We really appreciate you coming by," Waylon said as he and Boonie walked Lonnie to the door. "Let us know if there is anything we can do to help."

Waylon took the dog outside for a minute as Lonnie walked to the dock and then came back inside to join Burke who looked worried.

"I hate having to give this bad news to Mother," she said.

He sat down to finish off his last bites of pie. "I'll talk to Clifford and Henry in the morning, maybe to Henry's son Calvin, too. We'll need to pump up our security around the island, and you and your mother should stress to any women staying at the resort to not go wandering around the property by themselves." Waylon put a hand over Burke's. "That means you, too."

"You know I hate the idea of restrictions, but I'm not stupid. I'll keep the buddy system in mind when I go out." She wrinkled her nose. "I keep thinking there has to be some common thread with these women, some way the killer is connecting to them. Or maybe it's only random. I don't know."

"Well, I'll gladly be your buddy whenever you need one." Waylon got up to kiss her as she stood to gather up the dishes on the table to take to the kitchen. "And after you put those dishes away, I'll walk with you to the inn to talk to your mother."

"Okay, and call your mother and dad while I clean up. They need to know about this, too. So do Sally Ann and Don. We need to get the word around, even though I'm sure the media will splash this story across the news tonight or tomorrow."

At the inn a little later, they found Etta, Celeste, Lila, and Gwen sitting on the screened porch behind the family wing, talking together, while Chase, Leah, and Rose played with an old croquet set in the yard.

"Hey, come join the family." Gwen smiled as they came in the door with Boonie, following the sound of voices.

Burke glanced out into the back yard. "Isn't that our old croquet set the kids are playing with?"

"Yes, it is." Gwen smiled. "Clifford found it in one of the back storage closets and helped the kids set it up."

"We all joined in for a game or two teaching them how to play, but we're worn out now and taking a rest," Etta said, reaching out a hand to greet the dog, who curled up at her feet after she petted him. "There's some tea and ice on the sideboard if you want to fix yourself a glass."

"No, thanks, we just had dinner," Burke replied as she and Waylon settled into two of the chairs scattered around the large screened porch.

"How did that casserole turn out?" her mother asked.

"Excellent," Waylon replied.

Etta smiled. "Maybe you can copy it down for us to try here at the inn. If we make two casseroles it should be enough to serve the guests one night."

"I'll do that, and I'll help Novaleigh fix it if she'd like," Burke replied.

Celeste glanced over at them. "I would have thought you two love birds wouldn't come join the family tonight. Wasn't that the point of you sharing dinner at the lodge?"

Seeing Burke flush slightly, Waylon answered, "Burke and I had a visit from Lonnie Culler from the sheriff's department. We unfortunately needed to come tell you they've found the remains of another murdered woman, this one identified as the woman from Hollywood they've searched for all along."

"Oh, my." Etta put a hand to her heart. "Poor woman. Did they catch the murderer?"

"No."

Etta looked out toward the children playing happily. "Do the police think this will be an end to it?"

"Lonnie says with three women now found that it looks like the murderer may be a serial killer, which he says often means there will be more murders until he's caught."

Celeste shook her head. "This is such a quiet place usually. It's hard to believe murders could happen here. However, I've learned there are sick people everywhere."

"That's true, Celeste," he said. "Lonnie said serial killers are often people in the area, employed, often with families—not the sort of people you'd expect to commit crimes at all."

"It worries me for the children," Gwen said. "It's hard for them to understand. Usually when they come here they can enjoy more freedom, not need to be on such a tight leash."

"All of us will need to be more careful until this person is caught," Burke said. "Lonnie asked us to caution all the women not to go out alone around back areas of the island, or out walking or kayaking alone by themselves."

Celeste shook her head. "I came here to escape one crazy man only to find another on the loose."

"How sad that someone could become so sick in their mind and heart," Lila said, shaking her head.

Etta reached across to put a hand over Lila's, who sat beside her. "You need to heed these warnings, too, and not go off alone to sketch or paint. Talk to Myron and get him to go with you if he wants you to sketch a particular bird for his book. We all need to be careful for a time until this is resolved."

"It would be awful if anyone staying at the inn was targeted." Gwen shuddered. "The publicity would be horrible, too."

"I would hate to think of anyone at the inn, in our family, or even of another random woman we don't know suffering such a brutal death," Etta added. She shook her head. "Can you imagine the grief the families of these women are feeling? And I'm sure the police departments are under a tremendous pressure to resolve this with three murders now."

"Yeah, Lonnie looked haggard," Waylon put in. "Burke fed him supper because he hadn't even had time for lunch today."

Lila and Etta went out to check on the children and watch their play, taking Boonie with them, and leaving Waylon and Burke with

Celeste and Gwen.

"How are your problems with Dillon going, Celeste?" he asked.

"The divorce will be final soon, but Dillon is still angry. Some of the women Dillon knew in the past pressed charges for abuse they encountered with him. I imagine Dillon and his attorneys will pay them off but the publicity has been brutal."

"I'm so grateful you got away from that man," Burke said.

Celeste smiled at her. "I'm grateful you and Gwen came to rescue me. The time away has helped." She hesitated. "I hate the idea right now of going back to Nashville any time soon. I've received hateful, threatening emails and calls from Dillon—always camouflaged as from a random source, but I know it's him."

"Have you changed your email and phone?" Burke leaned forward, upset at this news.

"Yeah, yeah. I've done all that, but I still don't like the idea he's decided to blame me for all this mess that's hit the fan." She rolled her eyes. "Dillon has a twisted mind."

Waylon frowned. "I hope you've alerted the authorities and your attorney about these incidences."

Celeste sent him a smile. "Thanks for worrying about me, Waylon, but I pay big money to these attorneys, and to my agent and the agency, to take care of these things for me. I'm sure it will settle down, but right now it's disruptive to my career and my life. So far the press haven't tracked me down here at the island to hound me for details, but they might uncover me in time."

"If anyone comes to bother you, let me know, and I'll deal with them," he said.

She smiled. "It's nice having you around, being all protective over us like dad always was. I like that."

Burke turned to Gwen. "Do you know if Alex has resolved the sale of the restaurant?"

"Yes, he sent some information to the attorney I'm working with that he passed on to me. The house and business are both sold now. Alex is giving me finances from both, although debts had to be cleared first. But I'll have enough to get into an apartment or condo when I find a job and Alex has already agreed to child support, even when we haven't formally filed for divorce." Gwen hesitated. "I didn't want to push that on Alex until he got past some of these other problems and found another job."

"That was good of you," Waylon said, studying her.

She made a face at him. "I'm not an ogre and I can tell you feel more sympathetic toward Alex than me, Waylon."

He frowned. "I don't remember ever saying that or being unsympathetic toward you. But I can't help feeling sorry for Alex when I spend time with your children. I know he misses them."

She looked away from him. "I've let him know that he can come visit them. He has family in Beaufort. I've also told him the children can come to visit him. He and Josh are sharing a condo but they can make room and he knows friends who could help with childcare while he works."

"That sounds good."

"There are some straight flights from Charleston to Little Rock or I'd be willing to drive half way to meet him," she continued. "I'm not keeping him from them, Waylon. I'll work with him this summer so he can have time with Chase, Leah, and Rose. I know it's important." She closed her eyes for a minute. "But my heart is too hurt to personally want any time with Alex yet."

Waylon didn't reply, but Celeste did. "Betrayal injures the heart in a way that is hard to understand until you walk through it, Waylon. I hope you and Burke never have to walk through the pain of thinking you know someone well and then learning you don't know them at all. It's hard."

"I'm sure it is," he answered. "And I love you both and want only joy and happiness for your lives."

The children came running into the porch then, chattering and laughing, their game over. Gwen soon herded them off to the cottage to get ready for bed, Celeste going along with her. Lila excused herself, as well, to follow them out to walk to her own cottage.

"Celeste and Gwen have gotten really close in this time," Waylon noted as Boonie settled down at Etta's feet again.

"They were always close as girls," Etta said, pouring herself a glass of tea. "So much alike in many ways but their hard times lately have drawn them back together." She shook her head. "They hash over their bitterness and anger too much when together though."

Burke looked toward her mother in surprise.

"Don't give me that look, Burke. My love and sympathy are with them both, but they need to work on letting their anger and bitterness go, not continuing to fuel it with ugly talk. Celeste has cause, God bless her, with what she's experienced with Dillon, but I hate that Gwen is putting Alex in the same frame with that sick man. Gwen needs to work toward forgiveness."

Waylon felt glad to hear that Etta saw the situation so realistically.

Etta sat down and put her feet on an ottoman. "I want to thank you both for keeping close contact with Lonnie Culler and for bringing us this news about the new murder as soon as Lonnie brought it to you. I'm just heartsick about this and it worries me for our guests. I often have widows, single and divorced women, staying with me. They love bed and breakfasts. Can either of you think of anything else we can do here to keep them safe?"

"I think we're doing all we can, Mother," Burke replied. "And let's keep hoping and praying the police will find and arrest this killer. Surely with so much attention on the matter now, and with several police departments involved, they'll track him down."

"I agree with Burke that there's nothing more we can do than what we're already doing. We might insist, versus advise, that people stay more in pairs or groups in their activities coming to and from the island or when anywhere on the grounds. There's safety in numbers."

"I'll speak to all our guests at breakfast tomorrow," Etta said.

"That would be wise." Waylon stood. "I need to head back to the lodge. Especially now, it's good to have someone near the marina. If you don't mind, Burke, we'll skip our walk tonight. I need to make a few checks around the island and make some calls."

"Sure." She reached over to squeeze his hand. "We'll walk

tomorrow night. For tonight Mother and I will walk Boonie around the inn rather than on the beach. It will do us both good to stretch our legs."

Etta stood to kiss Waylon's cheek, surprising him. "I'm so glad you're in our lives now. It's a great help and comfort."

Waylon walked back to the lodge thinking about her words. He looked up toward the dark sky, scattered with stars, as he walked. "I'm working hard to fill your shoes, Lloyd Deveaux. Send some angels our way to help me keep everyone safe here."

CHAPTER 21

About a week later, to Burke's relief, life quieted down a little. Few clues about the murders had surfaced, the media coverage finally ceased, and life drifted back to an uneasy order around the Deveaux Inn and Lighthouse.

Today, Burke took a break from work to drive with Gwen, Leah, and Rose, to Beaufort for the day. Celeste had gone with Lila to help her present some of her paintings to two galleries in Charleston, and Waylon and Don Nagel had taken Chase and Don's boys deep-sea fishing.

"I'm glad you could come with me today," Gwen said, as she drove her SUV down Boundary Street into Beaufort. "We haven't shared a day together—just the two of us—in a long time."

"No, we haven't, and I was happy I could get away."

Gwen sent her a sunny smile. "I want to drive by two elementary schools in Beaufort, as a part of our day, to check them out before I have interviews with them. Since Chase got to go fishing with Waylon, Don, and the boys, I promised the girls a special day, too."

"We're going to the kazoo museum," Leah put in from the back seat. "What's the museum's big name, Mommy?"

"It's called the Kazoobie Kazoo Factory."

Burke laughed. "However did you learn about that?"

"Teachers research things and I remembered reading about it when I went to college in Beaufort. I always meant to check it out. It's not far to it now." She turned from Boundary onto the Robert Smalls Parkway. "I thought we'd take the tour that the museum offers. It should be interesting. They actually make kazoos at the factory and have a little museum, video, and demonstrations. Everyone who goes on the tour gets to make their own kazoo to take home, too."

"I seem to remember kazoos have a humming sort of sound and that you can play tunes on them."

"Yeah, when you hum a tune into the kazoo, the vibrations from your vocal cords travel down through the kazoo and come out with a funny humming sound." Gwen laughed. "We may regret getting the girls kazoos after they play them all afternoon."

"Oh, it will be fun," Burke said as Gwen turned off the road to travel down a side road to the factory building.

Looking through the museum did prove to be interesting, with its old instruments display and kazoo shop. They learned the history of kazoos from the tour guide, saw a video, and wandered through the factory store. They each made their own kazoo before they left, too, picking a favorite color for their little instrument and inserting the resonator. Afterward they learned how to play a few simple songs like "Mary Had A Little Lamb" and "Row, Row Your Boat," laughing at the silly sound of everyone playing along together.

"Some of these kazoos would be great to use for one of my elementary classes," Gwen said as they drove to Zaxby's nearby for lunch. In the restaurant, the girls picked their favorite kids' meal and Gwen and Burke decided on grilled chicken sandwiches.

"There's no point in going anywhere fancy with kids," Gwen said as they settled at a table to eat. "Children are either too picky, don't like what they order, or don't eat enough to make it worthwhile. They love places like this better, and I've learned to enjoy my fancy times out with adults only."

Giggling, the girls tried another song on their kazoos after finishing their chicken fingers. Gwen quickly shushed them and made them put the kazoos away, but Burke noticed several guests around them hiding smirks.

"Can we get one of those big chocolate chip cookies?" Rose asked, noticing someone eating one nearby.

"We could," Gwen said. "But I thought it would be more fun to go to Yo Yos by the Henry C. Chambers Waterfront Park for dessert. It's an ice cream store and we can get a big cone and eat it in the park while we watch the boats. There's a great playground at the park, too, and not far away on Bay Street there's a fun toy store called Monkey's Uncle. I thought we might buy a game there to take home and play later." She hesitated. "But of course if you want a cookie instead…"

No," Rose interrupted. "Let's go to the Yo Yos place."

"Okay," Gwen replied, "but first I need to drive by the two schools where I might get to teach this fall. If I get a job at either, we'd find a place to live nearby. You'd both go to school wherever I get a job, so see what you think, too. "

The girls were quiet for a minute, and then Leah said. "I like Beaufort. It's where Gramma and Grampa Trescott live. Will we ever get to see them again?"

"Of course," Gwen answered. "I'm sure when your dad comes to visit his parents that he'll take you to visit them. They'll be eager to see you again just like your dad will."

Leah and Rose grew a little too quiet for a time, but then they pulled out their kazoos to play with them while Gwen made her way to the schools.

"Did Elizabeth Nagel help you with contacts to these Beaufort schools?" Burke asked Gwen.

"Yes. She's been really nice to me. As an administrator, she knows so many people in the school system. Every time she hears of open positions she lets me know about them. I had one offer already at a Charleston school where I interviewed but I turned it down. I hope I don't regret it later but the school and the neighborhood didn't feel right for me or the kids."

"It's important that you like where you work so you'll be happy, I think."

"I agree, and I liked what I read about both these schools we're going to see," Gwen said as she headed down the Ribault Road towards them. "Maybe one of these will work out. Beaufort is a nice place to live, not as big as Charleston but pretty."

"It's not too far from us at the island either," Burke added. "Only about forty-five minutes."

"Housing near the city is expensive but toward Port Royal I saw some condos on the Internet I might be able to afford."

"You're brave to tackle this on your own," Burke said in a quiet voice, knowing the girls sat close behind them but were chattering away about the kazoo tour.

Gwen glanced toward Burke and said in a soft voice, "I really don't have much choice. I came to terms with that some time ago. Despite Alex's apologies and regrets, I simply don't think I could ever trust him again. And that's sad. I never imagined he could lie to me over and over, sign paperwork that would jeopardize our lives without even talking to me. For heaven's sake, Burke, if I'd had any idea about the problems with the restaurant I could have dropped out of school, gotten a job, and maybe helped salvage this mess."

Burke tried to think what to say but was saved from comment as they came to the first school on Gwen's list. Mossy Oaks Elementary sat in a nice community, a neat brick school with the Beaufort Middle School almost across the street from it. Gwen drove up and down some of the side streets around the school, checking out the neighborhood, and then headed down the Ribault Road again to find Port Royal Elementary.

"This is a really pretty school," Gwen said as they slowed to drive by it. "It's small but I like that, and I love the old Port Royal community and its historic homes and buildings."

Burke smiled as they passed green parks and colorful homes on the side streets near the school. "It's been a long time since I've been in Port Royal," she said. "Do you remember when Dad brought us here to the Sands Beach on the river? We walked that long boardwalk to the big observation tower, played in the water, and had a picnic on the beach."

"I do remember that. Lila wasn't much older than Rose and Leah then." Gwen smiled. "I remember happy times going to that beach with friends from my college in Beaufort, too. It's a favorite spot of the locals."

As they started back up the Ribault Road after checking out both schools, Leah asked, "Are we going to the park and the ice cream store now?"

"And the toy store?" Rose added.

"Yes, to both." Gwen turned around to smile at them. "And you'll love the park on the waterfront."

The next hours were pleasant, happy ones, playing with the girls at the park, sitting by the water eating ice cream, and walking down Bay Street to explore several shops. They picked out a Yahtzee game to take home at the Monkey's Uncle store, a cute shop full of children's books, games, and toys.

Rose held Burke's hand as they made their way back to the parking lot, Leah walking ahead of them with Gwen.

"Do you know how to play Yahtzee?" Rose asked.

Burke smiled down at her niece, cute today in a colorful shorts set with her hair in two ponytails.

"I haven't played Yahtzee in a long time, Rose, but I remember it's lots of fun."

"Will you play with us?" Leah turned to ask.

"Sure I will, but maybe not tonight. I've been gone all day and I'll need to do some work when I get back."

"Mom, will you play with us?" Leah asked.

"I will, and I know Chase will want to play, too."

The girls giggled and talked on the way back to the island, asking questions about Beaufort, and the schools they'd visited, and chatting about plans for their vacation days ahead. Gwen had nearly finished with their homeschooling year and the twins, like all kids, were excited about the summer days to come.

At the Jenkins Landing dock, they found Chase and Waylon waiting for them, Chase full of talk about his day deep-sea fishing, his nose a little red from a day in the sun. They'd caught a few fish but released them and, after fishing, they'd parked the boat at Shell Island, a sandbar across from Jeremy's Inlet, where they'd explored and gathered shells to bring home.

Gwen gave Chase the kazoo she made while the girls began to share about their day and visit to the kazoo factory. Then for the rest of the way down the river to the marina, Burke, Gwen, and Waylon were serenaded with kazoo tunes and giggles.

Waylon guided his boat into the dock about the same time as Myron Andric pulled his boat up ahead of theirs, tying it off, and waiting for them.

"Can I talk to you a minute?" he said to Waylon and Burke.

Burke hesitated.

"You and Waylon talk to Myron," Gwen said to her. "I'm going to haul these tired children back to the cottage. I brought a golf cart down earlier. You can walk back to the inn or Waylon can run you back later. Is that okay?"

"Sure, and I had a good time," Burke said.

After some goodbyes and hugs from the kids, Waylon invited Myron to walk up to the lodge with them. "We can sit on the porch and talk for a minute about whatever is on your mind, Myron. I could use a cola and a chance to put my feet up. Keeping up with four small boys all morning and then Chase this afternoon about wore me out."

Burke giggled. "I know the feeling."

Settled on the screened porch a short time later, Waylon said, "I can see something is bothering you, Myron. Spit it out."

"You know with all the police boats buzzing around the last week or so, it's upset and scared off a lot of the birds I wanted to study. So I boated down to Otter Island today. You know it's not far, just across the St. Helena Sound from the south end of Edisto Island. Have you been there?"

"Many times," Waylon said.

Burke frowned. "It's primitive on Otter Island beyond the coastal area facing the ocean. The island covers over 2000 acres of wilderness. I hope you were careful wandering around, Myron. There is a healthy population of diamondback rattlesnakes on that island, as well as other poisonous snakes and alligators."

"I was careful." Myron looked annoyed. "I know the safe places to anchor off shore, where the trails and designated campsites are. I've been on tours there with biologists and various people from the South Carolina Department of Natural Resources that help to protect the island." He leaned forward with excitement. "It's part of the St Helena Sound Heritage Preserve and Wildlife Management Area, basically an untouched natural place. Many birds make their homes there—Wilson's plovers and willets in summer as well as painted buntings. You can observe red knots and piping plovers on the shorelines at the right seasons, too. Bald eagles even nest there. I got some wonderful photos today."

He crossed his arms then. "But I saw a dog there. I walked all around the shoreline and back to the designated campsites, looking for anyone it might belong to. No one was on the island but me that I could find. Camping isn't allowed there except by permit and that's supposed to be only from November to the end of March." He rubbed his chin. "I think the dog might have been left there and it's been worrying me. I tried to look for him again before I left, spotted him a little inland near a campground on the island's north side near the Sound. It's easier to anchor a boat there, out of the ocean waves. I'd put my own skiff in there earlier. I whistled at the dog but he ran back into the scrub and forest."

"Did you contact the Department about the dog?" Waylon asked.

"No. Do you think I should? I thought maybe someone might come back looking for him. He didn't look like a stray, more like someone's pet. He was white, maybe a white lab, which was probably why I spotted him so easily."

Burke glanced at her watch. "It's already late today for the department to follow up on anything but an emergency. A lot of folks begin to leave the office around four, but I can contact the Department in the morning. I'm sure they will send someone to look for the dog."

"I'll call my friend Lonnie Culler with the Edisto Police Department, too," Waylon added. "They might have received a report of a missing dog. If he was left accidentally, someone might go to look for him again."

Myron looked relieved. "Thanks. Dogs may be illegal at Otter and in other protected bird sanctuaries and natural areas, but I like dogs. I didn't like the idea of going off and leaving that dog there. Like you said, the island has a lot of dangers and a pet dog wouldn't know how to keep safe there."

He stood to leave. "Would you let me know tomorrow if someone finds the dog? I've got a class at the college in Charleston and some meetings or I'd take food and try to go find him myself. I hated going off and leaving him there today."

"I'll call you if we learn anything." Waylon said, walking out with him and then coming back to sit down across from Burke.

"Poor dog." Burke sat forward. "We could take some food, a leash, and go and get him," she said. "You know how crazy busy the department and police are right now. They may say they'll send someone to check on that dog but then not get around to it." She sighed. "You know he'll be scared over there, hungry, too. He might get hurt. Bobcats have been spotted on Otter Island. It isn't a safe place for anyone past the beach unless they're knowledgeable about remote wilderness areas."

Waylon glanced at his watch.

"It's not even four yet," Burke put in." We can boat over in your Sea Chaser and be there in about fifteen or twenty minutes. I know the safe spot to anchor, on the north side of the island, that Myron was talking about. It's near a campsite not far from the beach. If we take water and food, the dog might be really glad to see us and happy for someone to rescue him."

As Waylon hesitated, she added, "I know you don't want me to go by myself, but I don't think I can sleep tonight knowing that poor dog is over there alone. What if it was Boonie?"

"You'd never take Boonie to Otter Island. You'd know it was stupid and illegal."

"Well, someone took that dog there, even if stupid and illegal, and then left him. What sort of person would even do that? What if they were only visiting Edisto and Otter Island for the day and don't even come back?"

"They might have dumped the dog there," Waylon added. "Some people are cruel like that, dumping dogs or cats they don't want anymore."

"So will you go with me? I know you don't want me to go by myself. And there's an extra dog leash in the closet and part of a bag of kibble. I brought it down when I cooked for you the other night, when Boonie came with me."

"I can see you're going to be upset about this all evening if we don't boat over to check on the dog." Waylon ran a hand through his hair. "Don't be upset if we don't find him though. Myron might not have seen his owners, even though he said he looked. It's a big island. Also, someone boating or fishing nearby might have left the dog for a short time and come back after him."

"If we don't find him, we'll call the Department in the morning. I'm sure they'll send someone out eventually." She smiled at him. "Thanks for going with me to check."

"Call your mother to tell her where we're going. We should be back in time for dinner, but if we're late she'll know where we are and not worry."

"Okay," she said. "I'll get the dog food, leash, and some insect repellent. Do you still have a first aid and snakebite kit in the boat, plus a knife in case we need to cut back some brush getting through the overgrown trails on Otter?"

"I have all that in the boat, except the dog food and leash."

"Good. I'll get that and call Mother."

A short time later they headed out of the marina toward the ocean, skirting south along the coastline of Edisto Island. After passing the island's Point, they turned right into the St Helena Sound and South Edisto River, keeping an eye out for the beach where they could safely put their boat in.

Burke pointed toward the spot a few minutes later and Waylon headed his skiff toward the bank. "This is a good spot for the boat," he said. "A lot of people put their crafts in on the ocean side of the island at high tide and then find their boats beached when the tide goes out."

"I've anchored here before with Dad, and this is near where Myron said he saw the dog last," Burke added. "As big as this island is, I thought we should look first where Myron spotted it last. Somehow I don't think a dog would wander too far inland in this harsh place."

After dropping anchor, they hung their socks and shoes over their necks to wade into shore, Waylon carrying a backpack with dry dog food in it, plus a leash, rope, more insect repellent, and the first aid kit. The knife from the boat he sheathed in a holder on the side of his belt.

They stopped first to sit on a dry spot on the beach to pull their socks and shoes back on and then started through thick sea grass and scrub into the maritime forest that covered most of the island.

"Look how rough this whole place is," Burke said as they picked their way down the path. "The underbrush is dense. I know there are five primitive campsites here on Otter Island but who would want to come stay here?"

"A lot of guys and girls like to rough it, hiking and camping in remote areas, getting off the grid."

"Well, this is certainly off the grid." She slowed to step over some brush and roots in the path.

"I read the military used this island for target practice during World War II," Waylon said as they walked on. "Dad and Dewey have a box of old brass bullet casings they found here years ago. Today, you're not supposed to remove any artifacts but in the past people used to collect buckets of old bullets and casings."

Burke paused to study the path. "I see some tracks in a few muddy spots in the path, like people might have walked through here recently. We must be close to one of the campsites."

A short distance later the trail curled right, moving into an open area on a ridge with a fire pit. A few worn tent stakes still remained stuck in the ground, and they saw a plastic bottle buried in the weeds and more footprints that seemed to indicate someone had been here in the past.

Burke looked around. "Camping season only runs from November thru March, but Dad said people often camp at Otter without permits anyway, even in the seasons when the campgrounds are off limits. It looks like someone might have camped here not long ago."

They walked around for a minute, before moving on, following along a trail out of the back of the campground. After scrambling through the brush for a time, Burke saw Waylon point toward a small side trail. "I think I just saw the dog."

"Where?" Burke asked.

He pointed down the pathway. "I saw a movement on that trail and a spot of white, like an animal. Let's walk that way and check." He whistled as they made their way down the rough side trail through scrub and trees.

"Hey, dog, if you're lost, your rescue group is here," he called.

Burke giggled. "I doubt he'll understand your message."

"Well, if we sound friendly, maybe he'll come out."

"We could get out some food and water to attract him. I put two small tin pans in your pack and …"

"Look, there he is." Waylon interrupted her.

Burke spotted the dog, too, in a small clearing not far away. He backed away as they came closer and began to growl.

Waylon put an arm out to stop Burke, who followed behind him. "Don't go further. I think I know why the dog's growling. I see a lump of clothing or something off the trail by the brush." He moved a little closer, talking to the dog as he did.

"Oh, mercy, Waylon," Burke exclaimed. "I see a leg and shoe sticking out from under the brush, too."

Waylon sighed. "It looks like we may have found the dog's owner as well as the dog."

"Do you think the dog will let us look closer?"

"Maybe. Get some food and water out for him, and talk real sweet to him. I'll see if I can move closer while he's eating." Waylon took off his backpack and handed it to Burke. "Who knows how long the dog's been out here. He looks dirty, but not thin."

She squatted on the ground to open the backpack and got out the food and water they'd brought, putting both into the small tin pans. "Look what I brought you, sweet boy," she crooned to the dog. "It looks like something sad has happened to your owner, but we're friends coming to help you. Don't be afraid."

Burke held out a hand toward the dog as she talked so he could move closer to sniff it. Drawn by the smell of food, he gradually edged forward.

"I think the dog's growl is a protective one, but be watchful getting too close to him," Waylon said. "A dog that's upset or scared might bite or attack."

After edging closer to Burke, the dog began eating the food.

"Looks like he's hungry and he seems friendly if scared," Burke said, continuing to talk in a soothing tone to the big white dog. "He's wearing a collar and a tag. That may help us." She looked toward Waylon. "I assume the body is a dead body."

"I'd say so. Let me move in closer to check. If the dog gets aggressive, let me know, and I'll move back."

The white dog looked up to watch Waylon for a moment as he moved nearer the body, but then resumed eating the food. He also let Burke pet him as he did and he began to wag his tail a little.

Glancing toward Waylon, Burke saw him wince as he squatted near the body. "It's a woman, Burke, and it looks like she's been murdered and more. Don't come and look. It's not a pretty sight. I'm calling Lonnie right now." He pulled out his cell phone and made the call.

"He'll get some of his officers and be on his way soon," Waylon said, putting his phone in his back pocket again. "I told him we'd walk out to the beach to watch for him so we can bring him back to this spot again."

"What a sorrow," Burke said. "Do you think we can get the dog to go with us?"

"Let's put the leash on him and see if he'll walk out with us. Maybe you can take a few handfuls of kibble along to lure him. I'd hate to leave him here, and once the police come it might upset him further to see more strangers showing up. He might run deeper into the island."

"Do you think the dog saw what happened?" she asked, looking around. "And what in the world was this dog doing here with that woman, whether she came willingly or not? It doesn't make sense."

"None of this has made sense," Waylon said, coming back to load the backpack and strap it over his shoulders again.

CHAPTER 22

As Waylon and Burke walked back to the little campground with the fire pit they'd found earlier, they were both startled by a man walking into the clearing on the trail from the beach.

Brown-haired with a short beard, he wore boots, jeans and an olive drab fishing vest over a faded shirt. Surprised to see them, too, he paused at first and then smiled.

"Hey," he said in a friendly voice. "It's seldom I run into anyone else around here, and I see you found my dog."

Waylon watched him, sizing him up.

"Did you guys come over to explore a little? I like to come here to fish and to camp." He gestured around the campground area.

"Do you have a permit to camp?" Burke asked.

"I don't see that's any of your business," the man snapped.

He frowned at Burke, and Waylon moved slightly to stand in front of her and the dog.

The man glanced toward the dog. "My dog took off on me the other day when I camped a night here. I was scheduled to work the next morning so I couldn't come back to look for him until now. I've got my boat pulled up at the beach though. I'll just take the dog and be on my way."

As he moved closer, the dog began to growl.

"A dog doesn't usually growl at his owner," Waylon commented, keeping a close watch on the man.

"Whatever my dog does or doesn't do, that ain't your concern either."

"Waylon, I don't think we should let this man take the dog," Burke put in. "Especially with …." She glanced back down the path behind her, wisely not saying more.

The man gave a low chuckle. "Looks like you two walked yourself into a real big problem today." He pulled a knife out of his belt, making Burke gasp.

The dog growled again as the man moved a little closer to them.

"I don't like people prowling around in my business, sticking their noses into things none of their concern."

In a calm voice, Waylon said, "I think it would be to your advantage to let us and the dog leave. To my way of thinking you have enough problems and potential questions to answer."

"You think so?" the man asked in a nasty tone, slashing out with the knife a little toward Waylon.

"Burke, why don't you walk around me to the right, take the dog and head down to the boat." He readied himself to fight if needed.

"I don't think so." The man pulled a gun out of the back of his jeans then, stopping Burke in her tracks.

A little frisson of fear dashed up Waylon's spine then. The demented look on the man's face worried him plus the way he waved the gun and knife around.

Waylon felt Burke move up close against his side, heard her breathing quicken.

"It's good to see a little healthy fear." The man sent a nasty, satisfied grin her way and then turned toward Waylon. "You might want to throw your knife off to the side now, mister. Funny how knives scare women but it often takes a gun to stir up fear in a man."

The man's eyes moved to Burke, seeming pleased to see the worry in her eyes. "You sure got pretty long legs, missy. I like pretty long legs in a woman."

Trying to divert the man and buy time, Waylon asked, "How did you come to know Otter Island so well? It's a remote, mostly wilderness area that most people don't visit."

"My Daddy used to bring me to the island and to other remote spots to help make a man of me. Sometimes he left me overnight." His voice took on a sick edge then. "You'd have thought my mama might have worried about that, me being nothing but a kid, but she never did. All she cared about were her little dogs. She worried more if my Daddy hit one of them than if he hit me or her. Daddy said women weren't good for anything but satisfying a man's needs and that even then a man sometimes had to make them do what they were meant to do."

Waylon heard Burke make an anxious choking sound, and he saw her reach down to put a comforting hand on the dog as the man moved closer, brandishing the knife and the gun.

"See there?" he said to Waylon. "She's worrying more about the dang dog than you, not seeming to realize I mean to shoot you and then knife her up good before shooting the dog. I regret it a little, but you two caused your own problems getting involved in what you shouldn't have today. What the heck brought you over here?"

"A man staying at the inn that my family owns saw the dog," Burke said with surprising spunk. "We came to see if we could rescue him."

"I'd have killed the dang dog the other night if he hadn't run off. I came back with my gun today to find him. You can't leave witnesses to things you need to see done, even dogs."

"Killing people or dogs doesn't need to be done." Burke spit back the words.

"You'll be wishing you hadn't smarted off to me so much, girl," the man snapped back, edging closer, waving the knife.

Waylon saw the anger building in the man. He knew he was sick deep into his heart, too. It didn't seem likely Lonnie and his deputy would arrive in time to be of any help in this situation, so he kept watching for a time when he could move in to attack and disarm the man. Karate training in the Navy had taught him how to take a weapon from a man but Waylon needed the right moment to make his move. Too much was at stake to err even a little bit.

The dog was growling more now as the man's voice rose.

"I think I'll kill this dog right now. I'm tired of hearing him growl at me." He started forward pointing the gun toward the dog but the dog, no fool, lunged at him, clamping onto his arm with his teeth, causing the shot to fire sideways, the gun falling from the man's hand. Waylon moved in quickly then to bend back the man's other arm, disarming him of the knife, and then felling him to the ground, turning him over to get his hands behind him.

"Burke, kick that knife far off to the side and get the rope out of the backpack so I can tie this man up. Hold the gun on him, too, while I do it. Can you do that?"

"Yes." She turned quickly to kick the knife away and to retrieve the gun. While keeping it focused on the man Waylon held down, she dug out the rope from the backpack to pass to him.

The man struggled and cursed, but Waylon had a firm knee in his back and pulled back on his arms as needed to keep him confined until he could secure him with the rope.

As he worked to tie up the man, he heard Burke praising the dog. "Good dog. You're a fine dog; your owner would be proud of you."

Just as Waylon got the man tied, they heard Lonnie's voice. "Hey, Waylon. Where are you?" he called. "Are you all right?"

Burke ran toward the path leading to the campsite to call out to Lonnie, helping him find the way to them.

Lonnie strode in to the clearing a few moments later with three other officers, including Ben Sutherland, the deputy they'd met at the Deveaux Bank. Lonnie pulled his gun as soon as he saw Waylon still wrestling to hold the man with his face to the ground.

"Get over there and restrain that man," Lonnie called to the officers, who were already moving in with handcuffs and more secure restraints.

"Who the dickens is this man and what's going on, Waylon?"

He stood, grateful to give the man over to the police officers. "I called you about coming to look for a lost dog and finding a woman's body in the woods. While you were on your way over to see about the woman, the killer came back to find the dog that had been with her and he ran into us. It's been an ugly scene."

"He's lying to you," the main tried to claim. "That's my dang dog, and this man attacked me with no cause."

Burke stood, crossing her arms, shivering even in the heat. "Lonnie, the man babbled away about killing the woman we found and the others, too. I think this is the man you've been looking for."

"Well, that's a high point to this mess but I'm sorry you had to deal with him and go through this." Lonnie eyed the gun and knives to the side. "Anybody hurt?"

"I got a knick from the knife and a few bruises, but nothing more," Waylon said. "I'll be fine, with credit going to the dog, who decided he didn't like this man or the idea of him shooting him. He attacked the man when he pointed his gun at him, gave me the chance I needed to move in." Waylon squatted to reach a hand toward the dog, petting and praising him. "He's got pluck, this one."

Waylon stood then to take Burke in his arms, who'd started to cry now that her adrenalin surge had passed.

"He could have killed us," she cried, leaning against his chest.

"But he didn't and we're okay." Waylon smoothed a hand over her hair and patted her back.

She looked up at him after a moment. "How did you learn to disarm a man and take him down to the ground like you did? It happened in only a flash."

"It was defense training I got in the military. I was glad to know how to use it today. I'd been watching for the right moment when the man was distracted to move in." He pulled Burke closer to hold and calm her. "It was the only chance we had, even with the dog helping. It might not have worked either, but I'm grateful it did."

Lonnie interrupted. "What can you two tell me before I let my officers take this man in? They're going to drive him back over to Edisto in that skiff of his anchored out by yours. They already found the keys on him. Ben and I will follow in our boat after I check things out here. Will you two be okay to drive your craft back to the inn or do I need to call for more help?"

"I'll be fine to boat back," Waylon said, watching the two officers take the prisoner away, the man still angry and spluttering denials and explanations.

After they left, Lonnie propped a foot on the fire pit, asking them questions about all that happened while Ben walked around looking for evidence. Then Waylon walked with them to where they'd found the woman while Burke sat on a big log, the white dog leaning his head against her knee.

When they returned, Lonnie said, "That's all I need from you right now. I'll get a team out here soon to follow up, retrieve the body, and check for any other evidence." He glanced toward the dog. "What about the dog? You want me to take him in with us?"

"There might be a family eager to get him back," Ben added.

"Let us take him for now," Burke said. "He's been through enough already and he's realized we're friends."

Lonnie glanced at Waylon for confirmation.

He nodded. "Yeah, let us take him. I'll get my brother-in-law Don Nagel, the vet on the highway in Edisto, to come check him. His tags may help locate an owner. I'll call you if we learn anything and you call me if you find out if anyone is wanting to claim him and pick him up."

"Sounds like a plan. We've got enough to deal with already." His eyes moved from Waylon to Burke. "I'm sorry you two ran into this, while just planning to check on a lost dog, but I have to say it's turned out to be a blessing to find this killer." Lonnie glanced back toward the side path. "I hate that another life was lost before we apprehended the man though. My officers found a driver's license and identification on him. We'll know a little more about the man soon."

"Will you come and share with us what you learn?" Waylon asked.

"I can't guarantee it will be tonight with all that's happened and with the legwork, checks, calls, and paperwork still to do, but I'll come by when I can." He reached out a hand to Waylon. "This is the second time you two have helped in this investigation."

"You showed good sense and resourcefulness both times, too,"

Ben added. "Lonnie and I thank you."

"We thank you both for coming when you did," Burke said, standing and smiling at them. "We'll all sleep better tonight knowing this matter is finally resolved."

Waylon and Burke were both quiet on the trip back to the island, probably experiencing a little after shock. Burke leaned her head against Waylon's shoulder most of the way back, the dog curled at her feet.

At the marina, Waylon called Don to see if he could boat down to check the dog and then he called Etta to fill her in, letting Burke rest on the sofa.

After Don pronounced the dog all right, health-wise, Waylon and Burke gave him a good bath, after his time in the wild, which he seemed grateful for and then fed him some more dog food, while they ate their own dinner. Novaleigh had sent Clifford to bring them dinner from the inn and it felt good to sit quietly on the porch to eat, listening to the night frogs tuning up in the marsh grasses by the creek and to a mockingbird in a big oak beside the house serenading them with a medley of bird songs.

"I think I'm still in a state of shock," Burke said quietly a little later when they'd moved to sit together on an old glider.

"We had a really close call," Waylon agreed. "Makes it all the sweeter to realize we're both fine and well. With someone sick and demented like that, you never know what they might do and when."

"How sad he took another life, though. At first he seemed like a normal person when he walked into the campground, friendly and smiling." She sighed. "But he was suspicious of us from the first and it didn't take long for him to feel threatened and grow nasty."

Waylon nodded. "As Lila said, God was watching over us."

"Yes, and that was a brave thing for the dog to do, don't you think?"

"It provided a good distraction so I could move in and disarm the man, but we were blessed, too, the gunshot didn't hit either of us when the man fired that wild bullet." He rubbed his neck. "That could have gone bad."

The dog looked up, seeming to know they were talking about him, and wagged his tail.

Burke smiled. "This dog's been following you around all evening. He likes you, Waylon. If no one claims him, will you keep him?"

Waylon reached down to scratch the dog's ears. "I've been calling him Patton, after the military combat general, instrumental in helping to defeat the Germans and saving many lives."

"He seems to like that name, too. He just perked up his ears when he heard you say Patton."

Waylon stretched an arm around her shoulders. "If I remember right, your mother has a strong 'No Pets' rule here at the island. I doubt she'd be supportive of me keeping a dog."

"As I told mother, when she and my sisters came down to check on us earlier, this dog all but saved our lives and helped to catch a criminal who was threatening our Lowcountry area. I have a feeling she might make an exception for Patton."

"You think so?" He grinned.

"I do, and Boonie likes Patton. He came with Mother to hear our story earlier and he frisked around happily with Patton. You saw them. I think Boonie would be thrilled to have a dog friend."

"What about Milo?" Waylon asked with a smirk.

"Milo is pretty settled in his dislike for dogs in general, despite Boonie's efforts to change his mind. I think Patton will be smart enough to keep a respectful distance as well."

Burke looked out the window toward the beach. "We could walk the dogs together on our evening walks, although we might want to use leashes for a time—at least until Patton is well trained."

"You're making plans that may come to nothing."

"Why? We know the woman was a divorcee and lived alone, and so far Lonnie hasn't turned up anyone wanting Patton," Burke argued.

"We'll see. Don is doing some checking at the office tomorrow. Lonnie is doing more research, too. Don't get too attached. Patton may have people of his own. He's a great dog, smart, personable, and well mannered. I'm sure anyone who owned him would want him back."

She snuggled closer to him. "Gosh, I'm glad we're safe and well. I was so afraid. We already knew what that man was capable of." Burke shuddered. "I believe he would have killed you and then me. He seemed to have no remorse for the other killings."

"Yeah, he was a sick one. Remember he talked about his father leaving him by himself as a small boy on remote islands, like Otter, even overnight to make a man of him. He seemed to focus his anger though on his mother who didn't try to protect him, who worried more about her dogs getting hurt than him."

"I remember that talk. How sad the things some people do to children." She sat quietly for a few minutes. "Do you think he might have been getting even with his mother, hurting women fond of dogs? I just remembered they found a dead dog with the first woman at the Deveaux Bank. Do you remember that?"

"I do. With a sick, twisted mind anything is possible. Perhaps Lonnie will learn more and share with us later what they find."

He changed the subject then, hoping to move Burke's thoughts in a new direction. "How is Maggie Bouls working out taking Rita Jean's place?"

Burke crossed her legs, leaning back to relax. "She's doing a fabulous job. She might leave a few dust bunnies in a corner or a smudge on a mirror, but she's such a delight to have around that it's easy to overlook. I visited with Rita Jean the other day, took her some books to read. She's cross and irritable at being laid up, worried Maggie isn't keeping up the work as she'd like."

"Henry hasn't had it easy dealing with Rita Jean either. She hates going to physical therapy, and Henry says World War II breaks out every time he makes her go."

He felt glad to hear Burke laugh and the rest of their evening passed pleasantly.

The next morning after breakfast, Waylon was sweeping out the garage by the dock and pavilion, where the golf carts and tram were kept, when he saw Lonnie Culler's police boat pull up. He waved as Lonnie tied off his boat and jumped onto the dock.

"Got a minute?"

"Sure. I'll even make a pot of coffee."

Lonnie glanced at his watch. "Well, I didn't get a second cup this morning with all that's going on, so I'll take you up on that."

He trailed Waylon to the lodge and the two men wandered into the kitchen, Lonnie settling into a chair at the table by the back window.

"You're in luck," Waylon said. "Novaleigh made what she calls Apple Pie Bread for the breakfast buffet at the inn this morning, and she gave me an extra loaf to bring home." He cut a couple of pieces of the loaf for them after starting the coffee.

"Man, you got a sweet deal here with all these free meals and women cooking for you."

"Maybe you need to find a wife and get married."

"I'm to the point where I wouldn't mind that. I enjoyed time with you and Burke the other night." He looked out the window. "It's been good having you back home. I enjoyed the day we spent fishing a couple of weeks ago."

"We'll do it again soon," Waylon said, putting half-and-half creamer and sugar on the table.

A few minutes later, when the coffee finished, Waylon poured two mugs out for them and sat down across from Lonnie.

His friend drank a little coffee while it was good and hot, and then said, "Well, I came to tell you about the man. His name is Denny Brett Eldrege. He lives in Meggett on Yonges Island, in the house he grew up in with his parents. They both passed some time ago. He works in the ship repairs services department at Metal Trades, Inc. on Highway 165 as a welder. From everything I've heard, he's reliable at work, if somewhat a loner in his ways. He's advanced in his company, gotten a certificate at a welding program, has a few friends he fishes and hunts with and shares a beer with down at the local bar. On the surface, a good citizen and a good person."

"So he was one of those people who had a second hidden side or something?"

"That's about it. By asking a lot of questions of neighbors and a few relatives we tracked down, Denny's family life wasn't ideal—cruel father with no respect for his wife, and a neglectful, abusive mother. The psychologist who talked to Denny said his past probably created a repressed anger and hatred for women, with a desire to humiliate and hurt them, taught to him in part by his father. He's sick enough in his mind to think the women somehow deserved abuse and murder. I'll leave the doctors to come up with words to explain that. They'll be a trial in time and whatever comes of it will put him away somewhere for a long time."

Waylon drank his coffee thinking about that.

"There are some sick people out there in this world and some purely evil and bad people, too," Lonnie added.

"Well, I'm glad for the information you brought me. I'll share it with the others." Waylon ate the last bite of his apple bread. "What about the dog?"

"Well, now that's an odd linked story." Lonnie looked down at Patton, curled up on the floor. "See, Denny met all these women inadvertently through the Edisto Canine Rescue. When he met a woman who volunteered with the rescue business and took in foster dogs, his mind would target them. He never had a chance to get even with his mother, so he got even with these women—living on their own and more vulnerable."

"Didn't the women see, after a time, that he wasn't quite right?"

"Evidently not. He'd build a little relationship with them, then lure them with a big sob story about seeing a poor dog that needed rescue, sometimes a dog they were already connected with, and he'd convince them to go with him to rescue the dog. Once he got them off at some isolated spot, he turned on them."

"And sometimes turned on the dog, too."

"If there even was one. Sometimes he'd just lie. But other times an actual dog would get involved. Denny didn't feel any more remorse killing a dog than a woman. That's where your friend Patton came in. The last woman, Marcy Brackman, lived near Bay Creek Park and worked for Pressley's at the Marina on Dockside

Road. Folks at the restaurant, once shown pictures of Denny, remember him coming in a lot, talking to Marcy. She worked as a volunteer at the Canine Rescue. Patton was one of their rescue dogs, found on Edisto. Nobody knows his story, since dogs can't tell you a lot about their past, but he was real smart. The rescue center said Marcy loved him, was thinking of adopting him. But one day someone broke in to the rescue property and took the dog. It really grieved her."

"So when Denny went to tell her he thought he'd seen Patton on Otter Island, she went right off with him."

"That's how he worked it." Lonnie looked at his watch. "I need to get back to the office." He looked down at the dog. "You can take the dog back to the rescue center. They said they'd take him, or you can keep him."

Waylon grinned as Lonnie walked back outside with him. "Somehow, it seems like a dog that nearly saved your life ought to be given a home. If I can talk Etta into it, I'll keep him."

"Well, let the rescue center know if you do. They have his shot records and stuff. They said he's also micro-chipped. They'll want to know if you take him in."

"I'll see what I can do. Thanks for coming by, Lonnie."

His friend grinned at him. "Invite me again sometime when Burke's cooking something special one night."

"I'll do that." Waylon went back inside to clean up the kitchen and then leaned over to pet the big white lab's head. "Looks like we're going to partner up, friend. It'll be good to have my own dog again."

CHAPTER 23

Burke found herself in an odd mood over the next days, contemplating life more than normal for her. Usually the busyness of her life kept her days full with little time for moodiness and it wasn't in her disposition to brood or overly reflect on life. Frankly, she'd always seen giving in to emotions like that as a weakness—and one she didn't admire.

On Monday after a busy weekend, with new guests coming and going at the inn, plus her tours on Friday and Saturday, and church with family on Sunday, Burke finally found a few moments to get off to herself.

Her usual Monday routine was to clean the lighthouse after the weekend, and when she finished that task she climbed back up the stairs to the high gallery room to record notes in the journal at the old keeper's desk. Deciding to indulge herself after she finished, Burke settled down on the cushioned bench against the wall with a book to read.

Waylon found her there a short time later. "I had a feeling I might find you here. You often come here on Mondays after you finish cleaning the light. Are there any tasks left I need to do?"

"No," she answered, studying him.

"I took time today to clean the ferry, after my morning run taking visitors to the landing. I washed and scrubbed it down. It looks better."

"Things always look better when clean."

He sat down beside her. "What are you reading?"

"An old book about women lighthouse keepers. Their stories amaze me. In the 1800s to 1900s one hundred and twenty-two women were appointed as lighthouse keepers in their own name. Many took over the job from their fathers or husbands and the work was harsh and often dangerous. Storms and hurricanes battered and often destroyed their homes and property. Far from medical help, many died or lost husbands or children from injury or illness, and explosions from the fuels and oils, used in keeping the light burning, brought a constant danger of fires."

She opened the book to show him some pictures of early women keepers. "Look at the clothing their times demanded they wear—these layers of petticoats and long skirts and these button-up boots. I can't imagine how they managed."

Burke pointed to another photo. "This is Kate Moore. She started assisting her father as keeper at the Black Rock Harbor Light Station in Connecticut when only twelve years old. Due to his ill health she took over his work and was keeper for fifty-four years. She saved at least twenty-one lives and lived alone at the Light until she was eighty-three years old. After she retired, she lived on to be 105 years old."

She ran a finger over a picture of the lighthouse. "Look at this place. It sat out on a rocky, desolate island—even more remote in the 1800s than it is now."

A streak of lightning with a loud rumble of thunder behind it made her jump.

Waylon smiled. "That was the other reason I came to find you. A storm is moving in."

She glanced toward the window to see rain now pouring down outside. "I'd say already moved in might be the more accurate term now. It's really pouring rain out there."

"Who's that?" Waylon asked, pointing to another photo in the book.

"That's Abbie Grant who helped her father and then her husband to keep Matinicus Rock Light Station in Maine before she became the keeper herself."

She looked at a winter shot of the old lighthouse. "Can you imagine what it must have been like caring for that lighthouse in Maine's severe winters with ice and cold, freezing rain and snows? Sometimes they couldn't get supplies they needed and they did dangerous rescues in inclement weather. Abbie did rescues at sixteen in nothing but an old lighthouse rowboat. She wrote that she wondered if the care of the lighthouse would follow her soul after it left her body."

"That's a little morbid." He looked at her with soft, concerned eyes. "You don't feel that way about keeping the Light here, do you? That it's a burden you wish you could step away from?"

"No, I love it with all my heart," she replied. "But when I read stories like these, I'm grateful for all the changes and progress made that make my life so much easier than what these women knew."

He sat with her in the quiet for a few minutes as the storm raged outside, lightning flashing across the sky, the wind blowing the rain against the windows.

Burke glanced down at the book before putting it aside. "They were so alone, these women. I don't want that life."

Waylon moved closer to her. "You won't have it. Don't let that be a worry for you." He kissed her lightly and then pulled her closer, deepening the kiss, running his hands through her hair, behind her neck, the feel and scent so sweet and soothing.

Burke felt her heartbeat kick up, her breathing quicken, and she pulled back to grab the front of Waylon's shirt. "I don't want to wait anymore, Waylon. I want to know love in every way."

He closed his eyes. "Burke, I promised my dad, your mom, even your father at the cemetery, that we'd wait, that I wouldn't take advantage of you until we married. I gave my word."

She moved closer to him, running her hands over his face, down his arms, then kissing him again. "Ever since we faced that killer at Otter Island, I've realized how precious each day is. I could have lost you. We both might have died there, and I'd never have known what it's like to really love you, to be one with you."

Waylon groaned. "You're killing me, Burke. Surely you know

how much I want to be with you. I lie in my bed every night and think about you, look forward to being with you and loving you."

"So do I," she whispered. "So why are we waiting?"

He winced, closing his eyes again.

"Waylon, why do we need to wait any longer? Let's get married now."

"Now?" He opened his eyes in surprise.

"I don't see why we need to wait. You told me if it got hard we could just get married."

He grinned at her. "I did say that."

"Didn't you mean it?"

"Well, yeah, but your mother and mine are working on these wedding plans already for August. We moved the date back once already, too."

"So? Whose wedding is it, theirs or ours?"

He looked at her, a little puzzled. "Is it only the scare at Otter Island that brought this on?"

She moved to settle herself closer against him and to trace her fingers over his face. "I admit it brought my feelings to a head and it made me wonder why we needed to wait. When you asked me to marry you and to get engaged, you questioned why we needed to wait to get engaged when we were sure. Do you remember saying that? Are you still sure?"

"How can you ask me that?" He traced his fingers down her arms, kissed her eyelids and cheeks, then moved his lips to her mouth.

Burke gave herself to the moment as he did, letting loose the emotions she often reined in. She pulled away after a time though, sensing Waylon was slipping over the edge of remembering and honoring any promises he'd made to anyone.

She studied him, breathing hard, trying to pull himself together, and she smiled. "Deveaux women can be rather passionate women. Do you think you can handle that?"

"You're really teasing me," he said, but he said it with a grin.

"I'm trying to get you to say we can get married now."

He shifted away from her slightly. "You really are serious, aren't you?"

"Totally and absolutely."

"Very well. When would you like to do this Now wedding? This afternoon, this evening, tomorrow? It might have to be with a justice of the peace or a wedding officiate. Or possibly with a minister who wouldn't mind being impulsive."

She grinned at him. "I like the idea of being impulsive and of crawling into that big bed with you at the lodge afterward. I've slept in a little twin bed all my life. I've always wanted to sleep in a big king-sized bed."

Waylon got up to go look out the window at the rain. "You don't need to keep convincing me and painting pictures in my mind, Burke. Give me a break. I'm saying yes to whenever and whatever you want."

She giggled. "Sorry. I'm just eager."

He shook his head. "Mercy."

Burke put her book away on a nearby shelf, thinking.

"Mother and my sisters, and your family, would be upset with us if we simply jumped into your boat and took off somewhere to get married today—appealing as that idea is. I'm thinking we could simply have something small right here on the island. Maybe tomorrow." She went to join him at the window where the rain had quit now, the storm moving out to sea.

She pulled him out the door to the gallery's balcony to point far below them. "See that big white pavilion? That would be an awesome place for a small wedding. We can move out the picnic tables, use the benches and some chairs to create a little chapel feeling, and we can get the old podium from the storage building to put in the front for the officiate. There would be room for our close family, the staff here at the island, and maybe a few friends who could manage a last minute announcement."

He chuckled. "Last minute is right. Any ideas for an officiate?"

"We could ask Wey Camp, the rector at our church at Trinity, or Dean Anderson, the chaplain at St Christopher's Camp who lives in our condo at the Bohicket Marina. I'll bet one of them could work something out to come over."

They moved back inside again. "I'd already planned to wear my Grandmother Eugenia's wedding dress, a pretty but simple white gown. I was named after her, you know."

"Yes. Eugenia Burke," he said.

"I assume you own a nice dark suit," she continued.

He nodded.

"Clifford can pick some flowers for me to tie a ribbon on and carry, and he can bring two of those flowering pots over to put on either side of the podium. That's all we really need."

"Do you think your mother will agree?"

Burke considered it. "She'll probably be upset again, like she was when we announced our engagement."

He'd settled into an old chair across the small room from her now instead of beside her, but he smiled at her with warmth. "I told you before I didn't need a long time to know you're the one I want to spend my life with. That's still true, and I love you more and more every day, Burke. I told you, also, that if we found it hard to wait, we could marry sooner. I meant that, too. It's been hard for me to wait every day. I'm rather pleased to find that true for you, too."

She hid a smirk. "Well, I guess our developing friendship has developed more quickly than we expected."

"I rather think that's a fine thing." He chuckled a little at his thoughts. "I guess we need to share your plans right away." He glanced at his watch. "You want to drop our bomb when all your family is eating on the screened porch as usual tonight?"

She made a face. "I guess we'd better."

"If it's tomorrow, Burke, we can hardly wait to announce it at a later time." He laughed. "After dinner we can make calls to Wey Camp and Dean Anderson to see which is available—or start hunting for another officiate. We can also start setting up the pavilion. Clifford and Henry might help with that." He hesitated. "You got any ideas for a honeymoon trip?"

Burke sighed. "It would be a hardship on everyone if we took off right now with the Memorial Day Weekend coming up and summer starting. How about if we take a trip in the fall instead? I'd love to go back to the Millhouse Resort outside Gatlinburg in the Smoky Mountains where Mother and Daddy took us when we were kids. There's a beautiful, gracious old lodge there, a wonderful dining room with a fabulous chef, mountain views out the windows, trails nearby to hike, and Gatlinburg and its shops to explore not far away. I always loved it there, such a change from our world here at the coast."

"You won't be disappointed to wait to go?"

She leaned toward him to whisper. "You know I already told you I've had fantasies for months about climbing into that big bed with you at the lodge, being alone with you there…"

"Enough." He stopped her, holding up a hand. "We'll honeymoon well enough at the lodge for now."

"I certainly hope so." She sent him a saucy grin.

He reached across to take her hand. "Be assured of it, Burke. I'll make you happy. It's all I've ever wanted to do since I came back and saw you again for the first time on that ladder at the lodge."

Waylon got up from his chair then. "I need to go get the ferry to do the four o'clock afternoon pickup at the Landing. A number of the guests went to Charleston to check out the tourist attractions today, and they'll be watching for me to bring them back to the inn. When I get back, I have some work to do, but I'll see you at dinner with the family at six."

Burke rolled her eyes, dreading it.

He came over and gave her a quick kiss. "Let me take the lead in telling everyone, okay?" He winked at her. "You caught me off guard with this today but the more I think about it, the more I like the idea. You can consider me well convinced."

Burke knew she blushed as his eyes moved over her with an intimate look. When he left, she sat for a moment, simply thinking. She'd soon be Mrs. Waylon Arthur Jenkins. How about that?

Later that evening, Burke smiled a secret smile at Waylon as she came into the family dining area on the large screened porch behind the family wing. The room was really what you might call an Arizona Room. Windows could close over the screens and a built-in heating unit made the room cozy even in winter. With Burke's sisters and the three children home, they needed the extra space at the porch table to seat them all since the smaller family table inside the family wing apartment only seated six. It was fun having so many to talk and laugh together with over their meals now.

Waylon waited to drop his news until the children ran outside in the yard to play croquet again, while the adults stayed behind, lingering over dessert and coffee.

In a lull in the conversation, he said, "Burke and I have decided to move the wedding date up again."

All eyes turned to him.

"What?" Etta asked. "You've already moved the date back once."

"We want to move it back again. Actually, you might say we need to move it back again." He rubbed his neck, showing his discomfort with this subject to a group of only women.

Gwen giggled.

Etta lifted her chin and gave Waylon a disapproving look.

Burke jumped into the conversation then. "Mother, Waylon and I agreed back when we got engaged that if we began to find it hard spending so much time together and working together like we do, and wanting more, that we'd just get married sooner."

"I see," Etta replied. "And when did you decide this sooner date might be?"

"Actually, we thought tomorrow might be nice."

Celeste burst into laughter and spit her tea all over the table, mopping it up afterward while she and Gwen passed each other significant looks, trying not to both giggle out loud.

Etta looked stunned. "You thought tomorrow might be nice?" She said the words slowly in disbelief. "Are you serious?"

"You might remember Waylon and I always wanted only a small simple wedding with family and a few friends, so it really shouldn't be a problem. I thought it would be nice if we just got married in the white pavilion behind the lighthouse. If we move out the picnic tables, arrange the benches and some chairs like a little chapel, and bring out that podium in the storage room for an officiate, it should be perfect. I already have Grandmother Eugenia's dress and Waylon has a nice suit. I don't see what else we need."

Burke smiled around at them. "All my family are here right now instead of scattered, and Waylon's family are nearby."

"We're in the middle of a work week here," Etta argued.

"Mother, we're always in the middle of a work week. But if we set everything up tonight or in the morning, we can have the simple service we want at 2:00 and be through before 3:00. It won't disrupt the day's schedule except for the need to rearrange a few factors in the day."

Gwen laughed again. "Well, I guess Celeste and I won't need to keep looking for attendant dresses."

"I am simply beyond words here," Etta said.

Waylon leaned forward. "Burke and I could simply go to a little wedding chapel and have a ceremony there if it would cause less disruption."

Etta glared at him. "Are you trying to further provoke me, Waylon? That suggestion hardly makes me feel better. I truly believe the two of you are being rather selfish here."

"Whoa," Celeste put in. "I married Dillon that way. Actually I ran off and married Nolan that way, too. Gwen ran off with Alex and got married and then went straight to Little Rock with him. At least Burke and Waylon have come to you, Mother, to include you in their wedding and to include us as well."

Etta crossed her arms to glare at Celeste. "Are you trying to say you're supportive of this idea?"

"If it's what they want, then yes I am," Celeste answered. "Isn't that the most important thing, Mother?"

Burke passed Waylon a glance, trying to decide what to say next while her mother stewed and made no response at all.

Lila cleared her throat to draw their attention and then smiled around at them. "I have a lovely compromise idea."

Burke raised an eyebrow.

Lila gave her a sweet look in return. "I'd like to ask that you and Waylon wait just a few more days to help the family better arrange their schedules, moving the date to Sunday afternoon at 2:00 instead of tomorrow. You can still have it at the pavilion like you want. I saw earlier today that the weekend weather promises to be sunny and mild."

She paused, turning her eyes toward Waylon. "Waylon, your father and Uncle Dewey probably have boat tours set tomorrow that they can't change at this late date. Sally Ann's husband Don may have surgeries at the vet clinic and the boys are in school. It would disappoint them not to get to come. It would help the Boals and Georges to make arrangements to come, too. The inn is always quieter on Sundays."

She smiled around the table at them all again. "Don't you think that would be nice?"

Burke glanced at Waylon, realizing the two of them hadn't given as much thought to others' schedules in their planning. She nodded at him as he raised his eyebrows in question to her.

"Lila, I think that is an excellent compromise idea," he said. "Feeling eager, Burke and I didn't think too far out."

Gwen tried not to giggle again.

Etta frowned at her. "Gwendolyn Yvonne, your sense of humor leaves something to be desired."

As Celeste started to laugh, too, her eyes moved toward her also. "As does yours, Celeste Jardeen."

"Honestly, Mother, this is a perfect answer," Celeste put in. "It will give Gwen and me time to zip over to Charleston to pick up dresses. Gwen and I already fell in love with some pretty, casual sea blue sundresses, in stock, that will be perfect for an outdoor wedding. We were already thinking in terms of an outdoor service at Trinity, so this isn't much different an idea. With the date change, Gwen and I will have time to decorate the pavilion real pretty now, too. I'm good at things like that. So is Gwen, and Lila is wonderfully artistic. We'll do all the work, so there won't be any inconvenience to you."

"Come on, Mother. Get excited about this," Gwen put in. "We all know Waylon and Burke are right for each other. Like Waylon said, why should they wait? They're in love. Let them get married. Hug and kiss them and wish them happy."

"You might not know, but I learned to decorate cakes at the Community," Lila put in. "I'll help Novaleigh make a nice cake for the day. We have glass punch bowls, cups, plates and tablecloths in the storage closet that we use for the luncheon events and weddings we host here at the inn. We can set up a refreshment table, and let Waylon and Burke cut a wedding cake."

She glanced at Burke. "Who did you and Waylon plan to officiate the ceremony?"

"We thought we'd ask Wey Camp, the rector at Trinity, or Dean Anderson, who's the Chaplain at St. Christopher's."

Lila put a hand to her chin, thinking. "It might be short notice for Wey Camp but I think Dean would be pleased to come and marry you."

"He comes to eat with us at the inn often enough," Gwen said.

Etta lifted her chin. "Dean was one of your father's dearest friends. He is always welcome here."

"More reason to ask him," Celeste added.

Etta sighed. "I'm sure he would be touched to be asked."

Her eyes moved to where Waylon and Burke sat together. "Will you two be agreeable to this slight delay in your plans?"

Celeste passed them a mischievous look. "If a few more days are a problem Gwen and I can keep you both away from each other if necessary."

At Etta's shocked look, Gwen snorted and she and Celeste both burst into giggles.

Etta rapped her spoon on the table. "Would you two girls try to keep your minds on a higher plane?"

They all sat quietly for a few moments after that.

Finally, Etta cleared her throat. "Well, I guess we have a small wedding to plan for Sunday afternoon," she said with only a twinge of resignation in her voice. "Actually, now that I consider it, I rather like the idea of having the wedding here at the island. I think Lloyd would have liked that, too."

Waylon gave her a grateful smile. "Burke thought she might ask my dad to give her away. Would you feel all right about that, Etta?"

"Yes, and I know Lloyd would like that, too," she said after a minute, trying to keep her emotions in check. "I also think Lloyd would like for Dean to officiate. I'll call to ask him after dinner. Would that be okay with you?" She looked toward Burke.

"That would be nice, Mother. Thank you."

Gwen looked out the window to check on the children and then said, "If we're going to be your three attendants, Burke, then Waylon will need three groomsmen for balance. Have you thought who you might ask, Waylon?"

He shook his head. "I hadn't until now, but I'll ask Don and my two friends from school who live over on Johns Island."

"What color is your suit?" Celeste asked.

"Black." He started to say he'd bought it for the many funerals he'd attended in recent years but thought better of it, knowing it would remind Etta of Lloyd's funeral.

"Well, ask your friends to wear black suits, too, and white shirts," Celeste added. "Gwen and I will pick up some nice blue bowties to match our dresses. After the service and pictures, you can all shed the jackets. I don't think, with an outside May wedding, anyone needs to dress up too much."

"What will we do about music?" Etta asked.

"Novaleigh's mother Mimi Beryl Hutchinson taught me the piano," Celeste said. "I'm sure you remember that. She taught Novaleigh, too, and Novaleigh's daughter Vanessa. I went to visit with Mimi and Orvis one day last week. She still plays piano at her church. I'll bet she would love to play for the wedding, since she worked here for so many years, or I can get Vanessa to come over. She lives in Charleston now. We had lunch the other day."

"And how do you plan to get a piano out to that pavilion?"

"The piano in the family wing is small, Mother, and it rolls.

Henry and Clifford can roll it out on one of those trailers they load golf carts on behind Henry's Jeep, take it to the pavilion and bring it back later," Celeste answered. "That's a really big pavilion on the hill behind the lighthouse. There will be ample room for a piano toward the front, for any guests we plan to invite, and for a little reception table and a white reception tent. You know we've used that pavilion and the tent for other events."

"Everything will be nice, Mother," Gwen assured her. "Celeste, Lila, and I will work together on this."

Etta offered a strained smile. "Well, I guess I have a daughter getting married on Sunday."

"It's a happy event for us, Mother," Burke put in with a wistful smile her way. "Please be glad for us."

"I know it is, dear. It's simply sudden and my mind hasn't totally adjusted to the idea." She glanced around the table. "In my heart, I still see four little girls with pigtails and missing teeth. It's hard to realize you've all grown up on me."

CHAPTER 24

On Sunday at a little after one, Waylon climbed into his golf cart and started up the sandy lane along the coast. Lighthouse Road wound along South Creek and the North Edisto River before turning right to pass the Signal House and arriving at the island's high point at the tall lighthouse looking out across the Atlantic Ocean, the big, white pavilion behind it. Waylon's suit jacket lay across the seat beside him. He saw no reason to put it on until time for the wedding.

Seeing the red-and-white striped lighthouse ahead, it came to Waylon more fully that he was not only marrying Burke Deveaux today but taking on, with her and her mother Etta, the role of Lighthouse Keeper. Together, they would keep the historic lighthouse, now over two hundred years old, going strong, helping it to continue to light the way for ships and travelers on the sea. It was a life Waylon had dreamed of for a long time and he smiled to realize it would become a reality today. And that Burke, whom he'd loved for so long, would become his wife.

"I'm a very happy man today," he said to the lighthouse ahead, simply needing to say the words out loud.

The pavilion had been set up, in part, the day before, with the finishing touches completed this morning after breakfast. Celeste, Gwen, and Lila, with Henry, Clifford, and Calvin's help, had hung silky drapes inside the pavilion with flowers and ribbons at the points where the draperies met in the middle. Beside the pavilion, they'd set up one of the inn's white tents for the reception area.

As Waylon walked closer to the tent, after parking his golf cart, he spotted a big wedding cake, mints, nuts, and pick-up snacks spread across the tables for the guests to enjoy after the ceremony. Burke's sisters had carried their blue and white decorative theme into the tent, also, with vases of blue and white hydrangeas, dusty pink roses, and some sort of pretty greenery on all the tables.

"Doesn't everything look gorgeous?" Celeste asked, coming up beside him. "You look very handsome, too," she added, looking him over and straightening his blue bow tie.

"You look nice, as well," he said, his eyes moving over her simple blue sleeveless dress with its graceful V-neck and a swirly skirt from waist to knees. "Not as fancy as your usual clothes."

She grinned at him. "No, but this is Burke's wedding, not mine. Gwen and I kept that in mind when we went to Charleston to shop, and of course we had Lila along to temper us."

"Well, everything looks truly beautiful." He glanced around. "I know Burke will be pleased, as I am. It's exactly what we wanted."

"Let me put this boutonnière on your jacket. We can sit down on that bench in the shade for a minute while I pin it on. I could use a rest." She glanced at her watch. "Besides you're early."

"It's an old Naval habit. Our admiral always used to say that if you're not fifteen minutes early then you're five minutes late."

"Well, you're more than fifteen minutes early, but it gives me one less thing to worry about seeing you here already."

She took his jacket after they sat down and began to pin on the boutonnière. "I won't give you a sister lecture about taking good care of Burke. I can see every day how much you love her, how kind you are to her, even how you look at her." She glanced away with a sigh.

"I'm sorry you met so much sorrow and hurt with Dillon."

She gave him a small smile. "I am, too, but I had a sweet, good marriage with Nolan before. So I know how nice it can be to have a good man in your life. And you're a very good man, Waylon."

"Thank you." He glanced across the room to see Chase sitting in a chair by himself toward one corner of the pavilion.

"What's Chase doing over there by himself, looking mad?"

Celeste laughed. "He's in what Gwen calls Time-Out." She shrugged. "It's partly my fault. When we were in Charleston this week I bought him some of these silly novelty, gag toys in a shop we visited." She shrugged. "How was I to know he'd drop the ice cubes with fake bugs in them into the ice bin here and put a whoopee cushion under one of those quilts we spread over the wooden benches to make them more comfortable?"

Waylon grinned. "What happened?"

"As you can already see, some people are here early. A lady staying at the inn sat on the whoopee cushion, screamed and got really upset. And, of all the luck, Rita Jean poured out an early cup of punch to taste it, dropping in a few ice cubes from the bin and freaked out when she spotted a fly frozen in one of them."

"I guess we can be glad it didn't happen during the wedding." He looked around. "Where is Gwen anyway?'

"Rose spilled punch down the front of her dress when the lady screamed. Gwen took her back to the house to see if she could clean it up. Poor little Rose was crying up a storm. I bought the girls sweet little matching dresses for the wedding and family photos and they were so proud of them."

"You've been generous in a number of ways with this wedding."

Celeste finished his jacket and laid it neatly on the bench beside her. "I always feel it's good to spread your blessings around."

"I agree and I believe you'll be blessed back for it, too."

An elderly black woman settled herself at the piano then and began to play.

"Who's that woman?" Waylon asked.

"That's Novaleigh's mother, Mimi Hutchison. She was so thrilled when I asked her to come to play for the wedding. She's known Burke, and all of us girls, since we were born and she's watched us grow up."

Celeste frowned, after a moment, as the music grew a little lively. "We asked Ms Mimi to play a medley of hymns before the service, not having a lot of time to think about choosing music, then to play a processional as the wedding starts and to play the traditional wedding march for Burke." She winced as a chord crashed. "I guess we should have specified she select more sedate hymns."

Waylon laughed, watching the smiling woman play away with zeal and pleasure on the piano. "I think that hymn is "When The Role Is Called Up Yonder," if I remember right."

"Great," Celeste said. "Do you think I should speak to her?"

"Absolutely not. Whatever she plays will be fine." He looked around. "Besides, I think the music is perking everyone up, bringing a few smiles, too." He pointed toward a woman across the room. "That lady from the inn is tapping her foot and nodding her head."

"Oh, well, I guess you're right."

Seeing his groomsmen and a few friends and family arriving, Waylon excused himself to go say hello and to get ready for the service.

Celeste put a hand on his arm before he left. "Tell your Dad, Don and your groomsmen, to get their boutonnières off that table by the corner of the pavilion." She pointed toward it. "I can pin them on if they don't have someone to do it for them."

"I'll tell them," he said draping his jacket over his arm to head their way.

A short time after greeting his family, Mimi Hutchinson moved into playing "Leaning on the Everlasting Arms" and "In the Sweet By and By" in equally lively fashion and Waylon wondered if a little afternoon revival might break out.

He noticed Dean Anderson's surprised glance toward the piano as he came to speak to Waylon near the time for the service. Dean wore white vestments for the wedding, the first time Waylon had seen him in anything more formal than fishing clothes.

Dean had counseled with them Friday about the service and dropped by last night on Saturday, too, for a brief wedding rehearsal and a casual rehearsal dinner afterward at the lodge. He and Burke had made what many in South Carolina called a Frogmore Stew. They'd spread the Low Country Boil of fresh shrimp, corn, potatoes, and kielbasa on newspapers across a picnic table in the traditional coastal way, along with plenty of garlic bread, coleslaw, melted butter, and homemade cocktail sauce—a feast and a good time for all.

Now, Dean waved and tapped his watch, reminding Waylon of the time, and they moved to take their places at the front of the pavilion for the wedding service. Gratefully, Mimi moved with soft ease into Pachelbel's classic "Canon in D" for the processional as Waylon's three groomsmen walked Burke's sisters down the aisle. Then Mimi paused dramatically for a moment and, after a little fanfare, began "The Bridal Chorus-Wedding March" by Wagner.

Waylon then forgot to notice anything but Burke, walking slowly down the aisle with her arm tucked into his father's. She looked so beautiful.

He hadn't seen the heirloom dress of her grandmother's she planned to wear but it was lovely, V-necked with short loose sleeves that drifted over her arms, the entire dress in some sort of lacy material with embroidered flowers on it, dropping gently to the floor. Waylon seldom saw Burke in a dress and the sight really took his breath away. She looked like she'd stepped out of an old movie set, with the soft ivory white of the dress perfect for her, and a simple circlet of pearls over her hair, which she'd braided in an elegant way. She carried flowers, tied with a ribbon, and he saw flowers at the back of her hair, too.

Waylon wasn't an especially sentimental man but he felt a lump form in his throat as he watched her walk toward him. He knew, too, he'd always remember this moment and the way Burke looked, so happy and smiling, her eyes focused on him with such joy.

As the rector offered the words asking who gives the bride in marriage Waylon's dad answered, "The bride's mother and I do." He turned to smile at Etta, adding, "I stand in Burke's father, Lloyd Deveaux's, role with deep honor, assured he is watching this special moment with warm pleasure from up in heaven."

And then Burke was standing beside him, with that ginger vanilla scent she wore tickling his nose, the nearness of her moving his heart.

Dean led them through their vows, sweet moments to cherish, but as they turned to exchange rings, a scream from the back of the pavilion interrupted the service.

"There's something crawling over my foot," a woman from the inn shrieked, jumping up from her chair.

A few moments of chaos erupted afterward as people scrambled about, but then Waylon heard Chase's young voice. "It's only an old green garden snake." He held it up in his hand, causing more gasps all around him. "I don't know how it got in here."

"Well, take it out and toss it near the beach somewhere," he heard Gwen say. "And do it now, Chase."

"Okay." Chase headed calmly out a side path from the pavilion, carrying the small snake toward the beach, and then Dean laughed, settling everyone back down with ease to continue the service.

"It seems like snakes have been causing problems since Adam and Eve walked in the garden together," he joked.

Turning back to Waylon and Burke he grinned at them before leading them back to the exchange of rings, adding, "And as you offer your rings in warm love may no evil or division enter the garden of your lives or come between you."

A few snickers could be heard at those words, but they lightened the service, making it easier to go on before Dean's final words pronounced them man and wife at last.

With pleasure Waylon kissed his bride and led her down the aisle to a somewhat lively recessional pounded out by Mimi.

That evening and the next day others at the Deveaux Inn and on the island took over his and Burke's duties so they could have what Leah called a "honeys moon." The night and the next day were certainly a sweet time for them both, and on Tuesday evening, after settling back into a catch-up day at work, they took the dogs for a walk on their leashes along the beach.

"Boonie isn't very happy about the leash," Burke noted as they strolled along in the moonlight.

"Well, he's better trained than Patton, but we're working with him. Maybe in time, we'll feel safe enough to let Patton run free with Boonie."

"Patton seems really smart," Burke commented. "Even at the rescue center, they thought he'd probably had owners who worked with him. He never gave them any trouble, but they said he always disliked the sight of weapons."

"I can't say I'm sorry about that."

"Do you think he might have been a police dog?"

"I don't know. He's still a very young dog, but he might have been in training with someone. I guess we'll never know." Waylon spoke to the dog to heel, patting his side as he did, and Patton stopped pulling on the leash, dropping back to keep pace beside him.

"Good dog," Burke said. As Waylon praised him, too, Patton looked up hopefully for one of the training treats Waylon kept in his pocket. Seeing Boonie walking along neatly beside Burke, and eyeing the treats, he passed one to Burke for him, too.

She stopped to pick up a shell to study it as they walked along.

"I still can't believe all the funny things that happened at our wedding. I missed most of it since I was at Lila's until the ceremony was scheduled to begin."

"You missed a lot of fun," he teased, "like Mimi's revival playing, Chase's whoopee cushion scaring one of the guests from the inn, and Rita Jean turning up a glass of punch to taste it and seeing a fake ice cube, with a fly in it, staring right at her."

She giggled. "Rita Jean is still in a snit about that. Gwen had to speak with her about continuing to give Chase a difficult time over it and sending him a dirty look every time she saw him."

"I said something to her about that, also. The boy is only eight."

Burke dropped the small shell back to the sand. "Lila says poor little Rose is still embarrassed about spilling punch down the front of her new dress, too."

"I thought Gwen said it cleaned up all right."

"Mostly, but there's still a small tell-tale stain."

"That wouldn't have bothered you at that age."

She smiled at the words. "No, but Rose is more girly than I was. You know I was always more a tomboy type."

"I loved that about you and still do." He leaned over to kiss her cheek. "I'll never forget though how beautiful you looked in your Grandmother Eugenia's heirloom dress. It was lovely and perfect for you. I'm framing one of those wedding photos of you in that dress to put in our room."

She sent him a provocative smile. "I love those words *our room.* They conjure up such pleasant memories."

He kissed her again, this time a little longer and with more passion. "Remind me to create some more memories for you to remember later after our walk."

"Maybe you can help me wash my hair again," she said, running her hands through his dark hair and giving him another kiss. "I could wash yours, too, if you like."

"An excellent idea," he agreed. "I'm so glad we have that big shower stall."

"I certainly do like married life," Burke added as they walked along.

Waylon didn't reply with more than a wink and a smile, taking her hand in his as they strolled down the beach, the moonlight forming a silvery pathway of white over the water. His life was so good right now, with Burke by his side and peace within, that he hardly needed any words.

RECIPES from *Light the Way*

Waylon's Low Country Boil

2 ½ lb large shrimp (appx 2 dozen)
1 pkg (1lb) Kielbasa, sliced in chunks
3 oz (half container) Old Bay seasoning
3 lbs Yukon gold and baby red potatoes
4 onions quartered
6 ears corn, halved
4 lemons, halved
3 quarts water

Directions:
Bring onion, lemons and Old Bay seasoning to a boil in the 3 quarts of water. Add the potatoes and let cook for about 10 minutes, or longer, until getting tender. Add the Kielbasa sausage chunks and the corn halves. Boil for 10 more minutes. Last, add the shrimp and cook for an additional 3 minutes until shrimp turn pink. After cooking, strain off all the liquid from the pot. Spread the boil out on a newspaper lined table to serve outdoors or put in individual bowls.

Novaleigh's Apple Pie Bread

1 yellow cake mix
1 can apple pie filling, mashed
1 medium apple, chopped
1 cup self-rising flour
4 eggs, slightly beaten
1 Tbsp each cinnamon and sugar

Directions:
Whisk together cake mix, flour, sugar, and cinnamon. Add apple pie filling and eggs and stir mixture together well. Pour in 2 greased loaf pans. Sprinkle some additonal cinnamon and sugar mixture equally over top of each. Bake in 325-degree oven for 35 to 45 minutes.

Burke's South of the Border Casserole

- 1 lb ground beef or chuck
- ½ tsp garlic powder or salt
- 2 cups broken tortilla chips
- ½ cup sliced green onions
- 1 cup cheddar cheese, shredded
- 4 tsp chili powder
- 1 can (15 oz) chili beans
- 1 tomato, chopped
- 1 can (8oz) Hunt's tomato sauce
- 1 cup sour cream
- 2 Tbsp taco sauce
- Extra tortilla chips, unbroken

Directions:

Cook ground beef or chuck in skillet and then drain. Add tomato sauce, beans, taco sauce, chili powder, and garlic powder or garlic salt. Heat all to boil. Spread the 2 cups broken tortilla chips in an ungreased 12x8x2-inch baking dish. Pour the beef mixture over. Spread the sour cream evenly over the top. Sprinkle with chopped onions, chopped tomatoes, and then the cheese. Bake, uncovered, at 350-degrees for about 20-30 minutes. Arrange the additional chips around the edges of the casserole dish. Serve with shredded lettuce and extra taco sauce and tomatoes on the side.

Etta's Three-Bean Baked Beans

- 1 (16oz) can baked beans
- 1 (16oz) can kidney beans
- 1 (16oz) can pinto beans
- 1 (16oz) can tomatoes
- 1 green pepper, chopped
- 3 green onions, chopped
- 1 pkg sloppy joe mix
- ½ cup shredded cheddar cheese

Directions:

Drain kidney and pinto beans and put in 9x12 oven dish. Add undrained baked beans, undrained tomatoes, chopped onion, and sloppy joe seasoning mix. Sprinkle cheese over top. Bake at 350 degrees for 30-45 minutes until bubbling. Great for outdoor cookouts with burgers and hot dogs!

A Reading Group Guide

LIGHT THE WAY

Lin Stepp

About This Guide

The questions on the following pages are included to enhance your group's reading of Lin Stepp's *Light The Way*

DISCUSSION QUESTIONS

1. Burke Deveaux grew up at her family's inn beside the historic Deveaux Lighthouse. As the book begins, what loss has Burke recently faced? How has this impacted her and her mother and their business? A good neighbor and friend, Hal Jenkins, has been pitching in to help the family but comes to offer a better, more permanent answer. What is that offer? Why does Hal think this is a good solution for all?

2. Lighthouses come in many shapes, sizes, and heights, and you can still visit many lighthouses maintained by individuals, state parks, and other organizations. Where is the Deveaux Lighthouse located? What did you learn about the history of the lighthouse and inn? What color is the Deveaux Lighthouse and most of the buildings around the Lighthouse Station? This distinctive color is called a lighthouse's Day Mark and the distinctive pattern of the lighthouse's beam at night is its Light Signature. Do you remember the specific pattern of the Deveaux Lighthouse's nighttime Signature? Have you ever visited a lighthouse?

3. The Deveaux Lighthouse has been in the same family since the lighthouse was built in 1870. After the lighthouse was decommissioned, the old keeper's house was renovated into an inn to provide a business income for the family. Etta and Lloyd Deveaux, are the sixth generation to keep the Light. They have four daughters—Burke, Gwen, Celeste, and Lila, and this book is primarily Burke's story. What did you learn about Burke as the story unfolds? What does Burke look like? What are her strengths? Which of her other sisters has recently returned and why? As the book progresses Burke's other sisters also return.

What brings each of them back? Who first called them The Lighthouse Sisters?

4. The Jenkins family live a short distance up the North Edisto River from the lighthouse and operate the Jenkins Boat Landing, offering ferry runs to the lighthouse and other locations and a variety of different boating and fishing tours. Waylon Jenkins left home after high school to go first to college and then into the Navy. How long has he been gone? Why is he returning? Why does Waylon decide to come to work for the Deveaux family? What childhood background do Waylon and Burke share?

5. An attraction flares quickly between Waylon and Burke. You soon learn they've carried hidden feelings for each other for a long time. Why did neither of them acknowledge those feelings before? Do you think Lloyd Deveaux was wrong to discourage Waylon's attraction for Burke? Have you ever had anyone break up or interfere in one of your relationships or in a growing relationship of someone you know? Was the interference good or bad?

6. Watch Island, a fictitious part of Edisto Island, South Carolina, is separated from land on all sides by creeks, marshes, the North Edisto River, and the Atlantic Ocean. On the island are the Deveaux Inn and Lighthouse, a gift shop, a variety of historic structures, an old lodge, five cottages, two homes, a marina and dock, and various outbuildings and pavilions. Two other families live and work on the island besides the Deveaux family. Who are they? What part do Henry and Rita Jean Bouls play on the island? What roles do Clifford and Novaleigh George carry? What do you remember most about these book characters?

7. Lila is the youngest of the Deveaux girls. She has only recently come back to the island. Where has she been and what has she

been doing since she left? Why did she choose to live in the small Inland Cottage near the inn instead of returning to live with the family in the inn? You soon learn Lila is an artist. What type of art and paintings does she create? How has she used her creative gifts to improve the Lighthouse's gift shop? Burke remarks that "Lila has always lived close to God." How do you see this relationship showing in her life in the story?

8. Waylon settles in easily to life at the island and into a sweet, comfortable relationship with Burke. At first Burke and Waylon don't tell anyone they're a couple but their love blossoms quickly and Waylon soon asks Burke to become engaged. Where are they when they get engaged? How does Burke's mother handle this news? Why does it seem especially shocking to her? How do Lila and Novaleigh help Etta to be more understanding and happy about Burke and Waylon's plans to get engaged and be married? Have you ever known anyone who met and got engaged very quickly?

9. A lot of interesting guests stay at the Deveaux Inn. Myron Andric, an ornithologist, is staying for several months at the inn while studying birds for a research project. Why is Myron especially interested in the birds at the Deveaux Bank? The Deveaux Bank is a real place. Why is it special and protected as a bird sanctuary? What does Myron find at the Deveaux Bank that gets him upset and causes Burke and Waylon to call the authorities and head to the island? What unexpected find do they also learn of? Who does Burke think the body on the island might be? Lonnie Culler, with the Edisto police, later informs them the woman found at the Deveaux Bank is a different woman than the one already missing. Why does this cause concern for all? How does this problem grow worse when a third body is found? Why does Lonnie Culler believe there will be more murders until the killer is arrested?

10. As Burke and Waylon are returning from the Deveaux Bank, Burke's mother tells them Burke's sister Gwen and her three children have just arrived and are waiting at the dock to be picked up. Why has Gwen unexpectedly come to the island from Arkansas? What has happened in her life? How is Gwen determined to resolve her problems? How would you feel if this had happened to you? Would you respond in the same way? How is Waylon a help to Gwen's young son Chase?

11. Many lighthouses around the U.S. and abroad offer guided tours, and Burke gives tours of the Deveaux Lighthouse two days a week. What did you learn about the lighthouse on the tour? What is the lighthouse's interior like? What difficulties and hardships did early lighthouse keepers face in keeping the light and making rescues at sea? What did you learn about old messages in bottles that many lighthouse keepers tossed into the sea? What did Waylon share about sharks and sharks' teeth that you might not have known before? Would you have walked to the top of the lighthouse or stopped with most of the guests at the first gallery?

12. The Deveaux sisters traditionally come home at Easter for a visit when they can. With Burke, Lila, Gwen, and the children already at the island, why is everyone concerned about Celeste as Easter approaches? How long has it been since any of them have heard from her? What do Burke and Gwen decide to do after Easter if they still haven't heard from Celeste? When they travel to Nashville to look for her, what do they learn? Where is Celeste and what has happened to her? What do Burke and Gwen do?

13. Over a month later, with Celeste, Gwen, and the children still at the island, Burke is growing upset that her sisters do so little to help with the work of the inn. What happens to Rita Jean that makes the situation worse? What other difficulties soon follow?

Do you ever have those times when everything that could go wrong does go wrong? How do you handle those times? Burke's mother, Maggie Bouls, and Waylon all help Burke feel somewhat better about the situation. What especially wise counsel does Lila also offer?

!4. During a big storm, Burke and Waylon look out the high lighthouse window and see a boat in trouble by the Deveaux Bank. What does Burke insist on doing? When Waylon's boat gets near the island, after battling through the storm to get there, he notices the boat looks familiar. Whose boat is it? What does Waylon find when he makes his way to the beached craft? Waylon and Burke eventually get his Uncle Dewey back to safety at the lodge, grumbling and unpleasant the entire way. Ever since he was a boy, Waylon has experienced trouble in his relationship to his Uncle Dewey. What does he learn this night that is behind this old animosity? Do you think Dewey's actions were justified?

15. Life quiets down, as it usually does after a series of stressful times, and Gwen shares a fun day in Beaufort and Port Royal with Gwen and the twins, Leah and Rose, while Waylon and Don Nagel take Gwen's son Chase and Don's three boys deep sea fishing. What new direction is Gwen beginning to plan for her life? How is she handling her relationship with her estranged husband Alex? Do you think her feelings and actions are justified?

16. After a long day, Myron Andric comes to Waylon and Burke with another problem. He's been bird-watching on remote, uninhabited Otter Island and has spotted a dog there. He says, "I think the dog might have been left there and it's been worrying me." After he leaves, Burke talks Waylon into boating to the island to take food and look for the dog. They find the dog but also another problem. What do they discover? After contacting the police and starting to leave they run into a man who claims

the dog is his. What happens in this encounter? What do you soon learn about this man and the dog? Do you think Waylon handled this situation well?

17. After her scary experience at Otter Island, Burke finds herself in an odd mood, contemplating life more than normal for her. What does she later talk Waylon into doing sooner than they'd planned? What are Burke's reasons for wanting this change? How do Burke's mother and sisters react to the couple's news to move up the wedding again? What compromise idea does Lila offer that smoothes out a tense and awkward situation?

18. For two conventional and practical people, Burke and Waylon's wedding proves to be full of unexpected events. What situations happen with the church music, Rita Jean sampling the punch, a guest sitting on Chase's toy, and a little green snake slithering into the outdoor pavilion? Who conducts the wedding ceremony and how does he smooth over the unexpected events in the service? Did you enjoy this story and do you think Burke and Waylon will be happy together? Who were your favorite characters in the book and what did you like most about it? Are you eager to learn what happens with Gwen, Celeste, and Lila in the next Lighthouse Sisters books?

Books by J.L. and Lin Stepp

The Afternoon Hiker
Discovering Tennessee State Parks
Exploring South Carolina State Parks
Coming next – Visiting North Carolina State Parks
Traveling Georgia State Parks

Books by Lin Stepp

The Smoky Mountain Series

The Foster Girls
For Six Good Reasons
Second Hand Rose
Makin' Miracles
Welcome Back
Lost Inheritance
Tell Me About Orchard Hollow
Delia's Place
Down by the River
Saving Laurel Springs
Daddy's Girl
The Interlude

The Mountain Home Books

Happy Valley
Downsizing
Eight at the Lake
Coming next – Seeking Ayita
Shop on the Corner

Christmas Novella

A Smoky Mountain Gift
In When the Snow Falls

The Edisto Trilogy

Claire at Edisto
Return to Edisto
Edisto Song

The Lighthouse Sisters Series

Light the Way
Coming next –
Lighten My Heart
Light in the Dark
The Light Continues

About The Author

Lin Stepp

Lin Stepp is a native Tennessean, businesswoman and educator. A *New York Times, USA Today, Publishers Weekly*, and Amazon best-selling international author, Lin has twenty published novels out now, including her twelve beloved Smoky Mountain novels, all set in different Tennessee and North Carolina locations, three Mountain Home books, a novella in one of Kensington's Christmas anthologies, and four South Carolina coastal novels, including her three Edisto Trilogy books and her first release in the new Lighthouse Sisters series.

Lin and her husband J.L. also write regional guidebooks, including a published Smoky Mountain hiking guide and a TN and a SC state parks guidebook, all filled with hundreds of color photos. Writing and adventuring are her joys and more new novels set in the Smokies and at the beach are on the way, as well as more colorful regional guidebooks. Lin's title *Claire At Edisto* was the *2019 Best Book Award Winner in Fiction: Romance*, sponsored by American Book Fest and her novel *Welcome Back* a finalist in the 2017 Selah Awards. Lin enjoys speaking for events, festivals, libraries, and book clubs. And she loves reading, hiking, exploring out of doors, and keeping up with her readers. Look for her pages on Facebook and Twitter and follow her monthly blog and newsletter, too, that you will find on her author's website at: *www.linstepp.com.*

www.ingramcontent.com/pod-product-compliance
Lightning Source LLC
Chambersburg PA
CBHW061334160726
47995CB00001B/31

* 9 7 9 8 9 8 5 3 6 8 1 2 3 *